Please return / renew this item by the last date shown above
Dychwelwch / Adnewyddwch erbyn y dyddiad olaf y nodir yma

Dedication

For my mother, Mary Willis. Where to begin, Mom? You taught me to read and by example how to enjoy reading. You shared your love of romance stories with me and supported me with great enthusiasm in this grand adventure of writing. You knew before I did that this was my passion! Thank you can never be enough for all the things you've done for me and our family, but thank you with all my heart.

Acknowledgment

Writing a book, while mostly a lone venture, often takes the help and expertise of others. Sometimes it's old friends or family that come to your aid. Sometimes it's an expert who is kind enough to share their knowledge with you. This is true in the making of Close To The Fire.

When I decided to include a domestic violence case in Close To The Fire, I realized I knew little to nothing of the statutes in the state of Ohio for such a trial. So, I did the first thing any modern day writer would do, I went to the internet. Luckily for me I came across a great website with loads of information. Of course, after reading the information on the law website, I realized I had more questions. The next thing I did was send an email to the website's owner, Stephen W. Wolf, Attorney at Law. It was a weekend and my husband told me not to expect any answer at all. But Steve not only answered my questions, but fielded a few more emails as I worked the details into the story I was writing. Thanks Steve! I hope I did you justice. (Any mistakes in the book regarding the law are mine alone.) Oh, and I owe you a book!

Two nurse anesthetist friends gave me valuable information in the use of Propofol. Thanks to Colleen

Wooldridge, CRNA and Carole Griffin, CRNA for all your help and quick answers to my messages. You guys rock! (And any mistakes I made in the use of the drug are mine alone.)

The Ferrell team always deserves a big thank you!

I'd like to think my cover artist, Lyndsey Lewellen of LLewellen Designs. Your covers are making the fictional town of Westen come alive!

My beta reader Melissa Kelley and critique partner, Sandy Blair who kept this story following the right path and my sanity on just this side of the narrow line into crazyville!

My formatters at Libris in CAPS. Mitch and Alison have done such a great job!

And my editor, Tanya Saari. Thanks for helping make my stories the best they can be!

Author's note

Dear Reader,

Thank you so much for trying my Indie published book. I understand that there are many options for you to spend your money on and am honored that you chose one of my books. For that reason my team and I strive to put out the best product we can from the awesome cover design through the entire editing and formatting process. For my part, I hope to deliver an entertaining story that keeps you wondering what's going to happen next.

If at the end of this book you find you simply loved the story and characters, please consider giving it a positive rating or review. In this brave new book world, the only way for a good story to find its way into the hands of other readers is if the people who loved it let others know about it. We authors appreciate any little bit of help you can give us.

If, when you reach the end of this story, you think, "Wow, I'd love to know what's next in Suzanne's world of characters," then consider joining my newsletter mailing list. I only send out newsletters a few times a year plus extra ones in anticipation of any new releases, so it won't be flooding your inbox on a weekly basis, but will keep you abreast on any changes I may have coming.

Also, I love to hear from readers. If you have any

questions or comments, or just want to say "hi", please feel free to visit my webpage for some extra tidbits or check out my Pinterest boards. You can connect with me via Facebook, Twitter or through my email: suzanne@suzanneferrell.com

Now the important part: Here's Deke and Libby's story. I hope you will love them as much as I did and enjoy revisiting Westen in CLOSE TO THE FIRE.

PROLOGUE

Flames shot up in front of him. Heat knocked him backward.

The noise deafening.

Smoke and cinders flew about in the firestorm like evil imps dancing to the tune of the monster raging around him.

Sweat ran down his face.

His mask fogged. Cleared.

His turnout gear plastered to his body. What little of his skin was exposed stung. Blistered.

Bill.

He had to find Bill.

"Bill! Where are you?" he said into the radio amplifier attached to his mask and gear.

Thick smoke and wild flames raged around him.

Which way had he gone? He tried to get his bearings. Where was the exit?

They'd been unable to get across the lower part of the warehouse and instead went up the side stairs to the metal bridge-like structure along the side of the building. There they split up, trying to see the kid they'd been told had been dragged into the burning building.

"Over here, Deke. To your left." Bill's voice sounded over the radio.

He swung his gaze that direction. There he was. About ten feet away, near the edge of the scaffolding they were standing on. Safe.

"Any sign of the kid?"

Bill shook his head no.

A rumble sounded above them.

They both looked up. A hole in the ceiling open up. Flames whooshed upward.

Another rumble shook the building. A timber gave way and half the roof on the far side of the warehouse came crashing down, throwing Deke against the outer wall of the building. Bill flew backward onto the shaky scaffolding.

Deke held on to a window ledge as he tried to get his balance. He glanced out. Two figures ran away from the burning building. The larger one had the smaller one by scruff of the neck, hauling him away in the opposite direction of the fire engines out front.

Damn, the night watchman had been right. There had been a kid with the arsonist.

"Kid's okay, Bill. We need to get out of here." He signaled down just in case his partner hadn't heard him.

Bill nodded. "Meet you down below."

Deke was halfway down the stairs when the loud creaking started above. He looked up.

The remaining roof broke into two parts. It dangled by a few metal beams. Right over Bill.

Another rumble.

The metal gave way. Hit the scaffolding.

One minute Bill was there, the next...only flames and twisted metal.

"Deke!" Bill said, then silence over the radio.

"Bill!" He tried to climb back up.

Another beam came loose. It hit him. Slamming him down the stairs, it knocked his headgear and mask loose. Flames all around him, hot metal landing on the side of his neck, something liquid seeping down into his turnout gear and searing his chest.

Screaming sounded in his ears.

His screaming.

Deacon Reynolds tumbled out of the bed and landed on the floor in a tangle of sweaty sheets. Willing his breathing to slow, he wiped his hands over his face.

"Dammit." His words were followed by hacking coughs.

Jeez. He must've been screaming again. He didn't do it every time he had the dream, but when he did his voice box complained with a coughing fit. The docs said the damaged vocal cords couldn't take the trauma of making harsh sounds. He thought he'd had it under control. At least the screaming part. The dreams hadn't been this bad in months, maybe even a year. What had triggered this one?

He ran his hand through his wet hair. His whole body was covered in sweat.

It had to be the summer's heat.

Untangling himself from the sheets, he strode naked across to the bathroom and poured himself a glass of cold water. Drinking it slowly, he worked on letting his throat relax as he stared at his naked chest in the mirror. The thick cords of scar tissue extended from his jawline down his neck, across the left side of his shoulder and chest. Docs said he was lucky the movement of his shoulder hadn't been damaged and that the burns hadn't gotten too deep near his heart.

He barked out a harsh laugh.

Lucky. Right.

Sometimes he wondered if it wouldn't have been better if the fire had claimed him right along with Bill.

CHAPTER ONE

"Want to be my best man?" Gage Justice said as he perused the morning menu.

Deke choked on the sip of hot coffee he'd just taken. Blinking at his friend, he sputtered and coughed. Setting down the coffee mug, he reached for the glass of ice water Rachel had set on the table when they'd taken their favorite booth in the Peaches 'N Cream Café for breakfast.

"Do I need to come over there and Heimlich you?" Gage said from across the table, with a grin on his face.

"Don't even think about it, Gunslinger." Deke cast his old football buddy a warning glare and swallowed half the glass of ice water to soothe his now-burned mouth and throat. After a minute he set the glass aside and picked up his menu. "You should warn a person when you ask a question like that. Not wait 'til they have a mouthful of Lorna's coffee."

"So, do you?"

Something in his friend's voice caught his attention.

Gage might be trying to play this off as no big deal, but the slight deepening to his voice and the way he kept staring at the menu they both knew by heart spoke of how much his answer meant to the other man.

"Might as well. Someone has to be sure you don't leave Bobby standing at the altar all by herself."

A smile split Gage's lips, all nervousness gone as he set aside the menu and leaned back in the booth. "As if. My daddy didn't raise me stupid. Bobby is the best thing that ever happened to me. Nothing I wouldn't do for her, including dressing up in a tux and standing in front of the whole town to make her mine."

"Man, you've got it bad." Deke shook his head, setting down his menu as Rachel approached.

"You two want the Monday special, like usual? Or you gonna take a risk and order something new?" the teenaged waitress asked as she set a carafe of hot coffee on the table. Her mother owned the café and Rachel had been working here since she was old enough to bus tables.

"We don't mess with Monday-morning specials, Rach," Gage said with a wink.

"You just don't want to mess with my mom." She wrote on the order book in her hand. "That's one heart-attack-on-a-plate for the town sheriff, what about you, Fire Chief?"

Deke gave her a shrug. "Hate to jinx our Monday meetings, so yep, I'll take the special, too."

"Okay, two Monday specials for the two old guys in

a rut," Rachel said, then headed back to the kitchen.

"Sassy brat," Deke called after her, then shook his head. "Kid's growing up to sound just like her mom."

"And who's she calling old?" Gage poured some more coffee into his cup then grinned at him again. "Must be you, since you graduated before me."

Before he could tell Gage where he could shove his younger status, the bells on the door jangled. He looked up to see who was entering and wished he hadn't.

Elizabeth Wilson.

Libby.

Beautiful as always. Her blonde hair pulled up into a fancy braid that ended just at the bottom of her neck, touching the collar of the pale-blue sweater that clung to her body in a loose, carefree way before stopping just below the tops of her black slacks. Damn. Even after all these years, seeing the soft curves of her hips, ass and long thighs, still made him want to grab her and pull her in close. But that would never happen again. She was off limits to him. Forever.

She glanced his way, her deep-blue eyes locking onto him. The half-smile on her lips froze and faded. A sadness clouded her eyes just before she turned and headed to the corner booth at the farthest part of the café from where he sat.

"So, what do you say?"

Gage's voice penetrated his brain, making Deke refocus on him and not on the worst mistake of his life. "I already said yes. Be happy to."

"Good. Told Principal Johnson you'd be happy to be my assistant."

Deke blinked then narrow his eyes at his oldest friend. "What the hell are you talking about? And what the hell does the high school principal have to do with your wedding?"

A slow grin spread over Gage's face. "Didn't think you were paying attention. Johnson asked me to fill in as interim football coach until they can find a replacement. I agreed, as long as I could pick my own assistant. And *you* just volunteered."

"You can't hold me to that. I thought we were still talking about your wedding," he groused as Rachel returned with their plates heaped full of breakfast.

Gage scooped up a forkful of fluffy scrambled eggs. "You said yes. Can't help it if you zoned out. Ya snooze, ya lose."

Deke took a few bites of his breakfast then swallowed it down with some coffee. Apparently he needed more caffeine than usual today. "I don't have time to babysit a bunch of wet-behind-the-ears kids for two-a-day practices right now, Gunslinger. It's been a dry summer and I've got everyone doing extra on-call duty for any brush fires in the area, including me."

Talk ceased between them and only the clink of cutlery on dishes sounded around them as they dug into their breakfast.

The bells on the door jangled again.

Out of habit, Deke glanced up to see a stranger walk

in. Tall, about forty, salt-and-pepper hair, sports shirt neatly tucked into his jeans. The man looked around, giving Deke a nod before scanning the rest of the room. Then with a wave and smile, he made a beeline across the café. Straight to Libby's booth. She greeted him with a smile and a handshake.

Deke forced himself to look away from how beautiful she was when she smiled and started shoving the now-nearly-tasteless food into his mouth.

"…just two weeks for two-a-days before classes start. We'll have the guys out early in the morning before you have to be at the office and late in the evening once the heat of the day starts to drop," Gage was saying.

Deke focused on the conversation at hand. It was none of his business who Libby had breakfast with. He'd lost that right ten years ago.

"As your assistant, what's my job going to be? 'Cause I ain't carrying your clipboard for your lazy ass."

Gage laughed, setting down his fork and reaching for the carafe of coffee to refill both their mugs. "I'll be dealing with the offense and formulating the plays. Thought you could handle the defense."

He nearly choked on the bite of toast in his mouth. Took a swallow of coffee to wash it down and narrowed his gaze at his friend once more. "I was the all-state wide receiver for three years running, what the hell do I know about coaching defensive players?"

When they were in high school, they were the dynamic duo. Gage was the best quarterback in their division, with a sidearm throw that was almost as accurate as his overhead spiral. Which was how he'd gotten the nickname Gunslinger. While Deke was not only a track star, but a wide receiver who could outrun any safety or cornerback in the state.

"You spent a lot of time dodging linemen, linebackers and the coverage team. Not to mention the fact that you were on our coverage team. You should've picked up a few defensive tricks for them to use," Gage said, setting aside his now-empty plate and leaning back in the booth to drink more coffee.

Deke finished the last few bites of his meal. Reaching for his mug, he shoved in another packet of sugar and a slow stream of cream.

He considered what Gage had to say a few minutes. Yeah, he'd learned some things he could pass on to the players. He'd loved playing football as a kid and all the way through high school. Maybe it was time to give back a little. He needed something in his life besides work. He glanced at Libby once more, who was in conversation with the stranger. "Sure, why not?"

Light laughter came from the far booth. Libby always did have an infectious laugh. The man's deeper responsive chuckle grated on his nerves.

Deke reached for the carafe to empty its contents in his mug. He took another long drink of his coffee to steady the tension in his hands. "So who's the guy over there with Libby Wilson?"

Gage looked over his shoulder then back. "New newspaper owner. Name's Callahan. Sean Callahan."

"How'd he come to own the newspaper? Wouldn't it go to Davis' family through probate?"

"Seems that despite all his grandiose plans and land-buying schemes, Davis neglected a few things." Gage's face lost all humor and he inhaled slowly, rubbing his left arm.

The topic was one Gage never liked discussing. Not that Deke could blame him, since he almost died at Richard Davis' hands last spring, the broken arm he'd sustained then still bothered him. The man murdered at least two people and nearly blew up the town with his illegal meth lab and crazed plans to take over the town. Gage had been trapped in an underground room and only the bravery of his fiancée, Bobby Roberts, and the teamwork of most of the town had saved him.

"Don't tell me he didn't have any relatives to inherit?"

"Better than that," and the hint of a smile returned to his friend's face. "Seems he forgot to leave a will."

Deke let out a low whistle. "Not smart."

"Oh, it gets even better. Not only did he spend all his time on buying land he helped foreclose with his late buddy over at the bank, but he also spent all his money on the land-grab scheme, ignoring the newspaper."

"And the bank had the note on the place."

"Yep. Lock, stock and all the contents within. So the

state and county now own all the land, which they're going to sell off to pay for repairs to the area, including some new highway access, according to our fine Mayor Rawlins. Tobias said the bank sold the newspaper and all the assets pertaining to it to Mr. Callahan. All the danger that bastard Davis put this town in, it seems a fitting epilogue to his life that we now benefit from his death."

"Couldn't have worked out better." Deke lifted his mug in a salute.

"Yep. May he rest in peace. Not." They clinked mugs and swallowed the last of their coffee.

"What are you two devils celebrating?" Lorna Doone asked, as she stopped by their booth. "Not more trouble, I hope."

The owner of the Peaches 'N Cream Café leaned one hip against Gage's side of the booth, her free hand holding a fresh coffee carafe. Her nearly-daffodil-colored hair piled in loose curls around her head hadn't changed since the day she'd moved into town nearly three decades ago. Lorna didn't take to change too easily. Although maintained and cleaned to her standards, the café still looked like the '50s diner it had been when she bought it, the cash register so old it probably could bring a small fortune at an antique mall. The menu was nearly the same as it was the day she took over, except for the healthy items Gage's cousin Emma had convinced Lorna to add when she worked here. But today something was different.

"You have a new apron," Deke said, not hiding the surprise in his voice.

"Sure do. And for being so observant, y'all get more coffee," she said with a grin as she switched out the carafes. She held out one edge of the top of the cream-colored apron so they could see the embroidered café name and three peaches across it. "New girl, Sylvie Gillis, over at the Dye Right Salon has a little side business doing embroidery. What do you think?"

"Nice image. Why the change?" Gage asked.

"With all the people coming through town these days helping with the rebuild, thought I might do some advertising. Get some T-shirts for the staff to wear round town and such. Just like in romance, gotta strike while the iron's hot." She gave them a quick grin and sauntered back behind the main counter.

Deke and Gage laughed.

"Don't encourage her. Next, she'll be having me wear a matching apron." Rachel made a disgusted face as she gathered up their empty plates. Then with a wink she laid their tickets on the table. "Remember when you're tipping, I have college tuition to save up for, guys."

Gage reached to fill his mug once more, his smile gone. Deke recognized that look. Time to discuss the business of keeping the town of Westen and the surrounding farms safe.

"What plans do you have for preventing any brush fires in the area? And how much of my deputies' help do you think you're going to need?" Gage asked.

"We're going to have to do some education of the farmers, especially the new landowners thinking to clear off dead brush by burning it."

The influx of former city dwellers looking for some rural land to spread out a bit added to the increased fire risk this year. Deke proceeded to outline his plans, the two of them coming up with a set patrol schedule for both the sheriff and fire department. Focusing on the important subject helped him keep his mind off the corner booth until Libby and the newsman paid for their food and left.

"I'll set up a town meeting with Tobias and get the word out to the rural families to come in. Maybe this Thursday? Seven at the town hall?" Gage said.

"Works for me. The sooner we're all on board to the dangers even a small fire can cause, the better. Since we're going to be at the high school anyways, might as well do a safety talk, too."

"Sounds good. I'd best be getting over to the office. You coming?" Gage asked, grabbing his bill and sliding out of the booth.

Deke shook his head, scratching at the old scars on the left side of his neck. "No, I think I'll stay a bit and maybe get Lorna to make me some lunch. Got a meeting with Harold Russett over at the county engineering department in the courthouse. We're coordinating installing siren triggers on the new stretch of highway they're putting in, then I'm headed out in the northeast part of the county most of the day, talking to the elders of the Amish community."

"Sounds like a fun day." Gage slapped him on the shoulder. "Don't forget about the football team. First meeting is tonight. Six o'clock at the practice field."

"I'll be there."

After his friend left, Deke gave Rachel an order for a sandwich to go then pulled out his smartphone. He plugged in the reminder for the meeting at the football field and one for Thursday at the town hall. He checked in at the fire station to let them know he'd be out most of the day and get the morning report. Luckily, it had been a quiet night as far as fires were concerned.

"Got your lunch, Deacon," Lorna called from the cash register station.

Shaking his head, he headed over. Time was, Libby had used that name as an endearment. Now, Lorna was one of the few persons besides his mother who got away with calling him Deacon. And when either of them called him that, it usually meant he was in trouble.

"Whatever it was, I didn't do it and it's not my fault," he said pulling out his wallet.

She took his money, rang him up then held his lunch in her hand, just out of his reach. "I've kept my mouth shut for years, but I'm fed up with you."

Surprise stopped him from laughing. She was serious.

He blinked. "What did I do?"

"Every time you're in here and that lovely woman

comes in, you do nothing but stare daggers her direction."

Great. She'd noticed how he reacted to Libby. This wasn't a discussion he wanted to have with Lorna—not now, not ever.

"Me? I don't stare daggers at anyone. Who are you talking about?"

She placed one hand on her hip, arched a hand-painted eyebrow and fixed him with her don't-give-me-that-innocent-look look. "You know who. Either fix whatever problem the two of you have or get over it. She deserves better than this."

Without another word, she handed him his lunch then headed back into the kitchen.

Her words playing over in his mind, he left the café and climbed into his truck where he sat staring at the dashboard.

Lorna was right.

Libby deserved better. She deserved love and happiness.

Lorna had it all wrong.

It wasn't hatred or anger that had him watching Libby so closely. It was desire and guilt. She was the only woman who ever made him happy. Probably would ever be, but his own stupid recklessness ended all that.

He tipped his head sideways, arching his neck and stretching the thick scars on the left side. A reminder of how much he had lost. How much he'd taken away from Libby. Nothing could ever repair the damage.

* * * * *

"Morning," Ashley Smith called over her shoulder to Libby as she entered her office on the third floor of the county courthouse. Always cheerful, the older woman was wiggling to the light-rock song playing on the radio as she watered the flowers that littered the reception area of the office.

Libby couldn't help but smile. "Morning, Ash. What's on the agenda for today?"

Her secretary put down the watering can and moved her computer mouse to bring up the day's schedule. "You have the Compton domestic abuse case at ten. Please tell me she's going to show this time."

"That's the plan, but get her on the phone for me in a few minutes so I can judge her mood."

Melissa Compton had been in and out of the hospital several times the past few years. Each time, the injuries had escalated, but she'd never followed through with getting the restraining order or getting her husband thrown in jail. She'd come close to pressing the charges the last time or two, but never seemed to make it inside the courthouse doors. The county prosecutor intervened the last time without Melissa's cooperation and Frank went to jail for thirty days, paid his fine and attended anger management courses—none of which seemed to make an impression on the man. The problem was,

Libby wondered if the next time Frank decided to "teach the little woman some respect" he'd kill her.

"Get me Sheriff Justice on the phone, too."

"Yes, ma'am." Ashley made a quick note. "You also have a meeting at the Senior Center this afternoon at two to plan the fall activities for the day care participants. Those little old people are so sweet."

"Yes, they are." Libby headed into her office, Ashley right on her heels.

"There was one more thing. Todd Banyon called. Wants to meet you for lunch, if you're free. Said he wanted to bring you up to date on one of his new residents."

Libby tried not to make an ugly look. Todd ran the new halfway house for troubled teens. A nice enough man, but Todd was such a stickler for rules and always had a complaint about something one of the kids was doing or not doing. She could make up an excuse to put him off, but heck, her day had already started off crappy. Seeing Deacon always brought back bad feelings. She might as well see Todd today, too. Then maybe the rest of her week would improve.

"Tell him yes, but I'll have to text him when we recess for lunch. I have no idea how long this case will take and I am scheduled to testify this morning. If he's agreeable to that, could you get some takeout sandwiches? He can meet me here. I'd rather not eat at the Peaches 'N Cream. I had breakfast there with Sean Callahan, the new newspaper owner."

"You did?" Ashley's face lit up and Libby knew what was coming. Only ten years older than her, Ash had taken over the place of her late mother in trying to get Libby married. "Was he cute?"

Libby thought about it a minute. "He's handsome enough. Pleasant to talk to."

"What did you talk about?"

Libby sat at her desk and turned on her computer. "He wanted to know about the Senior Center, the halfway house and any other services the county provided for the community. He wants to do an article for the paper. I answered his questions, including general information about the women's shelter but asked him not to publicize it or try to visit it as many of the women are there in secret for their safety. He promised not to."

"Good. Those ladies have enough problems. Think he'll keep his promise?"

"I don't see why not." She opened up the Compton family case file. "Let me know when you get Melissa on the phone."

"Yes, ma'am, boss." Ashley gave her a little salute then left the office, closing the door behind her.

Libby leaned back in her seat, rubbed the bridge of her nose and closed her eyes. Immediately, the image of Deacon's dark expression slammed into her, followed quickly by the ache in her chest. How had they gotten to this point where she couldn't even tolerate looking at him?

Wasn't time supposed to heal old wounds?

Not when seeing the person on the other side of your pain pulled the scab off to bleed fresh each time.

"Got Melissa on the phone, line one, boss," Ashley's voice crackled over the ancient intercom system.

"Thanks, Ash." She said, pushing the button to answer as she picked up the phone. "Melissa? This is Elizabeth Wilson. Just wanted to check in with you. How you doing today?"

"I'm okay. A little nervous." Melissa's voice sounded higher-pitched than usual and a little shaky.

Not good. She couldn't waver this time. Her life depended on getting Frank behind bars.

"Melissa, everything will be fine. You can do this. You're a very strong woman."

"Oh, I don't know. Seeing him in court. If the judge doesn't agree, and Frank finds me, he gets so angry…" Melissa's voice drifted off.

"Melissa Compton, don't you go there. Sheriff Justice will be right there beside you. Judge Rawlins is a just man and will give Frank the punishment he deserves for using you as a punching bag all these years. You just have to take the final step. And don't you dare say you're not strong." She put a little steel into her voice, willing some confidence across the airwaves to her client and friend. "A weak woman would've given up and let Frank kill her years ago. You can do this. I have faith in you and it's time you did, too."

Melissa gave a nervous laugh. "You make it sound so easy. I always feel more confident after your pep talks."

"I can call you daily, twice even, if it helps you through this." And she would. Whatever it took to keep her friend safe.

"I might have to take you up on that after today."

Relief surged through Libby. Melissa was planning to go through with the court appearance today. "Someone will be at the safe house to pick you up in about half an hour, and I'll be at the courthouse waiting for you."

"Libby?"

"Something wrong, Melissa?"

"No, I just wanted to say thank you for all your help and patience with me."

After they hung up, Libby pulled up the images in the computer file. She hit print to get the entire file printed.

Damn. Every time she looked at the images of Melissa's face, her stomach turned and her blood pressure shot up. Her left eye was nearly swollen shut, her cheek black and blue. Her swollen lips were bleeding and the bruise ran down her jaw. She clicked on the next set of pictures and hit print once more. Once he'd subdued her to the floor the bastard had kicked her. Bruises ran up and down her rib cage and hip.

When she told Melissa she was strong, it wasn't a line of horse manure. She'd meant every word of it.

Apparently, she'd gotten into a fetal position to protect her midsection and head. Self-preservation had been foremost in her mind, even during the beating.

"Sheriff's on line two," Ashley announced again.

Libby picked up the phone again, this time to talk to her best friend's cousin. "Hey, Gage. How goes the wedding plans?"

"Not bad. Bobby's pretty laid back about the whole thing, as long as her sisters don't get too involved. They tend to push her crazy button." He chuckled on the other end, telling her he really didn't mind his future sisters-in-law much. "I'm sure you didn't call just to talk about my wedding. What 'cha need?"

"I just talked to Melissa Compton."

"She gonna make it into the courthouse this time?" He asked, all humor gone from his voice. There wasn't any censure because Melissa had missed the first two court dates and dropped all the charges. More concern for her.

"I think so. This is the first time she's gone to the shelter and she sounds pretty sure she wants to finally put him behind bars."

"Good. The next time I might be arresting him for her murder."

"That's what we're all afraid of, especially Melissa." She leaned back in her chair and stared out the window at the little courtyard in the center of the courthouse building. "What I wanted to know was, besides you giving testimony, would you possibly be able to have another deputy in the courtroom? I think it might make Melissa feel more comfortable and safe."

"Already scheduled Daniel and Cleetus to be present. We also moved Compton to the holding cell at the courthouse earlier this morning. You want one of them to pick Mrs. Compton up from the shelter?"

"No. I think they'd make the other shelter residents nervous. I've already arranged for Emma to pick her up." Emma was Gage's cousin. She'd suffered emotional abuse at the hands of her ex, but was now happily married to the town doctor, who'd be at the hearing to give testimony to Melissa's injuries. Emma, a nurse in her own right, had helped Doc Clint perform the rape kit and taken their own set of pictures of her injuries. She'd be giving testimony, too.

"Good," Gage said. "Em will keep her calm and bolster her self-confidence all the way to the courthouse."

Libby couldn't agree more. "Your cousin will have Melissa believing she can do anything, even run for president by the time they get inside."

"That she will. Anything else you need?"

"No, we're set then and I'll see you at the courthouse in an hour."

They hung up and Libby started gathering the prints of Melissa's injuries, pushing down the anger that rose inside her at the stark brutality that her friend had suffered. Hopefully, if everything went without a hitch today, Frank Compton would go away for years and not be able to hurt anyone ever again.

CHAPTER TWO

Outside the courtroom, Libby paced past the long benches lining the hallway, watching for Emma Preston to arrive with Melissa. She glanced at her watch. Ten minutes until Judge Rawlins walked in and the case was to start. If they weren't here on time, he'd dismiss the charges just out of aggravation. Like she'd told Melissa, he was very fair and hated abuse of any kind, but he also hated his time being wasted, especially for a third time.

"Any sign?" A deep voice asked from behind her. She turned to see Kent Howard striding down the hall, his briefcase in hand. The county prosecutor always walked with a purpose, like he never questioned where he was going or what he was going to do. No questions. No hesitation. No regrets.

What must it be like to make decisions, have them always work out and never have any regrets?

Libby plastered her most positive smile on her face. "Not yet. Emma called and said they were on their way about fifteen minutes ago, so they should be here any minute."

"Good. I would prefer to have her here, but as you and I talked last week, the county can go after him with the felony domestic violence charges, given the nature of her latest injuries, without her cooperation. You can take the stand as her domestic violence advocate and we'll introduce the photos and hospital reports as evidence. Her testimony would be beneficial, but not crucial to getting him behind bars before he kills her. Although you know Judge Rawlins, he makes his own rules and could still dismiss the case if she's another no-show." He set his briefcase down on one of the long benches and checked his watch before fixing his intense, blue-eyed gaze on her once more. For some reason it always made her feel like she was under cross-examination. "Given the evidence of his escalation, if we don't get involved, I could be trying him for murder next time."

Libby couldn't agree more. "True. While getting him permanently away from her is the goal today, it would be in Melissa's best long-term mental health to participate in prosecuting her abusive husband. She needs to stand up for herself, not depend on someone else to always handle matters."

"Ah, here they are now," Kent said, looking over her shoulder.

High heels sounded down the hall. Libby turned to see Emma and Melissa hurrying towards them.

Melissa wasn't overly tall, about five feet, four inches. She had dark-brown hair that hung around her shoulders, large, dark-brown eyes in her pale face. In the month since she'd been admitted to the hospital, her facial injuries had healed to the point the swelling and bruises had disappeared. Doc Clint said her vision had cleared despite the injury to her orbital socket and she'd have to have dental implants for the teeth her husband had knocked out. She was very thin—thinner than any woman should ever be—which gave her a frail appearance.

The idea that Frank would use her as a punching bag shot anger through Libby once more.

"Sorry we're running late," Emma said. "I meant to have her here a lot earlier, but there was a truck and car accident on the highway and we couldn't get around them for a while."

"No problem, Mrs. Preston. You're here in time for the hearing, and that's all that really matters," Kent said, then turned to Melissa. "Remember what we talked about last week?"

She nodded, her long, dark hair bouncing around her shoulders. "Just tell exactly what happened as best as I can remember. And when Frank's lawyer asks questions, I'm just supposed to say yes or no and not give any extra information."

"That's right," Kent gave her a reassuring smile and patted her on the shoulder. "Doctor Preston, Mrs. Preston and Miss Wilson, here, will testify, too, to the extent of your injuries."

"And you're sure Frank will go to jail?" Melissa asked, twisting her fingers together. "He's going to be so mad that he had to come to court."

Libby slipped her arm around her shoulders and squeezed her in tight. "You're safe here, Melissa. Frank isn't going to do anything to you. Not here, in a room full of witnesses. Bullies never do. Besides, I asked Sheriff Justice to have an extra deputy in the room."

Melissa inhaled, looked at the three people surrounding her then seemed to come to a decision. "Okay. It's time he paid for hurting me."

"Good girl," Kent said, picking up his briefcase.

The door behind them opened and the bailiff stepped into the hallway and motioned to Kent. "Counselor, court is about ready to start."

They hurried in behind him, taking their seats just behind the prosecution side of the room. Emma's husband, Clint, already waited for them. Libby glanced around the courtroom. Gage and one of his deputies, Cleetus, sat in the next row back, as well as Sean Callahan, the newspaperman. On the defense's side were two businessmen, both salesmen from the same company Frank worked for in Columbus, about an hour's drive away. Libby guessed they were character witnesses. In front of them also sat Frank's mother, sister and two brothers, all dressed as if going to church in their Sunday best.

Along one wall sat the jury—six people: three men,

three women.

"Oh, dear," Melissa whispered, drawing Libby's attention. Her cheeks were tinged pink as she studied the people in the room. She knew what the other woman was thinking, her own mother had looked the same way once. She was embarrassed to have to tell these people what her husband had done to her and then admit to them why she'd stayed so long with him.

Libby took her hand and squeezed it firmly. "You can do this."

The door to the left of the judge's bench opened. In walked Frank Compton, dressed in a blue suit complete with red tie, fresh haircut and a confident smile on his very handsome face. His hands were cuffed in front of him and Daniel, dressed in his deputy uniform, escorted him to the defendant table before removing the cuffs. Frank shook his lawyer's hand, smiled at his family, and settled into his seat. Then he leaned back and stared across the room at Melissa, who seemed to shrink beside Libby.

Libby cast him a narrow-eyed look then moved to block his view and stop his intimidation tactic. The bastard gave her a smirk, then faced forward again.

If she could get away with assaulting him in a courtroom, she'd love to walk over and punch him in the eye, just like he'd done to her friend on more than one occasion.

Bet he'd cry like a baby.

Her brother Bill always told her all you had to do to

get a bully to stop was to step up and challenge them. He'd been the one to teach her to defend herself as a kid. She wished he was here now, he'd be proud of all the times she stood up to bullies. A little sorrow washed over her anger. Ten years and she still missed his solid support in anything she tried.

The door on the opposite side of the bench opened.

"All rise for the honorable Terrence J. Rawlins," the bailiff called.

The scraping of chairs against the floor sounded in the room as everyone stood. The silver-haired judge, complete with black robes entered, took his seat, and looked at the courtroom. "You may be seated."

Again, more chair scraping and a few murmurs as everyone resumed their spots. The judge flipped over a paper, then lifted a manila folder, opening it in front of him, then looked over his glasses at the bailiff.

The bailiff cleared his throat before announcing, "The State versus Franklin Compton, felony domestic violence in the first degree."

* * * * *

Deke closed the office door and stepped out into the crowded courthouse hallway, shaking his head to clear all the numbers bouncing around inside it.

For years he'd believed Harold Russett's anal-retentive tendencies bordered on obsessive compulsive, but ever since the man determined the safest way to dig

Gage out of the shaft he'd been buried in last spring and helped save his life, he'd been more tolerant of the county engineer's detailed meetings regarding the new road construction. Especially since Russett contacted him out of the blue about a traffic signal prioritization plan to help speed up the fire and EMS teams' response time to emergencies. But man, could the guy rattle off figures and numbers fast—so fast it made him dizzy.

He looked down at the folder of papers Russett had given him. It included maps of the current roads, those to be rebuilt after the meth lab explosion outside of town, and those gravel roads the county planned to pave and enlarge. One good thing to come out of that near catastrophe was the state's desire to help Westen rebuild, not to mention the added funding also pushed the state's embarrassment at not knowing the location of one of the largest meth kitchens in the state off the front pages of all the news sites.

The potential for fraud and greed from such a generous influx of monies into a poor county was huge. Lucky for Westen, Russett did take his job seriously and would use the funds allocated by the state to improve the lives of all Westen's residents.

Movement ahead caught his attention. He caught a glimpse of a familiar blonde ponytail as people moved from the crowded hallway through open doors into a courtroom. Standing off to the side were Gage and his deputies, Cleetus and Daniel. He strolled up to them.

"What's going on?" he asked, peeking inside to

confirm that the blonde was definitely Libby.

"Compton domestic violence case," Gage said, as the last of the crowd moved inside. "Judge gave a recess after Doc Clint showed the images of Melissa's injuries."

Deke arched a brow. "That bad?"

"Almost as nauseating as when I saw them in person. Now it's Libby's turn to talk."

"Libby has to testify?" The idea of her taking on a bully like Compton sent a chill over him.

Gage nodded, walking towards the door after his deputies. "She was Melissa's first contact."

Why the hell hadn't the woman called 911? Why call Libby?

Without thinking, he slipped inside the courtroom just before the doors closed and took a seat in the back row on the aisle. From that spot he could see the witness stand.

The room stood for the judge then resumed their seats. He gave the prosecutor permission to resume his case and Kent Howard called Libby to the stand.

Deke watched her stand and stride confidently to the witness box, drinking in every movement of her body— the bounce of the ponytail against her long, slender neck, the swing of her hands at her side and the gentle sway of her hips. There wasn't one inch of her body he hadn't known intimately.

That was a long time ago. She wasn't his anymore, and he shouldn't be remembering any of their time together. The mental slap-to-the-head reminder didn't stop him from watching her red-tinged lips as she held one hand on the Bible, the other in the air and swore to tell the truth, so help her God. He remembered what those lips tasted like beneath his. How they felt, not just kissing his mouth, but his body in various and intimate places.

He gave himself a mental shake again and focused on the courtroom as she took her seat. The bailiff stood at relaxed attention to the far left, but between the judge's bench and the defendant's table. Libby sat between the judge and the jury. The right side of the room held many of his colleagues and friends in the town, while the left side of the courtroom was filled with strangers—friends and family of Compton, he'd presume. Two men directly behind Compton's seat whispered and one nodded at Libby.

A tingling skittered across his senses and he sat up straighter in his seat.

"Please state your name and occupation for the court," the county prosecutor asked Libby from his seat to begin his questioning.

"Elizabeth Wilson. I'm the social worker for Westen County." Her voice was strong and confident, but still softly feminine.

"Can you please tell us your involvement with the events on the night in question?"

Only the slight swallow before she replied showed any hint of her nervousness at giving a public testimony. She'd always been that—delicately courageous. Even tagging along when he and her brother Bill went up to different rock climbing venues. They'd been using rock climbing to strengthen their muscles and skills for training exercises in preparation to enter the fire academy. While he'd strapped on safety harnesses he'd double-checked and triple-checked that she still wanted to give it a try. She'd swallowed just like now, then nodded, determination in her sky-blue eyes. From that moment on, they'd been a threesome as they traversed all the rock climbing areas in northeast Ohio.

"I received a call from Melissa Compton that she needed help," Libby said clearly, her eyes on the prosecutor.

"And what time was this?"

"My phone recorded the time as ten twenty-seven p.m."

"And what kind of help did Mrs. Compton need?"

"She asked me to come pick her up and she gave me an address."

"You mean her home address?"

"No. She was outside a local convenience store. I drove to the address and found her standing next to the pay phone."

Deke watched Libby as she gave testimony. Her cheeks turned pink and her jaw tightened almost imperceptibly as she spoke of to the condition she'd found Melissa Compton in, the injuries and how she'd had to help her into the car. Ever since he'd met her in high school—her brother was a sophomore while he and Libby were both freshmen—she'd always defended the underdog, taking on any bully, even someone twice her size. Of course, Bill, Gage and he had often been her backup.

Bill.

The deep ache started in his chest at the memory of his friend. His heart beat faster and the need to move hit him hard. His palms started to sweat.

Damn. He needed to get out of here. *Now.* Before the nightmare took over again.

When the defense objected to Libby stating that Frank Compton had inflicted the injuries to his wife as hearsay and the judge called both lawyers to his bench, Deke took the opportunity to head to the door. Just before he slipped out the double doors, he glanced at the witness box to see Libby watching him closely.

More guilt washed over him and he turned from the blue gaze he felt boring into his soul.

* * * * *

At the end of Libby's testimony and cross-examination by the defense, the judge dismissed the courtroom for lunch to reconvene in an hour and a half. She stood with the rest of the courtroom as he exited then turned and hugged Melissa, before Emma and Doc Clint whisked her out of the crowd. The plan was to take her back to their house—not too far from the courthouse, but far from any crowds that would gather at the small restaurants and the Peaches 'N Cream Café in town.

In the hallway, she stopped against one marble-tiled wall and considered her testimony. She'd been as factual and professional as she could. Told about the condition she'd found Melissa in, how she'd gotten her to Doc Clint's clinic and stayed with her all the way to the hospital and her first night. Even the defense had little to question her on other than asking her why Melissa had called her. Her answer for the record was that she was Melissa's court-appointed Domestic Violence Advocate and friend. The real reason was Melissa had been terrified.

"I can't go home." Melissa's voice was little more than a whisper in the phone. A car horn sounded in the background and the wind outside was making it sound like a static connection.

"I'll be right there." She was already gripping her purse and keys, heading out the back door. Thank God she hadn't gotten ready for bed yet. "Keep talking to me, okay?"

"I don't want anyone to see me. If they go to the house and wake him..."

"I'll be there before that happens." Once inside the car she set the phone in its cradle on the dashboard and hit the hands-free button. "How did you get to the store?"

"I walked. He has the only set of keys."

The bastard tried to make her a prisoner. "Did you bring any of your things?"

"No. I just wanted to get away." She inhaled and a moan sounded through the phone.

"Are you okay?" Libby asked as she ran the corner red light and turned onto Main Street, headed to the new area of upscale homes where the Comptons lived.

"It just hurts to breathe. I think he broke a rib this time."

It took five more minutes for her to get to the convenience store. Five minutes of her mentally cursing the bastard to hell and five minutes of calmly keeping Melissa on the phone talking to her.

Yes. Melissa had been terrified, bruised, battered, but not defeated.

She testified to Melissa's condition with confidence. She'd refused to let the defense rattle her or twist her words. In fact, the only time she'd stumbled while on the witness stand was when she saw Deacon in the courtroom and when he's abruptly left. Their eyes connected for a moment, and the sadness in his tore at her heart. His guilt was eating him alive and she couldn't help him, her own guilt keeping a wall between them.

With a sigh, she texted Ashley that she was on her way to her office.

Good. Todd is here. Starting to whine to me. Hurry.

Libby sighed at Ash's return text. Todd Banyon was

probably the only person who could make her normally optimistic secretary grouse. Which meant that their meeting wasn't going to be particularly enjoyable. She worked her way through the crowd outside the courtroom hurrying to lunch. Sort of like a salmon going upstream, she headed up the marble steps to her second floor office. Pausing outside the door, she took another deep breath and willed a smile on her face. If she was going to get Todd in and out of her office with any time to relax before going back to court, she needed to start the meeting with as positive an attitude as possible. Maybe it would improve his mood.

Yeah, and maybe cows would start giving chocolate milk.

"Hey, Todd. So glad you could meet me here for lunch," she said a little too cheerily as she stepped into her office with a quick consolatory look at Ashley, before turning her smile on the thin, dark-haired man seated in the uncomfortable waiting area chair. Ashley refused to replace it, saying it kept the idle problem makers from wanting to stick around more than necessary. Only those with tenacity or cast iron butts wanted to sit in that thing overly long.

"I don't mind at all, Elizabeth," he said, standing, a file clutched in his hand.

His heavy-scented cologne wafted over her and she fought hard not to gag at it. He always wore too much and it wasn't a good kind, some sort of smoky undercurrent to it.

He stepped closer. "I know you're very busy. But as I was telling Miss Ashley here, this really is an important case we need to talk about."

Each young man's case at the Colbert Street halfway house was important to her. Sadly, only the problem ones ever seemed to be of importance to Todd.

"Well, why don't you come in and we'll take a look." She led him inside, with Ashley close on their heels, a large shopping bag from the Peaches 'N Cream Café in her hands.

"Got you the chicken salad sandwich and fruit, boss." Ashley set the bag on the table and pulled out the contents. "Wasn't sure about you, Mr. Banyon, but Lorna assured me you like ham and cheese on rye with a side of homemade chips."

A rare smile settled on Todd's face as he eyed the luncheon Ashley spread out before him. "Yes. That's exactly what I get."

"Good." Ash beamed another overly bright smile at the man as she ushered him into the seat opposite Libby, who had trouble hiding her amusement at her secretary's ability to charm anyone. "Now, I'm heading to the vending machine for drinks. What would you like? A pop or bottled water?"

After Ashley got his order for a cola and Libby's for her usual bottled water, she left them alone.

"So, what's on your mind, Todd?" Libby asked, after she cracked a window for some fresh air and settled in her seat. Setting aside her files to clear a spot on her desk, she opened up her plastic container with the fruit inside. She speared a strawberry with the plastic fork and munched on it while Todd finished swallowing the bite of his sandwich and opened his file.

"The state has moved a new client into the Colbert House."

The halfway house sat on Colbert Street, within easy walking distance of both Westen High School and the town square. When the town council set up the house with state funding five years ago, they wanted to be sure the teens could attend school and find part time jobs without the excuse of limited transportation. Eventually, so many people called it the Colbert House, the council made it official.

"What's his name?" she asked, opening her sandwich, the sight of Lorna's world-famous chicken salad making her mouth water.

"Kyle Gordon. Sixteen."

Jeez. He was going to make her pull the information out of him.

"And why is the state sending him to us?" As the county social worker, she not only sat on the board of directors for Colbert House, she was instrumental in helping the boys get settled into the house, into school, and finding jobs. Most were minor delinquents the state didn't want to put into the system with more hardened offenders.

"That's the problem. They're not giving me a lot of information. As an orphan, he's a ward of the state—"

"The poor dear," Ashley interrupted as she brought back their drinks. "And he has no family at all?"

Taking a big bite of her sandwich, Libby hid her amusement at her secretary's kind heart and the frustrated look on Todd's face.

His cheeks turned quite pink and his lips pressed tight in a thin line beneath his bushy mustache. He narrowed his eyes at Ashley. "No. Not from what I can tell in his file, which really is quite sparse. That's why he's a ward of the state."

"Because his file is so sparse?" Ash asked with a mischievous gleam in her eyes and Libby choked on her food.

"No, Ms. Smith. Not because of the file. Because he has no family to take him in." If Todd turned any redder he'd be mistaken for the old-fashioned fire plugs that still graced the streets of Westen.

Libby took pity on him. "Ashley, if you'd give us a few minutes?"

"Of course." She gave Todd her friendliest smile and sauntered out of the room. Libby swore she heard a little giggle as she closed the door behind her.

Libby set her lunch to the side, took a drink of the cold water, then leaned her elbows onto her desk and looked the house supervisor in the eye. "Todd, I agree it's rather odd the young man's file has so little information in it. Did the state agency give you any reason for that?"

More relaxed now that Ashley had left, he settled

back in his chair. "They said his files were to be sealed until he was twenty-one by court order."

"I see." That usually meant some sort of juvenile arrest.

"Do you?" He leaned forward, real concern in his face. "I now have a hardened criminal among my residents."

CHAPTER THREE

The smell of cinnamon hit Kyle Gordon as he entered the café, sending his taste buds and salivary glands into overdrive. The rumble from his stomach warned him it had been hours since he'd scarfed down some nearly stale cereal back at the house. *Colbert House.* Yeah, that was the name of the new place they'd dumped him. Besides the usual rules of no drugs, no alcohol, no fighting and no girls above the downstairs living area, this place had another rule. Get a job.

Right. Everyone in this backward town knew he was new. New, with no parents, meant he was living at the halfway house. No way would anyone give him a job. He hadn't even bothered to go into any of the places on the list Banyon handed him this morning. He'd found the library and spent some time reading the old newspapers, trying to figure out the town. It was a little place. Sat on the edge of Amish country. Lots of articles about farming, the local county fair and high school sports. The newspapers stopped abruptly last spring.

He'd had to google on the library computer to find out why. Seems the newspaper owner ran a meth lab on the outskirts of town and nearly blew the whole place up. Now that was a surprise.

When the library was invaded by ankle-biters and their moms for story time, he'd evacuated the area and wandered around the square, finally sitting on a bench near the courthouse just watching the people come and go.

Now he figured he'd grab something to eat before going back and facing the pale skinny guy that ran the house and tell him he'd struck out. Maybe the state would send him to a city somewhere.

He walked through the café that looked like it had come straight out of a 1950s sitcom—complete with black-and-white checkered floor, chrome napkin holders, and turquoise-colored, vinyl-covered booths, chairs and barstools—taking a seat at the far end of the lunch counter. Out of habit he pulled up one of the laminated menus and pretended to peruse the items as he surreptitiously studied the other patrons, looking for any potential threats. At the other end of the counter sat two old men, drinking what looked to be iced tea and playing a game of checkers. Several tables in the center of the place had mothers and their kids eating dishes of ice cream.

The far corner held the biggest problem. Four guys. Looked like the local football big shots. They were wolfing down sandwiches and fries. If he was lucky they'd leave before noticing the new kid in the place. Yeah, and Hogwarts would be sending him an invitation by owl-mail any day now. He glanced up. Nope. No owl. Not happening.

"What's on your mind?"

Startled that someone had sneaked up on him so quietly, he looked over the top of the menu to see who spoke to him and swallowed hard. Across the counter stood a hot brunette about his age, with a bit of a smirk on her pink lips, staring straight at him. Her dark hair was pulled up in a ponytail, but he could see strands of it she'd dyed a deep purple. She wore a T-shirt with the shop's logo, Peaches 'N Cream Café, across a chest that hinted at breasts neither too big nor too small beneath. It was tucked loosely into a pair of well-worn, pale-blue jeans.

She leaned in closer, humor making her blue eyes sparkle. "And just so you know, I'm not on the menu."

His mouth went suddenly dry, heat filled his face and he had to work to sound natural. "Too bad. What would you recommend I have then?"

Good. That didn't sound like some lame ass.

She took a step back and sized him up and down, "Burger and fries and one thick chocolate milkshake."

Before he could protest that he didn't have enough money for all that she'd already disappeared in the kitchen part of the café. It wasn't that he didn't have the money, actually. Banyon had handed him part of his weekly stipend the State gave him as part of his spending money. But he didn't know how long he'd be here, and if he wanted to eat anywhere but Colbert House, he'd have to stretch every penny.

Maybe he could get her to take the milkshake back. Water would be just as good.

Movement from the far corner caught his eye. The four guys were sliding out of the booth and headed for the cash register. Great. He could study the menu some more and maybe they wouldn't say anything. But then the waitress might say something since she'd already taken his order.

A tall woman with hair the color of a yellow crayon piled on her head, wearing an apron with the café logo across the top part, stepped out of the kitchen to meet the four guys at the cash register that was so old, he swore it probably came from the 1800s.

"Hey, boys. Thought football practice started today?" she said, taking the first guy's ticket.

"Two-a-days start tomorrow, Miss Lorna," the dark-haired one said.

"Yeah, we're just having a meeting at the high school tonight," the tall, skinny one said then leaned onto the counter. "Gonna meet the coaches and probably pick which team we want to be on."

The redhead slapped the first guy on the shoulder. "Of course, old Brett here will be the quarterback."

"That's going to be up to the coach, Connor," the lady said as she rang up the first bill. "Sheriff Justice will wait to see how each of you play. Who knows, there may be someone better than Brett."

"No, way," Connor protested. "He's been the best passer in town for the past two years."

The lady shrugged and glanced at the counter where Kyle sat, then returned her attention to the cash register, but not before the shortest, lineman-sized guy focused in on him.

Kyle glanced around for something to look at so the foursome wouldn't think he'd been eavesdropping. A stack of fliers were on the end of the counter. He grabbed one.

The local craft show? *Crap*. With his luck one of those guys would wander over and comment on him being "crafty" like a girl.

"Here, this looks more your style," the cute waitress said, standing in front of him, blocking the view of the four football players. She set down the chocolate milkshake and a copy of a sports magazine featuring the Ohio State Buckeyes in front of him. Then she winked, turned and headed back into the kitchen. He couldn't help grin at her swaying bottom, the flyer for the craft show neatly tucked in the hip pocket of her jeans.

Out of the corner of his eye, he saw the shortest of the four guys say something to the guy they'd called Brett and both of them turned to stare at him. Looking them straight in the eyes, he took a big sip on the straw in his shake.

"That's seven-fifty," the cashier lady said, drawing

the short guy's attention. He fished out the money and the register made a clanking sound as she rang him up.

Quarterback Brett continued to stare his way.

Some hick town football player wasn't intimidating him. At some of the group homes he'd lived in, he'd bunked in with gang members—some he was sure had committed murder—thieves and general badasses. Slowly he lifted the magazine, unaware of what article he'd opened it to, his gaze still on the guy. Finally, Quarterback Brett gave him a small nod, then turned his attention back on his friends as they left.

"Cheeseburger and fries." The cute waitress slid the heaping plate in front of him, along with a glass of water. "Good milkshake, huh?"

He looked down to see he'd managed to drink half of it already. And it had been good. "Best I've ever had."

She leaned one hip against the counter. "That's 'cause we use real milk, real ice cream and old-fashioned chocolate syrup we make right here."

"Really?" he asked as he loaded ketchup over his fries. "Everything cooked fresh like that?"

"Of course, darlin'" the cashier lady, Lorna, said, sauntering over. "This is my place and I refuse to use frozen anything. Buy the vegetables and meat from the local farmers. Even buy the rolls from the bakery round the corner. Try a bite."

Not arguing with her pointed look, he sank his teeth into the burger. God, it tasted fantastic, with all the dripping cheese, perfectly grilled meat and the crisp veggies.

"Good, isn't it?" the waitress asked then laughed.

He nodded his agreement as he chewed.

The doorbell chimed again and in walked a woman with twin redheaded boys and a baby in a stroller.

"Hey, Emma," both the women said at the same time, leaving him to eat his meal as they met the mother and her kids.

As he ate his meal he tried to listen to their conversation, but got lost in the chatter of all three women and the little boys. What he did learn was the cute waitress was the café owner Lorna's daughter. Apparently, she also babysat on a regular basis for the family.

Slowing down his eating, he flipped through the magazine and watched as more people flitted in and out of the café, which seemed to be the place to meet and hang out in town. Even a few of the local deputies stopped in for an iced tea or milkshake. Finally most of the other customers had left. He looked down and realized he was on his last French fry. Time to pay up and head back to Colbert House.

Banyon would be all over him about a job. He was that kind of guy. Probably nag him until he got one or report him to the State and get him sent back to Columbus.

"You gonna eat that, or just hang out until dinner service starts?" Rachel was back, one brow raised in question as she slipped him his bill.

"Oh, sorry, I didn't mean to take so long."

She flashed him a little grin. "No problem. I'll meet you up at the register."

He popped the last fry in his mouth and looked at the bill. Great, he had just enough to pay for lunch and leave her a nice tip—and he was leaving her a good tip. For the first time in a long time, someone had made him feel welcome in a new place.

With more confidence than he'd had when he'd come in the café, he walked up to the register.

Once again she gave him that grin as she took the ticket and rang up the amount. "So, you're new in town or just passing through?"

Some of the air seeped out of his new found confidence. Once she learned he was at Colbert House he'd guarantee all her friendliness would disappear. But he'd decided long ago he'd make no apologies for who he was or what problems life had dealt him.

"Yeah. I'm the new kid." He pulled out his wallet and the lone ten sitting in it.

She hesitated before taking the bill from him. "Where are you and your folks living?"

"My parents are dead. I'm over at the Colbert House."

"So you're out looking for a job?" When she handed him his change, he looked up expecting to see scorn or even fear in her eyes. Nope. They were still clear blue, but maybe a little inquisitive.

What? Did everyone in this town know the house's rules?

"Yeah. House rules."

"Any luck?" She leaned one hip against the counter, her head tilted to the side. For the first time in his life, it felt like someone honestly wanted to know how things were going for him.

"Not really. Just sort of been looking around, mostly. Trying to get a lay of the land and see what might be available."

"Ever wash dishes?"

"Sure. Why?"

She gave him a wink and pushed away from the counter. "Hey, Mom. Come out here a second," she yelled into the kitchen.

A minute later the owner, Lorna, emerged from the kitchen, wiping her hands on a dish towel. "What's up, Rachel?"

Rachel. That was her name. He tried it over in his mind. Yep. It seemed to suit her. Smart. Friendly. To the point.

"I think I solved your help problem," she said, looking from her mother back to him. "This is...?"

"Oh, Kyle," he held out his hand to Lorna. "Kyle Gordon, ma'am."

The café owner shook his hand in a strong one of her own. "Glad to meet you, Kyle."

"Kyle's new over at the Colbert House and he's looking for work. Knows how to wash dishes," Rachel said with a head tilt at her mother.

"Does he now?" Lorna gave her daughter a shrewd stare then turned her attention back to him. "Ever worked in a café, Kyle?"

Might as well be up front, she'd figure it out soon enough. Better to not get the job, then have it pulled out from under him.

"No, ma'am. But the last house I was at, we were assigned chores on a regular basis. I've done my share of dishes."

She laid one hand on the counter, the other fisted on her hip just where the apron hitched up to tie in back, her lips pressed in a serious line as she studied him up and down. "Kinda scrawny. When was the last good meal you ate?"

Despite how nervous her look made him, he couldn't fight the grin as he answered. "About ten minutes ago when Rachel served me up one of your burgers, fries and chocolate shake."

That stern face of Lorna's cracked into a big grin of her own as she let out a cackle of a laugh. "Good answer, son. How about you show up here around five, tell Todd Banyon you'll be working for me. Money is minimum wage, plus a share of the daily tips. If you're a hard worker and as smart as I think you are, we might just make it permanent. Okay?"

"Yes, ma'am."

She started to head back into the kitchen, then stopped. "Rachel, give the boy back his money. You know the policy. Employees get all their meals free here."

"You got it, Mom." Rachel hit the keys on the register, popping the cash drawer open once more, took out his slip of paper and counted out the money to make his ten dollars whole again.

Stunned at his turn of good fortune, Kyle started to pocket the money, then stopped. Pulling off two crisp ones, he slid them back across the counter towards Rachel. "Here."

She held up her hands without touching the money. "You heard my mom. Food's free to employees."

"My food might be free, but you've more than earned a tip." Determined not to look like a mooch he pushed it towards her a little more. "Take it. Please?"

After a moment's hesitation, she nodded and picked up the bills. "Okay, this once."

"See you at five," he said, pocketing the rest of the money and heading out the door. The chimes sounded behind him as he stepped out onto the sidewalk. Suddenly, the little hick town didn't seem too bad. But he'd learned years earlier that appearances could be deceiving.

A chill crept over him. He glanced around to see if anyone was watching him. Not that he could tell. No use borrowing trouble. Bad news would find him soon enough.

For now he'd just enjoy having a job and maybe a new friend in Rachel. As he headed back in the direction of Colbert House he glanced up in the sky, expecting to see storm clouds gathering and lightning headed his way.

Not a cloud marred the bright-blue expanse. Maybe that was a good sign. For once maybe his luck had turned.

* * * * *

Despite the late-summer heat, Deke drove down the highway with the windows down and kept the air conditioning off. To fight the claustrophobic feel of the enclosed cabin, he needed the feel of the wind blowing on his face. After he'd nearly bolted from the courtroom and out of the building, he didn't know how long he sat on one of the benches that dotted the lawn of the century-old building and faced the town square.

Watching the ebb and flow of townsfolk and Amish-country tourists wander past from his shaded spot, he'd fought to get his breathing and heart rate under control. Thank God no one he knew well wanted to stop and chat. The last thing he needed to do was explain to someone how every time he remembered Bill Wilson, he broke out in a cold sweat and had flashbacks to the fire that killed his friend and nearly took his own life.

He hated seeing pity on people's faces, especially when he didn't deserve it. Right after the fire their sympathy ate at him as he nearly choked on his own guilt. So instead of facing them, he'd crawled into a bottle and drowned his pain and misery for months. Probably still be there if it hadn't been for Gage's dad.

The drumming in his head grew louder until the realization that someone was pounding on his door finally penetrated the groggy fog in his brain and pulled him up off the couch. He stumbled to the door and jerked it open.

"What?" The sound of his own voice made him wince. Squinting, he tried to focus on the man standing in the doorway.

Lloyd Justice, sheriff of his hometown fifty miles south of here, looked him up one side and down the other from behind his reflective sunglasses, his lips pressed in a firm line. "Put some pants on, boy. You and I are gonna have a talk."

He stumbled back into the apartment and his bedroom, searching for jeans among the pile of laundry littering his floor. Once he had them on and zipped he took a minute to grab aspirin from his bathroom, swallowing them down with just enough water to keep from choking on them.

Dammit. What the hell was Gage's dad doing here? Had he done something stupid while drinking?

A quick look out the bedroom window showed his pickup just where he'd left it. No dents anywhere he could see. At least he hadn't been drunk driving.

So what did the Sheriff want with him? No reason to stand here wondering. Gage's old man never pulled punches with either of them. He had no doubt the man would get to the point. Quickly.

Then he could get back to the job of pickling his liver with some Jim Beam.

The smell of coffee hit him as he walked back into the living room and slid onto one of the barstools at the island separating it from the kitchen.

Lloyd, minus sunglasses now, set a mug in front of him and some containers of creamer. Then leaned down over his elbows to stare straight at him. Ever since his father died in an accident helping a man fix a flat tire, Gage's dad had become like a second father to him. "Figured whatever you had in that fridge was curdled, so brought you something to lighten the coffee."

After doctoring his coffee with the cream, he took a few tentative sips of the hot caffeine, then a few bigger swallows, waiting for the jolt to hit his system.

Nearly all of his cup was empty when Lloyd spoke again.

"Your fire chief from up here in Akron called me a few days ago."

Yeah, he'd ignored calls from anyone from his old company.

"Gage said he tried to call you, too."

Man, he was a shit for not talking to his friend, but he just wanted to be left alone.

"Your mama was in to see me yesterday."

Deke took another swallow of coffee, preventing a frustrated groan to escape. Ignoring co-workers, friends and former bosses, he could get by with that. Not talking to his mama? No way would the old man let that one slide.

"Sorry. I'll call her today."

"Not drunk or hung over, you won't." Lloyd leaned back on the opposite counter, his arms crossed over his chest. "It's been six months since the fire and four since you were released from the hospital, boy. You've had time to come to grips with things. But all you've seemed to do was try to drink yourself to death. Is that what Bill Wilson died for? So you could wallow in self-pity and booze?"

Jeez. Talk about a gut punch.

"No."

"No, what?"

Suddenly he felt like a kid in school again. "No, sir. Bill wouldn't appreciate me not honoring his sacrifice." But he'd understand the guilt.

"Good. I want to see you at my office first thing tomorrow morning. I have a job for you."

"Thanks, but I'm not interested in being a deputy, sir."

"Good. Because I wouldn't have you." Lloyd slipped a piece of paper in front of him. "The county is starting a fire division in this area of the county. We want you to train our volunteers."

Train inexperienced people how to not die fighting a fire? No. He couldn't do it.

"Yes, you can, and you will." At Lloyd's words he

realized he'd actually been thinking out loud. "For Bill's memory and to keep my county's residents safe, you're going to pull yourself out of this pitiful-me funk and get on with your life. The life Bill died saving." He stood and strode to the door, stopping to put his sunglasses on and fix him with a don't-mess-with-me-boy stare. "And once you've sobered up, call your mama."

And that's just what he'd done.

Sobered up. Called his mom. Packed his things. Moved back to Westen. One step at a time, he'd tried to make amends for his mistake and make Bill Wilson proud. Then Bill's mother became ill and Libby came back to town. He'd never talked with her and couldn't beg her forgiveness—still couldn't after all these years.

As always, he pushed memories of Libby, their lives together before the fire, and the pain he always saw in her liquid blue eyes into the back corner of his mind. Some things were better left alone. What he needed to do was focus on the job of keeping Westen and the surrounding area from burning to the ground.

Newly mowed hay hit his senses as he turned off the highway onto the two-lane road leading into the farms owned by several large Amish families. Large horse-drawn wagons half-loaded with hay set in the middle of the fields, surrounded by piles of cut hay still drying. He was glad to see the farmers were getting their fields mowed and the dry stalks cleared out of the hot summer sun. The sooner they got the fields empty of potential fodder for burning, the less likely any stray spark would ignite it all.

Damn what he wouldn't give for a good ground-soaking rainstorm. Unfortunately, both the weather service and the farmer's almanac weren't predicting anything in the next week or so.

Turning onto the gravel road, he waved back at the small groups of farmers dressed in plain black pants and suspenders, white shirts with the long sleeves rolled up to show tanned arms, and straw hats perched on their heads. They reminded him of worker ants as they steadily walked up the road to Thomas Elder's farm. True to his name, Thomas was one of the elders of the community. As such, important meetings were held at his home, like this one Deke had asked Thomas to host.

The community's shunning of modern conveniences like televisions made word-of-mouth information in a face-to-face meeting the best way to get the fire warnings out to these farmers. He suspected they already knew what he was going to say, had been saying it over the years, but he wanted to be sure they knew the extra hazard they had this long, dry summer.

He pulled his truck into the gravel drive at Thomas' house. The tall, lanky farmer with the thick beard, who looked like he could be a direct descendent of Abraham Lincoln, stepped off the porch, one hand raised in greeting and a broad smile on his sun-wrinkled skin.

"Welcome, Deacon, welcome." Thomas shook his hand in a firm grip, then slapped him hard on the shoulder. "Always a pleasure to have you visit with us. My Naomi has made some cool lemonade and treats inside. You would like some, ya?"

"Can't think of anything I'd enjoy more, Thomas." Deke grabbed his notebook and followed the farmer into the house.

If Naomi was up to her usual standards, he'd be leaving with a basket full of baked goods, several jars of homemade jam and some freshly picked vegetables. He removed his hat as he entered the kitchen. Naomi Elder was as short as her husband Thomas was tall. No one looking at the tiny woman would guess she was the mother of eight. "Hello, Naomi."

"Welcome, Deacon. It has been too long since last you visited." She stood on her tiptoes to give him a hug then a pat on his arm as she moved away.

"I apologize. This summer has kept me pretty busy."

"It has been very dry, hasn't it? Perhaps you can come for dinner when you have time. The other men will be here soon. But you be sure to stop in here before you go," she said with a wink and pointed to the already-prepared basket before handing him a cold glass of lemonade.

Score.

There were a few perks to this job. Naomi's cooking was one of them.

He followed Thomas into the large living room area where Naomi had already set out a tray of small, homemade fruit-filled pastries.

"She likes to spoil you, Deacon," Thomas said, settling into what appeared to be his favorite leather chair.

"And I like letting her, Thomas. You're a very lucky man to have such a fine cook in your wife."

"Ya. My Naomi is very special." Thomas fixed him with a perceptive eye. "Do you not think it's time you found a good woman for your life?"

The image of Libby as she'd looked in the café and the courtroom this morning flashed in his mind. Then the sadness in her eyes hit him. "I don't think there's a woman out there for me."

"Nonsense. A man isn't complete without a woman by his side. It is how God intended, my friend."

Except the one woman for him was out of his reach forever.

"Maybe. Maybe not." He put Libby out of his mind once more and forced a smile. "Besides, I don't think there's a woman as fine as Naomi on my horizons. You wouldn't want to give her up, would you?"

Thomas laughed. "I could never live without my Naomi."

"Then it's a bachelor's life for me."

They both chuckled and sipped on their lemonade as the other farmers and the young men of their families filtered into living room. Once they were all present and greetings exchanged, Thomas stood.

"As ye've noticed the weather has been as dry as the almanac predicted this summer."

His proclamation was greeted with many "Ayes" and nodding of heads.

"Many of ye know Deacon Reynolds, the county fire chief. He's come to talk with us about fire safety. I know many of ye have already made sure you're doing everything ye can to prevent fires, but it never hurts to review all the steps we can be taking and Deacon always has ideas we might not have considered."

Deke stood in the center of the room. "We've been talking about fire prevention every year for the past ten years, haven't we?"

Many of the men answered with "Ya", or nodded their heads.

"And just today on my drive here I've seen the fields being cleared of dried hay and debris. I think you could teach some of us English how to maintain our yards and fields in a better fashion, that's for sure."

This got him some rumbling chuckles.

"I've asked the phone company to check the connections on your phone in the shanty." This was a small wooden structure the Amish community used to house a communal phone for business and emergencies, since this particular community didn't allow phones in their homes. "Everything is in working order and you know the number directly to the firehouse is 5-7-9." To decrease response time in the county one of the first things he'd done when he started the fire department was institute a direct number, since the usual 9-1-1 would have to go through the sheriff's office first.

"Everything is in working order there. As a precautionary measure during this drought, the sheriff's department and members of the fire department along with volunteers will be taking turns driving through the rural areas, watching for any signs of fire. If you have any concerns or hot spots, let them know and we'll check it out. How are you doing with maintaining water supplies around the barns?"

"The creeks and ponds are down several inches," Samuel Miller said. "But the deep springs are still flowing well. My sons and I have been filling barrels to feed the animals and keep near the barns."

Most of the other farmers said they were doing the same and would share with anyone who needed help. Another thing he'd always admired about the local Amish community. Their willingness to help others without question or complaint.

"Good. Until the rain comes, which the almanac and weather service agree for once won't be for a few more weeks, we'll need to keep from any burning outdoors."

"Tell that to the English," Josiah Miller, Samuel's younger brother said. "We found some boys camping in the woods not far from our back pasture and they were using an open fire instead of a grill. They put out the fire when we asked them to do so."

"How old were the boys?"

"Old enough to know better. They looked like what you'd call footballers."

Interesting. He'd heard of some teenagers in other

Suzanne Ferrell

communities who taunted and terrorized the local Amish, but they'd never had it in Westen County. "I'm giving a talk to the high school on opening day about fire prevention, but until then I'll see if I can find out who these boys were and make sure they know no open pit burns until we get some rain."

When there were no more questions or concerns, the informal meeting broke up, a few men remaining to talk about the crops and cattle. Deke excused himself, thanking Thomas before heading into the kitchen where Naomi and her eldest girl, who was about ten, were making dinner.

"Sarah, bring that dish." Naomi pointed to the small casserole dish on the counter then handed the wicker basket to Deke. "I've made you a shepherd's pie with homemade mashed potatoes, peas and carrots from our garden and sausage we set out last fall. It will fill you up."

"You shouldn't have." Deke took the dish and laid it on top of the basket.

"Of course I should. This way you have to visit sooner to return the dish," Naomi said with a grin and her daughter giggled shyly.

He promised he'd do just that then headed out to his truck. Tucking the food into the floor board of the seat, he made sure nothing would spill on the trip home. Thomas came over to lean in the window just after Deke climbed in the driver's side.

"Something wrong, Thomas?" he asked at the

serious look on the church elder's face.

"These boys that Josiah mentioned. Should we be concerned?" Deke knew he was speaking as an elder of the church now. Part of his responsibility as a community leader was protecting the members of their community from outsiders who might harm them.

"We've never had issues before, but I'll talk it over with Gage. Maybe he and his deputies can keep an eye out for them when they make their safety rounds. I'll give my boys a heads-up, too."

"Good. Good. Thank ye for talking to us. 'Tis always good to be made aware of the dangers and what we can do to prevent a fire."

"Anytime, Thomas. And if you have any problems, you let me or Gage know."

As he drove away from the farm and back down the gravel road, his heart was lighter than it had been before leaving the courthouse. Lloyd and Bill would both be proud of how he'd incorporated the Amish community into the county's safety plans. And Naomi's homemade food would certainly fill him up.

He glanced at the dashboard clock. Just enough time to get Naomi's goodies home before he had to meet Gage at the high school practice field. After talking to the farmers, assisting Gage in coaching might be a good thing after all. He'd get a chance to read the attitudes of the boys and also get some fire safety information in as well as defensive football moves.

* * * * *

The whirring of blow dryers and the friendly chatter of customers and hairstylists greeted Libby the next morning as she wheeled her mother's oldest friend, Mrs. Lafferty, into the Dye Right hair salon.

It was a lovely salon, with cotton-candy-pink-and-black damask walls, and black trim along the baseboards, crown molding and windows. Black-and-white checked curtains framed the three large street windows, while large black-and-white images of Parisian icons such as the Eiffel Tower, the Arc de Triomphe, and the Louvre hung on the walls.

The chairs, in Libby's opinion, were the best part of the salon. Instead of hard plastic that melted to your thighs in summer and felt cold and sticky in winter as some places had, the Dye Right had large wingback chairs with stand-up dryers behind them and overstuffed Queen Anne-style couches for those waiting their appointments. All were upholstered in various pink-and-black striped or black-and-white damask fabrics. Soft, comfortable, stay-a-while-and-chat furniture, with distressed tables to hold cups of tea and the lovely treats offered from the local bakery stationed beside them. She'd been bringing "Aunt" Julie here every Tuesday to get her wash and set ever since she'd had to move into the local nursing home. Now it was one of Libby's little pleasures.

"Morning, Miss Julie, Libby," the Miller twins

greeted them in unison from their seats under the driers, their grey hair rolled up in the same exact rows. Libby smiled. They'd been identical their whole lives and even got their hair done the same way every week so they'd continue the look, down to the last hair.

"Hey, Miss Julie. You're looking fit as a fiddle today." Twylla Howard, the owner of the salon came up to greet the octogenarian, helping Libby secure the locks on the wheelchair and assist the frail woman from the seat.

"Oh, you know how much I look forward to getting my hair done, Twylla. Have to keep those men at the home happy," Aunt Julie said with a laugh in her voice and a twinkle in her eye. Libby handed her the three-footed walking cane and the trio slowly headed over to Twylla's styling chair.

Twylla winked at her. "I bet you have to beat them off with that cane."

Aunt Julie shook her head slightly as she climbed into the seat. "Oh, dear, no. At my age, if they have a heartbeat and can feed themselves, they're a keeper!"

Half the salon laughed at her joke.

"Do you want something to drink while you're getting all pretty?" Libby asked.

Aunt Julie patted her hand. "No, dear. You just get yourself something or run your errands if you have any. Twylla will take good care of me."

"No errands today. I'll just grab some water and wait here. Maybe we'll go over to the tearoom and have lunch today?"

"That will be lovely, dear, if you're sure you'll have time." Julie patted her hand again.

"I wouldn't offer if I didn't."

She left her in Twylla's capable hands, grabbed a bottle of water and took a seat in the small waiting area near the front door. It was also the spot the stylists parked people who had highlights put in their hair to wait the required amount of time. Which is exactly what Bobby Roberts, the sheriff's newest deputy and more importantly his fiancée, was doing today.

"I know. I look like a giant antenna monster with all these aluminum foil sheets in my hair," Bobby said as Libby took the seat next to her.

Libby laughed. "Maybe we could hook you up to the radio and get the Cleveland baseball game."

"Whatever you do, don't mention that to Gage, or he'll have me hooked up like this at the office just to get football games."

They shared another laugh and Libby snatched up the newest gossip magazine. "Aunt Julie thinks I bring her here out of the goodness of my heart. What she doesn't know is this is the only time I get to indulge my need to live vicariously through the Hollywood stars and get my gossip fix."

Bobby held up the bridal magazine she was flipping through. "I'm under strict orders from my sisters to look through the pile of these they mailed me. I can't seem to get it through their heads that I'm not having a big elaborate, formal wedding. Gage and I just want something simple."

"Have you set the date yet?" Libby flipped through some pictures of the Kardashians' latest drama. She had enough over-the-top drama in her clients' lives. She didn't need it in her reading choices.

"If Gage could have his way, we would've done it the week after he asked me. But I wanted to wait until both my sisters could be here. Chloe can make up her own schedule as long as there's no big court case going on. Dylan is another story."

"Oh? Don't doctors make up their own schedules, too?"

"Once they're out of residency. But Dylan's an intern. She had to ask in advance to have any kind of vacation. Luckily, she got the time off at Christmas, but has to work every weekend for six weeks straight to get it."

"A Christmas wedding then?"

A soft look came over Bobby's face and tears filled her eyes. She dabbed at them. "Actually, December twenty-second. It was my parents' wedding day. I wanted to honor their memories by making it our anniversary, too."

"That's a wonderful idea." She knew that Bobby's parents had died when she was in college and she had to quit to take a teaching job to support and raise her younger sisters. Once they were out of college, she'd traded in her teaching career for one as a private investigator. Her first case landed her, quite literally, in Gage's arms. The pair fell in love and she'd even risked her own life to help save his. Sometimes happy-ever-afters did come true.

Just not for me and Deacon.

She shoved that thought back into the dark cave where it belonged. Some things just couldn't be undone.

"Aren't you testifying in Melissa Compton's spousal abuse case?" Bobby asked after a few minutes.

"That was yesterday." Holding her place in the magazine at the fall television previews, she leaned in and lowered her voice so that her words wouldn't carry past the two of them. As a deputy, Bobby knew the case, had even helped Doc Clint take the pictures of Melissa's injuries. The last thing Libby wanted was for any details of the trial to get picked up by the gossip community that lived at the Dye Right. "The prosecution finished their case yesterday evening. The defense was today, and quite frankly I didn't think I could stomach listening to Frank's friends and family testify to what an upstanding citizen he is."

Bobby's eyes narrowed and her lips pressed together in a thin line. "All anyone would have to do is look at those pictures and they'd know what kind of a son-of-a-bitch Frank Compton is."

"I know. But he's the epitome of a slick salesman. All flash and smile to the public." Just being in the man's presence made Libby's skin crawl. If she'd had to listen to glowing personal references in court, she'd been afraid she'd have been held in contempt for saying what she really thought of the man. That's the reason she kept her weekly appointment with Aunt Julie today and told Melissa she'd be there tomorrow.

"Well, I'm just glad Melissa is finally standing up to the monster." Bobby flipped a few more pages in her magazine. "I just hope she stands firm and uses this new courage to find a life for herself. She's such a sweet woman."

Libby nodded her agreement. "Thank goodness most of Frank's family has moved out of the area. Once he goes to jail, she might be able to finally hold her head up in town without worrying what might get back to him."

A short, willowy woman with spiky hair dyed several shades of red and orange approached them. "Okay, Miz Bobby, it's time to rinse you off and see what those highlights look like."

Bobby set aside the bridal magazine and stood. "Libby, this is Sylvie Gillis. She's the new stylist Twylla hired. Sylvie, Libby is the county social worker."

"Glad to meet ya, Miz Libby. Love to talk more, but if I don't get Miz Bobby under some water, she'll more than likely come out looking like me and I don't think the sheriff would like that much," the little woman said with a laugh as she took the deputy by her elbow and led her across the room.

Bobby gave her a wide-eyed look over her shoulder that said she prayed that wouldn't happen, too, and mouthed the words *help me*. Libby swallowed the grin that played on her lips. One thing about Westen. Newcomers, even multicolored-haired elves like Sylvie, were usually welcomed.

Which reminded her. She'd promised Todd Banyon she'd stop by and talk with his newest resident sometime this week. Once more she wondered what was in the young man's past that had his records sealed. Could Todd be right for once? Was there a dangerous criminal now living at Colbert House?

CHAPTER FOUR

A bunch of knuckleheads.

The words of Coach Turner, his old high school football coach, drifted into Deke's head as he watched this year's kids trying out for the team. Most of them had basic skills—probably drummed into them from the time they played peewee ball. Problem was they also had some bad habits, including showboating and laziness. Because most of these guys had grown up together, the hierarchy of the team, at least in their minds, was pretty well set. If they'd had the same coach as last year, they might be right.

Unfortunately for them, they had a new coach—the Gunslinger. The corner of Deke's mouth lifted in a half smirk. Yesterday the boys had been staring not only at the town's sheriff and recent hero, but at a town legend —the man whose records for passing completion yards still hung in the state's record books. This morning Gage had wiped the hero worship off their eyes with the conditioning drills he'd had them perform.

Gage learned from his father that every person had to earn their way through life, whether it was making a baseball or football team, or getting a job, or gaining respect of the people around him. If Brett Howard was going to be this year's starting quarterback, he was going to have to prove he could not only do the job, but lead the team. Same went for the star wide-receiver, Ethan Tanner. Long and lanky, with excellent hands, as long as the ball was thrown near him. Making an effort wasn't a priority for Tanner unless someone was on his heels.

"Damn, that kid runs like he's out for a Sunday stroll," Gage muttered beside him, then strode across the field, fire in his eyes. "Tanner, you think you could put a little more effort into that route? At the rate your running, the offensive line will have to take the defensive line out on a date and dinner before the QB can toss the ball your direction!"

Shaking his head Deke had to admit Gage was taking a page from Coach Turner's playbook. The old man had been devious in his attempts to weed out the slackers and undisciplined kids from the ones who had a passion for the game. Of course what he'd ended up with was a core team that made it to the State playoffs ten years straight before he retired. Gage had taken the drills and tweaked them. Instead of hundred-yard sprints—what they'd used to call *gassers*—he'd set up what he called *sprint ladders*. The kids ran ten yards up and back. Took a ten-second rest between sprints and then did a twenty-yard up and back sprint, working their way up to fifty yards up and back, then reducing the yards until they finished with the ten-yard sprints once more.

Time to get his defense moving. He'd had them practicing hitting the tackling dummies to get used to the contact.

"Defense, to me," he yelled, getting the fifteen guys' attention. Only half ran over. "Don't make me wait, ladies!"

That got the rest of them hustling.

"Next time I call you, anyone not running here on the double will do five laps of the field after practice. Got me?"

"Yes, sir!" they said with more enthusiasm than they'd shown running just now.

"Let's start with some back-pedal drills. I want you to keep your knees bent at a forty-five degree angle, heads up, back straight. Let your arms dangle at your sides. With your weight on the balls of your feet, push off with the front foot and back pedal ten yards, just like this," he said, quickly showing the form he wanted them to use and exactly how he wanted them to perform it. He figured he'd get their respect quicker if they were asked to do something he could do easily. Fewer complaints that way. He pointed to the first five guys, including Mike Cohn, the only senior of his group. "You guys first. Show the rest of us how you can do it."

They ran through the drill twice each with him

yelling to keep their chests over their feet, their feet close to the ground. "Pump those arms, Cohn. Make me believe you'll catch that wide receiver!"

"That one was better. One more time, then we'll switch over to some fade cover drills."

As the squad dropped back into formation and started the last set of back-pedals, movement from the corner of the field caught his eye.

Rachel Doone and some brown-haired kid he'd never seen before pulled a cart loaded with coolers onto the edge of the field nearest the locker room and parking lot exit. Her mom, Lorna, had been supplying afternoon refreshments to the team during two-a-days ever since he was a freshman.

As he watched the pair open the coolers and the foldable table they'd stowed on the bottom of the cart, another memory flashed in his mind. The first time he'd noticed Bill's sister, Libby, as something other than his kid sister. She'd worked at the Peaches 'N Cream all summer, and she'd been the one to haul the food with Lorna then. Hair pulled up in a sporty ponytail, hanging down her back, exposing the long slender column of her neck. Shorts that showed off long legs that should've been outlawed. Bill had hit him in the head with the football to distract him.

Libby. A dull ache centered in his chest.

They'd both been so innocent and carefree back then. The worst problem making sure to win all their Class A division games. Then how he was going to ask his friend's sister to Homecoming. Bill was a year ahead of him and would either tease him unmercifully or beat the snot out of him for liking his sister.

Dammit. For the past ten years he'd been able to keep thoughts of Libby at bay. Ever since seeing her yesterday morning with that new newspaper man at the café, she'd been popping into his head almost at will.

"Coach, how many more you want us to do?"

He blinked, coming back to the present. Mike and the other defensive players stood around him, half of them bent over sucking in air, sweat soaking the fronts of their T-shirts. Gage was right. He did need to give back to the team that helped center his teenage years. Besides, focusing on teaching the kids not only about the game, but life lessons might just get him out of this maudlin mood and his mind off Libby.

Leaning down, he snatched up a football. "Which one of you guys played defensive lineman last year?"

Four hands shot up from the older players.

"How many want to give it a try?"

Four more of the younger ones.

"Good. You guys are going to get some special coaching." He waved at the sidelines where Cleetus Junkins, still dressed in his deputy sheriff uniform, stood with his arms crossed over his chest like some giant sideline protector. The big man's face broke out in a grin as he jogged across the field.

Cleetus loved two things—the town of Westen and playing football. The year they'd taken their second

State championship, Cleetus had been a freshman while he and Gage had been seniors. It was like Cleetus was the missing piece to their threesome. Even back then, most people, including the coaches and the entire team, were misled by Cleetus' natural good-naturedness and affability. The gentle giant. That's what he was, until he donned a football uniform. Once he had on his pads and helmet, he made Mean Joe Green look like a lamb.

As he neared the group, the boys broke out in grins, and hailed him with, "Hey, Cleetus!" and "How's it going?"

Deke waited for all the greetings to die down. "Deputy Junkins is a former defensive lineman for Westen High. In fact, he was on the state championship team for four years of the ten year run that is still a state record."

Lots of cheering and whistles came from the boys and Deke again waited for quiet.

"He will be my assistant and the defensive line coach. I do not care how long you have known him, or how many times he's joked around with your or your daddies off the field. On this field he will be known as *Coach Junkins*. You will show him the same respect as you do me or Coach Justice. Do you understand?"

"Yes, sir!" the boys said in unison.

"Good. Coach Junkins will take the linemen to the sidelines to run some drills with them. The rest of you follow me and we'll practice coverage and tip drills. When Coach Justice calls us together, we're going to see what you can do against the QBs and the wide receivers before we break for the night."

Working the team, he saw some potential in the new kids and good skills in his older players. He just hoped when they went up against the offense someone could pressure Ethan Tanner and light a fire under the receiver's butt. Otherwise the team was going to have a rough first game.

* * * * *

It was Kyle's first full day working for Lorna at the Peaches 'N Cream Café and she had him helping make peanut butter sandwiches with Rachel, which was pretty cool. Then they'd loaded them into coolers with fresh apples and oranges, homemade oatmeal cookies and sports drinks. Lorna had him accompany Rachel as she drove the café's van out to the school and they'd dragged this all out to the field just so these guys could have a post-practice snack.

Really? These guys get fed breakfast before practice and snacks after? Talks about prima donnas!

How many times had he gone without a meal because someone bigger had decided to eat his, too? Or someone decided to use food as a punishment or reward system in their house?

Once they had the food out, Rachel took a seat on the ground near the cart full of food and pulled out her cell phone and book, putting her ear buds in to listen to music while she read.

He wasn't sure what to do. She hadn't invited him to

sit by her. Doing so would probably make him look pathetic. And he couldn't hang out by the food or someone might think he was taking some. Last thing he wanted to do was lose his job for stealing and risk Banyon kicking him out of Colbert House. So, he moved a few feet down the sidelines and stood watching the players go through their drills.

Like most Americans, he knew a little about football. One of the foster dads he'd lived with as a kid one year was an avid fan and while he didn't teach him much, he did get to watch lots of games while the guy cursed and carried on. Given all the temporary places he'd lived, no one ever took the time to get him involved with a little league team.

Surprise, surprise. He'd been lucky to get food and a clean bed. Hell, sometimes he was just lucky to stay alive in the places. The all-American little league experience wasn't for him.

So standing here watching them didn't make a lot of sense to him. Looked like they were in small groups, doing all kinds of exercises. When the heck did they start playing?

When the one coach had the guys start throwing passes to other guys, he moved a little farther down the line to watch them a little closer. He recognized the guy called Brett from the café yesterday, taking his turn to toss the ball. Seemed to have a good arm. Two of the other guys, the redhead and the tall, lanky guy were snagging balls passed their way. No one seemed to be working too hard.

On the far side of the field other groups were practicing. One coach, the one that looked like a small mountain and wearing some sort of police uniform, was showing kids how to come out of a crouch and rush forward. Pretty good moves for a big guy.

The other coach had his guys running backwards, then sideways, tossing the ball to them at the last second. Every now and then one of them would catch it.

"Look out!"

The warning came from the field about the time a football hurled towards the sidelines directly at Rachel, who still had her eyes down and her head bobbing to whatever song was playing on her phone. The tall, lanky guy was running after it, but his angle headed him right at Rachel.

Kyle took off at a dead sprint. His eyes darting from the ball to Rachel's spot and back again. The other guy was still running, his vision only on the ball and not Rachel. If he didn't do something the guy was going to plow her and the food over.

Checking the angle, he timed his jump, knocking into the side of the guy with his shoulders and his hands snagging the ball at the same time. Long-and-lanky landed about two feet to the side of Rachel, who jumped up with a scream just as Kyle landed on his back in front of her, the ball still clutched to his chest.

"You okay, kid?" the defensive coach asked, his voice deep and scratchy.

It took Kyle a minute to catch his breath as he stared up at the man with scars going up one side of his neck and along his jaw to his left ear. A flash of a memory hit him.

Rain. Pouring down in buckets. The priest saying words. Strangers standing on both sides of him. A lady to the left. She reached down to take his hand. A man to the right. He'd looked up. Scars, thick and red on his neck and jaw.

This man.

"You okay?"

The question knocked him out of the odd memory flash and back into the here and now. He nodded and took the man's outstretched hand to struggle to his feet.

"Great catch. What's your name?" the other coach said as he and the team circled around him.

"Kyle Gordon." He handed the ball back to the man.

"That was some interception. Knocked Tanner clean off his feet on the way down, too."

"I would've had it, Coach Justice," the tall kid said, half a sneer on his face and his eyes narrowed at Kyle.

Great. All he wanted to do was blend into the local scenery and now he'd made an enemy.

"Yeah, you would've caught it if you'd been running like you meant it," the short guy from the café joked and shoved his friend sideways a little.

Tanner shoved him back. "He blindsided me. Besides, we weren't scrimmaging, just practicing routes."

"Can it, you two." The other coach gave them a glare that said I'm-in-charge-and-you-will-listen-to-me and both guys stopped immediately. Kyle liked the coach. Then he turned that stare on Kyle, but softened it a little around his eyes. "Ever play defense?"

"No. Never played defense. Didn't mean to interrupt your practice, but he was gonna mow down Rachel."

He looked her way and she smiled at him. Something flipped inside his chest, almost knocking the wind out of him worse than landing with the football had.

"Hey, it's a football field, people get hit on the sidelines occasionally," Tanner continued to defend his near miss, this time in Kyle's face. "Ever watch a game on TV?"

"She didn't see you and you have her by fifty pounds," Kyle said, this time going toe-to-toe with the guy.

Quarterback Brett stepped up beside his friend. "I yelled look out."

"I didn't hear anything with these on."

Everyone looked at Rachel.

She twirled the ear buds by their cords to make sure everyone saw them. "Didn't know anything was happening until Kyle flew in front of me."

Again, he felt a swelling in his chest at her words. He'd protected her, done something good, and for once someone was acknowledging it publicly. Not just someone. Her. Rachel, with the sharp wit and cute smile.

"Okay. That's enough. We're done for the day. You guys go get something to eat," Coach Justice said to the whole team in a voice that brooked no argument. "Glad you're okay, Rachel. Next time, take a seat in the stands, okay?"

"Sure thing, Sheriff," she said then headed over to the food table.

Kyle started to follow.

"Kyle, wait a minute," the coach with the scratchy voice stopped him.

"I said I was sorry." His ingrained defensiveness popping up, he took a step backward, out of arm's length from either big man. Spending years getting blamed for things you didn't do, in homes and shelters where you really weren't wanted tended to do that to a person.

"No one's blaming you for anything. I just wanted to ask if you'd like to join the team?"

That surprised him, but he was careful not to let it show. *Never show someone you wanted what they offered. They could use it against you.* "You want *me* to play football? On your team?"

The coach gave a half shrug. "You did the fastest sprint of anyone all day, read the trajectory of the ball correctly, adjusted your route, leveled Tanner with a shoulder to his side, caught the ball and didn't complain when you hit the ground. I'd say you'd do great on the defense."

Yeah, right. Like that was ever going to happen. Best to stop him before he learned who he was, where he was living and anything about his past. "Sorry. Can't. Gotta work over at the café."

Before either man could question him further, he jogged over to help Rachel dish out food to the sweaty players.

Deke and Gage exchanged a look.

"Damn, that's one big *don't trespass* sign the kid just hung out, isn't it?" Gage said, crossing his arms over his chest as he considered the group over at the food cart.

Deke nodded, crossing his arms in the same fashion and shaking off the odd feeling of having met the kid before. He watched Kyle jog over to where Rachel was handing out food. The kid jumped in to help Rachel, but kept his distance from the guys, not really interacting with any of the members of the team. "Damn sure could use his abilities on the defense."

"Took out Tanner and didn't even seem to break a sweat doing it." Gage chuckled. "Maybe a little competition like that would light a fire under all the receivers' butts."

"Only if we can get the kid to agree to play against them." Deke studied Kyle. "Wonder what has him so defensive?"

"Back when I was working undercover in Columbus, I'd see street kids like him. Some were into drugs, gangs or prostitution. Others were just trying to keep out of sight, as if they were expecting anyone who made eye contact with them would cause them trouble."

Deke considered Gage's words. People dealing with gangs or dangerous friends didn't usually put themselves in physical danger to protect someone like Kyle had for Rachel. Something told him there was more to this kid.

"Might just have to talk to him away from here. Think I'll pop into the Peaches 'N Cream tonight and have a little chat with him, man-to-man."

CHAPTER FIVE

For a Tuesday night, the café was packed—even at eight o'clock when Deke walked in. A quick scan around the café told him all the tables and booths were taken. One seat was left at the dining counter. He took the seat and pulled up the menu, even though he knew the Tuesday special was Lorna's meatloaf, mashed potatoes and a vegetable. He glanced around the crowd. Rachel and the two older waitresses, Polly and Glenna, wove their way through the tables with trays of food and drinks, but no sign of Kyle.

What if he had the night off? Well, at least he'd get a good meal out of this.

"What'll it be, Deacon?" Lorna asked as she set a glass of ice water in front of him, her other hand holding the order slip pad and a pencil.

"I'll take the Tuesday special, with broccoli." He set the menu aside. "Met your new kid today."

"Kyle. Pretty good worker," Lorna said, slipping the pencil behind her ear, her-bright blonde hair trapping it in place. "Why? You want to talk to him?"

"Wanted to have a word with him about trying out for the football team. Any chance I can talk to him a moment?" He gave her his most sincere look, which only made her lift one painted brow at him.

"We're busy, in case you hadn't noticed. You can talk with him on his break." With a humph, she sauntered back to her kitchen.

The ching-chang of the antique jukebox clattered through the chatter as someone fed it change. Suddenly the place filled up with a nineteen-fifty's do-wop song. Deke smiled. He, Libby, Bill and Gage had spent many an evening listening to the oldies—both here and at Gage's house, where his father had the most extensive collection of classic fifties' rock and roll albums. They'd even dreamed of having a do-wop group, except none of them could really carry a tune. Well, all the guys. Libby had a very sweet alto and kept them from sounding like cows bawling to be milked.

Humming along, he was instantly pulled back to the first time he'd gotten Libby to dance with him. It was at Gage's house. They'd brought their latest girlfriends over and were trying to impress them with their singing. A slow dance popped up on Sheriff Justice's old juke box. Bill and Gage had their girls up slow dancing, leaving him and Libby sitting on the covered bar stools, just like the one he was currently perched on, in the kitchen, watching the other couples.

"Want to dance?" he asked, after a few minutes of

awkward silence between them.

She shrugged, giving him that shy smile that always hit him square in his chest. "I guess so, if you do."

He held out his hand and she placed her soft one in it. He'd never held anything so delicate in his life. He led her over to join the others, sliding his hands over her hips as she slipped her arms up over his shoulders. Her hair smelled of something lemony. Sweet and tart, just like her. He smiled as he lowered his chin onto her shoulder and held her slender body against his.

The song finished, dropping him back into the present and the sounds of families laughing all around him.

"Got your dinner," Rachel said, standing in front of him, holding a plate of mouthwatering food, complete with Lorna's special peppery brown gravy. "But Mom says you can't eat it here."

He blinked. Was Lorna throwing him out? He eyed the china plate and rolled up silverware in a napkin in Rachel's other hand. "That doesn't look like a take-out box, Rach."

"It's not. Come with me."

Curious, he slid off the stool, grabbed his water and followed her across the café to a corner booth.

Oh, hell no.

"Rachel," he said in warning as they approached the table and its occupant.

Libby looked up from the papers she was studying, her blue eyes wide with surprise.

"Sorry, guys," Rachel said as she slid his dinner on the table near the booth seat opposite her. "Mom says since you both want to talk to Kyle, you might as well wait together and free up a seat. Couldn't argue with her. She's the boss."

Before he could respond, the teen scooped up Libby's empty plate and headed back to the kitchen, leaving him standing there like a fool, not sure whether to sit, speak or just leave.

"Sit down, Deacon," Libby said, closing the files.

"Sorry about this, Libby." He slid into the booth, wanting to say more, to tell her how he was sorry for other things, but this wasn't the place.

"Don't worry about it. You know how Lorna gets sometimes." She rolled her eyes, gave him a whisper of her smile then took a drink of her tea.

Mesmerized, he watched her lips press around the lip of the glass, remembering how those lips had tasted against his. The muscles of her long slender neck worked as she swallowed and his mind turned to other memories. Fighting an urge to groan, he tore his gaze away. He picked up his knife and fork to dig into his meal. He glanced up to see her staring out at the rest of the café.

Damn. She couldn't even bear looking at him. He couldn't blame her. He'd killed her brother, for God's sake. The fact that she hadn't actually stormed out the minute Rachel marched him over to her table actually surprised him.

As if she knew he was watching her, she swung her head around and fixed him with that clear blue gaze of hers. "So, what is it you want to talk to Kyle about?"

Caught off guard by her question, he drank some water to wash down the meatloaf in his mouth before answering. "Football."

"Football?"

"Gage is the acting coach for the high school until the school board can hire a new permanent one. So, my good buddy conned me into being his assistant coach in charge of the defense."

She blinked at him. "Defense? You never played defense."

She'd remembered he played offense. Somehow that meant quite a bit to him.

"That's what I said. Gage told me that's why I'd be a plus to the defense. I could teach them how to defend against someone playing wide receiver like I did. Seemed like a good idea at the time." He shrugged, ate the last scoop of meatloaf and mashed potatoes, then set aside his cutlery. Wiping his mouth with a napkin, he sat back in the booth. "Anyways, we had a bit of an incident at the practice today and I wanted to talk to Kyle about it."

Her brows furrowed and she tipped her head sideways. Funny, he'd forgotten how she did that when something puzzled her.

"An incident? What kind of incident?"

Something in her voice got his attention and

awakened the hairs on his neck. Not a serious-kind-of-trouble reaction those hairs gave him, just an odd sort of curiousness. Setting his elbows on the table he leaned closer and lowered his voice.

"Why are you waiting to talk with the kid?"

* * * * *

"Do you think it's working, Mom?" Rachel asked her mother as the pair stood peeking out the order window into the café's dining area.

"I don't know," the café owner said, shaking her head. "Those two were made for each other and it's about time they figured out how to fix whatever's been wrong with them."

"I remember they used to date. I'd see them together when I was really little." Rachel pointed discreetly towards the corner. "Look. At least they're talking now. I wonder what about?"

"Well, whatever it is, all I can say is it's a good thing and about damn time." Lorna stepped back into the kitchen. "Come on, we've got food to serve. And you," she pointed at Kyle. "When you're finished with that pile of dishes you can take a break. I promised that pair they could talk with you then."

"Yes, ma'am." Kyle peeked over at the dining room corner. He recognized the coach from the football field, but who was the pretty lady sitting with him? Were they the people Rachel and her mom were talking about?

And what did they want with him?

Other than intercepting that wayward ball and knocking that ego-inflated Ethan Tanner on his ass, he hadn't gotten into any trouble. Hell, between Banyon's rules and Miss Lorna's working schedule, he'd been busy since the moment he stepped into Westen.

A sick feeling settled into the pit of his stomach. Had the past caught up with him here, too?

"Go on, get those dishes done, son," Pete, the cook, said as he flipped burgers over on the flat iron griddle. "You can find out what sort of trouble's going on when that's done. No use adding Lorna's wrath on top of it."

"Yes, sir."

"No, sir, here, kid. I'm just plain old Pete."

Kyle went back to the sink and started scrubbing a stack of dirty plates. He studied Pete out of the corner of his eye. The man wasn't too tall—just under six feet, if he had to guess—skinny as a meth user, with a scraggly beard and wild, grey-and-black hair he held out of his face with a faded red, white and blue striped bandana. He was a bit of an odd duck, as his mom used to say. "How long have you been working here, Pete?"

Pete lifted the toasted bun top onto the burger, then set the whole thing on the bottom half of the bun resting on the plate to the side of the stove. Taking the plate over to the fryer, he tossed half the basket of double-fried crispy French fries on the other half. He set the nearly overflowing plate in the serving section along with the ticket and started serving up two Tuesday specials. "Been here a while, came into town right after the doc and Miss Emma got hitched. Lorna needed a cook, I needed a job."

"Where are you from?"

"Here and there." Pete dinged the bell to tell the waitresses another order was up. "Mind those dishes get clean or Lorna will have you doing them again."

In other words, mind your own business.

Kyle set a plate into the drying rack and picked up another one, not even noticing the heat of the sudsy water anymore. Doing the work kept his mind off what trouble might be waiting for him at his break.

* * * * *

"I'm waiting to talk with Kyle as part of my job, actually," Libby said, gazing into those coffee-brown eyes of Deke's. Every time she stared into the dark depths, she'd swear she could see straight to his soul—a place where she'd felt loved and desired.

This time, he'd closed that off to her. The knowledge helped her put the shutters on her own emotions. Calm and cool was all she'd let him see. Not the hope. Not the guilt. Certainly not the sadness.

"You're meeting this kid here in the café for your job?" The curiosity and doubt in his voice almost made her smile.

"As the county social worker, I sit on the board of town administrators for Colbert House, and part of my job is to interview and keep in regular contact with any of the young men living at the house. Per the rules of the house Kyle got a job here and I'd thought it would be nice to chat with him on neutral territory." And she didn't want to do it in front of Todd Banyon. The guy just seemed to naturally bring out the antagonism in the young men that stayed at the halfway house. There was no reason, however, to let Deke know this about the man. After all, Todd did help young men find more stable lives.

Deke seemed to be processing what she said, which had her replaying her words to see if she'd said anything odd that would send off his alarm bells. A moment later he nodded, and leaned back in the booth once more. "So what's the kid's story?"

"I can tell you why I'm here to talk with him, but not anything about Kyle's personal life, past, present or future." She gave him her patented, this-subject-is-closed look, the same one she gave nosy neighbors of her elderly clients or abusive parents or husbands making rude threats.

Deke didn't get upset, just nodded. "Fair enough. From what I can tell, he seems like a conscientious kid. Lorna certainly likes him or she wouldn't have hired him."

"True. Lorna was always a good judge of character." She remembered how nervous she'd been when she'd applied for a job at the age of fifteen. Lorna had sized her up one side and down the other with her one brow arched like Mr. Spock and her lips pressed in a thin line. *You'll have to do a lot of heavy lifting between the supplies and tubs of dirty dishes. I won't tolerate any whining. You work here at the Peaches 'N Cream I expect you to work as hard as me.* And she had, but Lorna was a tolerant boss and a fair one. She paid above minimum and everyone shared all the tips, even the dishwashers, so she knew Kyle was going to make a decent wage while he worked here. He'd also get free food and some free life lessons.

"Kid's got a protective instinct, too. Stopped a six-foot ball player from crashing into Rachel this afternoon, without blinking an eye after he hit the ground."

"Ah, the incident."

"Yep. Kid laid him out flat." The corners of Deke's mouth lifted in a half-grin.

"And you enjoyed every second of it." She couldn't help smiling. He always did have a warped sense of humor and strong sense of karmic justice.

He shrugged, a true grin on his face now. "Can't say I didn't like seeing the prima donna end up on his ass. Will do the guy and the team some good for him to realize he has to give a hundred percent." He paused a moment, his face growing a little more pensive. "Thing is, the move Kyle made on Tanner was instinctual. Said he never played football, but he ran the interception route to perfection, hit Tanner with his shoulder—hard enough to hurt, but not injure him—caught the ball, and landed with as little impact to his body as possible."

"Sounds like a natural."

Staring out the window, he reached up and rubbed the thick scars that laced his neck and jaw. How he must have suffered during the healing process. An ache started in her chest, and she blinked back the moisture that threatened to fill her eyes. She'd known he'd been injured in the fire that killed Bill. He'd been in the hospital for months refusing to see anyone, even her. The pain at that rejection after the loss of her brother had cut her deep, wounded her in ways he could never imagine. For the first time she got to see those scars up close. They stretched over his throat and she had to wonder if that was why his voice was a deeper, scratchier version than the one she remembered.

"I thought so, too. Funny thing was, when I asked him about joining the team he turned me down flat. No discussion, as if joining the team wasn't an option."

"So you wanted to try an end around and catch him here?"

"True." He gave a soft laugh at her use of a football analogy.

What did he expect? She'd grown up with the testosterone trio of him, Gage and her brother. Football was a second language to her.

"Might be better than cornering him in front of his parents."

"Since he's a residence of Colbert House, I have the ability to grant him permission to play on the team and sign any medical waivers," she held up her hand when his eyes lit up like he'd just won the lottery. "That is, *if* he really wants to play. The three main rules he must follow to stay at Colbert House is first to stay out of trouble, second is to get passing grades and third is to have a job. You'd be asking him to add a time-intensive sport to his already full plate."

Deke looked around the room and she followed his gaze as it landed on Kyle, cleaning off a table of dirty dishes, smiling at something Rachel said as she passed by, then hefting the heavy tub of dishes off to the kitchen. Slowly he turned back and gave her a whisper of the grin she'd so adored as a teen. "Something tells me the kid can handle it."

* * * * *

Sylvie Gillis paced the front of the Dye Right, stopping every third time to peek out the window and check her watch. It was Tuesday night, the night the Deputy Junkins walked the streets of town and checked that all the storefronts were secure. The first week she worked late on a Tuesday she'd seen him.

The memory made her smile. She'd been in the back cleaning up the wash bowls and rods from perms they'd done that day when he stepped inside to check with the owner Twylla that everything was okay. He looked very out of place in such a dainty women's salon—seemed to take up half the space in the waiting area. Not one too shy to meet new people, she'd hurried out of the wash area to where Miss Twylla stood talking easily with the big man.

And oh, she did like big men.

"Cleetus, this is my new girl, Sylvie Gillis," Twylla *said, introducing them. "Sylvie, this is Cleetus Junkins. He's one of the deputies here in Westen."*

"Nice to meet you, Deputy," she'd said, holding out *her hand with her newest nail art.*

"Pleased to meet you, ma'am," he'd said, taking her *hand in his big firm one.*

And oh, she did like men with firm handshakes.

"Pleasure's all mine," she said with just a bit of a *flirty giggle.*

The man blushed from head to toe.

And wasn't that the sweetest thing?

From that moment on she'd been determined to get to know the deputy better. That's why she'd been volunteering to close up on Tuesdays. Even if there were no late-night clients, she did some extra cleaning just to get a few minutes to talk with Cleetus. Of course, she had to do most of the talking. He seemed not quite sure what to say to her flirting.

Tonight he was late. Maybe she should just close up and head home. She'd hoped he might at least walk her down the street to the little rooming house where she stayed. She uttered a little sigh. The man was not only the size of a mountain, but apparently moved as fast as one, at least when it came to the world of romance.

She turned out all the lights but the one near the front door—Twylla always kept that one lit. Grabbing her bag from where she'd set it by the front door, she flipped the open sign over to closed and stepped outside.

"Evening, Miss Sylvie," a deep voice said from over her right shoulder.

She jumped and turned with a little gasp. "Dear Lord, Deputy Junkins, you startled me."

"Didn't mean to scare you," he said with a little grin, telling her he actually had meant to surprise her.

And wasn't that just the littlest bit intriguing?

Well, he might be getting interested, but as her mama always said, *best to keep a man guessing, keeps them from thinking you're a sure thing.* So as she turned her back and locked the door, she put a pout on her lips and scrunched up her brows a bit—not enough to look really mad, but enough to make him think she wasn't very happy about his sneak attack.

"I was going to ask you if you'd walk me home, but I don't think I will if you're planning to scare me like that," she said, giving him a disgruntled look from head to toe, then strode off in the direction of her rooming house.

"Wait a minute, Miss Sylvie," he said, catching up with her in less than a few strides. "I really didn't mean to…I was hoping…I mean I'd planned to…um."

She came to a halt and stared at him with one hand fisted on her hip. "Is there something you wanted to say to me, Deputy, or are you just planning to scare me more?"

For a moment all he did was stare down at her. In fact, she was beginning to think he'd been shot with a freeze-ray from some sci-fi show, but then he swallowed. "Ma'am, I'm truly sorry that I surprised you. I'd meant to stop by the Dye Right and ask if you'd want to join me for a slice of pie over at the Peaches 'N Cream?"

He looked so sad that she might refuse him—like a giant puppy dog.

"Pie?" she said, giving him an opening.

He smiled. "Yes, ma'am. Miss Lorna makes the best pies in the whole world. It's nearly apple picking season, but I know for a fact she's got some strawberry-rhubarb today."

"Well, I do like a nice piece of pie." She unclenched her fist and slid her arm into the crook of his elbow. "Just remember I'm still mad at you."

"Oh, yes, ma'am, Miss Sylvie. I know you are," he said, leading her across the street in the direction of the café.

* * * * *

In the shadows of the big oak tree across the street, he watched the pair inside the café. When she made him smile, he ground his teeth together.

How dare she flirt with someone else? She was *his*

goddess, had been since the first time she looked at him with those blue eyes. It was one of the things he loved about her.

He took a drag from his cigarette, his anger rising with every moment he watched her with another. And it was righteous rage he felt right now.

She belonged to him. From the moment he first laid eyes on her, he knew they were destined for one another. Fate had decreed it. He wasn't letting someone else come between them.

He stepped into the alley and slowly headed home. Time to make plans.

Secrets. That's what he needed. Everyone had some. Even his new enemy. He'd find them, and when he did —he glanced at the glowing embers on the end of his cigarette—he'd make sure the guy burned.

CHAPTER SIX

"Lorna said you wanted to talk to me," Kyle said to the couple as he approached their booth. He knew the coach from practice earlier in the day. Didn't have a clue who the pretty lady was, but she had kind eyes.

The coach slid out of the booth and held out his hand. "Didn't get a chance to introduce myself this afternoon, Kyle. Name's Deke Reynolds," he said in that raspy voice of his.

Kyle shook the man's hand, a sick feeling settling into his stomach as he tried not to stare at the man's burn scars.

"This is Miss Wilson." Deke nodded towards the lady, who smiled.

"Nice to meet you, Kyle," she said, extending her hand. He shook it quickly.

"Why don't you join us for a bit?" The coach motioned him to slide into the booth and Kyle got the idea it really wasn't a request as much as an expectation that he had no choice but to do so. He took the spot just vacated by the man.

"That was some catch you made today, Kyle," Coach said, sliding in to sit next to the pretty lady.

Before he could apologize again, Rachel walked over to the table and slid a burger and fries in front of him, smiled, then turned to stare right at the big man. "Mom said to remind you guys he only gets an hour for his dinner break."

"I'll keep that in mind, brat."

She laughed and walked away. The corners of Kyle's mouth twitched and he focused on shoving a fry in his mouth so the adults wouldn't see how much he admired her ability to put them on warning.

"Too much sass in that kid," the coach muttered.

"She has a lot of her mother in her," Miss Wilson said and the twinkle in her eye made Kyle relax. Whatever this woman wanted, she didn't seem to be ready to ship him back to some juvie squat house in Columbus, or worse, up north in Cleveland. He'd spent one cold-ass-snow-up-to-your-balls winter there and didn't like the prospect of doing it again anytime soon.

"You said you never played defense this afternoon. Did you play offense sometime?" Deke directed the conversation around to football once more.

Man, the guy was like a dog with a half-chewed steak. Kyle took a drink of the soda Rachel had set down with his plate. "No, sir. Never played football."

The man's right eyebrow lifted in question. "Never? Not once?"

"No, sir." He took a big bite of his food to keep from saying more. He'd figured out years ago it was best to let the other people, especially adults do most the talking. You learned information that might keep you out of trouble that way. You could also read when a situation was going to escalate to punching and you could move faster.

"How'd you figure out to take Tanner out?"

He chewed slowly, studying the man. The scars on his neck and lower face were like thick cords. He knew what they were from. He'd seen them on someone else a long time ago. Burns. Wonder what he'd done to get them. Between the scars and the man's intensity, he suspected he could be a bad-ass when he wanted. This was not someone you blew off with a grunt.

"Like I said this afternoon, I didn't want him plowing into Rachel and the food. The guy wasn't paying attention to where he'd end up. Hel—" he glanced at the lady, "I mean, heck, he wasn't even really trying to catch the ball."

"Which would've nailed Rachel," Deke filled in for him.

"Right. So I just checked the angle and took off at a dead run, turned to reach out for the ball and knock him out of the way at the same time." He took another drink of his soda. "Like I said earlier. I'm sorry I interrupted the practice."

"I'm not here to give you grief, kid," Deke leaned back in the booth, angled so he could look him straight in the eyes. "If you wanted to, you could really help me out."

The big man wanted his help? Yeah, right.

"Doing what?" he asked, more out of curiosity than any real interest in getting involved.

"My defense is pretty solid, but having a safety or corner who can take out the offense's main wide receivers is something we're lacking."

Tempting as the idea was of being able to strip the ball away from glorified a-holes like that Tanner guy, he knew better than to get involved in anything resembling a commitment. Nothing in his life had ever been that permanent.

"Can't. Got to work." He took another big bite, leaving the ball in the man's court.

"True. But Lorna is a big supporter of the high school team. If you decide you want to give it a try, I can talk with her to work your schedule around practice and games."

He wiped his mouth and set the burger down. "Coach, I see what you get out of this, an extra player to fill the roster. The team gets a player not afraid to take some pain to stop the offense. Not really sure what I'd get out of it."

The lady across the table half choked on her tea then smothered a smile with her napkin.

Deke shot her a half-warning, half-amused look, before focusing back on him. "I could tell you being on the team would get you the attention of the cheerleaders," he glanced across the café at Rachel then back. "But somehow I don't think you're too interested in them. I could tell you being on the team will get you some great friends, but that may or may not happen. I could tell you being on the team will get you a scholarship to college, but I have no idea what your grades are going to be like, so I won't lie to you."

He paused and leaned in on one elbow to stare straight into his eyes. Kyle didn't read any bullshit in them, just the honest truth. "I will tell you that every day in practice you'll run routes against Tanner and the other receivers. You'll get a chance to take the ball every day." Then he lifted the corner of his mouth on the unscarred side. "You will have a chance every day to knock the crap out of each and every one of them."

"Deke," Miss Wilson said, her eyes wide. "You can't tell him that."

"Sure I can, Libby. It's the truth. What guy doesn't want to knock the arrogance out of some other guy? It's a male thing." He finished his drink and set his napkin on the table. "You think about it, Kyle, and let me know what you decide. I'm going to leave you to talk with Miss Wilson now. Listen to whatever she has to say. You can trust her."

The coach slid out of the booth and headed over to the now nearly deserted lunch counter.

Kyle nodded and refocused on eating his dinner, surreptitiously watching the lady across the table as she stared at the coach's retreating back, a sort of hunger and sadness in her face.

Wow, bet there's a story there. And none of his business, that was for sure. He'd gotten close to a foster family once, only to have them turn their backs on him the moment his past was known. The pain at their betrayal had cut him almost as deep as losing his mom. Never planned to trust anyone like that again.

* * * * *

Libby had always loved the slow ripple of muscle in Deke's retreating form.

Gage might've had the nickname of Gunslinger on the football field, but she'd always thought Deke moved more like one of those old-time western cowboys—slow, measured and dangerous. There'd been a time when just seeing him approach her would have her body heated like a hot August day. Her hands had known every inch of his body intimately. Now the scars on his neck and jaw had her wondering what changes lay beneath his clothes, but that was something she'd never know. Despite the quiet conversation they'd had tonight, too much of the past lay between them. Even if he could ever forgive himself for Bill's death, he'd never forgive her the secrets she kept.

With an internal sigh, she forced her attention away from the man of her past and on the young man seated opposite, quietly devouring his dinner.

She wasn't fooled by the apparent focus he had on

his food. There was a wariness about him. She'd seen it in others over the years. Those waiting for the next bad thing to happen. Women expecting a loud male voice or a strong slap for any minor infraction of rules that changed daily. Children who didn't know safety at home. Runaways expecting a stranger to commit violence in every shadow.

But she'd seen something in Kyle's face missing in so many others.

Hope.

He'd shown a glimpse of it when he talked with Deke about the football team. He might've said he didn't have time, but having Deke tell him he was good and would like him on the team had struck a chord with the teen.

Then there was the way he interacted with Rachel throughout the evening and when she'd brought him his food. The girl had sparked a different kind of hope in him. Hope that she saw him as something more than another down-on-his-luck kid needing a job. Maybe more.

"Kyle," she started, as he finished his burger and scooped a fry full of ketchup into his mouth, "I'd like to welcome you to Westen and hope you'll find a home here with us. How are you settling into Colbert House? Everything okay?"

He swallowed and took a long drink of his soda before answering her with a half-shrug, half-nod. "S'okay."

Okay. He might have some hope deep down inside, but she was going to have to break through the typical teenage shell that most of the boys at Colbert House had to get to it.

She opened the thin file beside her and fixed him with her most sincere look. "I'm not just some nosy woman. Not only am I on the Colbert House board of directors, but I'm the county social worker."

He nodded at the file. "Figured as much."

Wow. Three whole words. She was making great progress. Deke had more success with football.

"Part of my job is to look out for your welfare here in Westen and at the Colbert House. Since you already have a job here at the Peaches 'N Cream, I assume Mr. Banyon already ran through the house rules with you?"

"Yep. Stay out of trouble, show up at curfew, show up for classes and get a job. Got it."

"Any questions? Any problems you've had since you got here?"

"Nope."

She resisted the urge to roll her eyes. No use both of them getting belligerent. She flipped the first page of information to his very, very brief family history. Normally, she had a thick file that gave her details as to what trouble each member of Colbert House had been in to get them sent to the group home. In Kyle's case the file was so thin and sketchy as to be almost non-existent. Which of course had her curiosity piqued.

What had happened to his parents? Why was there

no family claiming him? Why was he moved around so many times? Had he caused trouble at the other places the state had placed him in? If so, why wasn't there pages telling her what offenses had gotten him moved on to their site?

She glanced up to find the young man staring out over the café's main room, which was emptying as families were headed home for the night. Only a few late-night truckers, Cleetus and Sylvie, and Deke remained. Rachel walked over to set pie slices in front of the deputy and hairdresser. Kyle's eyes followed her every movement.

Again, she saw a quiet hope in him, a yearning. Not just the yearning of a young man for a pretty girl. Libby got the sense that he yearned for the connections that seemed to be strong in Westen.

Time. That's what she needed to give the kid.

Slowly she closed the file and took out one of her business cards and slid it across the table. "Kyle, most of the residents of Colbert House have family that can come visit or they can go visit on furloughs. Since you are an orphan, I'd like you to feel free to come talk with me anytime. Whatever is said between you and me will be confidential. Not even Mr. Banyon has a right to know about our conversations."

He picked up the card. "Not much for talking."

"I noticed," she said with a smile and his mouth turned up at the corners just a notch.

Score!

"Just keep the card. It has my office address and my cell phone. You can drop by Monday through Friday or call any time. No big deal. I do have to meet with you once a month, but we'll make it kind of informal like tonight, if that's okay with you?"

"Sure. I need to get back to work. Miss Lorna only gives me an hour for dinner."

"Of course." She gave him another I-like-you-and-I-mean-you-no-harm smile as she extended her hand. "It was good to meet you."

He shook her hand then slid out of the booth. For a moment she thought the whole effort might have been a mistake until he slid her card into the back pocket of his jeans.

Touchdown!

She gathered up her things and headed to the cash register and nearly came up short when she saw Deke standing near it, talking to one of the older truckers. Was he waiting for her? No. He was just chatting with a frequent visitor.

Damn her heart for doing a little flip. The traitorous organ delighted in torturing her.

Stopping at the register, her back slightly angled away from Deke's direction, just to show her heart who was really in charge, she focused on trying to find her bill just as Lorna stepped up to the register.

"Something I can do for you, Libby?"

"Um," she flipped open the file folder slightly. Maybe she'd put her check slip inside. "I think Rachel forgot to give me the check."

"Nope. It's already been taken care of," Lorna gave her a wink.

"Lorna, I can't let you do that."

"Wasn't me. Talk to the big man," she said and nodded in Deke's direction before turning and leaving. Her part of the discussion over.

Great. Sometimes Lorna could be so high-handed. Now she'd have to take up her bill payment with Deke, because she sure wasn't going to let him pay for her meal. That part of their lives ended ten years ago.

Inhaling slowly, she straightened and turned on her heel, to find him waiting for her.

"Deke—"

"Thought I'd walk you to your car," he said, that low, raspy voice of his warming her.

What was he up to? They hadn't talked in a decade and suddenly tonight he's paying for her dinner and wanting to walk her to her car. She had two choices. Refuse and make a scene, and wouldn't that make fodder for the gossip mill? Or let him walk her to the car and find out what was on his mind.

She gave him a nod and headed to the door with him, feeling Lorna's watchful eyes on her back the entire way.

* * * * *

Cleetus watched Sylvie scoop a forkful of pie and

slip it between her dark-red lips. Closing her eyes she seemed to sink into the lemon meringue. He'd have thought she'd be a cherry pie girl, but somehow the tartness of Lorna's lemon pie suited Sylvie to a tee.

He could watch her forever. She enchanted him. Heck, she was about the most fascinating person he'd ever met. Kinda like a little sprite with her pert turned-up nose, big green eyes and spiky red hair. She only came up to the middle of his chest, but her smile made her seem to fill a whole room.

When he walked into the Dye Right late one Tuesday night a month ago, he'd only expected to find Twylla working late. He'd expected to just say hi and that everything was okay before heading on down Main Street on his security rounds. Then out of the back came this orange-headed ball of energy. All he could do was stare at her. Even after Miss Twylla had introduced her as the new girl at the salon. He'd managed to say hello. Then she'd smiled. And dang if his tongue stopped working completely.

It took him two more visits before he could do more than stare and stumble through hello. But catching her by surprise tonight had let him get the invitation for dessert out before his tongue and brain lost their function. Now here he was, watching her enjoy her pie.

With a smile, she opened her eyes as if she'd just come out of a really good dream.

Heat filled his face and he swallowed hard.

"That's about the best thing I think I've ever tasted."

She tipped her head to the side with a little smile. "Aren't you going to taste yours?"

He blinked at her question, sliding his gaze away from her to the cherry pie on his plate. Usually, he devoured his favorite flavor almost after it hit the table, but tonight he suddenly wondered what the lemon meringue tasted like. Picking up his fork, he took a big bite. He chewed, swallowed and went for a second, hoping to come up with some sort of smart thing to say when he finished.

"Do you like being a deputy?" Sylvie asked, another forkful of pie halfway to her mouth.

He swallowed the bite in his mouth and reached for his water, trying not to stare at her mouth as she slid it over the fork and pie once more.

"Um, yes. Gage's late daddy was the sheriff when I started." He tucked into another mouthful of cherry goodness, relaxing a bit. If she did the asking he could talk to her, easy.

"What do you like about it?"

He thought about her question a moment. "Well, I like helping people."

"Oh, like being a hero," she said with a little twinkle in her eye and the heat flushed back into his face at her teasing.

"No, I ain't a hero. Gage and Deke are the heroes. Heck, even Miss Bobby, Gage's fiancée, is a hero, saving him last spring. I just like making sure everyone is doing okay and the town is safe. Like that time when

Miss Isabelle was still living with Doc Clint and Emma and was out walking on the highway."

"Why was she on the highway?" All the tease was gone and her eyes opened wider with real concern.

"Miss Isabelle would get confused. Doc Clint and Emma finally had to get her into a nursing home, with Miss Libby's help. She had Alzheimer's."

"That is so sad. So how did you help her?"

"She was out on the highway with Emma's two little boys. I was making my rounds in the patrol car and stopped. She thought I was a taxi driver. Didn't tell her no different, but got her and the boys in the car, then took them home all safe and sound."

She smiled big at him, her whole face full of admiration. "Well, I think that's very heroic."

He smiled shyly, but sat a little straighter as he took the last bite of his pie.

"What else do you like to do? You know, for fun?" she asked after a few minutes.

"Started helping coach the high school football team this week."

"Really?" Her eyes opened wide in surprise again. He liked the way they did that. It let him see the green in them better.

"Yeah. Used to play lineman there, so Gage and Deke asked me if I'd like to help teach those guys some of my tricks."

She gave him another of those teasing smiles. "Somehow I thought you'd be a football player."

Before he could answer, the alarm on his cell phone went off.

"Crap," he said, leaning back and pulling it out of his jeans pants' pocket.

"What's that?" she asked, laying her fork back on the plate, her brows scrunched down in concern.

"The fire alarm." He looked at the number. "It's the Amish alarm. Some kind of fire out there." He slid out of the booth, whipped his wallet out and tossed a ten on the table. "Sorry to have to run, Miss Sylvie—"

"No, no. You go. I understand. Go."

He hesitated just a moment then hurried out, hitting the door at a run.

* * * * *

Deke held the door for Libby as they left the café, not quite sure why he'd insisted on walking her to the car or even why he'd picked up her check for dinner. Sitting across from her tonight, while it hadn't felt comfortable, it did feel familiar. He could say his actions were a habit from the days when they'd been together, but habits didn't continue after a decade had passed.

Maybe he was tired of pretending they were strangers. Or maybe he just plain missed her. Whatever the reason, he'd just known he wasn't ready to just walk out of the café and not see or talk to her again for days, or weeks, or even years.

"So, what did you think of Kyle?" he asked, looking for something to break the quiet between them.

"Kyle?" She blinked in surprise and stopped walking to look up at him.

"Yeah. I can't seem to shake the feeling I've met him before."

She tilted her head. "He looks familiar?"

"Not exactly. It's his eyes." Deke ran a hand over the back of his neck. "Not too many people I know with grey eyes."

"They are unusual," she said as they walked along.

"So, what did you think of him?"

She laughed, the softness of it running over his senses like cool air. "I think you got more information from him than I did."

It was his turn to be surprised. "You're kidding me. All we did was talk about football."

"Yes, but it wasn't what you talked about, but how he reacted to your questions that spoke volumes."

"And what did his reaction say?"

"That even though he turned you down, it meant a lot to him that you singled him out to ask him to join the team. That you saw potential in him. That you saw him more than just someone on the sidelines."

"You think he heard all that?" He shook his head. "I know you have to use a lot of psychology working with people, in particular these at-risk kids, but I'm pretty as up front as you see me. No secret codes. No hidden messages. What I saw was a kid who could take on

Ethan Tanner, one of the best wide receivers in the state, and lay him out flat. And I said so."

"You always were pretty up front about what you thought." She reached into her purse and pulled out her wallet. "And you didn't have to pay for my dinner."

"Put your money away, Libby. I paid, no big deal. Used to do it all the time." The words were out of his mouth before he could stop them.

"That's when we were a couple." She got that stubborn look he knew all too well in her eyes and her lips pressed into a thin line as she held the money out to him. There was no talking to her when she got like this. Might as well try to shove his head through a brick wall.

He took the money and shoved it into his back pocket. She nodded then turned and headed towards the parking lot once more.

Conversation stalled again, because the big Pink Elephant between them had joined them on their walk.

She was right. He'd never pulled any punches or kept his opinions to himself, at least when asked. One of the reasons he hadn't been able to face her after Bill's death. He'd known it would destroy what they had. Hell it already had and he'd never even said a word.

Dammit. He'd never been a coward before that fire. Had been living in its shadow for far too long.

The truth hit him smack in the face. He'd waited to walk her to the car, because it was time to crawl out from under that specter and start living his life again.

She stopped at her car. A nice silver SUV. Safe. Sporty. Very Libby.

After opening the door, she tossed the file and her bag onto the passenger seat. Turning, she held the door for a moment, staring up at him with those beautiful blue eyes. "You didn't have to walk me to the car."

"I know." He laid his hand over hers on the top of the door. Her fingers were cool beneath his and they trembled just a little. "Libby, we need to talk."

"I know." She slowly pulled her hand from beneath his. "But not here, Deacon."

"I could follow you home."

She hesitated, a shadow passing over her face, then she nodded. "You're right. There's things we need to talk about."

He took a step back to give her room to climb inside the car. Suddenly, Cleetus came running out of the café at the same time Deke's phone sounded a high-pitched alarm from his jeans' pocket. Blood drained from his head as it had anytime an alarm sounded since Bill's death.

"What's wrong?" Libby said, already back out of her car.

"That's the fire signal. The special one for the Amish community."

Quickly, he hit the number for the fire station, where Brandt Outman was manning the phones. "It's Deke, Brandt. Where's the fire?"

"The Zimmer farm out on county road 79. The trucks are on their way."

"I am, too." He closed the phone, looking at Libby. His pulse raced with the need to act, but his heart wanted to stay with her. "Libby…"

"Go," she said, holding up her hand. "We'll talk later."

With one last glance at her, he turned and ran for his truck, already dreading the coming firefight.

CHAPTER SEVEN

Libby stayed standing between her car door and the driver's seat, watching Deke, who'd gone pale when he got the call on his phone, climb determinedly into his truck and do a U-turn in the center of the road. When he lifted his hand briefly to her, she raised hers, wishing he wasn't going to a fire.

Ever since Bill's death, she'd dreaded fires. Had nightmares of him and Deke trapped in one. She'd needed to talk with him about them, but then he'd closed her off and she'd had to come to terms with that loss on top of the others. And now Deke was headed into one.

Stop it. It's his job.

Yes, but she didn't have to like it and knowing how badly he'd been injured before, her fear for him increased.

You should head on home and pretend it's not happening, like you always do. He's been doing this a decade since those injuries, and you haven't been this concerned.

She shook her head, knowing the voice in her head was a liar. She had worried, she'd just tried to not know he was in danger. Now he was going into danger, even though it was his job, and her fear had been let loose. She'd lost Bill, she didn't know what she'd do if a fire consumed Deacon, too.

"What's the rush?" a voice said from behind Libby.

At the sound she jumped slightly, gripping her door handle tighter as her heart raced. She whipped her head around towards the sidewalk outside the café. Walking along, half in the shadows of the maple trees that lined Main Street and periodically blocked both the moonlight and the street lights, was the new newspaper owner, the glowing ember of a cigarette in his hand.

"Sean," she said, letting out the breath she'd been holding. "You startled me."

"Sorry. Didn't mean to startle you. I was just out for an evening stroll. Saw the deputy and now Chief Reynolds bolt out of here. What's going on?" He took one last drag on his cigarette, then ground it out beneath his foot on the sidewalk.

She wished he wouldn't litter the sidewalk with the butt. She'd always been proud of how clean Westen was, but she wasn't going to sound like some old prude by saying anything. Instead she glanced back down the road where Deke's taillights turned off the main road and onto the State road toward Amish country. "There's a fire out on one of the Amish farms."

"Really?" Sean asked, coming to stand near her. "How far out?"

"It's the Zimmer farm, northeast of here about five miles or so."

"Damn. I'd love to go out and get the lowdown, but haven't memorized the roads yet."

Libby shook her head. "That's not going to do you much good anyways."

"Why not?" He looked down at her, curiosity in his grey-green eyes.

"Once you turn off the State road on to the township road, you still have to find the right farm road, which are usually gravel and in the Amish farm areas aren't marked very well."

"I figure I'll just follow the bright flames in the night sky."

Libby shook her head. "I don't know how high the flames might get, but that area has ancient forests with some massively tall trees. You might drive in circles trying to find it."

"Great. Biggest story since I got here and I'll get lost trying to get there."

Libby glanced back down the road where Deke had driven just moments before. Maybe she'd be less scared if she saw him and knew he was all right. "I could take you," she said, looking back at Sean.

"How about you let me drive and you give me directions?"

"I don't know," she hesitated. After all, she hardly

knew the guy.

"Look, I'll never remember if you do the driving. But if I do, I can get back out there in daylight if I have to do any follow up with the farmers about the fire. I'm a tactical learner." He gave her a hopeful smile and she couldn't help but relax.

"Okay."

"Great! Let me get my laptop and car. I'll be right back."

As he took off at a jog across the street, she pulled her purse back out of the front seat and locked the doors. A truck went flying past and she caught a glimpse of Doc Clint and Emma in the front seat. A moment later, Lorna's catering truck pulled out from behind the café. Just like last spring when Gage had been trapped in the meth lab tunnels, the town would gather around to help the firemen and any injured people out at the farm. It was one of the things she loved about Westen. The people were so willing to help each other, no matter their differences.

"You ready?" Sean asked as he pulled his SUV up beside where she stood.

Her fear for Deke and concern for the farmers she visited regularly out that way propelled her around the front of the vehicle and she climbed into the passenger seat. "We'll try to get close, but we can't interfere with the firefighters."

"I understand. I'll be sure to park on the periphery," he said, heading down Main towards the light, then turning right, following the same route Deke had taken. "Thanks for being my navigator. You won't regret it."

The image of Deke's face filled her mind. She hoped not.

* * * * *

Flames lit up the night sky as Deke pulled up to the fire area. The tanker truck and the quint—a large truck capable of not only breeching tall buildings with its ladders, but storing its own water or pumping water from the tanker truck—arrived on the scene right behind him. Given that there were no fire hydrants in this rural location, they'd need the extra water from both trucks.

The smell of burning wood and debris wafted into the summer night, reminding him for a moment of the bonfires they'd light every fall for homecoming. Shaking off the odd reminiscence, he grabbed his gear from the bed of his pickup and quickly shucked his shoes. He stepped into his pants and boots—the combo already together for just such an emergency—quickly donned his coat and grabbed his helmet, then headed to where his men and the county fire volunteers were gathering.

Ahead of them they could see the farmers doing an old-fashioned bucket brigade into a century-old hand-pump wagon, which they were using to pump water onto the fire. It would take at least ten more such devices and as twice as many more men to cover what looked like several acres on fire. He needed to get his crew and equipment busy to control the fire before it covered much more ground.

"Aaron," he yelled to the young man climbing off the side of the quint. "Let's get some hoses out there and get those farmers some help. One on each side and two in the middle."

"Yes, sir, Chief," Aaron Turnbill said, opening up the side where the hoses were stored and handing several off to the other volunteers.

Deke and John Wilson, the quint driver, attached the hoses to the quint's pumping system while Cleetus helped haul the hoses past the water wagon. Like all the other county deputies, Cleetus had joined the volunteer department and attended their regular training sessions. Now all that training would come into play and hopefully keep them all safe.

Once the hoses were securely fastened to the quint, John started flipping switches, and water surged through the huge lines which uncoiled like huge jerking snakes. It took several men on the end of each to control them and direct the flow towards the fire. As the trained firemen moved beyond the Amish brigade the farmers shifted their equipment out of the way, but continued to pump water on the surrounding area, hoping to keep the fire from spreading. One tall shadow left the group of farmers and slowly approached Deke.

"Good to see you, Deacon," Thomas Yoder said. His

face was covered in soot, his shirt stuck to him from all the perspiration caused by the heat. He wiped his hand on one cotton pant leg before offering it to Deke.

Deke shook it. "I'd hoped we wouldn't have to meet out here again so soon, Tom."

"Ja. I did too. But the alarms, they worked well. You are here now." He looked beyond Deke's shoulder. "And here's the sheriff."

"Tom," Gage said coming up behind, Bobby by his side, both dressed in firefighter gear. "Any idea how this started?"

The Amish elder shook his head. "Jacob Zimmer—this farm is his—said the field had been cleared of dry hay weeks ago. Very little debris was left, so a hay fire is highly unlikely. I think."

Deke nodded.

One of the first things he'd learned about having a fire department in a rural setting was how easy barn fires could happen in barns stocked with hay bales. If the hay wasn't dried completely before being baled, microbes could grow inside them. The growth of these organisms gave off heat, which in turn heated the internal temperature of the hay. If that temperature reached one hundred and eighty degrees or more, and oxygen from the microbes was trapped near the hot spots, the probability of spontaneous combustion was good. All the local farmers, who had been farming for years or grew up on farms, knew about letting the hay dry thoroughly before baling it. They also cleared debris from the fields as soon as possible.

Which meant there might be a more nefarious reason the fire started. But that was something he'd have to look into later, once the fire was put out and danger to the farmers and their families was put to rest.

"Jacob also listened when you talked about firebreaks the other evening. He had plowed trenches every few acres, just like you suggested."

A firebreak was a barrier, whether natural or constructed, that could stop a fire or provide a control line for the firemen to work from. In this case, trenches of newly plowed earth with no dead debris to fuel the fire.

"Good. That's probably what kept the fire from spreading too quickly. You can have your men move farther back, Thomas. Let us take it from here."

"Ja, I will do," he said, walking back to the fire wagon and calling to his men with a wave of his hand.

"What do you need Bobby and me to do?" Gage asked, slipping on his volunteer-fire coat.

"If you can take the team in the center, I'll work with the ones on the periphery. We want to coordinate where the water is aimed and be sure no hot spots are left."

"Got it." Gage gave his fiancée a quick, fierce kiss.

"Be careful," she said.

"Will do," Gage said then trotted out along the side of one of the hoses to the front of the firefight.

"Bobby?" Deke pointed to a stream of cars starting up the road. "If you can keep any gawkers from getting in the way that would be a help. And watch for Doc Clint. I imagine one of those trucks will be him and either Emma or Harriet. They might need to check out the farmers."

"Yes, sir," she said and headed away from the fire to head off civilians, no questions asked.

Bobby had been trained in firefighting, just as the other deputies had. In such a small town the deputies were expected to do double duty during emergencies. He wasn't discriminating about her being a woman by sending her out to handle the crowd. No, his choice to keep her back from the fire was two-fold. Since arriving in Westen, Bobby had proved on more than one occasion that she could handle people, with either sweetness or a strong word. She'd do an excellent job curtailing the gawkers and not take any grief from anyone. The other reason was more for Gage's benefit. No way would the Gunslinger concentrate on what he was doing if his woman was in the middle of the firefight, too. Keeping her out of harm's way was a safety issue for Gage and the other men.

He wasn't losing another friend to the monster that was a fire.

* * * * *

Bobby stood in the middle of the farm road, motioning for cars to turn off and park in another empty field several hundred yards away from the fire. The first car held the Mayor, Tobias Rawlins, son of Judge Rawlins. The second held county District Attorney, Kent Howard. Both men climbed out and headed her way.

Great. Just what she needed. Gage, Deke and the firefighters were out there in danger, trying to prevent it from spreading, and here were two politicians getting in the way. Probably looking for sound bites.

Okay. That wasn't particularly charitable. Tobias had helped save Gage's life. So she'd cut him some slack, for now, and assume he was here out of concern for the farmers and the firefighting crew. Kent, she wasn't so sure about.

"Tobias, Kent," she said, holding her hands out in front of the pair. "Sorry, gentlemen. Can't let you past this point."

They both stopped, craning their heads to the side to see around her.

"Any idea what started it?" Kent asked.

She waved another car to the side, then focused on the would-be politician. Ever since she'd met the viper that was Gage's ex-wife, she hadn't been too keen on district attorneys. Especially ones who showed up at major events that might mean a case or publicity for them. "It's too early to tell at this point. Once the fire is out Chief Reynolds will investigate the cause."

"Anyone hurt?" Tobias said, his face filled with concern, hands on his hips.

Okay, the Mayor gets bonus points for actually

caring about the people out there.

"Not that I've been told. But again, everyone's focused on getting the blaze under control."

Tobias nodded. "Okay. We'll be back here. Let me know if there's anything we can do." He clamped one hand on the DA's shoulder and they moved back towards their cars. Two tall, lanky figures bounded out of a truck and headed for them. She recognized one as Kent's son, Brett, the high school quarterback.

What the heck were he and his friend doing here?

Before she could find out more, another pair hopped out of an SUV that had parked closer than the other vehicles but still out of the way of the fire trucks. They headed right for her. Doc Clint and his wife, Emma. Each carried a duffle bag she assumed held medical equipment. Finally. Someone who would actually be of help.

"How's it going, Bobby?" Doc Clint asked, looking past her to where Deke was shouting orders. Gage's team were shooting water high over the center of the flames while the ones flanking him were concentrating their hoses lower and to the periphery.

God, she hated that Gage was in the center of things. But then, the big lug always had to be in front of others, protecting them. Probably the only one worse was Deke.

"Best I can tell, it hasn't spread since we got here with the fire trucks and pressure hoses."

"Any injuries?" Emma asked.

"No one's come back here, yet. But I'm not sure if any of the farmers were hurt before we got here."

"Emma," Doc Clint took the duffle bag from his wife. "You get back to the truck and get out the mini oxygen tanks and masks. Don't turn them on until you need them."

"Where are you going?" she asked, worry lacing the corners of her eyes.

"I'm going to see if there's anyone that's inhaled too much smoke up there." He nodded towards the fire fighters then looked at both Emma and Bobby. "I promise not to get in the way. Won't be much good to anyone if I get injured."

With his promise, Bobby nodded and waved him through. Emma hesitated a moment, watching him move forward.

"He'll be careful, Emma," Bobby reassured him.

"I know. And he's in less danger than Gage or Deke."

"Yeah, those two see danger and raise their hands saying, *sign me up!*" Bobby said with more humor than she felt.

Emma gave a shaky laugh. "They were always like that."

She should know. Gage was her older cousin and she'd spent more time with the pair growing up than anyone else. No further words necessary, the nurse headed for the truck and Bobby went back to doing crowd control. Worry set aside for duty.

Another truck arrived, pulling right up beside the doc's SUV, but instead of getting annoyed, this time she smiled. The truck was more like a van with the sides painted in flamboyant pink, red, yellow and shades of peach and the new logo for the Peaches 'N Cream Café blazoned on the side.

Lorna.

Bobby couldn't help but smile as the café owner climbed out of the driver side, her bright yellow hair glowing from the reflection of the fire. Out of the passenger side came…not Rachel, but Pete, the line cook. Lorna said something to the apparently aged hippie, who nodded then came around the back of the truck. Lorna made a beeline straight for her.

"I brought water and sports drinks to keep the guys hydrated. Some stuff for sandwiches, too, in case this turns into an all-nighter," she said in way of a greeting. Trust Lorna to think of things beyond rescues and injuries, to other needs the crew might have, especially this far out in the boondocks.

"Sounds good. Right there by where Emma is setting up their makeshift triage should be good."

"That's what I thought. Told Pete to get out the table. We'll set up the drinks in an easy spot for the crew to get ahold of. 'Course, gonna have to keep the gawkers out of the supplies," Lorna said, casting a disparaging look at the group gathering near the mayor and DA.

Of course, if she was lucky, Lorna would march over and disperse the crowing crowd of spectators with marching orders.

* * * * *

Libby directed Sean to take the last right turn onto the gravel road that ran beside the Zimmer farm—a farm she visited biannually, like all the other farms in the area, to check on the welfare of the kids, visit with the parents, and often came home with a basket of fresh produce or baked goods—but by this time he no longer needed her directions, since the flames and smoke up ahead announced the farm and fire's location.

Jacob and Anna Zimmer had four little children. The whole drive out here in the near dark, she'd prayed that nothing terrible had happened to the family. While a fire in the field might be terribly frightening, a house fire or the injury of a child would be devastating to the young couple.

She strained to look beyond the field to where she knew the house was. Lights were on inside, but the fire was nowhere near the farmhouse.

Thank God.

"Park here," she said, pointing to the line of cars off to the side. "We don't want to get in the way."

"No problem." Sean swung his car into the field, parking alongside a pickup truck.

She made to get out, but he stopped her with his hand on her arm. She blinked and looked back at him. "What?"

"Thanks," he said, honest appreciation in his eyes. "You really didn't have to come out here. I probably could've found it by following the others."

"Probably, but you could've gotten lost, too." She shrugged, feeling a little awkward. "Can't have the town's only news source wandering around lost in the dark, not when we just got you."

"True. Hate to be the source of a rescue mission with this going on." He laughed and released her arm. "But I just wanted to be sure I said thanks anyways, in case I don't get a chance later."

"You're welcome."

They climbed out of the car and headed up the path to where other town folks had gathered, many of them spoke or nodded hello.

"Everyone always come out for fires like this?" Sean asked, looking around at the crowd, most of whom had worried expressions on their faces.

"We don't get a lot of this kind of emergency too often, thank goodness." She paused, staring directly at him. "The series of murders and meth lab explosion that nearly leveled the town and almost killed Gage last spring a definite exception. I think that made majority of us, and definitely the town council, realize how much we needed to pay more attention to each other's needs. Sort of a wake-up slap to us as a community. And it took a community to save him."

"Yeah, no help that my predecessor took a header over the line to crazyville, from what I've learned."

"And until Bobby came here asking questions, none of us saw it coming."

They continued closer to the spot where Lorna stood talking with Bobby Roberts, who was dressed in volunteer fire gear and keeping everyone not essential out of the way.

"It took that near catastrophe to bring our core value to light."

"And that is?" he asked.

She shrugged. "Unlike the big city, most of the people here care about not only their next-door neighbors, but those in the community as a whole."

"Even the Amish?"

"Even the Amish. I know that in some other areas, even here in our state, harassing the Amish about their lifestyle choice borders on bigoted. But we've always been accepting and friendly with those in our community." She laughed slightly. "Besides, some of the best produce comes from these farms."

"That is does," Lorna said as they stopped beside her. "Get my honey from Jacob's farm here. Hope this fire doesn't hurt his bee colony. Make sure Deke and the others know I have the hydration station up and ready." She squeezed Bobby's shoulder and headed back to her van.

Libby took a moment to introduce Sean to Bobby.

"Can you give me any official report, Deputy Roberts?" Sean asked, going into professional-reporter mode.

Bobby gave him a slight shake of her head. "That would be something for Chief Reynolds or Sheriff Justice, Mr. Callahan. Right now, they're both busy out there working the fire."

Sean nodded. "I'll talk with them later. Do you know if there's any chance this will spread?"

"That's one of the things we're trying to prevent, besides getting the monster under control," Bobby said, half-turning to look at the firefighters behind her. "Jacob Zimmer, the farm's owner, plowed up firebreaks after the hay was cleared from the field to help prevent just such a fire jump from occurring."

While Sean talked with Bobby, taking notes and asking questions, Libby took a step away to get a better look at the crew working the fire. They'd divided up into four groups. The Amish farmers were grouped together off to one side, all in white shirts, suspenders and black pants. They seemed to be using their old-fashioned cart to wet the area not in the fire. One crew of the volunteers was shooting water high over the center of the flames, a tall figure that had to be Gage was at the head of their hose. Two other crews flanked them, sweeping their water lower from the edges in.

She strained to make out more of the firemen. Then she saw him.

Deacon.

And damn her for feeling a lightness of relief, seeing him unharmed.

Using a large rake he hauled debris away from the

edges of the fire that had been put out, stepping back to let the left team use their hose to soak it down more, preventing any smoldering flare-ups. Then Deke stepped back in to rake away more from the edges of the fire, which seemed to be contained—at least, to Libby's untrained eye.

Suddenly, several figures moved away from the area back towards the safety line.

Doc Clint had two of the farmers with him, both of whom were coughing—hard. Libby and Bobby hurried up to meet him.

"Libby, can you get Jacob and Eli over to Emma for me? Tell her just some oxygen and to check their vitals. I'm going to go back and check out some others. Okay?"

"Oxygen and vitals, maybe more to come. Got it."

Taking both men by the elbows, she helped them over to the makeshift triage area where Emma already had folding chairs and oxygen tanks out with masks at the ready. Libby repeated the instructions that Clint had sent to his wife, then followed her movements by getting a mask over Jacob's head. Eli, who was older than Jacob by at least two decades, was having the most trouble getting his coughing under control, so Emma focused on him.

"Any burns?" Libby asked Jacob, who started to remove the mask to talk. She stopped him. "No, just nod or shake your head. The oxygen is important."

He shook his head no, which she took to mean he

didn't have any burns.

"Is your family all safe up at the house?" she asked.

He nodded.

"Good. I'm going to go get you some water from Lorna's van. Anything else I can get you?"

He shook his head.

She retrieved two bottles of water from Lorna, opening them and handing one to each man. She took a moment to locate Deke in the fire crew again, where he was now directing the teams to move closer together. The fire was definitely shrinking. This need to see that he was still uninjured and working hard disturbed her, but before she could focus on it and analyze it to death, Doc Clint was headed back with more men. Focusing all her attention on helping him and Emma with the firefighters, hoping no one was too seriously injured. She prayed that Deke would be sensible and not take any unnecessary risks—this time.

CHAPTER EIGHT

Sweat trickled down Deke's face and he swiped at it with his free hand to keep more from dripping into his eyes. He set down the fire rake, leaning the handle against his thigh, removed his helmet for a minute to wipe more sweat from his forehead and neck, shook his head to fling more moisture from his hair, then slammed the helmet back in place. The intense heat and exertion from the battle with the fire had the clothes beneath his fire-retardant turnout gear plastered to his body.

Damn, he needed a shower.

"Looks like we're getting a handle on it." John Wilson, Libby's uncle stepped up beside him, the face mask of his self-contained breathing apparatus hanging to one side of his helmet. Taking out a kerchief, the older man wiped the soot and sweat from his own face. The pair of them stood downwind from the smoke, watching the hose teams focus on the small area of fire still ablaze.

"The major portion for sure and it's not spreading, mostly thanks to Jacob's preparedness in clearing the field of major debris and the firebreaks he plowed." Deke pointed to the edges of the fire. "Once we get it out, we'll need to work from the cooler edges into the center to be sure there are no hot spots to flare and reignite. I'll keep a team of the volunteers here for a while doing that. You and the on-duty crew can head back to the station. You'll need your rest, in case any other emergency comes in."

"Want us to fill up the hand-pump cart before we go?" John cleared his throat with a hard cough.

"Sounds like you might need to have Clint and Emma take a look at you first. Have Aaron fill the cart while you do that."

"Will do, Chief," John said, signaling the young farmer-turned-firefighter to join him as he moved away from the fire.

A few more minutes of water spraying the area and the last of the flames were out.

Deke inhaled and exhaled slowly. His body relaxing slowly with the action.

Thank God. It could've been so much worse.

Gage came over to stand next to Deke. "Why don't we get a head count of our men, while Cleetus and Wes finish dousing the embers?"

"Got any idea how many turned up?" Deke turned to scan the triage area.

A group of the Amish farmers who'd been fighting

the fire when they got there were gathered in one area, several of them seated with oxygen masks on their faces. Doc Clint and Emma hovered around them. The farmers hadn't had breathing apparatuses so smoke inhalation was a problem for them. His own men seemed to be more in need of hydration and stood off to the side drinking bottles of electrolyte-filled sports drinks or water. No one appeared to have been badly injured.

"I counted your crew of five, fifteen volunteers, including you and five of the Sheriff's department, including me and Bobby."

"Twenty-five. Not a bad turnout."

"Not including the Amish that were already here."

A movement at the triage area caught his attention. A flash of blonde hair.

Libby?

What the hell was she doing here?

"Helping Doc Clint and Emma, looks like," Gage said beside him, making him realize he'd said the words out loud.

"Shit. After Bill's death, she shouldn't be anywhere near a fire."

"Technically, she's not near the fire, but behind the boundary line *you* set for civilians."

He shot Gage a scathing look. "You know what I mean."

"Yes. But she wasn't in danger back there. She's helping the medical team with the injured, which is more than I can say for some of our other town council members," Gage said, nodding to where the mayor, DA and others of the council stood watching, but making no move to help. "Besides, the fire is out now. So what's your beef with her being here?"

Guilt. Over her brother's death. Regret. That the fire might bring her bad memories. Fear. That he'd lose her to the monster, too.

He didn't voice those thoughts to Gage. The pain they caused was too personal for him to give them more power by saying them aloud. Instead, he picked up his fire rake, slapped his mask back over his face and returned to the fire.

Time to focus on what was important for this moment. All his feelings about Libby would have to go back in the vault of his brain where he'd been keeping them for the past decade.

Over the radio and headset attached inside his mask, he talked to his men and volunteers still working. "Gage, Cleetus and Daniel, keep the water spraying for another thirty minutes. Aaron, Martin and Wes, let's focus on checking any large piles of charred debris. Look for embers still glowing and get them snuffed out. Let's keep this baby from flaring back up on us."

* * * * *

"Do you have any idea what might have caused the fire, Mr. Zimmer?"

Libby heard Sean ask the young farmer seated at the triage table. Doc Clint was busy bandaging up his left forearm with a while cream beneath it. Thankfully, Jacob had been the only one with burns from the fire. She was no expert, but from what Clint and Emma had said, they were mostly first-degree burns and should heal easily.

It could've been so much worse.

She shoved that thought out of her mind, at the same time glancing up to see Deke talking with Gage near one of the fire trucks. Taller than most of the other men, their forms were always easy to find.

Neither one had taken a break in…she checked her watch…the nearly two hours they'd been fighting the fire. Even now, Deke was headed back in, his arms waving as he gave directions to the other men still working the water hoses.

"No. The hay had been dried thoroughly and moved into the barns two days ago," Jacob replied with the rhythmic cadence common among the Amish community. He shook his head, unshed tears in his eyes. "I followed Chief Reynolds' instructions for fire safety and still we had this."

"Sometimes God gives us problems even when we plan to prevent them, Jacob," Thomas Elder said, laying a hand on the younger man's shoulder from behind. "His blessing is that now you don't have to clear the hay stubble from the field."

Jacob gave him a weary smile. "A blessing in the

chaos, Thomas?"

"Ja. And your family is safe."

"Ja. That is truly a blessing."

Jacob nodded more solemnly, his smile fading as he apparently thought of what could have happened to his young family. Libby's heart went out to him.

"Thank you for talking with me, Mr. Zimmer," Sean said, closing the cover to his computer tablet and shaking both the men's hands. He headed her way.

"Did you get all the information you needed for the newspaper?" she asked when he stopped beside her.

He nodded. "I think so. A couple of the firemen gave me the lowdown on the usual causes of fire. I had no idea that spontaneous combustion was a real thing, especially in rural areas."

"I didn't either." She handed him a bottle of water.

Taking it, he cracked the lid and took a long drink. "It can happen when the freshly cut hay is baled and stored in a barn. When the core temp gets too high, poof. Fire."

"So that's why the hay is left out to dry for days, or even weeks. I'd always wondered." She soaked down a cloth with water from the ice chest Lorna had provided and handed it to Andy, another of the volunteer firefighters, who sat holding an oxygen mask to his face. "This will help cool you down," she told him.

With a smile of appreciation beneath the mask, Andy slapped the cloth on the back of his neck.

"How much longer do you think they'll be here?"

Sean asked, staring out at the fire area.

"I imagine they'll want to stay a while to be sure there are no flare-ups. Maybe an hour or so," she said, gathering some empty water bottles into a trash bag for recycling. "Why?"

"I need to get this back to the paper, so we can put it out for tomorrow's edition. But I don't want to drag you away."

The town had gone without a paper since the previous owner had literally lost his mind. Having Sean put out a bi-weekly paper had brought some normalcy to the town that it had been missing for months.

Libby looked around at the men still needing attention. "Why don't you head back to town? I can get a ride with someone here. That is, if you think you can find your way back."

He gave her a smile and tapped the water bottle to his head. "Tactile learner. Once I've driven somewhere once, I have no problem getting back or there again. If you're sure?"

"Yes. I'm sure." She laughed and waved him on his way, returning to her task of cleaning up the bottles and checking on the firefighters still in the triage area. As she worked she noticed the spectators' cars starting to trickle out of the area, including most of the town council members. The volunteers were hanging around, but finally the on-duty crew loaded up the quint and tanker trucks after filling the hand pump cart with water, and headed back to town.

"Looks like everything's under control here," Mayor Rawlins said, strolling over to the triage table. He'd been over several times to talk with the firefighters and the farmers. Tobias could be pompous at times, but the town knew he loved the citizens, so most tolerated his self-interested moments. Tonight wasn't one of them. He'd sincerely come to check on the injured or those requiring some hydration or oxygen.

"Yep. Just the cleaning up left to do, Tobias," Lorna said, handing him two bags of trash. "You want to toss those into one of the dumpsters on your way into town? Might as well be of some help, Mayor."

"Be my pleasure, Lorna." He smiled and took the bags good-naturedly. Turning, he looked at Libby. "Want me to take those, too?"

"Nope," Lorna answered first. "We're gonna recycle those in the café's recycling bin. Every little bit helps."

Tobias looked a little embarrassed. Libby gave him a half shrug in sympathy. As he walked back to his car, she closed up the second bag of empty bottles. Carrying them over to Lorna's van, she set them in back next to the other supplies that Pete, the cook, had loaded into the van.

She headed back to the triage table and started putting the unopened bottles back into the cooler.

"Can I get one of those?"

Her heart skipped a beat at the raspy, deep voice from behind her.

Deke.

Inhaling slowly to calm her sudden nervousness, she grabbed a bottle and turned to him with a smile. "Of course."

"Thanks," he said, taking the bottle. He popped the top.

His eyes closed as he drank, she took the opportunity to study him. He'd pulled his helmet, hood and mask off, his short, sandy-colored hair curling in waves from the heat and sweat. Soot streaked his face in spots and down his neck. Watching him swallow as he drank, his muscles working hard, she swallowed too, and licked her suddenly parched lips.

"Man, that was good." The bottle completely drained, he handed it back to her.

"Want another?" she asked, her voice sounding a little shaky in her own ears.

Great. Now she'd reverted back to an awkward teenager in his presence.

He shook his head. "No, I'm good. Thanks."

"Everything under control?" she asked, to fill the awkward pause between them.

Idiot. Of course they were under control. He wouldn't be here getting a drink if they weren't. His sense of responsibility had always been one of his driving forces. And she'd both loved and hated that about him.

"The major fire is out." He scanned the charred field, his eyes taking in every man still out there, working. "We've still got some work to do. Checking for hot spots under the ashes. Don't want any flare ups to set the whole mess off again."

"Does that happen often?" she asked, drawing his dark eyes back to her.

"Not as much with a nearly empty field like Jacob had here. Structural fires are more at risk, with all the debris still acting as fuel for any smoldering embers. With the dry summer we've had, I'd like to be extra sure we don't have anything to worry about this time."

Pete interrupted them as he stepped over to the cooler. "Y'all done with this, Miss Libby?" he asked.

"Oh, yes, Pete." Smiling, she slipped the last bottle of water back in the cooler and closed the lid. "Thanks. I was going to haul it over to the van."

"No problem, miss," he said lifting the cooler and giving her a wink. "It's my pleasure and why Miss Lorna keeps me hanging around."

After he stashed the cooler in the café's van, he came back, folded the metal table and loaded it in, too. Then he climbed in beside Lorna, the pair waving as they pulled out to follow the caravan of vehicles toward town.

"He's a nice man," Libby said, watching him walk away.

"What's his story?" Deke asked, bringing her attention back to him.

Not knowing what to do with her hands, she shoved them down in her jeans pocket and shrugged. "Not really sure. He wandered into town not long after

Emma left to go to nursing school. Lorna gave him a chance as the line cook and he's just sort of stayed on."

"No family in the area?"

She shook her head. "Not that I'm aware of. Why?"

It was his turn to shrug. "Nothing really. Just curious, I guess. For someone who's been in Westen for nearly two years, I've never really talked with him."

"Deke," Doc Clint said, stepping over with Emma's hand in his. "We're about done here."

"Any serious injuries?" Deke asked, his brows drawn down in worry.

"Nothing too serious. A few of the farmers have some smoke inhalation, but none serious enough to take to the clinic for the night. I'll come out and check on them tomorrow."

"Any burns?"

Clint shook his head. "A few minor ones. Embers getting under clothes on arms and necks." He looked at the group of farmers slowly walking up to the Zimmer home. "Jacob Zimmer seemed to have been the only one to sustain anything worth worrying about. We put some burn cream on it and dressed it and we'll check it tomorrow, too."

Gage nodded. "Jacob and the others came over and thanked me a few minutes ago. I saw his bandages. Anyone in his family harmed?"

Emma shook her head. "I took a few minutes to walk up to the house. Anna and the children were shaken up, but otherwise okay."

"Fires can be very frightening, but when your home and family are threatened…" Deke paused, swallowing and looking away.

Libby blinked at the sudden tears that filled her eyes as she turned away from the pain that crossed over his face, knowing he was thinking of Bill. Emma sent her a sympathetic look. She returned it with a very shaky whisper of a smile.

Clint clamped his free hand on Deke's shoulder. "True. But everyone is safe tonight. We can be thankful for that."

Gage, Bobby and one of the other deputies, Daniel, approached. The seven of them were all that was left of the town's people. A small group of the farmers still hovered on the edge of the field, talking quietly with Jacob.

"We've turned over every charred pile across the entire burn area. No signs of smoldering embers, Gunslinger," Gage said, dropping an arm over Bobby's shoulders and hauling her into his side. "We're going to head out of here. Got an early morning tomorrow with the football team before court."

"Thanks for being here," Deke said, shaking hands with all three.

"No problem," Gage said. "Got your back always."

Deke watched them walk to their trucks then turned to Libby with his brows furrowed again. "Where's your car?"

"I didn't bring one. Sean wanted to come out, so I

played navigator for him."

"Sean?" he asked, sounding oddly aggravated.

Seriously? Was he jealous? The idea both irritated and thrilled her. It had been a decade since they'd been together. Whatever right he had to be jealous had long passed its expiration date by now. But a little part of her, that part she'd carefully tucked away in her heart, did a little-girl-excited-squeal inside her head.

"You want a ride back with us?" Emma asked, before Libby could explain why she didn't have to justify time she spent with any man besides him.

"She'll ride with me," Deke said, without even asking her if it would be okay.

She started to protest, but the silent plea in his eyes that she ride with him stopped her. With a smile she turned to Emma. "Thanks, but I'll come back with Deke. He knows where I left my car."

Emma and her husband exchanged a quick glance. "Okay, we'll see you both tomorrow," she said and the pair headed to their truck.

When she turned back, Deke had stalked over to his truck and was stripping off his coat. He tossed it into the back of the truck. Still dressed in his turnout pants, boots and suspenders over the shirt he'd had on in the café, he wandered over to the edge of the burned field once more. In the moonlight she could see his silhouette —the ramrod spine, shoulders straight, his hands on his narrow hips.

She gave a little sigh.

After all this time, how could he still make her heart yearn for him so deeply?

* * * * *

She'll ride with me.

Could he have sounded more caveman-ish? Why didn't he just open his pants and mark her like a dog claiming his territory?

Deke shook his head slightly. He couldn't help it. When she'd called the newspaperman by his first name, something had gone off in his head. Like a warning shot. And the caveman had thumped his chest and roared. *Mine.*

He'd done his best to stay away for the past ten years. It would be best for both of them if he could let her go permanently, but hearing her say another man's name so familiarly had reawakened that part of him that had loved her above everything else.

The ground behind him crunched. Her lemony scent rode over the smoky ashes in front of him, blocking their acrid smell from his senses.

The caveman relaxed.

She was here. With him.

"At least the crops were out of the field."

"Yep. Jacob's preplanning to plow fire breaks in the fields was a godsend." His eyes fixed on the dark ground in front of them, he didn't dare look at her. "Kept it from spreading or heading straight for his home."

Despite how easily they'd managed to subdue the fire, it was still a bad one. It had been years since he'd had to fight more than a small kitchen blaze in the county. Nothing this big, this potentially dangerous. It slammed home the loss of his friend, not to mention his own fight to get free of the burning rubble, and the months of painful rehab.

"When I think of what could've happened to Anna and the children…"

Her voice caught and he finally looked at her. Standing to his left, her arms wound around her torso just beneath her breasts, drawing the thin material taut over them. A tremble made her blouse shuffle to the sides. Moonlight shone on her pale face and the tears in her eyes.

Bill.

She was thinking about Bill's death.

Aw, hell.

He reached over and pulled her into his arms, feeling another tremble run through her. In an effort to soothe her, he stroked his hands over her back. The effect worked. It not only calmed her, it took the edge off his own raw emotions. He leaned his chin on the top of her head, the softness of her blonde hair cool against his skin.

How many times had he held her just like this?

Her arms came around his body, her hands clutching the back of his shirt.

A sound escaped her, muffled by his chest and shirt. Then another.

A soft sob.

Aw, hell. She was crying.

He'd never known what to do when she'd cried. Thankfully, that hadn't been too often. In self-defense, he'd always just held her, which, as it turned out, seemed to be enough for her.

Who had held her when the news came about Bill?

Certainly hadn't been him. He'd been in the burn unit for three months. In isolation for his own protection. No visitors. Alone with his own pain, his own guilt, his own grief.

"I missed his funeral," he whispered into her hair. The words seeming to force their way out of him. The pain over it bubbling to the surface. The tears that had filled his eyes slid slowly over his cheeks.

She nodded against his chest, inhaled. "I know."

"He was one of my best friends, my partner, and I couldn't even be there to bury him. To hold you like this."

She pulled back slightly, tilting her head so that he had to move his chin to the side. He stared down into her blue eyes wet from her own tears.

Bringing her hand up, she cupped his cheek. "You couldn't be there. You were in the hospital. All alone."

And that's all it took.

He dropped his head onto her shoulder.

Sobs wracked his body. His legs wobbled and he

would've collapsed had she not been strong enough to hold him up.

The pain so deep, so raw, it was as if Bill had died just yesterday.

And for him he had.

A deep wail filled the air around them.

It was from him.

"Oh, God, Lib! He burned to death. Died in that fire. I let him."

"It wasn't your fault," she whispered. "You didn't set that fire."

"I couldn't... get to him..." His voice broke on another sob.

"Shh, it's okay," she crooned softly, stroking his face with her hand.

"No. I tried...to save...couldn't." He stopped, swallowing hard, willing his head and heart to focus past the pain. It was time to let go of some of it. "He was...right there." He reached his hand out as he saw Bill reaching out for him again, their fingers separated by mere inches. "I almost...had him."

Another round of sobs hit him. He clutched her tighter as once more Bill slipped away from his grasp, over the side of the burning floor, into the fiery abyss below. His last word, *DEKE* coming over his radio mic as he went.

She continued to hold him, crooning more words to him, her hands stroking over his face and back, her warmth penetrating the coldness of his grief—a grief he'd been living with for ten years, unable and unwilling to share it with others. Until now. Until her.

Slowly, his tears ended. His body weak from the effort of purging itself of the pain. Inhaling and exhaling a few times to help gain control once more, he released his tight hold on her shirt and wiped his nose and face on his shirt sleeve. "I'm sorry. I don't know why I did that."

"Yes, you do," she said, staring at him with soft sympathy in her face. "You never really got to grieve for him. Not like the rest of us did."

That was it. But it was so much more. And when she knew the truth, would she ever look at him with such tenderness? Or would it change to hate?

He couldn't go there. Not tonight.

Coward.

Yes. He was a coward. He'd faced that truth years ago. He'd hid it from everyone, including Libby.

"What's going on in there?" Libby asked, quirking her head to one side to stare at him.

Damn. She was way too perceptive.

"Nothing," he said, and she lifted one brow expressing her doubt in that statement. "No, really. Just amazed how hard that hurt."

"It's bad enough when the loss is fresh, but to hold onto that grief for all these years," she paused. "I can't even imagine it."

She shivered and he realized the night had gotten a bit chilly, even for late August.

"I'd best get you back to town," he said, releasing his hold on her back and taking a step away. His arms feeling emptier now than they had the past ten years. How would he ever be able to leave her alone again?

CHAPTER NINE

"That's it," Rachel said, locking the front door to the café and turning the closed sign out. "Last customer fed and on his way home happy."

Kyle wheeled the bucket and mop out into the center of the floor. He'd already cleaned the dining room and stacked the chairs on the table, leaving a clean path for mopping.

"That's my usual job," Rachel said, stepping forward to take the mop.

He held up a hand to keep her away as he dropped the mop into the soapy water. "Not tonight. Miss Lorna said I was to stay and help close up or until they got back." He slopped the mop into the wringer and squeezed the excess water out before dropping it onto the floor in the far-right- hand corner of the room.

"Ah, my knight in shining armor," she said with her hand to her chest, delighted when he blushed.

That was something she'd liked from the moment she'd teased him about looking her over at the same time he was considering the menu. Most guys, you teased them or flirted with them, and they went all I'm-too-cool-for-you douche on you. Not Kyle. Or the guys got out their phones and spent so much time telling everyone how video-star they were, you couldn't even hold a conversation with them. She was pretty sure Kyle didn't even own a phone. Of course, since he started working here, they hadn't had much time to talk, not that he said much anyways.

"I get the floors," he said, looking over his shoulder at her with a half-smile. "You get to do receipts."

She pressed her lips together and made a face at him. "Thanks. I take back the knight comment. You're more like Sauron."

The rhythm of the mop paused and he stared at her, a blank look on his face. "Who?"

She blinked. "Sauron," she repeated, expecting it to make sense this time.

He shrugged. "Still no clue."

He was kidding, right? "From the *Lord of the Rings* books and movies, you know, super-bad entity bent on destroying the world?"

"Sorry, never saw them or read the books." His cheeks were red, this time from embarrassment rather than charming bashfulness.

And didn't she feel like a real ass.

Play it cool, like it's no big deal.

She put a smile on her face as she opened the cash register and removed the final till for the night—she and Mom always emptied it several times a day, especially on busy ones like today. "So you're sending me off to do horrible office chores, just like an evil king torturing the fair maiden."

That brought a light back to his grey eyes, if not that whisper of a smile she'd kinda gotten to like seeing the past few days.

He pointed the mop toward her. "Hie thee off to the dungeon, fair maiden, and finish the receipts."

Laughing at his command and that he'd joined her in good-natured role-play, she clutched the tray of money to her hip, laying the back of one hand to her forehead. "I don't think I can take the torture."

"You must or there will be a worse fate for you."

She stuck her chin up in the air and with a toss of her ponytail retreated to the office. His deep laughter followed her into the room.

Inside the office, she locked the door as her mother had always insisted she do while handling money. Seated at the table, she counted out the bills, recounted them for a second and a third time, finally slowly writing the numbers on the paper ledger Mom insisted she keep. She counted the money a fourth time, then checked that number against the ones she'd written down, one column at a time, just like her tutor had taught her.

Crap. She'd written the figure wrong, again. She'd mixed up the five and the three. Of course that made her question her counting, so she set about counting the bills and change for a fifth time. Yep, she'd put the three where the five should be and vice-versa.

Dang dyslexia. Numbers just seemed to jump around at will and at the stupidest times. It's why she hated math class and math in general.

Also why Mom insisted she work in the office and on the books. The more she did, the easier it was for her to find and correct her own mistakes. At least she didn't have the same problem with letters and words like some people.

Next, she counted out the minimum that her mother always started the morning's business with and refilled the till tray. After that she opened the safe, set the tray inside and deposited the remainder of the money into the Tuesday money pouch. Mom would make her bi-weekly trip on Thursday to the bank to deposit it. Payday was on Friday, so she'd want to have the week's money in early so the staff's paychecks, including Rachel's, would be available for cashing the next day. Cash tips were kept by the waitresses at the end of their shifts. Tips written on credit card transactions were put into a special account, and Mom always divided them up between all the staff, Pete and Kyle included, on their paychecks.

Now that the money was secured, Rachel opened the door to work on the computer part of her job. She'd heard Kyle moving the mop bucket around the front dining room while the door was closed. He'd moved into the kitchen just behind the dining room and across from the office. She swiveled in the chair to watch him scrub the big, flat-top grill to Pete's demanding specifications. For a man who was so laid back about his own appearance, Pete had surprised both her and Mom when he'd started working for them and kept his kitchen in tip-top, military shape, grousing that cleanliness and organization couldn't be overlooked in a kitchen.

Watching Kyle lean into the scrub brush he was using to slosh soapy water over the large gill, she realized Pete's instructions had made an impression on him. Seemed he took every aspect of his new job very seriously. In fact, it was as if he was afraid that if he missed one step or had one dish out of place someone might take the job away from him.

She smiled when she thought about the conversation her mom had with her just before she and Pete had left for the fire.

"Rachel, there's only one customer left," she said, nodding at old man Russell, seated at his usual counter spot eating his nightly slice of pie. "I was going to take the new boy with me out to the fire with supplies, but he got so pale when we heard there was a fire, I'm thinking it might not be such a good idea."

"I know," she said. "He must have a real fear of fires to get that upset about seeing the fire trucks fly past."

"Well, that settles it." Mom nodded her head the way she did whenever she came to what she considered

a done deal. "I'm leaving you and Kyle here to close up. You feel comfortable staying with the boy? If not, I'll have Pete stay, too."

She'd glanced at Kyle, who was bussing the last table of all the dishes the family of six had left behind. "I know we haven't known him long, but I trust him, Mom."

Her mother had smiled and said, "I do, too. You keep your phone in your pocket, in case there's any trouble, okay?"

She'd agreed, and with that, Mom had scooted Pete out to the van and they'd left.

A deep rhythmic sound pulled her out of her reverie.

Singing?

Listening closer, she realized Kyle was doing the bass part to one of the old do-wop songs Mom kept stored in the old-fashioned jukebox. Turning back to the computer, she started entering the figures from the credit card receipts, joining her own alto harmony to the song. Mom might keep the old-time-diner feel out where the customers could enjoy it, but her business inside the office was very twenty-first century. She like to tell Rachel, *"Manage your money or you'll be trying to figure how to manage without it."*

Rachel smiled as she entered the nightly figures into the spreadsheets, using her finger on the screen to check each figure one number at a time to be sure they were correct. The town council and local bank might not know it, but Lorna Doone had invested in several of the small, lucrative business that had popped up in town in the past few years. Usually the owners were former employees of the café. Twylla over at the Dye Right, Becky Hodges, owner of the Quilt Shop, Trudy Fisher at the Broadway Boutique dress shop, as well as Joe at Murphy's Antique Mall on the edge of town all owed their startup success to her mother's belief in helping her neighbors.

The clatter of pans behind her made her look to see how far Kyle was to being done. Looked like four big pots left to do. Refocusing on the bookkeeping program, she hurried to get all the data entered before Kyle was finished with the pots. She didn't want him thinking she couldn't work as efficiently on the computer as he could in the kitchen.

Besides, she glanced out into the dark night outside the office window, walking out to the parking lot at night by herself, even in small-town Westen, gave her the creeps. Especially after the crazed-newspaperman-turned-meth-kingpin had been on the loose in town last spring. You never knew who or what might be out there.

After glancing at the clock, Kyle focused all his attention on scrubbing down the last pot. It had been more than an hour since the fire trucks had gone screaming down Main Street. Ever since he could remember, he hated the sound of fire trucks or fire drill alarms in schools. A shudder ran through him. His breathing hitched. Sweat broke out on his face again. Same as it had with the first siren tonight.

The psychologists called it a visceral response to how his parents had died.

Yeah, right. For all their fancy letters behind their names, those docs didn't know squat.

He'd been having the same response long before that ever happened. Probably the smell of smoke on his dad was the trigger. He'd reeked of smoke every time he came in drunk to beat on him and his mom—always after fire trucks would shatter the quiet night.

For all their training, no one ever asked him that.

He'd kept his secret.

He'd come outside to get Leo for dinner. The door to the shed was open. He wasn't supposed to go inside. Ever.

What did Leo do out there?

He peeked inside. There was a work table with all kinds of things on it. Spools of wire. Pieces of clocks. Bottles.

Suddenly he was grabbed up by the back of his shirt, his feet dangling from the ground.

"What are you doing, brat?"

He gulped hard and stared at the huge work boots, too scared to see Leo's face contort with rage. He'd seen it too many times in his life already. "Din... dinner," he managed to whisper.

"You know better than to go into the shed." The monster that was his father shook him hard.

"Didn't...didn't go...in."

His feet hit the ground as quickly as they'd left. The shadow switched and a hand came to force his face up to meet his father's scarred one.

"Don't tell anyone, boy. Forget what you saw. Understand me?" Eyes the same steely grey as his bored into him with an intensity that warned of dire consequences should he fail to heed the warning.

He'd nodded and never went back to that shed again.

"You're gonna scrub a hole in the bottom of that thing."

He jumped, sloshing water over the side of the tub and down his shirt.

"OMG," she said, running to grab a dish towel.

"No biggie," he said as he set the pot back in the water, gathered up the bottom of the shirt and wrung out as much of the water into the empty side sink as he could.

She held out the dish towel. "I'm really sorry. I thought you heard me coming up behind you."

He took it, wiping the water off his arms and the front of his jeans. He looked up to see her smiling at him, laughter in her twinkling eyes. She wasn't laughing at him. Not like so many others had over the years. No, she was laughing at what had happened and that she'd managed to surprise him.

Earlier he'd been surprised to hear her singing along to that old song that got stuck in his head. She had a great voice and picked up the harmonies without any effort. Of course, he shouldn't be surprised. There didn't seem to be anything she wasn't good at.

Great. Now he sounded like some stupid crushing noob. Bad enough that when she teased or flirted with him he could barely talk.

"Thanks," he said, handing her back the towel then turned back to the pot. "I'm just about done."

"I really didn't mean to make you get all wet."

Something in the way she said it—a slight hesitation in her voice—made him look over his shoulder at her.

"Yeah, right," he said, but softened it with a wink.

She blushed.

His hands froze in the hot, soapy water. His heart kicked up a notch. God. She was even prettier with her cheeks all pink like that.

"Um, I could make it up by giving you a ride home." She licked her lips and then bit down on her lower lip.

Kyle tightened his grip on the pot. "Um. Okay."

She smiled, the odd sense of nervousness gone from her face once more. "Okay. I'll get my stuff and turn out the lights in the front while you finish up."

She whirled around and almost ran from the kitchen.

He continued to watch the space where she'd just been, wondering what had just happened. Because something had happened. He was sure of it.

Blinking, he turned back to finish scrubbing the pot. Didn't want her to come back finding him staring like some stupid statue. Finished scrubbing away the last of the cooked cheese from the macaroni and cheese Pete had made earlier, Kyle rinsed and dried the pot. Finally, he set it in the big rack under the kitchen-prep island, right where Pete had told him it went.

The guy reminded him of some of the old homeless vets he'd seen on the streets of Columbus and Cincinnati when he'd lived in those cities. But Pete wasn't confused or strung out. Nope. He was a great cook and liked his kitchen just the way he wanted it. Kyle wasn't going to mess with his process. Especially if it meant he got free meals.

The sound of jingling keys to his left caught his attention. Rachel came to a stop in the doorway.

"Here," she said holding something out to him.

He looked at the dark-grey cloth. "What is it?"

"A dry shirt. One of the new ones my mom has for sale." She stepped closer, still holding it out to him.

He held up his hands, palm outward. "Nope. Can't take anything. She might think I stole it."

"Don't be ridiculous. She bought tons of them and expects the staff to start wearing them as free advertising starting next week. You are staff here, right?"

"Yeah."

"Okay, I'm giving you yours early." She stuck it out again, this time hitting him in the chest with it. "Go on. Change shirts," she said, sounding every bit as tough as Miss Lorna. "Besides, if she knew I caused you to get soaking wet and didn't offer you one, she'd tan my backside."

"Yeah, like I believe she'd ever hit you," he said, whipping the wet shirt over his head and dropping it on the floor. He took the shirt from her. After he pulled it over his head, he found her staring oddly at him. "Rachel?"

"Um, yes, well, Mom never *hit* me." Rachel stepped away, turning her back to go retrieve her backpack from where she'd left it in the doorway. "Not like in a mean way or out of anger. More like spanked me when I was in need of one, usually for blatantly disobeying a safety rule. And I can count those times on one hand. Mom is very just and only metes out punishment when it's deserved. Always explains why. When I was little I'd go to the time out corner. Now, mostly I get grounded or my phone taken away."

"That's good," he said, picking up his wet shirt and following her to the back door.

"It's good I got my phone taken away?" She set the alarm and the two of them stepped out into the alley. The light over the back door lit up the porch and doorway so she could see to lock the two deadbolts. The alley was dark, except for the light over where Miss Lorna's car sat. "It's over there. Mom will drive the van to our house."

He walked silently with her to the car and climbed into the passenger side, thinking about how she could count the exact number of times her mother had spanked her, while he'd dodged Leo's fists so many times, the number seemed infinite.

They drove on with only music from her phone playing through the speakers breaking the silence. It didn't take long for them to pull up outside the Colbert House.

"Thanks," he said reaching for the door handle.

"You never answered my question," she said, laying her hand on his arm, stopping his exit.

"No. I don't think it's good your mom takes away your phone. I think it's good she's never hit you. No one should ever get hit in their own home."

Before she could say anything more, he got out of the car and jogged up to the door. The sympathy in her eyes fueling his escape.

CHAPTER TEN

They rode in silence all the way back to town. Libby stared out into the dark night, her nerves and emotions still raw from holding him as he'd cried. Old wounds she'd been sure were good and healed felt as fresh as if someone had torn the scabs right off them.

How must he feel?

At least she'd had her mother and friends to help her grieve for Bill. But Deke had held his grief close, closing out his mother same as he had her. Probably hadn't shared his pain with her before she moved to South Carolina last year. He'd lost his father right after finishing college. She doubted he'd even talked with Gage about the fire or Bill's death. No, he'd been the lone wolf, nursing his own wounds.

"Why didn't you let me come see you at the hospital?" The words were out of her mouth before she could stop them.

"I was in the burn unit, Libby." His tone suggested his comment needed no further explanation.

Well, dammit, she wanted some answers.

"You mean no one was ever allowed to visit anyone? Ever?" she snapped, unable to keep her frustration in check.

He didn't answer for a few moments. "Visitors were limited. The risk of infection was very high."

"So no one came to see you?"

Another long pause, as if he were measuring his words. "My captain and a few of the others came by."

"So, it was just me you didn't want to see." This time it was hurt in her voice and she hated sounding so childish.

He pulled up beside her car in the empty parking lot. "Libby, it wasn't like that—"

She held up a hand to cut him off. She turned to look at him, the street light behind him casting shadows over the planes of his face. "I wanted to be there for you. To know you would survive. That the fire hadn't taken both of the men in my life from me."

Tears started afresh.

"Libby."

He reached for her again, but this time she bolted from the car before she turned back into a sniveling wimp, incapable of controlling her own emotions.

As she fumbled for her car keys, she heard the slam of a car door.

"Dammit, Elizabeth." Deke stepped up behind her, his arms coming around her once more, imprisoning her between his warm body and the metal of her car. "Let me take you home. You're not in any shape to drive."

She started to shake her head no at his pity, but his lips landed on her temple.

Such a simple touch. A kiss of comfort.

Suddenly, he turned her, cupping her face with his big, work-worn hands. Pain and desire warred in his deep-brown eyes. "Ah, God, Libs," he moaned a second before his mouth descended on hers.

A hot, searing kiss that shot right through her. She clutched his shirt in both her fists, parting her lips and meeting his tongue, thrust for thrust, wanting to get closer to him.

So long.

It had been so long since he'd held her, kissed her. So long since she tasted the essence of him, the pure male scent of him and the smokiness from the fire mixed to fill her head with such desire. So long since she'd felt this alive.

He lifted his lips for a brief moment, took a breath and claimed them again, tilting her head in the other direction with his hands. It was as if he couldn't decide which angle gave him better access to her, his need to claim her more powerful than the distance he'd tried to put between them all these years.

Why had he hidden from this? From her?

She pulled her lips away from his. "Deke," she said through a breath, making her sound whispery.

It didn't stop him. Moving his hand, he simply traced his lips along her jawline towards her ear.

"Mmm," he murmured as his lips pulled on the lobe, his breath teasing that spot just below that he knew drove her crazy. He'd always used it to get her to bend to his desires, his needs.

Anger shot through her.

Not this time.

She released his shirt, wiggling her hands between them to land on the hard planes of his chest. With all the strength she could muster, she shoved him back. "Stop!"

He stumbled back a step, releasing her, confusion clouding his eyes. As if not believing she wanted him to really stop, he reached for her again. "What the—?"

She planted her hand in the center of his chest and locked her elbow. "No, Deacon. Not this time."

His first name in the pissed-off tone finally got through to him. He'd always had a love-hate relationship with the name. Taking a step back, he shoved his hands through his hair then to the back of his neck. A sure sign of his frustration.

"What did I do?" he asked, the word half question, half accusation.

Slowly she inhaled, then let it out before focusing on the now irritated male standing an arm's length—her arm's length—away. What she said next would either give them a step to healing this rift between them—and there was a lot to fix—or send them back to the point of ignoring each other for the rest of their lives.

"Libby?" he asked, this time a little gentler.

"You don't get to do this, Deacon." She pointed one finger of her free hand at him. "You don't get to turn your back on me when I needed you most, ignore me for ten freaking years, then suddenly kiss me like your life, my life, *our* lives depended on it."

"Lib—" He growled softly, starting forward again, but she pushed her hand hard against his chest, forcing him to stop.

"No. Not without answers. *It's the rules, Libby*, isn't going to really work for me. Until you're ready to talk, really talk about the fire, Bill's death and why you closed me out, we can't move on. No matter how wonderful it feels to be in your arms, kissing you. I deserve better than that."

He stared at her, his mouth slightly open.

Blinking again, but this time to focus her anger, she fumbled with her purse a moment and snatched up her keys. She unlocked the door and climbed in. After starting the engine, she rolled down the window to look at him. His mouth pressed in a firm line, his hands shoved in the front of his jeans, he was as stiff as an ancient oak.

"If the man I loved is still somewhere in there, you know where I live and you'll respect me enough to come talk with me. Honestly and openly. Otherwise, I'd rather live my life without you in it."

She put the car in gear, pulled out and drove away, praying all the way her ultimatum hadn't just destroyed their future.

* * * * *

Deke slammed the kitchen door behind him. Dropping his keys on the counter, he pulled a glass out of the cupboard then reached in the far back corner of the pantry for the bottle of double-blend scotch he kept hidden back there. He'd made a promise to Gage's dad that he'd get sober and he had. He'd climbed out of that bottle and had no intentions of ever going back in. But sometimes he just needed something to take the edge off.

Like tonight.

He opened the bottle, poured just two fingers' worth into the glass, deliberately put the lid back on and stored the bottle in its spot behind the jars of spaghetti sauce and cans of baked beans. Out of sight, not easy to reach for a second helping.

Carrying the glass loosely in his right hand, he strode into his living room and collapsed onto the leather couch. He took a sip of the amber liquid, letting the slow burn ease down his throat, then leaned his head back. Staring at the wood beams that ran across the width of the ceiling, all he could see was the taillights of Libby's car as she'd driven away.

He'd stood there in the dark parking lot, stunned that she'd not only stopped him in the hottest kiss he'd had since the last time he'd held her in his arms, but that she'd sounded upset. No, not upset. Pissed.

It had taken him a few minutes to close his mouth, calm his own anger and really hear what she'd said to him.

Until you're ready to talk, really talk about the fire, Bill's death and why you closed me out, we can't move on.

How could she ask that of him? Didn't she know he lived with Bill's death every day? Saw the fire in his head, Bill slipping over the edge into the fiery abyss blow? Was reminded every time he looked into the mirror, saw the scars? His own guilt eating away at him every time he heard the scratchy sound of his own damaged voice?

No. She didn't know that. She couldn't know that because he'd never told her, never told anyone. He took another slow sip of the whiskey, picturing her beautiful face looking at him with determination as she'd pushed him away.

No matter how wonderful it feels to be in your arms, kissing you. I deserve better than that.

Yes, she was right. She did deserved better than the way he'd treated her the past ten years. Hell, she deserved better than him. She deserved someone solid, unscarred, safe—like that newsman Sean Callahan.

The idea of her with anyone else hit him like a sucker-punch. He couldn't stand the thought of her with the newsman. Hell, it wasn't just Sean. He couldn't stomach the idea of Libby with any other man, no matter how good they might be.

You know where I live and you'll respect me enough to come talk with me. Honestly and openly.

Could he do that? Could he tell her the truth about how her brother died and his part in it? Would she ever forgive him once she knew?

If the man I loved is still somewhere in there.

Was he? Was that man somewhere still inside? Could he be that man again? For her?

He swallowed the last of the whiskey and set the glass on the table, the urge to pour another one coursing through him. With all his will he got up and walked to his bedroom, turning his back on the call of the alcohol. It had taken months, but he'd crawled out of that bottle. One hard step at a time. Facing the truth with Libby would be an even harder journey.

The man I loved.

Her words rang through his head just as the feel of her body against his and the taste of her on his lips thrummed through his body. It would be a long, painful journey, one he might not survive if she couldn't forgive him, but what if she could?

She was definitely worth the effort.

* * * * *

The fire had surprised him.

Not the size or scope of it. He'd been prepared for how fast it spread, especially after he doused it in kerosene. The internet was full of pictures of wild fires.

No, it was the rush of pleasure he'd gotten when the blue fire danced across the top of the field after the timer went off, then the shock of the red flames that shot up into the dark sky.

It was almost orgasmic.

And the heat. God, the heat had licked at his skin, even from his hiding spot in the creek bed.

A chortle escaped him.

Those damn Amish farmers had almost stumbled into him as they'd raced to set up their stupid water bucket brigade. Who knew they'd run so fast when the bell up at the main house started clanging in the night?

At first he'd laughed when he saw their puny efforts to haul buckets of water from the creek. Then he'd seen that odd contraption they'd hauled out. Instead of pouring the water over the quickly growing fire, they were loading that wagon and using four men to pump the water over the flames.

His ire piqued again. They'd mucked up his plan.

It hadn't stopped the fire, but they'd managed to slow it down enough for the firemen to arrive and really work on it. He'd hoped to have a bigger blaze, maybe even get that farmhouse before the trucks arrived.

The sirens ripping through the night signaled his time to fade into the distance. He'd moved deeper into the trees, watching as the men jumped out of the trucks, milling about like worker ants trying to put out the flames. Then people from the town arrived, acting like they were doing something important.

Didn't they see? Didn't they realize that for once *he* was in charge? He and his fire had them all under his control, jumping to try and contain the monster he'd let loose. Standing back in the dark cover, he'd given in to the urge and stroked his cock through his pants, enjoying the feel of his power.

As the fire slowly died, he controlled the urge to come, saving it for later when he was alone and could fully enjoy it. He walked into the night past his neighbors. Nodding to them, just one of the crowd. Climbing into his car he'd followed the long caravan back to town, then parked down the alley from the café.

For a first attempt, he'd been successful in gaining attention. Like a warning shot. He'd also hoped to get the goddess by herself, but that hadn't happened. This time. Next time he'd find a way.

Now, seeing her in the car with *him*, he ground his teeth hard. She was meant for him, not that interloper.

The groundwork for his plan was set in motion. Secrets were all so deliciously fun to uncover. The next fire would be twice as fun, knowing the trap for his adversary would be set. The internet was so easy to manipulate and find out the information he'd needed to expose those secrets. His enemy's past would come to light then.

How long would it take the fire chief to find that timer? Would it trigger memories?

He giggled with glee. Oh, what he'd give to see his face when he recognized the signature.

* * * * *

Libby locked the front door and set her purse on the coffee table. She dropped onto the old, over-stuffed couch and pulled the soft, well-worn afghan over her, curling up in fetal position. All the emotions of the evening weighed hard on her.

The shivers had hit her on the short drive from the café parking lot to her home. Which, in her mind, was better than tears. At least body-wracking shaking could be blamed on the adrenaline response of the fire. Or the emotional stress of being with Deke again, especially after he wept for—what she suspected was the first time —Bill's loss. Even that damn searing kiss and Deke's body pressed against hers caused more of the hormone to surge in her system.

Tears on the other hand meant sadness. They meant grief, pain and loss. Grief for Bill. Pain over the long rift between her and Deke. Loss, oh God, the loss they'd both suffered.

The ache started in her lower stomach and reached up to strangle her heart.

What if Deacon didn't come to her? What if he couldn't find that place deep inside him that would only heal once he was honest about why he'd closed her out? Could she stick to her resolve and turn her back on him? Her choice to bury what hopes their future might have this time?

What if he did?

Fear quickly followed the pain, pushing all other thoughts aside.

Could she be as honest with him? And would he ever forgive her for keeping her secret?

CHAPTER ELEVEN

Just after dawn the next morning, Kyle wandered onto the football field, still wondering what had possessed him to crawl out of his warm bed at such a stupid hour and haul his butt over here.

Near the fifty-yard-line bleachers the other players stood in a semi-circle. In front of them were all three of the coaches. Four dweebie-looking guys—the water boys and trainers—were off to the side. He'd probably be better off joining their quartet than trying to compete with these guys.

What the hell did he know about football? Or playing on a team for that matter?

Zilch. Zip. Nada.

And he was about to gloriously humiliate himself proving it. He already stood out. Everyone else, even the training crew, wore matching team tee-shirts in the school's maroon-and-gold colors, while all he had on was a faded, nearly-thread-bare scarlet-and-gray one.

As he neared the group, Coach Reynolds turned his

Oh great. He's going to call my name, point me out. Make me look like a fool.

Only he didn't. All he did was give him a slight nod. Anyone not paying close attention, which thankfully was all of the team, would miss the acknowledgement.

"How many of you've looked at your playbooks?" Head Coach Justice asked—Kyle still thought it funny that the sheriff's last name was Justice.

A few hands shot up, mostly the offensive players.

"Every one of you guys needs to study that playbook. Every day. You don't know my system and I don't know, nor do I care, what the last coach had you doing. Got it?"

"Yes, sir," they said in unison.

"Same thing as yesterday, we're going to start with warm-ups," the coach continued. "Then we'll divide into offense and defense. After, we're going to do a few plays with offense and defense together. Let's get to it."

As the crowd broke to get in lines, they noticed Kyle standing off to one side.

"Hey, what's he doing here? It's not food-break time," the tall receiver he'd knocked on his ass the day before said, loud enough for everyone to hear, which garnered him a bunch of laughter.

Kyle locked his jaw and pressed his lips together. He wouldn't react. He had as much right to be here as the rest of them. Hell, more. The coach had made him a special invitation.

"Probably here to put you on your ass again, Tanner," the stocky defensive guy said. The laughter this time was louder.

Kyle relaxed a little.

"Knock it off. Get in your lines or plan to run extra laps after practice," Coach Justice said, getting everyone's attention again as Coach Reynolds headed for Kyle.

"Glad you changed your mind," he said, stopping in front of him and extending a hand.

Kyle shook it, feeling a little odd shaking hands like two men respecting each other. "Not really sure why I'm here. I won't know any of the plays."

Deke barked a raspy rumble of a laugh, nodding back at the group of teens sitting on the ground, each with one knee bent behind them, the other leg extended out in front as they stretched over them to touch their toes. "Apparently, no one else has bothered to learn them yet, either."

Kyle relaxed more and lifted the corner of his mouth. "So, what now?"

"First, let's get you a team practice shirt. Then I'd like to see how fast you sprint."

"Never did that before," he said walking one step behind and an arm's length away from the coach towards the locker room.

"After our conversation last night, I didn't suspect you had. We'll measure you running the forty-yard dash a couple of times and average them. That should give us your number."

"What if it's not very fast?" He'd probably get cut from the team immediately.

Deke opened the door and stopped to look at him. "Tanner can run the forty yard dash in just under five seconds. Given he wasn't going full speed, which is part of my problem with the kid, but you took him out without too much effort. I'd say you had to run almost forty yards to do it. I think your speed will surprise you."

Inside the locker room, the coach opened a box and pulled out a shirt and shorts. He tossed them to Kyle. "Put these on."

Gripping the material in his hands, Kyle held his breath, judging the distance between him and the door. More than one foster parent had used the guise of new clean clothes to get him naked. Learning quickly how to flee before they could get their hands on him got him the reputation of *a runner*, one of the reasons he'd been in so many different homes.

Deke walked over to the desk. He pulled out a box of funny looking keys and searched through them. Finally, he tossed one at Kyle, who caught it in mid-air. Grabbing a stopwatch from the desk, he turned and headed for the door, saying over his shoulder. "When you're done, lock your belonging in that locker, then meet me out on the field."

Kyle stared in open-mouthed astonishment at the man's retreating back.

Deke's jaw clenched tight as he strode out of the locker room. He made sure he cleared the corner of the building before giving in to the rage that surged through him.

The kid had been scared shitless just now. *Of him.*

Never in his life had anyone been that frightened of him, even with his scars, and certainly not a kid. He slammed his open palm against the concrete wall. The sting took some of the heat out of his anger.

The fear started out on the field when they'd walked away from the others. Alone. The way Kyle kept his distance. Just far enough that he'd see any threatening move made his way. Deke suspected Kyle had learned that lesson one too many times before. Inside the locker room the tension in the kid was almost visible, his eyes darting from him to the door and back, especially after he'd told him to get changed.

Bile rose in his throat and he leaned against the wall as he suddenly understood what Kyle had thought he'd planned. No kid went immediately to something so vile without previous experience.

Someone, somewhere had taken advantage of that kid. Physically. Quite possibly sexually.

The idea that someone in charge of a kid could do something that frightened him from simple acts of kindness appalled him.

Why hadn't someone done anything about it? Is that why he was moved to Colbert House? Did Libby know? Was that what was in the file she'd been looking at last night?

Libby.

He needed more information about Kyle and Libby was the only one who could help him. Closing his eyes, he rubbed the back of his neck. What the hell was he going to do about her? Hell, what was he going to even say to her after what happened between them last night? She was right, though. She did deserve the truth, no matter how much it killed him to tell her what happened in that fire.

Then there was last night's fire. Another problem on his plate. At least he'd get some kind of answer today when he met with Mike Feeney, the arson investigator from over in Columbus. He'd called Mike last night and they'd agreed to meet out at the fire scene after the morning's football practice.

He shook his head as he walked back to the football field. Mike had gotten a good laugh over him and Gage coaching football, especially when he learned Cleetus was one of their assistants. He'd let him have his laugh before telling him why he'd wanted him to come look at a field fire. Something he hadn't mentioned to anyone else. The smell of fuel had permeated the ground. Not crisp like gasoline, but something.

At the edge of the field, he stopped and watched the kids run through their drills. So many problems already on his plate and now he was worrying about Kyle.

Hell, his life had just gotten complicated.

Well, one problem at a time. First the team drills and whipping these guys into some sort of shape. Then he'd get more information about the fire. Which could be his imagination going wild or turn into a bigger problem. Finally, he'd go talk to Libby in her office about Kyle's past. He needed to know more about this kid. At least that way he could see her without getting personal, again.

Coward.

Not really. He'd give in to her ultimatum, just not yet.

* * * * *

The small courtroom was packed again that morning as Libby sat next to Melissa, holding her cold hand. What was it like to be so afraid of someone you thought you loved? She willed some of her strength into her friend. Everyone in town seemed to want to hear the verdict and sentencing for Frank Compton. Once again, the seats behind the defendant's table were filled with family and business associates, while the prosecution's side held Melissa, Libby and members of the community.

Libby glanced around, half-hoping to see Deke in the room somewhere, then cursed herself for being a fool. She'd told him to leave her alone until he could talk honestly with her about Bill's death and the reasons he had kept her at arm's length. How could she then expect him to follow her around like some lovesick fool?

Besides, this hearing wasn't about her. It was about Melissa's future, heck, even her life.

She squeezed her friend's hand. Melissa looked at her with huge, frightened blue eyes and Libby gave her an encouraging smile.

"Madam Foreman," Judge Rawlins addressed the young brunette woman who had been elected foreman of the jury, "will you please read the verdict?"

"On the charge of felony domestic violence in the first degree, we, the jury find the defendant, Francis Compton guilty," she said in a clear, confident voice.

"Oh, God," Melissa's whisper was almost lost in the shouts and gasps from the other spectators in the court.

"On the charge of felony kidnapping, we find the defendant guilty," the jury foreman continued with more gasping scattered around the room.

"And on the final count?" Judge Rawlins asked.

"On the charge of felony assault, we find the defendant guilty."

"You did it, Melissa." Libby whispered and squeezed her hand tight, as her friend sagged against her.

It took three loud bangs of the judge's gavel, followed by his commanding, "Order," before the room once again was quiet.

"Thank you, Madam Foreman and members of the jury," the white-haired judge said with a formal nod, then turned to look at the papers on his desk.

The rustle of the papers and a few low murmurs were the only sounds in the nearly silent room. Libby gripped Melissa's hand tighter to help calm the small nervous tremors that shook her body.

Finally, Judge Rawlins looked over the room full of people, his focus coming to rest on Frank. "The defendant will rise."

No please, no hint of a request. It was an order. Cold and commanding. He wanted to be sure this excuse for a man know he was no longer in charge.

Frank rose, his hands folded in front of him, like a petulant child called before the principal.

"Francis Compton, you've been found guilty of domestic violence in the first degree. This is your third such offense. The maximum sentence for this is eighteen months in jail and a fine of five thousand dollars. You've also been found guilty of felony kidnapping, for which you will be serving the maximum sentence of eleven years. And finally, for the charge of felony assault, you will serve another eight years, for a total of twenty and a half years to be served consecutively."

A wail rose from behind the defendant's table. His mother collapsed in the arms of Frank's oldest brother. The defense lawyer reached behind Frank to grasp his elbow and keep him standing as his knees wobbled.

The judge slammed his gavel again, calling for order and waiting for the room to settle once more.

"You will be remanded into custody and wait transfer to the Lucasville State Penitentiary."

"Thank God," Melissa whispered beside Libby.

She slid her arm around her relieved friend, hugging her close. They remained that way until Frank had been taken from the court in handcuffs. Even after Frank's family had left, casting disparaging glares her way. Finally, Kent Howard, the DA, turned in his chair and took Melissa's hands in his.

"It's over, Melissa," he said in a kind voice. "He'll be in jail for years. You'll be safe."

"I don't know how to thank you," she said with tears in her eyes.

"There's an old saying. The best revenge is to live a long and happy life." He squeezed her hand and smiled. "You do that and it will be thanks enough."

He's going to make a great governor someday. The idea wasn't a surprise at all to Libby.

Kent released Melissa's hands and stood. "Now if I know Lorna, she's probably expecting you two over there for a celebratory lunch. And I have an appointment back at my office."

Standing, Melissa grabbed his hand one more time. "Thank you so much."

"Believe me, it was my pleasure." Kent squeezed her hand one more time, then picked up his briefcase and looked at Libby. "Elizabeth, I'm sure I'll be seeing you around."

He escorted them out of the courtroom and left.

Libby watched him stride up the hall. A man on a mission. And he was right, she was sure she'd see him again. At the women's shelter there were more women in the same situation as Melissa. Each case would end up in court either to protect the woman or prosecute her murderer. Thankfully, that wasn't the case for Melissa.

"I can't believe it's over," Melissa said quietly beside her.

Libby grasped her hands in hers. They were still so cold. "Believe it. He's going to go to the penitentiary and stay there for years to come."

"What will I do now?"

"First, we're going to go to the Peaches 'N Cream and have lunch. Kent was right, you know. Lorna will be wanting to celebrate and spoil you rotten." She released her friend's hands and put an arm around her, turning her towards the exit. "If we're lucky, she'll have made some chocolate cake with buttercream icing and we'll get to score a slice."

Melissa laughed. A solid, happy laugh. Something Libby hadn't heard out of her friend in years. It lightened her own troubled heart.

Sometimes things worked out just as they should.

CHAPTER TWELVE

The charred field looked even worse in the daylight as Deke pulled his truck up beside it. Jacob Zimmer and several of the church elders, including Thomas Elder, stood on the edge of the field watching a man in jeans and pale-blue sports shirt slowly walk the perimeter. Mike Feeney, the state arson investigator, was a meticulous man. A detective with the Columbus police for years, he always worked a fire like it was a crime scene, until he determined arson was not the cause.

Deke climbed out of his truck and went to talk to the famers first.

"Gentlemen," he said, shaking hands with each of them, ending with the land owner. "I'm sorry this happened to you, Jacob."

"Ja. It is ugly, but thanks to you and God, at least my home and family were spared," the young farmer said.

"What is Mister Feeney looking for out there, Chief Reynolds?" one of the elders asked.

"Since we haven't had any storms lately, and since

Jacob was diligent about clearing his fields once the hay was dry," Deke said, measuring his words carefully, "I've asked Mike to come out and be sure there was nothing intentional done to cause the fire."

The group considered this, exchanging worried looks between them.

Finally Thomas spoke, saying what they'd all been thinking. "You believe that someone set this fire on purpose?"

It was more a statement than question.

Deke looked him straight in the eyes. "I don't know, Thomas. The way it burned, the fact that the chance of a natural cause is small, I have my suspicions. For everyone's safety, I have to check it out."

"Do you think it is the young town men who did this?" another elder asked.

Deke gave them a half shrug as he shook his head. "I hope not. But right now, if it was intentional, I have no suspects in mind." He looked out to the field. Mike waved at him to come forward. "If you'll excuse me, I'll go find out what Mike has to say. Then I'll be able to tell you more."

He strode off across the charred field in a direct line to his friend, leaving the small worried group behind. Like he told them, he had no clue who might've done this and he sincerely hoped the area teens weren't engaging in harassing the Amish, especially in such a dangerous way.

"Mike," he said, coming to a stop beside him and

extending his hand.

"Deke." Mike shook his hand. "Hate to tell you this, but your gut instinct was right. You've got a firebug."

"Fuck." He rubbed the back of his neck, trying to relieve the sudden tension there. "You're sure?"

"You were right about the accelerant. Diesel or kerosene, if I had to make a guess. I've taken samples to see if we can determine which for sure."

"Shit. I'd hoped it was just some kids smoking out here who forgot to be sure they'd smothered their butts."

Mike shook his head. "No. And what's more, this guy planned this out."

The tension in Deke's neck tightened and his heart lurched. "How?"

"Found the makings of a timer," Mike said, holding up a plastic bag. "I'm betting the farmers wouldn't have electronic devices of any kind."

Deke took it, studying the small bits of electrical components inside. "Good bet. Anything else?"

Mike handed him a smaller bag. "Our guy's a smoker. Found these over there," he pointed towards the trees, several feet from the field and down near the creek bed.

"The bastard was watching." Deke gave the evidence bags back to his friend and the pair walked over to the trees.

"They usually do. Probably getting off on it, too." Mike stopped and crouched down, pointing to an area of footprints. "This is where he was standing. Found several cigarette butts scattered around. I'll send them for DNA testing, but that can take a while to get results."

"And only if we're lucky enough that he's in the databases somewhere." Deke stepped back and studied the area. "Lots of footprints and damage to the foliage about three feet to the left."

Mike stood, shaking his head. "Yeah, I saw that. Figure he was still hidden here when the farmers started their bucket brigade."

Deke clenched his hands into fists and worked the muscles of his jaw in silent rage, knowing someone that rotten would get his kicks out of watching people risk their lives. "Damn. They were so focused on stopping the fire from spreading, I doubt anyone saw anyone, but I'll ask anyway. Did he stay this close the whole time?"

"No. I think at some point he got nervous and moved farther back. I'd need a tracker to know for sure. Tim Carter of the state dog rescue society lives pretty close. Want me to have him come see what he can find?"

"Yeah, I guess we better cover all our bases. We'll have to bring Gage and his people in on it."

"Okay. I'll give Tim a call, and I'll get some castings of these footprints, then meet you over at the sheriff's office this evening."

"Make it after dinner. Gage and I have practice again today," he said, lifting a brow at Mike's chuckle. "Don't suppose you'd like to take on the special team players for us?"

"No way in hell. I have three teenage daughters. That's enough punishment for anyone."

They started over to the farmers. "You think this could be a hate crime?"

Mike shook his head. "Too early to tell."

"Meaning?" Deke asked, even though he knew what his friend was going to say.

"Meaning we won't have too much information until the guy does it again."

Deke stopped him a few feet from the farmers. "Mike, you didn't find any...?" He lifted his eyebrows suggestively.

Mike shook his head. "No, no body fluids. If the guy got off on this, he did it somewhere else."

"Good."

For some reason, the idea of the guy masturbating on the farmer's land after setting fire to it triggered Deke's personal ick factor.

Mike left him to go store the evidence and make his call to the tracker. Deke headed over to the group of farmers, delivering the news that it was, indeed, an intentional fire.

"Until we've processed all the evidence we found, I can't tell you if the fire was a hate crime or not, gentlemen," he finished.

"It must be," Esau Yoder, the youngest of the elders said. "Why else target Jacob's farm? He has no enemies."

The others nodded and voiced their agreement.

"Gentlemen." Deke held up one hand to get their attention. "First, there is no evidence of this being directed particularly at Jacob. His farm is on the remote edge of both the Amish community and the town itself. The person responsible for this could've chosen the area simply for that reason. Also, while I know there have been terrible crimes committed on members of your faith in other communities, we've never had any such activity here in or around Westen. I've always believed our two communities have gotten along quite well."

This got him some nodding and cooler heads.

"Mike and I are going to meet with Sheriff Justice this evening and go over everything we've learned. I'll ask him to add some extra patrols out this way for the deputies, if that would be okay with you."

Again, he got lots of positive responses.

"Is there anything we can do, Deacon?" Thomas asked in his thick Dutch-English accent.

Deke thought about it a moment before answering. "Keep your eyes open for strangers in the area. Cars stopping for a long period down the side roads. Especially after dark. If you notice a pattern, let me or Sheriff Justice know. Do not approach this person. Although most fire starters are cowardly, I don't know what he'd do if threatened."

"We will begin our watch today," Thomas said.

Deke shook hands around and headed to his truck.

Not much more he could do until Mike had some more information for them. He'd head home, grab a shower and put on some clean clothes, since he'd worn his workout clothes from practice right out to the fire scene. Once he was cleaned up he'd tackle the problem of Kyle. A half smile turned up one side of his mouth.

Nothing like ambushing Libby in her office.

* * * * *

Cleetus walked past the Dye Right Salon for the third time that hour. He'd volunteered to foot patrol the downtown business area today in the hopes of getting a chance to talk to Miss Sylvie again. Last night he'd enjoyed their conversation over pie until the moment he'd had to run out to the fire.

Gosh, he hoped he hadn't scared her.

"Deputy?"

He froze, his face heating at how nice her voice sounded. Swallowing, he turned and smiled. "Miss Sylvie. Nice day, isn't it?"

She grinned at him, her pixie eyes twinkling and dimples appearing on both her cheeks. "Must be, if you're spending it outside patrolling the salon's sidewalk."

His face grew hotter at her teasing, but he wasn't going to go all tongue-tied this time. "I confess I was hoping to catch you going to lunch. I wanted to apologize for leaving you at the café last night."

"Oh dear, no. You were doing your duty. There's no need to apologize for that," she said laying her hand on his forearm.

He liked the way her hand felt on his skin.

"Then would you like to join me for lunch?"

She dropped her hand, but gave him another dimple-filled smile. "I think I'd like that very much."

"Did I leave enough money for the bill last night?" he asked as they strolled down the sidewalk and around the corner onto Main Street where the café sat.

"Yes, and I told Rachel to keep the change as her tip," Sylvie said.

"Good. I was worried about it."

He'd slowed down so she wouldn't have to walk too fast. She wore those big high heels and her legs being shorter than his and all. *How did women walk in those tall heels?*

"Was the fire a bad one?" she asked after a few more steps.

"Well, it was pretty big, but no one got hurt. I mean, some guys got a burn or two, and of course some of the farmers had to have oxygen since they were fighting it before we got there. But for the most part, I guess it wasn't too bad." He said, then stopped and held open the café door for her.

They headed towards a booth on the side of the room.

"Hey, Cleetus," Wes Strong called as they passed his table

Cleetus stopped to speak to the other deputies. "Miss Sylvie, I'd like you to meet my friends, Wes Strong and Daniel Löwe. Wes, Daniel, this is Miss Sylvie Gillis."

"Pleasure to meet you," Sylvie said, blushing as she shook hands with both men.

Cleetus didn't like watching her get all flustered by his friends.

"You want to join us?" Wes asked.

Sylvie looked up at him, with her eyes wide in question.

The last thing he wanted to do was share the little lady's attention with his friends. Cleetus shook his head. "No, thanks, guys. Miss Sylvie's on her break and I'm sure you guys have to get back to work."

Wes and Daniel exchanged a look and Cleetus was sure they were going to make some wise-ass comment. What would he say then? He didn't want Miss Sylvie to think he was rude to his friends. Or worse that he was ashamed of being seen with her. He wasn't. He was damn proud she'd agreed to have lunch with him.

"You're right," Daniel said, pointing to their nearly empty plates. "We're just about done anyways."

"Maybe next time," Wes said.

Cleetus took Sylvie's elbow and steered her past another table or two.

"Hey, Libby, Melissa," Sylvie said, stopping by the social worker's table, where she sat with Mrs. Compton. "How did it go today?"

"They found him guilty," Melissa said quietly.

"Oh, that's good, isn't it?" Sylvie asked, looking from one woman to the other.

Libby smiled. "Yes. It is a very good thing. Frank won't be able to hurt Melissa any more. In fact, we're celebrating with Lorna's chocolate buttercream cake." She lifted a forkful to show them. "It's on the house, so be sure to ask for a slice."

"Oh, we will." Miss Sylvie said, reaching out to squeeze Mrs. Compton's arm. "And I'm glad things worked out for you."

"Thank you. I am, too. Even if it will take a while to get used to."

Cleetus tipped his cap at both women then they finally got seated in their booth.

Glenna, one of the waitresses, joined them almost immediately, gave them a friendly greeting, and took their orders for the Wednesday specials of fried chicken, au gratin potatoes and cooked greens.

"You sure you didn't want to check out the other lunch items?" Cleetus asked after the waitress had left. "I love the specials, but you could've had anything else you wanted."

"Don't be silly. I adore Miss Lorna's fried chicken plates, especially the greens." Sylvie gave him one of those dimple smiles again and his heart turned over hard in his chest.

"They say greens are good for you. Make ya regular."

She blinked and opened her eyes wide at him.

His face grew warm.

Crap. Why'd he say that? You don't talk about body functions with ladies.

"I mean…um…" He didn't quite know what to say.

"Do you have to go to fires often?" she asked, turning the conversation around.

Thank goodness.

"It's part of the job of being a deputy. We're required to take the volunteer courses and train right alongside the other volunteers. 'Course, we don't have as much training as Deke and his career firefighters, but in a small county like ours, we have to take on extra duties to help keep people safe."

Thankfully, Glenna came back with their drinks. He took a long drink of his usual sweet tea, wondering what it was about Sylvie that had him either stumbling over his words or making long speeches like that one.

"Well, I think it's very heroic of you to do both jobs, but my, they're both dangerous."

She thought he was heroic. He sat up straighter, his chest puffed out a little bit.

"Most of the time is like today, walking around just checking on people and things. Not always as exciting as fighting a field full of fire."

"Have you ever been injured?" she asked.

Before he could answer the waitress returned with their food. "If you need anything else, just give me a holler. Enjoy."

The aroma of the food had his mouth watering and

he took several bites before he realized Sylvie was watching him, waiting on his answer to her question. He swallowed his food, then wiped his mouth with his napkin, just like his mama had taught him years ago.

"Up until last spring, I'd never gotten so much as a sprained ankle."

"What happened last spring?" Her violet-blue eyes had gotten big as saucers, and her thin little eyebrows had crinkled towards her nose with worry.

"I got shot in the leg."

"Oh, no." Her fork clattered on the china plate and customers nearby stopped their chatter to stare at them. She leaned in closer to whisper. "How did that happen?"

"We had this crazy man who ran the paper. Thought he should own the whole town. Nearly blew it up when his meth lab partner had booby-trapped their hiding space. Gage nearly died in the explosion. Daniel got koshed on the head with the man's gun and I chased after him, that's when he shot at me." He took another bite of his food and ate before adding. "Like I said, though, stuff like that doesn't happen around here much."

* * * * *

Deke took a deep breath outside Libby's office in the county courthouse building. Westen had decided to combine the courthouse with all county offices to efficiently use the taxpayers' money when they built the facilities nearly fifty years ago. It had proven to be quite forward thinking, since many times the people serving in the county positions had to make an appearance in court for one thing or another. Especially Libby, who testified in domestic cases.

Opening the door was like walking into a hothouse. Lush green plants sat on every surface, even the desk situated near the window, but facing the outer door.

"Hey, Chief Reynolds!" Ashley, Libby's secretary, looked up from her computer and greeted him from the center of all the greenery. "Whatcha doin' here?"

"I was hoping to talk with Elizabeth if she's not too busy."

Damn. He should've called ahead. What if she was out on a visitation? Or testifying in court again in the Compton trial?

No, wait. He'd heard that SOB Frank Compton had gotten a virtual life sentence earlier in the day.

Ashley flashed him a big smile. "If you'll have a seat, she's in a meeting, but I imagine it's just about through."

He started for one of the plastic chairs that looked like it was invented in a nineteen-sixties' torture factory when the inner door to Libby's office opened.

"Thanks for your time, Libby," the self-assured district attorney, Kent Howard, said, turning back to look over his shoulder. "I've had word that the defendant has skipped bail and the state. Hopefully, he'll stay gone."

Libby followed him into the outer office. The pair stopped when they saw Deke standing there. A desire to demand an explanation why they were alone in her office hit Deke. He mentally shook it off. This was her business and he had no right to demand anything from her, let alone explanations. Still, it didn't sit right seeing her with the lawyer.

"Chief Reynolds," Kent said, extending his hand. "Heard you're helping the sheriff with the football team this year. How are things coming along?"

Of course he had. The man's son was the star quarterback.

He shook the other man's hand. "Sort of got roped into it, but the team seems to be finding its mark."

"Good. Think we'll take the state title this year?" the man said with a slight narrowing of his eyes.

In other words, do you think my son will get a scholarship and offers from major universities this year?

"You never know. We're planning to give it our all."
In other words, I'm not making you any promises.

"Good. I'll be looking for the first game."
My son better be the starting quarterback again this year.

"Looking forward to it."
He will if he earns it.

They stared at each other a moment longer than necessary, then the other man, realizing Deke wasn't the least bit intimidated, broke eye contact, turning back to Libby. "You'll have your deposition next week, then?"

She nodded, glancing at Ashley a moment. "We'll get with your office to set that up."

"Yes, ma'am," Ashley said, quickly focusing on her computer.

"Good. I'll see you then."

And with that, the room seemed cooler. Probably because all the hot air had left with the district attorney. Deke glanced at Libby's face, her lips pressed together in a thin line and her arms crossed beneath her breasts. Maybe the temperature drop had something to do with the pissed-off woman and not the loss of the other man.

"Did you need something, Chief Reynolds?" she asked.

Ouch. Cool and uber-professional. Not a good sign.

"I wanted to talk with you," he said, glancing at Ashley, who seemed to be paying acute attention to the two of them, despite her fingers flying over the keyboard. "It's about one of your clients."

"Oh. Okay." She blinked, her face softening in confusion. Obviously she'd thought he'd come to continue their conversation from last night.

He meant to do just that, but later, in a more private venue.

"Can we go in your office?" he asked when she hadn't made a move.

"Of course." She opened the door, then looked at her

secretary. "Ashley, hold any calls for a while, okay?"

"Sure thing, boss."

Libby rolled her eyes and shook her head at the casual comment as she walked into her office. He followed her inside. It wasn't your typical county office. Unlike the outer office that held hard, plastic, uncomfortable-looking chairs, there was an overstuffed loveseat near the window. Bookshelves lined one wall, and the filing cabinet had several small, very-healthy-looking plants—obviously Ashley's green thumb had trickled into Libby's space. On the walls hung pictures of children, some with Libby in them. *Probably some of her happier clients.* The office chair behind the desk was leather and plush. The large desk had a neat stack of files, a computer and a jar of colorful hard-shelled candies. He took one of the two large, cotton-covered wingback chairs that faced her desk.

"I suppose this is about Kyle again," she said, already thumbing through her files and pulling out the thinnest one. "I told you last night that everything in here, what there is, is confidential. I'm really not at liberty to discuss it with you."

He sat back and lifted one leg to rest his ankle on his knee. "After an incident that happened during this morning's practice, I thought I might have some information for you to add to your file, or what's in there could confirm my suspicions."

"Really?" She tilted her head like she always did when something had her curiosity. "What happened?"

He relayed the incident in the locker room to her. "Which made me think somewhere along the line the kid's been abused..." Uncomfortable with the subject, he paused to swallow. "Um, possibly sexually."

Her shoulders had gone rigid and her mouth pinched. She was as angry as he'd been when he first comprehended what the exchange between him and the teen had meant. She opened the file and studied it a moment.

"Quite honestly, there's not a whole lot of background on Kyle in this file. What the state sent to me and to Colbert House was sketchy, his records sealed."

"Like a juvenile delinquent? I thought that would only happen with a kid who had committed some heinous act as a kid."

"That's the most common reason to seal someone's records. Sometimes, it's to protect them from unfair prejudice."

He thought about it a moment. "Could it be done to protect them from an abusive parent finding them?"

She nodded. "It could, but not in this case."

It was his turn to be surprised. "Why not?"

She exhaled slowly. "I can't tell you details, but it will be common knowledge as soon as the first day of school anyway. Kyle is an orphan, a ward of the state. Has been since he was seven."

Slightly stunned, Deke leaned back in the chair, idly rubbing his jaw. "Poor kid. There was no family to step up and take him?"

"Apparently not."

"I don't suppose you can tell me how his parents died?"

"That's one of the odd parts of his case."

"What is? How his parents died?"

"Not exactly." She hesitated as if deliberating on how much she could share with him. "The cause of his parents' deaths is part of what's sealed."

And didn't that open up a whole can of what-ifs?

"I can't believe Kyle had anything to do with it." He'd like to think he could read people, especially the kids on his team. And between the conversations he'd had with Kyle before today and the frank fear he'd seen in the kid this morning, he was even more positive he wasn't behind what had happened to his folks.

"I can't, either." She tapped a finger on the file.

He'd seen her do this many times over the years when she was weighing a decision. This time she seemed to be thinking about how much she could tell him. One thing he'd always loved about Libby, she'd follow the rules as long as they made sense to her.

Waiting patiently to give her time to come to her decision he studied the woman she'd become over the past ten years. Her hair was the same pale shade of blonde, but around her eyes there was one or two fine lines near the corners. She'd lost weight. Nothing shocking to indicate an illness or depression to the average observer, but to someone who'd know her body as intimately as he had, the small signs were visible. Her fingers, while always long, had a more delicate look. The line of her jaw a bit more sculpted. The hollow of her neck slightly more pronounced—just enough to allow him to watch the bouncing of her pulse just to the left.

Memories of kissing down that long column of her creamy neck to that exact spot hit him hard. She'd always arched her neck, pressing her breasts up into his chest, moaning softly as he suckled on her skin and traced her pulse with his tongue. Usually he'd be buried deep inside her at the time.

"If you believe Kyle has a history of being sexually assaulted it would explain one thing," she said, her voice drawing him out of his erotic memory.

Clearing his throat, he adjusted his seat against the sudden tightness of his jeans. "I'm no expert, but I can't figure out any better explanation for the kid's sudden fight-or-flight response to my actions, which I can assure you were in no way threatening."

"Oh, I believe you, Deacon," she said with a hint of her smile. "You would never take advantage of someone under your protection like one of the boys on your football team. No, what I meant was, it sheds light on one of the mysteries about Kyle."

"Mystery?"

"Yes, the reason given for him being moved around so much. While the details of his past have been sealed, the chronology of his life since coming into the system is rather lengthy." She took a sheet of paper from Kyle's file and handed it to him. "As you can see, since being placed in the state's custody, he's traveled around quite extensively, never staying in any one home more than a year. Some no more than a few months."

She was right. According to the paper she'd given him, in the nine years since Kyle had been a ward of the state, he'd been in no less than twelve homes, including his new lodgings at Colbert House.

"Why would the state move him around so much?" he asked, handing her back the paper. "It makes no sense. Do they give any reason for placing him in so many foster homes? Is he a troublemaker?"

She lifted another page of the file. "All that is stated here is that he has a tendency to run away from every place they tried to house him."

"Why didn't they do anything about the people abusing him?" Anger for the young child placed in such peril ate at him.

"The state takes complaints of abuse and neglect in the foster homes very seriously. It's one of the things I have to look for every time I visit one of my kids." With a sigh, she closed the file. "If he was molested at a young age, he might've been too frightened to say anything."

He nodded. "Afraid that the punishment might be worse."

"Exactly. He might've even been threatened with worse if he told anyone. His natural instinct to protect himself would be to flee any situation that felt menacing. And thus the pattern of running to save himself is reinforced each time."

"He certainly had that look on his face this morning when I told him to change clothes, his eyes measuring the distance between me and the door." His stomach churned once more with anger that a young man should feel that threatened by a simple act of kindness. An idea hit him. "Do you suppose he could've been assaulted by one of his parents? Could that be why his past and all mention of his parents' deaths have been sealed?"

She shrugged, frustration apparent in her eyes. "I have no idea and I'm bound by my job and the courts not to try and have them opened."

"Where was his first foster home?"

She looked in the file once more. "Near Massillon. Why?"

"You're under obligation to pursue no further investigation, but I'm not."

"How will you get around the court order to keep his past hidden?" she asked, resting her elbows on the table and leaning forward, her eyes alight with such curiosity she reminded him of the young woman he'd once called his.

"There are lots of sources open to someone doing a discreet inquiry these days. The internet, for one. Plus, I still have a few contacts in the area who might be able to look up some records for us." Massillon was a moderate-sized city almost an hour and a half due north of Westen, which butted up next to Canton, where one of his old station mates ran his own fire division.

"Yes, other firefighters." The light in her eyes dimmed as the specter of Bill entered the room between them once more.

"Libby," he said softly, laying his hand over hers where it lay on Kyle's file. Their eyes met, hers bright with unshed tears, and he felt the urge to take her in his arms once more. "About Bill—"

"Don't," she said, cutting him off before he could start. Slowly, she slipped her hand out from beneath his. "This isn't the time or place for that discussion. If you really want to talk, then come by the house tonight."

"I have a meeting with Gage and the State arson investigator after football practice. I don't know how late it will run."

"If it's important to you, then you'll come by." She stood and walked to the door.

He had no choice but to follow her, but he held her hand on the knob, staring into her beautiful blue eyes. "I'll be there," he said, before claiming her lips in a hot, fast kiss, sliding his tongue into her startled lips to taste her once more, her lemony scent filling his senses. As abruptly as he'd started it, he pulled away.

Opening the door, he stalked out, almost smiling at how breathless he'd left her.

CHAPTER THIRTEEN

"So what's your take on this fire?" Gage leaned back in his office chair, looking at the others gathered around to listen to what Mike Feeney and Deke had to say. All his deputies had been called into the sheriff's office for this meeting and Bobby sat perched on the corner of his desk, her favorite place these days. Normally that would bring a bit of a smile to his face. Not tonight. The last time Mike had come to town, they'd thought they had a possible firebug on the loose, only to find out it was a crazy psycho determined to own the town or destroy it.

"Definitely arson," Mike said sipping on his coffee-to-go cup from the Peaches 'N Cream Café. "Like I told Deke at the site today, an accelerant was used, along with a delay timer."

"What kind of accelerant?" Wes Strong, one of his deputies, asked. One of the things Gage had learned to count on since taking over as sheriff was Wes cataloguing and focusing on details. He didn't know a lot about the guy's background, other than he'd been in Army Special Forces for a number of years before coming to Westen. A fact his dad had whispered to him on his deathbed.

Mike took another long drink of the coffee. "Definitely kerosene. Some firebugs like to use it because they say they like to watch the way the flames dance across the scene before bursting into higher flames."

"That sounds rather perverted," Bobby said.

Gage reached over and squeezed her hand. A former teacher and now a licensed detective, Bobby was still learning the intricacies of police work, part of which was that there were a lot of sick people in the world.

"You don't know the half of it, ma'am," Mike said. "Some of these guys really get off just talking about the fire. I won't tell you what they do while watching them."

"Please don't. I don't even want the mental image." Bobby made a face and gave a shudder, which sent a low rumble of male chuckles and groans through the room.

Gage relaxed a little and gave his fiancé a half smile. She winked in response. Despite the seriousness, it was good to have some of the tension relieved in the room. Bobby was good at that. It was one of the things he loved about her.

"You said there was a timer?" Wes asked. The guy was like a bloodhound with his nose to the trail.

Mike handed him the plastic bag full of burnt electronic bits. "Found this at the edge of the field. Probably the only reason there was anything left of it. Which tells me two things."

"What?" Deke asked.

"That he's not a professional at this."

"Using kerosene and a fancy timer suggests pro to me," Daniel Löwe, another deputy asked, taking the bag of parts from Wes and looking at them.

"A pro would've put the timer in the center of the field where the fire would've obliterated any evidence or it," Mike said, then drained the last of his coffee.

"What's the second thing it tells you?" Deke asked.

"Given that he started the fire from the edge of the burn, but very close to the trees and creek bed, I think he was afraid he might get trapped. He wanted to be sure he had an escape, especially into the water source." Mike pointed to the plaster casting of footprints on Gage's desk. "That's from where he stood and watched the fire and the Amish farmers trying to fight it. Put all that together and I'd say he's a novice."

"You think this was his first fire?" Cleetus asked from his desk in the center of the room.

Mike nodded. "If it's not his first, I'd say it was no more than his second."

"If it was his first fire, how did he learn about timers?" Bobby asked, now holding the bag. "Isn't this a little on the sophisticated side?"

"Yeah," Daniel asked. "Why not just light a match?"

"A match would put him too close to the flash point," Deke said.

Mike nodded. "Right. A timer lets him move back out of the way. Less likely to get injured."

"So how'd he learn about timers?" Cleetus asked.

"More than likely reading on the internet."

Mike's comment sent another low rumble through the room, this time one of disgust at the availability of dangerous information at the fingertips of any psycho that wanted to experiment.

"So, this would be his signature?" Bobby asked, watching Mike for confirmation.

"I can't answer that. If this is his first fire, he may be experimenting. Trying to figure out what gives him the biggest rush. Learning how the fire reacts. He may not have liked the results or might tweak his timer and placement next time."

"You think there will be a next time?" Gage already knew the answer from the knot in his gut.

"We didn't catch him. He'll do it again." Deke said, his face almost as still as solid stone.

Angry enough to kill. Gage had only seen him look like this once in his life—the one time he visited him in the burn unit. He'd asked him to send Mike to see him. He was going to hunt down the SOB who'd set the warehouse fire and killed Bill.

Mike exchanged a look with Deke. "Right. These guys are like drug addicts. They'll always try to repeat the rush they got from their first fire. Often escalating their efforts. If I were you, I'd be planning on getting another call. Then we'll have more evidence to start seeing a real signature."

Gage ran his hand over his short-cropped hair and let out a long breath. "Any idea what time frame we'll have before he gets the urge to burn something else?"

Mike shook his head. "Not after one fire. It's going to depend on his own psyche and the depth of his need to experience the rush of the burn again. Anywhere from a day to a week or two would be my guess."

"Any idea what set him off?" Deke asked.

Again, Mike shook his head. "Who knows? It could be a hate against the Amish since it was started on one of their farms. It could be something else. Again, the second fire will tell us more. I know that's not what you want to hear, but until I know more and have more evidence, there's no other answer."

"So, what? We just sit around and wait for him to do it again?" Bobby asked.

Gage shook his head. "We'll do what we can. Increase our patrols, try to track down the purchases of cell phones and kerosene in the area. Do some background checks on any new residents."

"Kerosene sales aren't really going to help," Cleetus said. "Most folks around here use it for backup generators, farm equipment, oil lamps for when the power goes out in ice storms."

"Any idea what kind of a timer he used?" Wes asked, pulling them back to the evidence.

"The lab will analyze it to be sure, but I'm guessing a cell phone. Easy to tie into the ignition fuse and a simple phone call from the safety spot would set it off."

"Anyone use this kind of timer before?" Gage asked.

"There was one guy about a decade ago who used kerosene and cell phones in his fires. Made a name for himself as an arsonist for hire across the northern third of the state for people looking to commit insurance fraud with their businesses." Mike glanced at Deke then looked back at Gage. "Can't be him though."

"How can you be sure?" Bobby asked. "He could've gone dormant or been doing business in another state, couldn't he?"

"That's not possible," Deke said.

"Why?" Gage didn't like the sudden sense of dread creeping up his spine as he stared at his oldest friend.

Deke raised his cold, hard eyes to him. "Because I killed him nine years ago."

* * * * *

Kyle stepped out into the alley carrying two bags of garbage from the café, heading for the dumpster. Of all the jobs at the café, this was the one he hated the most. Not so much because he hated trash. Nope, it was the fact that he had to haul this stuff out down an alley, in the dark, behind the small picnic area where the staff ate their meals.

Thirty long strides halfway down the alley to the

dumpster and he had the lid open. It was a habit, counting strides to places, knowing how fast he had to move to be out in the open. Always, his eyes darted from side to side, looking for movement—any danger coming at him. One counselor thought it was from being moved from place to place. He knew the truth. From the day he learned how hard his dad's fist felt connecting with his cheek and how much his arm hurt after the old man twisted it, he'd learn to be aware of his surroundings.

The dark was the hard part. Monsters liked to hide in the shadows.

He tossed the sacks in the dumpster, letting the lid slam to break up some of the quiet of the night.

Thirty more strides and he'd be back inside the safety of the café. Back to listening to old bee-bop music with Rachel. He smiled as he started back inside. When he'd walked inside today wearing the café's logo T-shirt, she'd grinned and made a big deal of showing her mom how good they looked. Next thing he knew everyone else, including Pete had one on. It was like they were all part of a team.

Movement up ahead caught his attention.

He froze.

Two tall forms blocked the path between him and the back door of the café.

He looked behind him.

Yep. There were the other two, blocking the exit of the alley behind him. Shorter and more squat than the ones up ahead. His football teammates.

Trapped.

"Well, look what we have here," the quarterback and leader, Brett Howard, said in front of him. "The showoff taking out people's garbage."

"Sort of fitting," Tanner sneered as the pair took a few steps forward. "Garbage taking out garbage."

Kyle flexed his fingers, then drew them into fists, taking one slight step to widen his stance, ready to fight since his first choice of taking off at a dead run was no longer an option.

"Seems the new kid needs to learn his place," one of the guys behind him said.

Kyle didn't recognize his voice, so he assumed it was the redheaded offensive lineman, Connor Riley, which meant the other one was the linebacker Mike Cohn, who was decidedly silent. Was that a good thing or a bad one? In Kyle's experience no one was ever on his side, so the silence had to be bad.

"Yeah, not so intimidating now that he can't run," Tanner said. He and Brett moved forward, trying to crowd his space.

"Hey man, I was just doing what the coach told me," Kyle said, taking a step backward in response.

"Coach," Brett, now only a foot away, pointed at him, "didn't tell you to go out there and make us look like fools."

Actually, Coach Deke told him to *make those guys play hard.* And that's exactly what he'd done, intercepting balls that were meant to float into Tanner's hands, reading the routes telegraphed by Howard watching the receiver, and running the ball back for a touchdown. It had felt good making them look like chumps.

Now, it didn't look like such a good idea. Hell, he'd never fit in anywhere before, why did he expect to do so here? He glanced from one to the other. Yep. He was going to take a beating.

"Can't help it if you guys aren't as special as you think."

That was all it took. They blitzed him from both sides.

* * * * *

Libby glanced out the window into the dark summer night. No sign of a car coming up the street.

Stop it. If he seriously wanted to talk to her, he'd be here. Pacing the floor and watching the street weren't going to compel him to magically appear. Normally she wouldn't be this anxious, but ever since the kiss he'd planted on her before walking out of her office she'd been as jittery as a June bug on a griddle.

How had she ever forgotten the effect his kisses always had on her? Breathless. Wanting more.

She let the curtain drop. Determined to curb her anxiety, she went to the kitchen and focused on—what?

The fridge.

Grabbing a plastic trash bag, she started emptying the refrigerator of any old or moldy vegetables. Years ago, she'd learned to put nervous energy to work in the form of housework. Cleaning the fridge wasn't her favorite chore, but tonight she'd do anything to take her mind off the conversation to come. When she'd issued the challenge to Deke she'd been angry at him. Now she had so many consequences of that ultimatum to face, not the least of which was finally telling him the secret she'd held inside for ten long years.

Hard, brisk knocking shattered her thoughts and she dropped the bag on the floor with a slight yelp. Slimy, smelly spinach popped out of the plastic bag and onto her tile floor.

Great. Just what she needed before having a heart-to-heart talk with the man she'd loved forever.

She stomped over to the door and jerked it open to find him standing there, hand halfway up to knock again. "Come in. I have a mess to clean up," she said, not waiting for a response. Leaving the door open for him, she headed back into the kitchen. She snatched a handful of paper towels, wet them under the faucet and sank to her knees.

"What the hell is that smell?" Deke's deep raspy voice rumbled over as she scooted the offending greens back into their bag and then into the garbage bag.

She gave him a *duh* look and went back to cleaning the slimy drippings from the tiles. "Bad spinach. Don't tell me you've never had spinach go bad in your fridge before?"

"Nope."

Again, she paused to look at him like he was crazy. He leaned against the door frame, his hands in his jeans' pocket and the whisper of a smile on his lips. Then it hit her and she laughed. "Of course not. What man would have fresh spinach in his refrigerator to begin with, let alone have it there long enough to go bad?"

He shrugged.

"Men," she muttered and scrubbed at the last bits of mess. Finished, she scooped the paper towels into the bag, too. Before she could close the bag, his hands closed over hers.

"I'll take it out to the trash," he said, taking it from her without waiting for her to protest and walking out the back door. No need for him to ask where the trash was stored. This was the house she and Bill had grown up in. Deke had been here so often, it was almost his second home when they were young.

She quickly washed her hands in case any of the nasty stuff had managed to get on them. Funny thing, as soon as the bag had left the house the smell had, too. She pulled her hair out of the hair tie, letting it fall down around her shoulders the way he always liked. Picking up the bottle of Zinfandel she'd opened earlier, she poured herself another half glass of wine. A moment later, Deke stepped back inside, closing the door and locking it behind him.

"I don't have any whiskey in the house. Want a glass of wine?" She held up the bottle.

"I don't drink very often anymore," he said. "Maybe just some water?"

When they'd been together it wasn't uncommon for them to finish an entire bottle with their dinner, and he'd often enjoyed a whiskey neat after work. A lot of things changed in ten years. Without asking about his decreased alcohol consumption, she poured him a glass of water, then led the way into the living room. She sank onto the sectional and waited for him to pick a spot.

He stood in the middle of the room, taking in the changes she'd made. The old, cotton-covered couch and loveseat had been replaced by the sectional with its soft-as-butter leather upholstery. The old console TV was gone. In its place sat a modern credenza with a large flat-screen TV on top. She'd painted the wood paneling an off white, but left the family pictures in place.

Finally, Deke sat on the sectional, two cushions away. "I like what you've done with the place."

"After the fire, I came home to live with Mama. Her Alzheimer's was aggressive and before I knew it, she was in the nursing home. So, I thought why not update the old home to sell." She took a drink of her wine. "Funny thing was, after I made changes, I decided I liked how comfortable it was and decided to just stay."

"Nothing like coming home. My mom sold the old

place of ours before she moved to her condo in South Carolina a few years back."

Silence filled the next few minutes.

"What happened at the meeting over at the sheriff's office?" she asked, mostly to avoid the hard conversation she knew was coming.

He shook his head, staring at the fireplace across the room. "Nothing good."

She waited. Despite the years apart she knew Deke well enough to know he'd talk once he'd weighed the information in his head. Finally, he turned and focused his gaze on her. "Mike confirmed what I thought. The fire was set intentionally."

"Kids playing around?" she asked, hoping it was some only teenagers being careless or thoughtless.

Again, he shook his head.

"An arsonist?" she nearly whispered the word. What little she knew about the fire that caused Bill's death and nearly taken Deke's life was that it was the work of an arsonist for hire. In fact, the only contact she'd had with Deke since that fateful night, was a letter a year later telling her how he'd tracked the man down, but he'd died in a fire before Deke could bring him to justice.

His dark-brown eyes fixed on her, he slowly nodded. "Trouble is, Mike hasn't seen this guy's work before. He thinks it's his first fire, but won't be his last."

"Dear God," she said, setting her glass aside, her fingers shaking. "We were lucky no one was seriously injured this time."

"Mike said our firebug could escalate his enthusiasm and his deadliness." His mouth pressed into a thin line and she could see his jaw muscles working hard as he fought his own anger. "We think he's been studying someone else's style of arson. His signature is one we've seen before."

"Who?" she asked, even though she knew what he was going to say.

"Leo Harkin."

"The man who killed Bill." The need to move had her bolting from her seat to pace the room. "You told me he died in a fire he'd set himself."

"He did. I promise."

She stopped and whirled to face him, pointing right at him. "How do you know for sure? He could've escaped, couldn't he? Do you know for sure his body was the one in the fire?"

"Trust me, Libby, Harkin died in that fire." He rose from the couch and stood just an arm's length away.

"How? How do you know?"

Deke went completely still, His jaw once more hard as granite, his hands in tight fists at his side, eyes narrowed. "Because I watched him burn."

Startled by his confession, she blinked and gaped at him for a moment. Then she gave her head a shake to clear the confusion that had his words had set off. "Excuse me?"

He took a step back from her, absently running his

hand over the scars on his neck as he took a turn at pacing. "From the moment I got out of the hospital I'd been chasing down the leads that we had on the guy. We knew he'd been active in the northeast part of the state for months before the warehouse fire."

She didn't have to ask which warehouse fire. The only one that mattered to either one of them was the one in which Bill died. Slowly, she sank back down onto the couch as he continued to talk.

"It took me several months, but slowly a pattern started to emerge. Every time a fire with his signature appeared, there was a robbery days before, usually just blocks away at an electronics or phone store. So I started watching the surveillance tapes of those stores. And I found him. The local cops cornered him at his home."

"What happened?"

Eyes bleak, he slumped onto the sofa beside her, staring into the empty fireplace once more, as if he were back at the scene. "The man was paranoid on top of being a sick bastard. He'd booby-trapped his home and kept his wife and son virtual prisoners inside. When he saw the police outside surrounding their house, he yelled out the door that if anyone came inside, he'd burn the house down with them all inside it. The SWAT team was called in, but before they could talk him out or take him out, the front of the house was engulfed in flames."

"Oh, dear God," she whispered, suddenly nauseated.

"He killed his whole family?"

Deke shook his head. "We thought so at first. The place burned fast. When we went through the rubble we found him and his wife, but no sign of the son."

"He'd escaped?"

"Apparently the wife suspected what was going in her husband's mind. There'd been years of abuse on both her and the son. Somewhere along the way she'd gotten enough courage to provide a trap door beneath the pantry's floor that dropped to a space under the back porch. She'd hidden the boy, he was all of about six or seven and told him to get out, to run to the woods behind the house and not to come back until she called him." Deke closed his eyes a minute, inhaling slowly, his jaw muscles flexing again. When he opened them again, unshed tears glistened in them. "We found him the next morning. Poor kid had been out there all night in the cold winter weather, barefoot and in his pajamas, while his parents burned to death.

"We took him to the hospital for exposure and they took a little of his blood for DNA testing against those of the couple inside the house. Both were his parents."

"Do you think this could be the son? Come to exact revenge?" she asked.

He shook his head. "Gage asked the same thing. Told him I had no idea what happened to the kid. He's going to look into it in the morning. In the meantime, we're all going to go on alert. There will be another fire. No question."

They sat in silence a few more minutes.

"It was my fault, Libby," he said in almost a whisper, his shoulders slumped as if he were collapsing into himself, his deep, raspy voice adding its own pain to the statement.

She narrowed her eyes at him. "Horse crap. You didn't make him kill himself or his family, Deke."

"I know that. That's not what I meant."

"Then what was your fault?" she asked, her heart pounding at the ache in her chest.

"Bill's death."

CHAPTER FOURTEEN

"It was my fault. We were out," he said, staring down at his hands clenched tightly in his lap, unable to stop the words now that he'd started. "We were safe. But then the night watchman asked us if we'd seen the guy and the kid."

"What kid?" Libby's quiet voice asked beside him.

He gave a harsh sound—half laugh, half choke. "That's what Bill and I said, almost in unison."

Suddenly he was back there, standing in his turnout gear, sucking in oxygen, the fire raging behind him, even as the rest of the team fought to contain it.

"The boy the man dragged inside with him," the burly night watchman said, sweat dripping off his thick moustache. "I saw them on my camera. Little guy, dirty-blonde hair, maybe light brown. The man had a duffel bag in one hand, his other had the kid by the shirt collar, dragged him in behind the building."

He slammed his hand into Bill's chest. "Come on. We've gotta go back in."

"Wait," Bill said, grabbing him by the arm and looking at the watchman again. "You're sure they went into the building? Not around the back? Maybe over a fence?"

"Doubt it. Was headed in to check it out and the next thing I knew flames were shooting up inside the warehouse. I ran to call 9-1-1 as fast as I could."

"Come, on, Bill. We have to go now." He was already putting on his mask and hat, ready to head back into the inferno, but he had to wait on his partner.

"Okay, okay. We go. But we tell the captain first."

The rush hit him as they got the "go" order from the cap. They went in the side door on the first level. The heat was intense, the fire hotter than any he could remember. Bill grabbed his arm from behind, signaling to stay with him and they'd go to the right, away from the initial burn point up front.

"Deke."

"Deacon."

Libby's voice.

The memory fading, he blinked, slowly raising his eyes to meet hers, knowing the hatred he'd see there. He'd killed her brother.

Only, it wasn't hatred he saw there. Simply tears.

"Deacon," she whispered again, her soft, gentle hands cupping his face.

"I'm sorry, Libby," he whispered, his own eyes hot with unshed tears.

"You didn't kill him, Deacon," she said, leaning in to

press her lips against his.

The softest of kisses and the pain in his chest—the one he'd been living with for so long—threatened to swallow him up, the tears finally flowing down his face.

She pulled back to stare at him, compassion in her beautiful blue eyes, her thumbs wiping at the wetness on his cheeks. "You did your job. Neither you nor Bill would've stayed out of that fire if you knew a child might be in danger."

Again she kissed him. This time slower, a little deeper. Repeating the motion. Kiss after kiss. Moving her mouth on his, pulling back slightly to hold his lower lip between hers, then coming in again. With each one his ache eased a little more, his breathing now ragged, not from the pain inside him, but from the need for this woman, *his* woman.

Finally, he let the need to hold her take over and untangled his fingers to grasp her hips and draw her up to straddle his lap.

"Libby," he murmured, finding hope and strength in her kisses.

"It wasn't your fault," she whispered, as she trailed her lips along the left side of his jaw, her fingers sliding down over the thick scars on his neck.

Grasping her hand, he stilled her movements. She leaned back, the question in her blue eyes. He wanted to let her continue, to feel her touch him in the one place that reminded him daily of what had happened, but he couldn't, not until he explained. "You were right."

Her eyes narrowed and she tilted her head as she stared down at him.

God, how he had missed that little quirk of hers. It told him she was both confused and curious by his admission. Some women would gloat over being told they were right. Not Libby. No, she'd want an explanation.

"I was right about what?"

"You could've come to visit me in the burn unit."

"Then why didn't you let me?" she asked softly. No accusations. No recriminations.

"Guilt." He held her hand in his, lightly rubbing his thumb over her knuckles. "I'd pushed him to go back in. I'd lived. Bill hadn't. Your brother died. I couldn't take the pain of you hating me on top of the pain I was already going through, both mentally and physically."

"I wouldn't...didn't hate you, Deacon," she leaned in and kissed him again. Quick. "I don't hate you now."

He lifted the right corner of his mouth. "I know that now, but then. Seeing your pain and grief, knowing I'd caused it. I just couldn't do it." With a groan he leaned his head back and looked up at the ceiling. "I'm such a coward."

"Stop that." Both hands on his shoulders, she raised up until she could stare straight down into his eyes, hot anger in them. "You are not a coward. No one—I mean no one—running into a burning building to find a child, has *ever* been classified as a coward."

"But Bill—"

"Bill didn't go into that building because you made him. You need to get over that. Bill went in because It. Was. His. Job. Same as it was yours." She slid her hand up his neck, resting her splayed fingers over his scars. Her softened gaze never left his face. "You chose to suffer alone. You chose that for both of us. That was the pain I suffered with the most. I didn't just lose Bill in that fire. It was as if you'd died, too."

"God, I'm so sorry, baby," he said, a new pain hitting him. He tried to pull her in closer for another kiss, but she stopped him with her fingertips on his lips.

"It's like there are two ghosts—Bill and our grief— between us and we can't let either one go." She took a slow breath in, then exhaled just as slowly. "I miss him. I do. But I've missed you more. I want you back in my life, Deke. You. The man I loved then, the one I still love."

He opened his mouth, but she shook her head, stopping him once more.

"I forgive you. I forgive you for Bill's death."

She leaned in and kissed him.

"I forgive you for getting yourself nearly killed."

Another kiss.

"I forgive you for shutting me out."

A slower kiss as she slid her hips over his thighs, getting closer.

"I forgive you for making us both grieve alone."

This kiss long, heated.

"I forgive you for making me ache to be in your arms night after night."

And with that, need slammed into him. Need to let her forgiveness wash away the guilt. Need for her, the woman he'd never been able to forget. He wrapped his arms around her and crushed her to him. Sliding his tongue between her parted lips to taste her essence, he was rewarded by the soft, muffled moan from deep inside her.

Suddenly, it became a chaotic frenzy of hands and fingers. Shirt, blouse, bra, shoes, socks, his belt, her shorts, his jeans. All went flying to scatter on the floor beneath them. He ran his hands up her arms, the smooth softness of her skin teasing his palms. Then he slid them down the front of her to cup her breasts. They were slightly larger than he remembered, but still delightfully pert, with their pointed nipples. They'd darkened, too, over the years.

"You're still so beautiful," he murmured against her lips as he pinched and plucked at both nipples, feeling them grow even tauter. "I've missed you. Holding you. Touching you. Loving you." He accented each statement with a short kiss, pulling her lower lip between his teeth with the last one.

She rocked her hips so her panty-covered heat stroked across his aching erection, straining against his boxers to be released. Another moan escaped her, and she clenched her hands on his shoulders. "Deacon, please."

"Please what, baby? This? Is this what you want?" he asked. Sliding one hand down her stomach to slip inside her panties and gently grasp her mound in his palm. He crushed her lips with his again as he pressed upward and she began to ride his hand. Even though it had been ten years, he knew her body's needs and desires so well. He slid one finger between her slick folds, finding the spot just above her clitoris that always brought her to orgasm. Like a guitarist with a fine-tuned instrument he slowly let her tension build.

Releasing her lips, he ran his mouth down the long elegant column of her neck to the juncture of her shoulders. The spot where he'd watched her pulse earlier in the day. He ran his tongue over it.

Soft mewing sounds filled the room as her rhythm increased.

"That's it, baby," he murmured against her neck. "Give it to me."

Suddenly, her fingers dug down into his shoulders as she arched forward, her body taut like violin strings. Then, slowly, she shattered in his arms, the sound of her orgasm ringing in his ears. She dropped her head on his shoulder, her blonde hair covering them both. Her breasts moving against his chest as she sucked in air.

He held her tight as the last shudders of her release ran through her. His own aching need throbbed just below her, his erection wanting to find its home inside her. Reality hit him. He hadn't brought any protection with him, and the last thing he'd do is get his own pleasure while putting her at risk. Counting to ten, then to twenty, he willed his body to relax.

"You okay?" he asked, soothing her hair from her face.

She rose up to press her forehead against his. Passionate blue eyes stared down at him, her cheeks flushed from her release. A slow, satisfied smile spread over her face. "Oh, I am better than okay."

He returned her smile. "I've missed that."

"Me, coming apart so hard?" A wonderful pink blush covered her body.

"Well, yeah, I missed that," he said, watching her wiggle her brows.

"Me, sounding like a cat in heat?"

"Oh, yeah, I missed that, too. A lot," he said with half a grin.

She playfully slapped his arm, then buried her head against his shoulder. Her body shook, but he could still her laughter. Cupping her head in his hands, he slowly raised it once more until their gazes met. The humor faded as the bond between them grew.

He wanted her to know he hadn't reconnected with her just because he was as horny as a kid on his first date. Given the fact that he'd been celibate since the last time he'd made love to this woman, it wasn't too far off the mark. That wasn't the reason he was here, what he wanted from her.

"Your laughter."

"My laughter?"

"Your laughter, your smiles. I've missed them." She opened her mouth, but he stopped her with a soft kiss before continuing. "I've missed talking with you—about anything and everything. I miss holding you, especially at night and waking up to hear your gentle snores."

"I do not snore," she said, slapping his arm again.

He caught her hand in his. "I even miss you smacking me on the arm when you think I'm wrong. And yes, you do snore. Okay, maybe it's more like a gentle purr. But I can't tell you how many times I've woken in the middle of the night wishing I would hear it and I could pull you in to spoon a while."

She lowered her head a little and peeked up at him through her slightly lowered lashes. "I've missed that, too."

"You have?"

She nodded. "I miss watching sports with you. It's no fun yelling for our teams or against the refs when you're not here to back me up."

He laughed. "You have an unhealthy bias against refs who don't call in favor or our guys."

"Whatever," she said, her usual reply when she was out of arguments. She leaned in and kissed him slowly, then pulled back. "I've missed the way you always checked the doors and put on the alarm before crawling into bed with me. The way you'd call me while on shift to be sure I'd done the same, then talk to me until I was ready to fall asleep." The corner of her lips lifted again and she slid her hips back so she could stroke the thickness of his still-happy-to-be-here hard-on. "I've missed other things, too."

"You have?" he asked, enjoying the slow torture of her movements.

"Oh yes. The feel of your muscles," she said, running her hands over his lower arms, then slowly upward, stopping to briefly massage his biceps. "The feel of your skin against mine." Her fingers stilled over the scars that extended from his jaw, down his neck, and across his left shoulder and chest.

He reached up to grasp her hand. "Don't."

"Does it still hurt?" she asked, all her teasing gone.

He shook his head. "Not like it did. The scars get tight sometimes."

"Then why don't you want me to touch them?" She stared at him with those clear blue eyes and he knew she wasn't going to let this go.

Holding her hand pressed against his chest, he closed his eyes and leaned his head back on the sofa again. "They remind me of Bill's death."

"It's time to let him go, Deacon."

Beneath his hand he felt her fingers move slightly and he relaxed his hold on her hand. Libby could be one very stubborn woman. Especially when she thought what she was doing was the right thing to do. And maybe she was right. It was time to let Bill go, to let the pain of losing him go and the memories of that damn fire.

Gently, she traced her fingers over the edges of the scars. From his outer shoulder, slowly over his collarbone, then up his neck. There, she let her fingers get a little firmer, massaging the corded muscles beneath them. A moan escaped him at how good that felt. The she moved, and her lips traced across his jawline, moving downward towards his chest. When her tongue traced over the thick lacework of the scar tissue he sucked in his breath.

"Did that hurt?" she asked, her breath teasing his skin.

He shook his head. "It felt good."

"Oh good. Because I've always loved the way you taste," she said, sliding her tongue back over his chest at the same time she feathered her fingers over the upper part of his torso.

And the erection that had been waning seemed to surge back to life beneath her. If she kept this up, he wasn't going to keep from sinking deep inside her, protection be damned.

"Libby," he said hoarsely, leaning up to capture her face once more.

"Yes?" She picked that moment to dart her tongue out and lick her lips as if she was savoring the taste of his skin.

Willpower was so highly overrated.

"Libby," his voice croaked this time as he fought to do the honorable thing. "Sweetheart, I haven't got a condom with me."

"Hmmm, I don't have any here," she said, looking at him with almost innocent eyes, then her smile turned the look on her face into something much more sensual, seductive. "But you know I've *always* loved the taste of you."

"Oh, God, baby," he whispered.

Giving in to the devil on his shoulder telling him to enjoy what she was offering, he released his hold on her and watched her move farther down. A soft chuckle of triumph escaped her as she licked all the scars, until she came to the smooth skin of his muscles. Her hands trailing behind her mouth, still teasing his chest, scars and nipples.

"Oh, baby," he moaned.

"Like that?" she whispered.

"You know I always have."

She wiggled back until she was kneeling between his spread thighs. Just as she reached for the opening of his boxers, the room shattered into the ringtone of her phone lying on the table beside the couch.

They froze, eyes locked on each other.

"Sorry, I have to see who it is," she said, reaching for it. Then she was standing and reaching for her bra, giving him an apologetic shake of her head. "Hey Emma, what's up?"

I'm sorry, she mouthed to him. He stood, grabbed his jeans and stepped into them, almost glad for the interruption. Well, most of him was. He wanted so badly to be with her again. To make love to her. And the phone call forced him to see how important that was going to be to the two of them. Way more important than a blow job on her couch. Of course, he knew it would've been one hell of an experience with Libby, but not really what he wanted for their first time back together.

"He's what? Is he okay?" The tone in her voice changed and her gaze shot to his.

Something was wrong.

Deke paused—jeans around his hips, the fly open—completely focused on her face. His internal warning bells going off.

Kyle.

"No, no. Don't bother Todd. I'd rather you called me, too. I'll be right over." She hung up and wiggled into her shorts. "I'm sorry, Deke. I have to go to the clinic."

"What's up?" he asked as he jerked on his sports shirt and was finally able to zip up his jeans.

"It's Kyle. He's been beaten up." She put on her blouse and quickly pulled her hair into a ponytail. "He doesn't have a guardian, and as part of the board of Colbert House, it's my duty to see to the residents' welfare along with Todd. Emma called me first, thank God."

"I'm coming with you." He'd gotten his shoes on and stood holding the door open.

"You don't have to." She grabbed her purse and phone.

He stopped her at the door, one hand on her shoulder. "Yes, I do. The kid doesn't have too many adults on his side. I figure his coach ought to be one of them. Besides, I want to hear what he has to say happened. And for another thing. I'd feel better going over there with you."

Neither one of them said it, but once again, the peaceful little town of Westen seemed to be a dangerous place to live.

CHAPTER FIFTEEN

Thank God, Emma's call had stopped them. Thank God, Emma's call had stopped them.

The words kept running through Libby's mind like an old record with a scratch in the vinyl. Heat filled her face in the darkness of the truck cab as they drove the short distance to the medical clinic.

How could she have been so stupid? Quick sex wasn't going to mend this thing with Deke. *Unprotected* sex. What an idiot! Hadn't she learned her lesson years ago? Every action had a consequence and some were more devastating than others. She laid her right hand over her lower abdomen and glanced at Deke.

The truth. That could be the only thing between her and Deacon from now on. Secrets and feelings long hidden were going to come out. What if they couldn't get past them?

She thought back to that final day when she'd gone to the hospital asking to be admitted to the burn unit.

From the moment he'd been admitted, she'd spent whole days in the waiting room—first to see that he'd live, then hoping to see him, to talk with him. She'd watched other families go in to visit their loved ones, but every day she was turned away.

Then came the day the young doctor sat down beside her in the empty waiting room.

"I'm sorry, Miss Wilson. Mr. Reynolds isn't accepting any visitors."

"Does he know it's me?" She couldn't believe he would turn her away.

The doctor laid his hand on her shoulder. "I'm afraid he does. He's refusing all visitors at this time, including you and his mother, and it's his right to do so."

"Is he burned so badly?" Dear God, was that why he wouldn't let her in? Did he think she wouldn't love him if his face was scarred?

"I'm limited by law not to discuss details of his case, however, I think I can assure you that while his injuries are extensive, his general appearance hasn't changed considerably." A softness came over the man's features. *"Often, our male patients don't want their loved ones to see them in any kind of pain, especially the kind that can come with the healing process involved with third-degree burns. With time, and as the healing process progresses, he may be more willing for your company."*

From the moment he'd uttered the words so sympathetically, she knew they were a lie.

Deacon would never let her back into his life. She knew him that well.

They said deaths came in threes. First she'd lost Bill. Then Deke was as good as dead to her from that moment on.

That night she'd been sound asleep in the bed she shared with him when the bleeding started. Almost three months into a surprise pregnancy, she'd miscarried their child.

"How bad was it?" Deke's gravelly voice broke the silence, his words making her catch her breath.

He couldn't possibly know?

"The injuries to Kyle?" he said, laying his hand over hers and clarifying his question. "Did Emma say how badly he was hurt?"

Libby's heart dropped back into a regular rhythm and her body relaxed. Her secret was still safe—for now. "No, she didn't give me details. She thought someone should be there for him and Todd Banyon wasn't really a good choice."

A harsh bark sounded from Deke.

She turned to watch him in the intermittent light and shadows cast from the passing streetlights. "What?"

He glanced at her, shaking his head slightly. "I can't imagine that guy giving anyone comfort, much less understanding. Emma was right. You are a much better choice to be there for Kyle."

Something in his voice caught her attention. "You like him, don't you?"

The corner of his mouth lifted slightly. "He's had it tough, but so have lots of kids. It doesn't look like he's letting it keep him down. He seems to be responsible and determined." He paused. "Yeah, I like him. There's something about the kid. A kind of connection."

Before she could ask him more, he released her hand and turned into the parking lot next to the Westen Medical Clinic. A fancy title for the two-story Victorian that Doc Clint's uncle and aunt had converted into the clinic decades earlier. Clint and Emma had converted the upstairs rooms from a live-in apartment to an overnight stay for minor cases that needed watching, but not hospitalization. They'd also expanded the lower level to have several more exam rooms. All the lights in the front of the downstairs were on and one upstairs.

The van from the Peaches 'N Cream Café sat in the lot. Deke parked next to it. As they climbed out of the truck, the front door to the clinic opened and Doc Clint met them on the wide front porch that extended across the front of the house.

"Sorry to get you out here so late," he said, shaking hands with both of them. "Kid got the shit beat out of him outside of the café. Lorna and Rachel brought him to me."

"How is he?" Libby asked, wrapping her arms about her. The news that someone could attack a young man so violently in their small town sent a shiver through her despite the warm summer night.

"Mostly, cuts, bruises, broken nose. I'm keeping him

overnight. Just to be sure I'm not missing any internal injuries." Clint shook his head. "Hands are a mess. I think the kid gave as good as he got."

"Good," Deke said, conviction and anger lacing his words.

Anger surged through her. "Good? A boy gets beat up and injured badly enough to have to be observed overnight and you think it's good he hurt someone else?"

The two men exchanged a look that said their pride in Kyle for defending himself at risk to his own safety was justified.

Men. Did they ever really crawl out of their Stone Age caves? Shaking her head, she swung open the screen door and stalked into the clinic, not looking to see if either of them followed.

Harriett, the irascible nurse Doc Clint had inherited with the clinic from his uncle, stood at the foot of the stairs, holding out a bag of frozen peas to her. "Upstairs. Cover with a towel. Right hand. Twenty minutes."

Without another word she turned and headed into the back of the clinic.

Libby shook her head again. It had taken her years to get used to Harriett's limited conversation. She was blunt, succinct, almost to the point of rudeness. But Libby had also learned the older lady loved every one of her neighbors and patients.

Hearing the low rumble of conversation between

Deke and Clint as they entered the clinic, she hurried up the stairs. She wasn't in the mood for any more male chest thumping.

Outside the overnight room, Lorna sat in a chair. "Hey, Libby," she greeted her, but not with her usual sass. No smile. In fact, she hadn't ever seen the other woman this quiet or angry.

"How is he?" she asked, peeking inside to see Kyle in the hospital bed and Rachel sitting by his side, talking quietly to him.

"Doc thinks his injuries aren't too bad, at least he doesn't think there are any internal ones, but he's keeping him overnight."

Libby nodded. "That's what he told us downstairs."

"Us?" Lorna tilted her head slightly and lifted one brow.

Great. She was going to tell the center of the town's gossip about Deke. "Deke was at my place when Emma called. As his football coach he wanted to come check on him."

"Good." Lorna gave a hard nod, delivering her approval—of what, Libby wasn't quite sure. Deke being with her or him being interested in Kyle's welfare. Knowing Lorna's busybody ways, it was probably both. "That boy in there could use a man in his corner."

Left unsaid, but the intense look in her friend's eyes spoke that she, too, could use a man like Deke in her corner. She also suspected she thought Deke needed someone, too—her. While she couldn't agree more, there were a few more bridges they had to cross before that could ever happen. If only her libido would listen to her heart and brain.

"Better get those peas on his hand before Harriett comes up here. You know how she can get when her orders aren't followed exactly." Lorna said with a wink, as she stood and looked into the room. "Rachel, we have an early day tomorrow. Kyle, you listen and do what the doc and Harriett say. No arguments. I expect you back at work tomorrow night."

"Yes, ma'am," he said. Relief crossed his face. Apparently he'd been worried he'd lose his job over this. "And thank you."

Softness crept over Lorna's features. "No need to thank me. I'm just sorry this happened to you, especially outside my café."

"See you tomorrow." Rachel patted Kyle on the shoulder, then walked to the door.

Kyle's eyes never left her, even after the pair headed down stairs. Libby hid the smile. The boy was head-over-heels for the young waitress. She had to admit he had good taste. Pretty, practical and smart. Hopefully, she wouldn't break his heart.

"Harriett sent this up to you," she said, holding up the bag of frozen peas and crossing over to the bedside, trying not to wince at his injuries. She lifted one of the washcloths folded neatly on the side table, wrapped it over the plastic bag and laid it gently on the boy's right hand, which was swollen and the knuckles red from the multiple abrasions.

He hissed at the contact, but laid his other hand, much less injured, over the makeshift icepack.

"Sorry. It will help." She sat in the straight-back, woven-cane-bottom chair Rachel had vacated. "Harriett said to leave it on twenty minutes. And I'd recommend you don't take it off one second sooner. She has eyes everywhere."

"Yeah. She had some on my face a little bit ago. The look she gave me said I'd better not complain." He laughed. Then stopped with a catch and a moan. "Sorry. It kinda hurts to laugh."

"I imagine it does," she said, studying everything she saw in the dim lamplight of the room.

Whoever had done this, they seemed to have concentrated on his face. His left eye was already showing signs of being bruised. Both cheeks had bruises and cuts on them. His lip was cut and swollen. His nose was cut and swollen.

"Did you break your nose?"

"Yeah. The doctor put it back in place."

Libby winced. "I bet that hurt."

"Not too bad. He said it was because it was already damaged, putting it back in place would make it feel better." He closed his eyes and leaned back in the bed. He looked so alone and so helpless in the hospital bed.

What had he done to make someone want to hurt him so badly?

"Who did this to you, Kyle?" she asked after a few minutes.

"That's what I'd like to know," a gravelly voice asked from the door.

 Deke strode into the room, grabbed the other cane-bottom chair and came to sit on the other side of the bed.

"Coach," Kyle said, a look of surprise crossed his face and he struggled to sit up.

"Don't move." Deke laid a hand on his shoulder stopping his efforts. "Doc Clint said you took a couple of kicks to the side, as well as all this," he said as he waved at Kyle's facial injuries. "You want to tell me what happened?"

The hopeful light in Kyle's eyes dropped and a mask of teenage stubbornness dropped over his face. "I was taking out the trash and some guys jumped me."

"And you didn't recognize any of them?" Deke asked, watching Kyle.

The young man looked down at his hands. "No, sir. It was too dark."

 "I don't know what's in your past, Kyle," Deke said. "But we all come with some kind of baggage. Sometimes you just got to take the chance and trust people."

After a moment Kyle shook his head. "Like I said, didn't see who they were, sir."

Deke looked at Libby, one brow lifted in doubt at the boy's reply. She had to agree. Kyle knew exactly who had done this, but he wasn't going to tell them. They weren't his parents or legal guardians, so they had no recourse to force him to tell them.

"You're going to have to stay here overnight, Kyle," she said.

His head snapped up at that. "Colbert House has rules about not making curfew."

"Your health is the most important thing. I'll handle Mr. Banyon and the house rules."

"You're sure it will be okay?"

She smiled and patted his arm in a spot that wasn't bruised. "I'm on the board that made up those rules. I think I can get them amended to cover a night in the clinic."

"Uhm. Thanks."

Deke pushed his chair back. "You get some rest and Doc Clint will have to clear you to return to practice tomorrow."

"You mean I'm still on the team?" The hope in the young man's face nearly brought tears to Libby's eyes as she stood, too.

Deke pointed to his injured hands. "Anybody who can take a beating like this and still have enough fight in him to give some of it back is gonna be one helluva defensive player and I want you on the team."

"I'll be there, Coach. You can count on it," he said as he lay back in the bed.

"Okay, you two. Out. Kid needs some sleep," Harriett said, bustling her way into the room, a cup of small pills, glass of water and two more bags of frozen peas on a tray.

Libby and Deke didn't waste any words arguing with her. Everyone in Westen knew, when Harriett was in nurse mode and giving orders, it was just best to obey. They'd been trained since childhood to do so.

* * * * *

They drove a few blocks in silence again. Deke hadn't asked if she wanted him to take her over to Colbert House, he just was. He had a feeling he knew exactly who'd been behind the beating Kyle took, but just in case he was wrong and it was someone at the halfway house, he wasn't letting Libby go there by herself so late at night.

She hasn't needed your help for the last ten years.

True. But until last spring he'd never thought anyone was in any kind of danger in Westen. Now he realized evil could be anywhere, even a sleepy little town like theirs. Besides, now that he'd gotten a taste of her after all these years, and a feel of her in his arms, he wasn't sure he could walk away again.

"He was lying, wasn't he?" Her quiet words were more a statement than a question.

"You got that, too, huh?"

"Fairly obvious when he wouldn't look either one of us in the eyes. If he knew who did this, why wouldn't he tell us? Is he afraid of them finding out and repeating the attack?"

"I don't think its fear. More like a rite of passage and pride. He was outnumbered, but he didn't give in to them. In fact, I suspect some of them have a few bruises of their own."

He felt her gaze on him in the darkness. Even after all these years, his body was attuned to every little thing she did, even just looking at him.

"You know who did it, don't you?"

He shrugged. "I have my suspicions."

The silence stretched between them as they pulled in beside Colbert House. Only one light was on near the back of the house on the main floor. Apparently, Todd Banyon kept a tight curfew on his residents, it was just barely eleven.

Libby didn't make a move to open the door even after he turned off the engine.

"Are you going to tell me who you think beat Kyle?" she finally asked, one hand on the door handle.

"Nope."

"Why not?" She paused and let out a very un-ladylike snort. "Let me guess, it has to do with the whole male-pride thing. If Kyle won't tell me, you won't either."

"Pretty much." For some reason, getting her riled up took some of the edge out of his own anger over what was done to the kid.

"Will you at least let Gage know, so he can investigate the beating?"

"Depends."

"Depends on what?" Her voice had gotten more edgy and he had to fight the urge to grin at her.

"On whether or not I need help handling it."

She shook her head at him. "It's just like when we were in high school. You, Bill and Gage wouldn't let me know what you did to Ryan Tompkins after he ripped my dress at the freshman mixer dance. I told you then it was a sloppy drunkard's kiss and I'd already decked him for trying it. The ripped dress happened when he tried to grab my arm. I walked home and that was it. But you guys did something to scare the bejeezus out of him. Guy never looked me in the eyes again." She threw open the door and stomped up to the porch.

He swore he heard her mutter *cavemen* as she went.

She was right. He, Bill and Gage had scared the guy so badly he'd actually wet his pants. The fact that they all had about five inches and thirty pounds on the guy might've had something to do with it. But when he'd seen her walk into her house where they'd all been watching football film—her dress torn, lips swollen and cheeks pink from anger—he'd known exactly what had happened and immediately seen red.

So had the others.

Then she'd cried. At first they thought it was because she was hurt or the guy had done more than get handsy and kissy with her. Then they realized she was pissed. She'd gone into the kitchen, come out with a bowl of ice water, and shoved her right hand in it, just like she'd seen them do after a football game. Apparently, she'd taken their lessons on how to hit with a fist so your thumb didn't get broken to heart.

Tears. Torn dress. Swollen lips. Iced hand.

Yep. It has all added up to Ryan Tompkins needing a lesson on how to treat a girl, especially one that Deke would do anything to take to a dance. And while they were at it, the three of them had let it be known that no one, *no one* messed with Libby Wilson. Ever.

He smiled as he watched her talk with Todd on the porch.

Making Libby off limits to every other guy in school hadn't been a bad move on his part. It opened the door for him to date her.

A moment later, she walked back across the grass, her hips swaying softly and her arms crossed over her chest, pushing her breasts a little higher. The image of her naked except for her panties, and kneeling between his spread thighs earlier in the evening slammed into him.

"What did Todd have to say?" he asked as she climbed in the truck cab, forcing himself to think of Kyle's problem and not a nearly naked Libby.

"I told him what had happened. It took some effort to convince him that Kyle was the injured party here and not the instigator. That he was staying the night at the clinic under Doc Clint's supervision seemed to ease his worry over Kyle breaking the house curfew rules."

She gave another one of those snorts. "He is such a tight-ass over rules, he probably gets constipated going over the speed limit."

Startled, he barked a laugh at her comment. "He's that bad?"

"You have no idea," she said, shaking her head.

Chuckling still, he pulled out and headed back to her house. "How many residents does old Todd have at the house right now?"

"Including Kyle, four." She paused a moment and he could almost hear her thinking. "Is that who you think might behind the attack on him? One of the other residents?"

"Do you know anything about them? Backgrounds? History of violence?" he asked, making a left turn onto Main Street again.

"I'm not supposed to talk about it, but if Kyle's safety is at risk, I guess I can tell you the general information as to why they're here," she said, turning slightly towards him. "The three of them are kind of loners. One just got out of drug rehab. One is there to protect him from his father, the mother is in a women's shelter near Cincinnati, but her son is too old to be housed there. The last one got caught in an identity fraud case. He was too young to charge as an adult and the courts felt his older brother, who was the ringleader of the group, had pressured him into participating. Kid's been a straight-A student before and since his arrest."

"Are all three from the Cincinnati area?"

"Nope. One is from Columbus and the other is from over near Youngstown."

"So, they have no prior connections. How long have they been at the house?"

"Our check fraud boy has been there a year. The boy under protection about four months and the other one got out of rehab about six weeks ago."

"Not long enough to really become a gang then." He turned onto Libby's street, slowing as he came to her drive and pulled in.

"They could be, but they've all had to be employed within the first week of arriving. The rehab graduate has to do a drug test every few days, randomly at Todd's discretion, so he's under a tight leash. The check fraud kid has to report to his parole officer weekly and is taking summer courses on top of working to make up what he missed while in the juvenile detention center."

"So no time to bond. Little time to plan and attack Kyle." He shut off the engine and turned to face her. The streetlamp gave them a little bit of light.

"That's what I'm thinking. I'll check with Todd as to what their activities were tonight if you want me to."

"Let's wait. Sounds like those kids in the house have enough on their plate right now without us getting Todd worked up over something that might not be their fault. I have a feeling I'll be finding out who did this later today."

For a moment he thought she was going to continue the question-and-answer period. He hoped not. If he was right, and the gang that attacked Kyle were members of the football team, it would be best for everyone if he handled the issue quietly and with little outside help. Of course, Gage was going to know immediately who'd been involved, if the condition of Kyle's hands were any indication.

"I'll leave it to your judgment then," Libby finally said. "As long as it doesn't happen again."

There it was. That little bit of defiance she always had when championing an underdog. It was one of the things he'd always loved about her.

He reached out and tucked a wayward strand of her hair behind her ear. "Libby—"

She caught his hand in hers, the street lamp showing the shadow in her eyes. "Deke. I want to be with you, but the phone call about Kyle saved us. We still have some things to discuss before we can be together."

His heart clenched. "I told you everything about Bill's death and my part in it."

"I know. It's just…" She looked away and he could see the unshed tears glistening in her eyes.

"What is it, Libby?" He cupped her chin and turned her face back to his. "You can tell me anything."

She stared into his eyes and swallowed. "Not tonight. It's getting late. Could you maybe come by tomorrow evening?"

He was torn between wanting to insist they have whatever talk she wanted now and relieved that she was giving him time to come to grips with this rekindling of the spark between them. And of course the thought of a spark made him remember that he had to speak at the town hall meeting the next night. "It would be late. I have to appear at the town hall meeting tomorrow night and talk about fire safety."

"I'll be there, too. Could we talk afterwards?" She licked her lips and he found himself thinking more about tasting her again than the meeting, or fires.

He slid his hand along her jaw to the back of her neck. The distance closing between them until her mouth was just a hairsbreadth away from his. "I'd like that very much."

Then he had her in his arms once more. Her soft lips parting beneath his sent heat coursing through his veins like fire coursing through a building. The coolness of her skin beneath his hands and the pressure of her breasts against his chest fueled his need further. The soft little moan that escaped her thrilled him.

We have some things to discuss.

The solemn sound of her voice as she'd spoken those words burst through his growing lust. She'd asked him to wait and he would, even if the effort nearly killed him.

Slowly he eased back on the kiss, releasing her mouth and bracing his forehead against hers. "Damn, baby, you still make me forget everything."

Her hand came to rest on his face, her fingers touching the burn scars on his neck. "You still make me want things I shouldn't."

Sitting back behind the steering wheel once more, he closed his eyes and inhaled her scent. "You'd best get inside or I can't promise I'll wait until tomorrow night to continue this."

He heard the car door open and close before he looked her way again. He watched her all the way to her door and still didn't move, until he saw the living room light come on—same as he had when they dated. Once he was sure she was safe inside her home, he pulled out and headed home.

If he was right, tomorrow was going to be a very interesting day and heads were going to roll.

* * * * *

She was with *him* again.

With a growl he threw the cigarette onto dirt and ground it out under his heel. Exhaling the last of the smoke from his lungs, he pulled another butt from the pack, lit it and inhaled. God, he loved the rush that came with the smoke as it whirled around him and then filled his lungs. Damn, just like he'd loved the smoke of the fire the other night. And the flames. The way they'd moved, almost as if it were an erotic dance the fire was doing just for him.

Closing his eyes, he could see the blue of the flames, the same color as her eyes.

She belonged to him. No one but he deserved such perfection. No one.

Apparently the bastard hadn't heeded his warning. He'd have to send another one. A little closer to home this time.

He took another long drag on the cigarette.

And this time she'd see how he'd do anything to have her. That he had all the power. That he was the master and only he could command the beautiful creature that was the fire. That he could get it to do his bidding.

Even kill for him.

CHAPTER SIXTEEN

"You're sure about this?" Gage asked from across the desk the two of them shared in the coach's office at the high school the next morning.

It was just after the crack of dawn and they sat drinking coffee Deke had picked up at the café on his way over to the school. He hadn't slept well. The dream awakened him again and then he'd lay there, thinking about the evening before with Libby. He'd confessed his part in Bill's death and it hadn't destroyed her.

Instead she'd forgiven him. That was the part of her he'd forgotten about. Her ability to look bullshit in the eye and call it for what it was. He'd also felt there was something more she wanted to talk about. Probably his recovery. He hadn't quite confessed his cowardice in keeping her from seeing his pain.

Maybe something good would come out of it. Hell, her response to his description about Bill's death had not only surprised him, but freed him of some of his guilt. Some, because the dream was still there.

Something about it kept drawing him back to the place where he saw the man dragging the boy into the dark.

"Where'd you go?" Gage's words pulled him back to the problem at hand.

"Sorry. Had a bad night last night, trouble waking up today." He took another swallow of coffee, hoping his friend wouldn't question him more. "And yes, I'll be interested to see what those four look like this morning."

"You're sure it was all four of them?"

He shrugged. "You've seen them, not just on the field, but around town. Thick as ticks on a hound dog."

Gage huffed out a sigh. "Just what I need. Not only do I have to discipline them as their coach, as sheriff I'll have to arrest them for assault. And since Brett Howard's dad is the county DA, that's going to open a whole can of bad shit my direction."

He didn't envy his friend the job of not only arresting the DA's son and his friends, but having to bench four of their best players before the season even started. "I could be wrong."

"Kyle didn't tell you who attacked him?"

"Nope."

Gage filled his mug again. "If he's not going to name his attackers there's little chance he'll want to press charges."

"Libby says the three other guys at Colbert House aren't up to this kind of blitz attack. Besides, it smacks of a gang mentality. That's what's got me thinking it's our guys."

"You think it was some sort of initiation ritual our guys put him through?"

"Could be," a voice said from the door. They both looked over to see Doc Clint standing in the doorway.

"What're you doing here?" Deke asked.

"And what do you mean by *could be*?" Gage asked.

"I'm here," he said, walking in and pulling a chair over to the desk, "because Harriett woke me up at the butt-crack of dawn to handle a problem."

Gage nearly spewed his coffee over the desk. "Harriett had a problem she needed help with?" He and Deke couldn't have been more surprised if Clint had told him the Titanic had surfaced in the Mohican River outside town.

"Yep. Seems your new defensive end was trying to leave my clinic this morning, even if he had to climb out a window."

"He what?" Deke sat straighter in his chair. "You didn't let him, did you?"

"Caught up with him halfway down the block." Clint picked up an empty mug and held it out for Gage to fill with coffee. He took a long drink, sighed with pleasure, then fixed his gaze on Deke. "Kid said he had to be at practice on time or you'd make him do extra laps afterwards. Seems you've made an impression on him. I get the idea he doesn't want to disappoint you, as well as to show his attackers he's tough inside as well as out."

"Well, he can't play if you don't clear him medically."

"That's what I told him." Clint shrugged as he drank more coffee. "Only thing that got him into my truck and back to the clinic."

"Good. He can sit on the sidelines until he's healed enough to play." Deke set his own mug on the desk and leaned back in his chair, lifting both front legs off the floor like he did as a kid. Obviously, there was no question that the kid couldn't practice after the beating he took last night.

Gage nodded his agreement.

"I cleared him medically."

Both front chair legs slammed down hard as Deke came forward to stare at the Doc. "Are you kidding me? Why would you do that?"

Clint held up a hand. "Because other than some bruises, lacerations and dinged up knuckles, there's no real injury to keep him off the field. Hell, he's no more banged up than some of your guys after a game."

"What about his broken nose?" Deke asked.

"Checked his O2 sats. He's oxygenating just fine." Clint gave a shrug and shake of his head. "Kid said it didn't hurt."

"I thought you were watching him for internal injuries." For some reason, the kid coming to practice had him feeling both pride in the kid's guts and determination, and the need to protect him from any real harm.

"That's what I told him last night to keep him at the clinic overnight. Safest place I could think of at the time. Like I said, he can play if he's bent on proving to his teammates he's not easily intimidated."

Deke and Clint stared at each other a moment, then both looked to Gage. As both head coach and sheriff, how they proceeded was ultimately up to him. He seemed to consider the situation a few moments.

"Way I see it, if the kid doesn't want to name his attackers, I can't legally press charges. If he wants to return to practice and Clint's already cleared him medically, I have no real reason to sideline him. So, let's let him play and see how the others react to him."

Deke knew Gage was right, but the need to protect the kid was eating at him. "Okay, but as his defensive coach, he shows one sign of not being up to it and I'm benching his ass."

"Fair enough," Gage said as he stood, the others following suit. A slow grin spread over the Gunslinger's face. "Besides, might be interesting to see how our four wannabe thugs react when their victim shows up ready to play ball."

* * * * *

Kyle sat on the bench in the early morning light, trying not to shiver and remember how warm and comfortable he'd been in that bed under that quilt over at the clinic.

Maybe he should've stayed there for the day. The doc said he could.

No. He knew how to handle these guys. You let them know they beat you down and you were their punk for the rest of the time you were in town. No matter what, he was going to be out on that field letting them know each time he took the ball away that they hadn't hurt him last night.

While he waited for the coaches and the other members of the team to arrive he took inventory of his body.

Every muscled ached, along with all his injuries. He hadn't pissed blood at any time during the night, so he knew the kick to his side hadn't damaged his kidney. That knowledge had come to him at the ripe old age of ten in the first group home the state had tried him in. This morning the doc told him that his ribs weren't broken, but he already knew that. He'd kept his elbows in tight like he'd learned when he was twelve. His nose felt like it was three times bigger than usual, but other than being clogged with dried blood, it hurt way less since the doc reset it. *And damn hadn't that hurt?* His vision was clear, despite the punch the lazy wide receiver had dealt his left eye. Guy could take lessons on punching from his old man—that is, if the bastard was still breathing.

Everything else was a cut or bruise, and he knew from experience they'd heal with time. He was just going to hurt until they did.

That's what he tried to tell that nurse—Harriett…that was her name. The look she'd given him when she found him sitting in the chair tying up his laces had almost gotten him back in the bed, it wasn't mean. More like disbelief that he wasn't doing what she'd told him. Apparently no one in town had ever defied the old lady. He'd been getting around doctors and nurses for years. One nurse with an attitude wasn't keeping him in bed if he didn't want to be. She'd huffed and puffed at him all the way out the door like some irate dragon.

He smiled at the image, then winced as his cut lip pulled with the effort. The taste of fresh blood seeped across his tongue.

Dammit.

He held his hand over it to stop the bleeding before the doc and the coaches came out. He'd gotten past the nurse, convinced the doc he was okay to play, but he had a suspicion Coach Reynolds wasn't going to cut him any slack. One wince, one sign that he wasn't one hundred percent, his ass would be sitting on this bench all week.

Yeah, he hurt like hell, but it was going to be worth the effort to show those four that it would take more than an ambush in the alley to get him to quit.

The door to the coaches' office opened and out walked Coach Justice, the doc and finally, Coach Reynolds. The trio made a beeline straight for him and he stood, forcing his body to be as straight as possible.

"Gordon," Coach Justice said, stopping in front of

him, "Doc Clint says you're medically sound to practice."

"Yes, sir," he said, moving his busted lower lip as little as possible.

"And Coach Reynolds says you refuse to name your attackers. Still feel the same way this morning?"

"Too dark to really see them, Coach." He forced himself to stare straight at the big man while telling that lie. Even though both coaches had treated him fairly so far, he'd had mistrust of the law drilled into him. Hard to unlearn that lesson. Besides, who would take his word, the word of a virtual stranger, over the words of the home-grown football heroes?

Coach Justice exchanged a look with Coach Reynolds. Deke nodded and Kyle knew they weren't going to push the issue.

As they'd been talking the rest of the team streamed onto the field in small groups. As each group got a look at him, they'd whisper, some staring openly at him. He'd laugh at their shock if it wouldn't hurt him so bad.

Finally the last group of four approached the circle around the coaches and bench.

Kyle looked each one of them in the eye. Two—the quarterback and wide receiver—sported black eyes to match his. Good. He'd hoped he'd landed a few good punches before they dropped him to the ground. The redhead who played running back but had good enough hands to catch passes held his side like he'd been kicked there, which he had. The last one, his defensive teammate Mike Cohn, had a busted lip to match his own.

The first three looked surprised to see him standing there, then dodged their eyes sideways.

Yeah. Bitches. It'll take more than you guys to beat me down.

Cohn looked him right in the eye then nodded.

Well, okay. At least one of them wasn't hatin' on him anymore.

"…since some of you need some extra outlet for the natural aggression football gives you, we're running laps after practice," Coach Justice was saying. "Now get started on your warmups."

As the team started to spread out on the field, Coach Reynolds held up his hand. "Howard, Tanner, Gordon, Reilly and Cohn to me for a meeting first."

Schooling his features to show no emotion, Kyle didn't wait for the others and stepped over to the coach.

Once the rest of the team was out of earshot, Deke motioned for the five of them to take a knee in front of him. He didn't say anything at first, just looked each one of them over with a look that said he was pissed-off enough to take someone's head off.

"Gordon refuses to name who attacked him, so I'm going to assume y'all ran into the rogue group of strangers who apparently wants to destroy this team. And I'm assuming it was some unknown strangers, because if I or Coach Reynolds learn that any member of this team is beating the shit out of another member of the team, we'll be forced to suspend said players for the entire year."

That snapped four heads up to stare at Deke. Kyle had never taken his eyes off him.

"The Gunslinger and I know that scholarships are on the line for you seniors. So, from now on, you five are going to be sure nothing, and I mean nothing, happens to another member of this team, down to the water boys and trainers until the end of the season. Do I make myself clear?"

"Yes, sir!" they said in unison.

"Good. Get your asses out on that field and show me you deserve to stay here."

Kyle grabbed his helmet and shoved it on his head, jogging just behind the others, glad the coach had included him in the lecture and not made him the reason for it. The guy had street smarts.

Once they were near the others, Cohn slowed down as if waiting for him.

Great. A side threat. There always was one with bullies.

"Sorry about last night," the linebacker said.

"Yeah. Right," he muttered, not stopping as the kid fell into a jog beside him.

"No, really, dude. Besides, you held your own." He pointed to his lip and gave a half laugh, then winced.

Kyle took a spot in line. "Might want to avoid laughing for a few days. Takes that long for it to heal up."

"I get that."

"No more talking, ladies, unless you want five extra laps added on," Coach Justice said.

Not risking being the reason for more exercise, Kyle dropped down and started stretching with the rest of the team. Cohn had offered an olive branch. Maybe he should take it.

* * * * *

Memories hit Libby the moment she stepped onto the edge of the running track that encircled the football field.

Years ago, she used to sneak onto the field in the mornings to watch Deke do his warmups and the first practice of the day. If anyone asked, she would've said it was because she wanted to be close to her boyfriend. The truth was she liked watching him work out. The way his gym shorts clung to his buttocks as he stretched and ran, the way the T-shirt rode up to show glimpses of his abdomen and ribs as he reached for a pass. The sweat glistening on his tanned skin.

Watching the young Adonis that was Deacon Reynolds had sent her teenage body into such a frenzy she often had to remind herself to breathe. Was it any wonder that her heart fell so hard and fast for him? And how thrilling it had been to know she was the only one who could touch that body so intimately?

And now?

Damn if he didn't still make her heart race. Gone was the lean body of a young man, replaced with the more mature, firmer body of a man. A man who worked regularly to keep his body fit for duty. And damn if the shorts still didn't mold themselves to his still-firm ass.

"Doc Clint must be losing his skills."

Libby jumped and turned to see Lorna and Rachel standing just behind her, both of them watching the field.

"Harriett said he cleared Kyle to come play ball," she said turning back to watch the practice, concentrating on finding Kyle's form and off Deke's backside.

"Harriett ain't any happier about it than I am. She's going to be giving the doc hell for days over this, you can bet on it."

Libby tried not to grin at the suffering the nurse would cause her boss. "What are you doing here? Aren't you supposed to be up at the Peaches 'N Cream for morning service?"

"Got up early. Had a hankering to make pecan cinnamon rolls today before checking on the boy over at the clinic before bringing breakfast out here for the team. Pete and the girls can handle the morning rush for a little while. Didn't think I'd be wanting to smack Clint, Gage and Deacon's heads together for letting Kyle get hurt worse."

"Look, there he is."

Rachel pointed to the pair running towards them as

the ball sailed through the air. Just as the ball got near them, Kyle twisted into the other player, knocking him down and snatching the ball before it hit the ground where they both lay for a minute. Kyle moved first. Slowly, guarding his side with the arm holding the ball. Then he held out a hand to the taller player still on the ground. The receiver hesitated a moment before putting his hand in Kyle's. He rose and the morning sun picked that moment to shine on the pair.

Libby sucked in her breath.

He had a black eye nearly as bad as the one on Kyle's face.

Deke had been right. The members of Kyle's own team had been behind the attack on him last night. She clenched her hands into fists, wanting to march out there and give the boy a piece of her mind. They could've injured Kyle much worse, or even killed him. For what? Some male macho-ism or slighted egos?

"Well, I'll be damned," Lorna said beside her as they watched the other kid pat Kyle on the back and say something. The pair grinned at each other and ran back to the main part of the team.

"Guys," muttered Rachel, shaking her head at what had just occurred. "One minute they're beating the snot out of each other, the next they're laughing like best friends."

"Yep. They're haven't got much sense until they hit twenty-five, and even then it's still questionable. Time to get their breakfast out." Lorna said, turning to leave,

Rachel on her heels.

Libby smiled at the pair. With Lorna as a mother, she doubted Rachel had one impractical romantic bone in her body. Maybe she'd be lucky and wait to fall in love until she was old enough to handle the heartbreak.

Did one ever handle heartbreak well? What was the alternative? Never trust someone with your heart again? Shut yourself up from love? Live in loneliness and fear of being hurt again? Been there. Done that for an entire decade. It sucked.

Looking back at the field, she saw Deke had his players gathered around him, holding up a tablet and pointing at it, then back at a couple of his players. He was a good teacher. She could tell that by the way the players listened to him. He was patient and she knew he cared about the boys, especially for Kyle. She'd seen it last night and the way he'd talked with him the night of the fire.

He was coming out of his own isolation. He wanted to reconnect with her, but would he still want to when he learned what she'd kept from him all these years?

She inhaled and exhaled, willing the ache in her chest to ease. Her mother hadn't raised her to be a coward. She'd hidden from this long enough. Tonight, no matter what, she'd be telling him what they'd both lost.

CHAPTER SEVENTEEN

Shrugging on his T-shirt, Kyle hurried to dress at his locker. Even though the other guys were walking around in their boxers and some of them naked from the shower, he'd learned early on to be ready to book it out of a building if trouble started.

"So, what, our colors going to be black and blue now?" one of the linemen joked, looking at his, Brett's and Tanner's black eyes.

"Maybe, want one to match?" Redheaded Conner Riley said, getting in the guy's face.

The lineman threw up his hands, palms out. "Hey, no offense. I mean, kinda looks cool because you're tough guys."

"Yeah, besides," Cohn said, coming over to drape one arm around Riley's shoulder. "In a few days our colors are going to be purple, green and yellow."

The locker room filled with laughter.

Kyle smiled, then sat on the bench to tie his shoelaces. He had to be at the café in fifteen minutes for his first shift to start. Lorna had him working mornings after practice and again in the evening. He'd seen her, Rachel and Ms. Wilson standing on the edge of the field earlier and serving breakfast to the guys after practice ended. If she knew he was well enough to make it to practice, then she'd expect him to make it to work. And for some reason, people in this town seemed to care about him enough to make him want to live up to their expectations.

He toweled off his hair and ran his fingers through it real quick. Picking up the towel and his backpack, he slammed his locker door. He tossed the towel in the hamper with the other wet ones and headed out the locker room door, stopping short when he saw Tanner and Brett Howard standing on the sidewalk smoking and blocking his exit.

"Good practice," Brett said, exhaling smoke.

"Thanks," he said, approaching them slowly, he was ready this time. They attacked and he was making like a train straight out of there.

Tanner stepped towards him, holding out the pack of cigarettes. "Want one?"

Kyle shook his head. "No, thanks. Those things killed my parents." *Literally.*

"Yeah, the big C," the quarterback said. "My dad keeps telling me about it, even when he's lighting up." He took another drag on the cancer stick. "Sorry about last night. Coach is right, we need to keep our attitude for just the other team."

"Yeah." *Where the hell was this leading? Just a peace offering, or were they setting him up for something worse?*

"Besides, if I have to work that hard to keep you from taking the ball, just think how easy I'll have it against the other teams' sorry defenses," Tanner said and grinned.

Kyle nodded, lifting one corner of his mouth in response. Maybe it was what it looked like, teammates accepting him. Not as a best bud, but as at least a member of the team.

The door behind him opened and the other pair of his attackers approached. Out of habit, he moved to the side, keeping all of them where he could see them.

"Coach Justice sees you guys with those things and he'll bench you before the season starts," Riley said, coming up to take a drag off the one Tanner offered him. "Especially after Coach Reynolds' talk on fire safety yesterday."

Deke had started out the evening practice last night with a lecture on responsibility, looking out for neighbors, including the Amish community, the dry season and fire safety. At first Kyle had thought yeah, this guy is just doing his job. But as the coach kept talking, he knew he believed what he preached, that it was everyone's duty to protect their community from fires, smoldering cigarettes apparently a problem out in the rural areas. It wasn't just his words that said he respected the dangers of fire. The scars on the man's

neck and jaw spoke that he'd been in at least one fire—
a bad one.

Kyle's stomach clenched. Every time he got a look
at those scars, he wondered, *had his old man been the
cause of the fire that injured the chief? Was it the one
he'd been at? The one he'd watched the old man start?
The one when he learned just what a monster his father
was?*

"Don't worry, I've got water to put it out," Tanner
said, holding up a bottle of water.

An alarm sounded and Kyle grabbed the cell phone
Colbert House had provided him as a new resident.
Shit. He had ten minutes to get across town to the café.

"What's up?" Cohn asked, the others looking at him.

"Gotta go. Work in ten minutes." He started down
the sidewalk at a trot.

"Hey, wait up," someone called from behind him.

He turned to see Mike Cohn, his linebacker and
squad captain, jogging his way. "You're gonna have to
run like hell to get there. Let me give you a ride."

Kyle stopped and studied the other guy. Seemed to
be in earnest.

Might as well take a chance and get the ride. Deke's
words from the night before sounded in his head.
*Sometimes you just got to take the chance and trust
people.*

* * * * *

The Dye Right was hopping when Libby entered at lunchtime. Aretha Franklin played overhead. Blow dryers and stand dryers were running full force. Above it all could be heard the chatter and laughter of women enjoying each other's company.

"Hey, Libby," Twylla called as she came around the corner carrying a load of clean towels. "What can we do for you today?"

"Hey, Twylla. I was hoping I could get a pedicure today. My toes are a mess."

Twylla nodded to an empty chair up front. "Have a seat and let me see if Sylvie has some time open. Want a foot massage to go with the pretty toes?"

"That sound wonderful, if she has time."

As the shop owner strode down the center of the shop handing out towels to her stylists, Libby took the empty chair and picked up the gossip magazine on the table next to it. She felt rather frivolous taking her lunch hour to come get her toenails done. Rarely did she spoil herself with pedicures at the salon. Her frugal self couldn't justify the expense, so she usually took care of it herself at home. But while she'd been working on case file reports something her mother used to say kept playing over and over in her head.

A good pedicure could give a woman confidence and confidence gives you courage. Courage to do anything. That's something men will never understand.

Courage. That's what she needed.

Facing Deacon tonight to tell him her secret would

take all the extra courage she could muster. So here she was, waiting to get her toes colored blood-red. A foot massage would relax her and help build up more courage, right?

"If you can give her about ten minutes, Sylvie says she'll have time to take you," Twylla said, standing behind the reception desk and flipping through the old-fashioned paper schedule.

Libby smiled as she flipped through the pages of the magazine. Computers were making their way into Westen. PCs and laptops in the homes and businesses, especially over at the courthouse. Teens with their smartphones. Tablets everywhere. But some things would never change. Lorna's antique cash register over at the Peaches 'N Cream. Twylla's paper appointment book. And that was what she loved about Westen. The old and the new mixing together.

"And he came home with a black eye," a high-pitched voice carried over the noise.

Libby peered over the top of her magazine in the direction of the voice. Yep. Tiffany Howard, the DA's socialite-wannabe wife.

"What happened?" the little brunette stylist, Cara, asked.

Just the opening Tiffany was looking for.

"I was sure someone had beaten poor Brett," she said a little louder so her audience would grow, "but Kent said it was probably nothing more than a football injury. Seriously, I know Brett is the best quarterback ever in this town, but I worry about him getting injured."

"Aren't the sheriff and fire chief the coaches this year?" the stylist asked as she took the straight iron to the fake blonde's unruly curls.

"Well, yes. And you'd think they'd be more careful with our children, but honestly, they aren't really trained coaches, are they?"

Libby saw red. She knew the truth. The woman's son had tried to bully a new team member who'd stood up for himself, not gotten injured in practice and certainly not under Deke and Gage's watch. Slowly, she closed the magazine, sharpening her focus on the other woman.

Tiffany let out a long, dramatic sigh. "And I can't believe they have Cleetus as one of their assistants. I mean, seriously. What could that man possibly teach our children?"

Out of nowhere, Sylvie came barreling up the aisle, knocking Cara's arm and causing her to jerk on the flat iron.

"Oww!" Tiffany yelled as her head was jerked sideways.

"I'm so sorry," Cara said, quickly removing the flat iron and looking ready to panic.

"Oh, no," Sylvie said, dramatically, feigning surprise at her actions, her Appalachian accent getting a little thicker. "I'm so sorry, Ms. Howard. I just don't know what got into me. I'm such a klutz, sometimes. Not like you, you're always so graceful and beautiful."

Libby quickly opened the magazine and hid her smile behind it hoping no one could see it tremble as she laughed.

"Oh, well. No real harm done Sylvie." Tiffany said, her voice softening as she suddenly realized everyone in the room was watching to see what she was going to say. Her husband was a public figure and it was her job to keep him in the community's good graces.

"How about a nice glass of sweet tea," Twylla said, coming up with a crystal goblet full of her special tea and getting between Tiffany and Sylvie.

"Why thank you, Twylla. You know just how to soothe a client's nerves."

While Tiffany took the glass Cara exchanged an eye-roll with Sylvie then went back to work on the curls.

"Hey, Miss Libby," Sylvie said as she approached, her eyes twinkling and her cheeks pink. "Let's get you right back to the nail area."

Libby swallowed her own mirth and set aside the magazine to follow the pixie stylist to the back of the salon. "I hope my sudden need for a pedicure didn't make you rush too much, Sylvie," she said just as they passed Cara's station and the now-much-more-subdued DA's wife.

"Well, I was in a hurry to get you going, you being on a lunch break and all," Sylvie said over her shoulder with a wink.

She opened the door to the nail room and waited for

Libby to enter first. Tywlla had wanted this to be a restful spot for her clients, separated from the rest of the salon by glass walls. The door closed and only the sound of peaceful jazz music could be heard.

"I hope your run-in with Cara wasn't really caused by my adding to your workload," Libby said as she sat in one of the three leather pedicure chairs and took off her dress sandals.

"Oh, no. I did that very intentionally," Sylvie said, her cheeks getting pinker and her lips tightening. "That woman was saying the worst things about the sheriff, Chief Reynolds and Cleetus. Someone just had to get her to stop and poor Cara couldn't afford to say anything. So I just thought I'd step in."

Libby distinctly heard the little woman's voice soften over Cleetus' name. She'd seen them together the night of the fire, eating pie in the café. Apparently Sylvie had a soft spot for the big deputy. *Wasn't that interesting?*

"And besides, for all her highfalutin' ways, she's a lousy tipper."

Libby snorted a laugh and made a mental note to be a good tipper where Sylvie was concerned.

"Besides, you'll be my last appointment today. I'm going house hunting this afternoon," Sylvie said as she set a bowl of warm water at Libby's feet. Gently she picked up Libby's feet and set them into the water one at a time.

"Ah." Libby couldn't help the sigh as the warm,

soapy water encased her feet. "That feel heavenly."

"Just wait until I start the massage, you're gonna love it."

She bet she would. "So what has you out looking for houses?"

Sylvie sat on a rolling stool and slipped up close. "Well, I've been staying over at the Tumbolt sisters' boarding house, but I'd really like a little place of my own. They're sweet and all, but a girl needs her privacy, you know? Especially after taking care of other women all day long."

Libby could imagine. Ida and Lucy Tumbolt were in their seventies and had been running the boarding house two blocks north of Main Street and the heart of Westen for nearly fifty years. She stopped by monthly for a spot of tea and to check on the ladies. They did love to chat and poor Sylvie probably wanted nothing more than peace and quiet after a day at the noisy salon.

"Any place you're looking at in particular?" she asked, resisting the urge to purr as Sylvie massaged her left foot. The firm strokes and organic lavender cream making her almost melt into the chair.

"There's a few rental places around town. I need something close by. Not too far a walk to here. That's important since I don't have a car yet."

Twylla had told Libby that Sylvie had stepped off the bus outside town, walked to the Dye Right with her suitcase in hand and promptly asked for a job. The salon owner had liked her spunk, not to mention her orange, yellow and red spiked hair, hiring on the spot. Libby like her, too.

An idea hit her.

"You know Chief Reynolds' mother moved to a seniors' center down in South Carolina last spring. I believe her little house is up for rent."

"How far is it?" Sylvie asked, drying Libby's foot then lifting the right one out of the tub to begin her magic on it.

"Only a few blocks west of downtown." She smiled at Sylvie. "I believe Deputy Cleetus could show you exactly where."

The twinkle returned to Sylvie's eyes. "I believe I'll just see if he's free this afternoon."

* * * * *

Cleetus stared at the spreadsheet on his computer screen. Ever since Ms. Bobby came to town and showed him how to use the computer, he'd started listing things on spreadsheets. He could stare at written reports forever and not see any pattern in the information. But put it in columns and lines and it was like someone hit his *on* switch. All the pieces would fall into place, the pattern coming into focus. Sometimes it was as simple as accidents happening ten miles out of town on certain days of the week, or a ring of candy bar thefts that turned out to be a confused elderly man with diabetes. He always saw the pattern.

He'd been sure once he put all the reports of kerosene sales into the computer, the pattern would stand out. Only it hadn't. Nothing. No one seemed to be buying extra kerosene this summer. And since the weather had been so dry, no one worried about needing fuel for their backup generators this year either. There had to be something he was missing. Something just out of his reach. He looked closer. The numbers and words shifted, grew sharper—the bell on the office door rang.

The puzzle piece disappeared again.

"Dang it."

"Is there something wrong, Deputy?"

The soft southern drawl sounded behind him and he jumped out of his chair, nearly knocking it into Sylvie. He stopped it with one hand. "Miss Sylvie, didn't see you come in the office, ma'am."

"You were concentrating so hard on that computer screen I hated to surprise you," she said, even though the twinkle in her blue eyes said she'd actually enjoyed surprising him.

A slow heat filled his chest. No lady had ever wanted to surprise him, let alone tease him about things.

Sylvie did.

The clearing of a throat at the other side of the sheriff's office where Wes sat working reminded him he was still on duty. "Is there something I can do for you, ma'am?"

"I was wondering if you could give me a lift over to look at a house to rent. Miss Libby said Chief Reynolds was looking to rent out his mother's old house."

She laid her arm on his and Cleetus' knees wobbled.

"I know you're awful busy and everything, but Miss Libby said you'd know right where it was and I'd sure hate to get lost looking for it." She smiled at him, dimples and all, then looked up through those big dark lashes.

He swallowed hard. At that minute, she could've asked him to take her to the moon and he'd have said yes.

"He'd be more than happy, too, Miss Sylvie," Wes said, coming to lean one hip on Cleetus' desk and giving them both a smile. "Wouldn't you, Cleetus?"

"Um, I was supposed to get this information to Sheriff Justice," he said, torn between helping the little lady staring so sweetly up at him and doing his job.

Wes handed him his baseball hat and sunglasses from the side of the desk where he always kept them. "Go on, Cleetus. I can finish the report and get it to Gage."

"You're sure?" he asked, even as he slipped the ball cap on his head. Gage's daddy had always wanted them to wear cowboy-style hats and full uniforms, but since Gage had taken over as the town sheriff, he'd relaxed the regulations, allowing the deputies to wear jeans and baseball hats, as long as the hats had the official sheriff's department logo on the top.

"I'm sure. Get on out of here," Wes said, sliding into the desk chair and looking at the spreadsheet Cleetus had left open.

Cleetus reached into the top drawer and pulled out a large key ring full of keys. He smiled down as Miss Sylvie slipped her hand in the crook of his arm and he led her over to the office door. Holding it open, he looked over at Wes. "Tell Gage there's something weird in that sheet, but I just can't figure out what it is... maybe I should stay—"

Wes swiveled the chair around to face him. "Cleetus, I've got this. Besides, when a beautiful lady asks you to do her a favor, you don't keep her waiting."

Cleetus couldn't help the big grin that split his lips or the heat that filled his cheeks as he joined Sylvie on the sidewalk. Wes was right. It wasn't every day when someone as sweet as Miss Sylvie asked him to help her. Whatever he'd started to see in the spreadsheet could wait until he got back.

* * * * *

Hidden in the copse of trees that flanked the detached garage, he stood outside the mid-century craftsman cottage. His view of the street and side yard unobstructed. Close enough to watch the fire dance its way up the path of kerosene he'd laid, but far enough away to escape and blend in when the crowd gathered. And there would be a crowd to watch his masterpiece.

He'd be sure of it. He had the fire station number plugged into his phone. Once they were here, he knew his goddess would come to see what he'd created.

And what a better way to show his adversary who was really in control, than burning down his childhood home?

After his goddess saw who the more powerful man was, she'd never look at the other man again.

He tried not to giggle at the idea of besting the big man. And if he timed it right, they should find the little surprise he hid inside the house. Something that would have them looking for answers to the secret he'd uncovered.

A sound on the street caught his attention.

A truck drove past.

Now. He had to start the fire dance now before someone saw him.

He pulled out the cellphone and dialed.

Less than fifty yards away, another phone sounded.

The spark shone in the shadow of the bush where he'd hidden it.

Flames the blue of the goddess' eyes appeared. Quickly, they danced up the path to the house.

* * * * *

"I really appreciate you taking time from your responsibilities to show me the house. I wouldn't have known which one it was. So many of them look the same."

Cleetus smiled as he pulled his truck to a stop in

front of the one-and-a-half story house. Sylvie hadn't stopped talking the entire short trip over to the old house Deke's mama was renting out. Not that he minded. Sylvie's soft southern accent sounded sweet in his ear. He could listen to it all day long. And when she'd smile up at him with those big dimples, he had trouble finding words to answer her. So best she did most of the talking.

"It's my pleasure, ma'am." He turned off the engine, hopped out and hurried around the truck to help her out. She was so tiny, he'd almost had to lift her up into the truck cab back at the sheriff's office.

"You have the nicest manners, Cleetus," she said as she slipped her tiny hand with the bright orangey-red nails into his. Everything about her was small. Heck, when she landed on the pavement beside him, her head barely came to his shoulders, and that was including all the spikey tips of her hair.

"My mama always insisted I be extra careful around ladies, me being so big and all."

Now why did he say that? Stupid. Reminding him how big and awkward he was. He let go of her hand so she wouldn't get scared of him holding it, even though he liked how nice it felt in his.

"Well, I find it right nice." The smile she gave him eased some of his embarrassment. Then she started up the walk to the house. "This was Chief Reynolds' mother's home?"

"Yes, ma'am," he said, slowing his long stride so she

wouldn't have to run to keep up with him. "Miss Callie, Deke's mom, moved to a seniors' community in South Carolina a year ago and Deke's had Joe from over at the hardware store restoring the inside."

He pulled out the large ring of keys and flipped through it until he found the one with the house number taped on it.

"You have a key to the house?" Sylvie asked, watching him. "Isn't that a little unusual?"

"This is the ring that has keys to all the empty properties in and around town. After last spring, the Sheriff got all the realtors and the bank to make a copy of the keys for us. Said we needed to keep a closer eye on what might be happening in them." He opened the door, then stood back to let her pass. He liked the small whiff of spicy scent that hit him whenever she walked past. "Once a property is rented or sold, we give the occupant the key."

"I heard about the meth lab outside of town. It was in an old abandoned farm, wasn't it?" she asked, then stopped and stared wide-eyed, her lips in a perfect "O" for a moment. "Oh, my, this is so lovely."

All thoughts of last spring's calamity gone, Cleetus leaned against the wall and watched Sylvie walk into the living room, her high heels clicking on the hardwood floors. She ran her hands along the wainscoting and then the big mantle over the fireplace like she was stroking a favorite pet. Suddenly, he felt warm all over.

Sylvie walked over to the corner of the room, lifting up some kind of cloth and looking at it curiously. "How did this get here?"

Her question had him pushing off the wall to see what she held. Then the smell hit him.

Something was burning.

He changed course and marched towards the kitchen, the smell of gas burning his nose.

"What is it?" Sylvie asked, stepping up behind him.

He didn't answer her, just shook his head, focusing like a coon dog on a hunt in the woods, following the scent.

Not gasoline. Not natural gas. Something stronger.

"Kerosene," he muttered.

At the kitchen door, his foot slipped on something wet on the tile floors. He grabbed the counter to keep from sliding onto his knees. Outside the big picture window behind the sink, a trail of fire snaked up the backyard.

A face appeared for a moment in the smoke, then was gone.

In a whoosh, flames shot up the back of the house.

"Dear God!" Sylvie whispered behind him.

"Out! Get out now," he shouted, turning and pushing her towards the door.

The window and back door blew in, and smoke rolled through the room. Choking, turning everything dark. Then flames flared up. Someone had doused the kitchen with kerosene.

Without thinking, Cleetus picked Sylvie up in his arms and ran like he was chasing down a quarterback towards the front door.

Just as she wrenched it open, a rumble sounded overhead.

The house shook.

Suddenly, they were shoved by some unseen force through the door.

Cleetus tried to turn as he hit the ground, pushing Sylvie away from the blast.

The windows shattered.

Sylvie screamed.

He looked up just in time to see the door headed like a bullet toward his head.

The world went black.

CHAPTER EIGHTEEN

"What's up, Mike?" Deke said as he hit the Bluetooth feature of his phone. Driving back into Westen's town limits, he'd just finished doing a drive-through of the Amish area of the county, happily finding nothing suspicious or out of the ordinary there.

"I got to thinking about that arsonist case you had me looking into right after your injury," Mike Feeney said over the speakerphone.

"Yeah? What about it?" Deke tightened his fingers around the truck's steering wheel.

"You said you killed him?"

Deke inhaled slowly, then let it out. "In a manner of speaking. I didn't pull a trigger, but thanks to your information, the police were able to track him down to where he lived. Bastard had it rigged to set fire. Killed him and his wife."

"Yeah. That's the thing that's bothering me. The guy had a son." Mike sounded thoughtful.

"I know. A kid of about six at the time. We found

him out in the woods behind the house the next morning." God he hated thinking about what that poor kid went through all night in the forest alone, in the snow. "We were lucky he didn't get some kind of frostbite from the exposure."

"Do you think the kid could be copying his dad's signature?"

"Anything's possible." The image of the arsonist dragging the kid away from the industrial fire that killed Bill filled his head. "I know of at least one fire the kid was at. Why?"

"Thought I should check it out, just to be sure we're not looking at a fire-for-revenge scenario with the kid."

"What did you find?" Deke really didn't like the way this conversation was going.

"Funny thing, I can find where the kid entered the foster care program as an orphan, but it's as if the system completely swallowed him up. They could've changed his name. It's as if the kid was placed in the Witness Protection program or something."

Now the hairs on Deke's arms were standing at attention as he drove past the football field on his way to the downtown area. An image of Kyle Gordon popped into his head. "Mike, any idea what the kid's name was back then?"

"Last name was Harkin. The father was Leo Harkin."

There was a long pause and Deke could hear papers being shuffled in the background. He had a feeling he already knew what Mike was going to say.

"The kid was named Kyle."

* * * * *

Stretched out flat on her office sofa, Libby dangled her feet over the arm like when she was a teen. Funny what blood-red toenails and a thorough foot massage could do for a woman's spirits. When she went into the Dye Right, she'd been anxious, on edge, knowing she had to face her own past with Deke. Afterwards, she'd felt so good that she'd given Ashley the rest of the day off and decided to spend the afternoon reading files and studying her toes in the glints of later-afternoon sun shining on them.

Whatever Twylla was paying Sylvie, it wasn't enough. The girl had magic hands.

And she'd repaid the pixie nail expert by giving her an excuse to spend the day with Cleetus.

Libby let out a giggle.

They were so opposite of each other.

Sylvie was tiny, perky and chattered on like a child on a sugar rush. But she didn't gossip like some of the other stylists and had been a blessing to Twylla's growing shop. Cleetus, well, he was one mountain of a man. He didn't talk a lot. In fact, he didn't really say much to her besides, *Morning, ma'am,* or *Hello, ma'am.* And yet, he was the gentlest of men. She'd seen him with the town's elderly residents, carrying groceries to the car or helping them safely across the street. He'd even brought more than one aging parent home in his cruiser when he thought they were confused. Yes, Cleetus deserved a woman with a heart of gold and Libby suspected Sylvie might just be perfect for him.

A knock sounded on her office door.

Ashley must've forgotten something.

Setting aside the file on the table by the sofa, she smoothed her skirt into place and padded barefoot over to the door. "What did you forget?" she asked as she opened it, only to find Deke standing on the other side.

"How sexy your toenails were painted red," he said, staring down at her feet.

"Deke. I thought you were Ashley I decided to give her the afternoon off since I had no appointments. Thought I'd relax a little bit."

"I can see that." He smiled a half-smile, which made her heart take a little leap.

"Come on in." She hurried to open the door and stepped back so he could enter.

He had other ideas. Instead of walking past her, he came closer, like a tiger stalking its prey. Sliding one hand around her to pull her up close, he traced his other hand over her arm to loosen her hold on the door and pushed it closed. "Did I ever tell you how turned on I got whenever your painted your toes?"

She smiled up at him. "Why yes, I believe you did."

He nipped at her lips, his eyes hot with desire. "And

did I ever tell you my favorite color?"

She leaned in close, wrapping her arms around his neck, kissing him a little deeper, letting her tongue tease his a moment before pulling back. "I believe that would be fire-engine red."

He leaned back to look down between them at her toes. She wiggled them so they'd glint in the sunlight.

"And what color would you say those are?"

"I believe Sylvie called it…fire-engine red."

With a low growl that sounded even sexier with his raspy voice, he crushed her to him and covered her lips with his. She melted into the powerful feel of his body against hers, all the toned muscle holding her like she was everything in the world and he'd die without her. And with that the last hold on her heart snapped and she lost herself in the feeling of being home. Home, with Deke. Where her heart had always belonged.

One hand gripping his shoulders while she slid the other up into the short, dark-blonde hair, she moaned into his mouth.

Like kindling, he bent her back and his hand slipped down to cup her ass, pulling her in tighter. His full erection pressing into her stomach like a branding iron through their clothes. And why did they still have their clothes on? She slid her hand down between them to grasp the hem of his polo shirt and pulled it up. He released her long enough for her to get the thing off his body.

Sucking in her breath at the sight of his scars in the

daylight, she laid her hand over them, his heart beating right beneath her hand. Tears filled her eyes.

"You could've died," she whispered. Yes, she'd known how close he'd come. In her head. But now her heart understood how much more she could've lost that night.

"But I didn't, sweetheart." He laid his hand over her cheek.

She looked up at him through her watery eyes. Her fingers lightly caressing the scars. "The pain you must've suffered…all alone."

"I screamed, Libby," he murmured, laying his forehead against hers. "Every time they had to do a treatment. Every damn time. I couldn't handle it. And I couldn't let you hear that. I couldn't do that to you. That's why…" He swallowed hard and she raised her other hand up to stroke his face.

"That's the other reason why you wouldn't let me come visit, isn't it?"

He nodded.

Tenderly, she wrapped her arms around him and led him over to her sofa. He collapsed down in her arms. This strong, brave man needed her. She held him to her chest, felt the silent wracking of the sobs he kept inside, the tension of his muscles beneath her hands as he tried to hold on to that external veneer of courage he'd shown the world for so long.

He protected so many people. Who protected him?

He was hers to protect. Always had been.

"It's okay, Deacon," she murmured as she held him close. "I'm here. I've got you."

And still she held him. Even after his body relaxed in her arms.

A low rumble sounded outside. Libby glanced out the window at the clouds in the sky, wondering if they were finally going to get some rain.

Slowly, he raised up and sat back on the couch. "I'm sorry. I didn't mean to break down like a little kid all over you."

"I didn't mind," she said, turning to face him.

He gave a half strangled laugh. "It's not what I came here for, that's for sure."

"What did you stop by for?"

He stood, retrieved his shirt and pulled it back on.

So much for getting physical. Dang it.

"Is this about Kyle? Did you want to talk to me about what happened at practice today? I did notice that several of your prime players had unusual cuts and bruises."

"Yes, it's about Kyle, but not his injuries or who might've been involved in the beating." Deke sat down again, keeping a little distance between them this time. Then he ran a hand over his face.

A tension started low in Libby's abdomen. Whatever Deacon was here to talk to her about, it had him tense. "What is it, Deacon?"

"I need you to see if you can get that seal on Kyle's records lifted."

"I'd need a very, *very* good reason. No juvenile judge is just going to lift that seal, especially if it's been put on there to protect someone who is still a minor."

Deke turned slightly and took her hand in his. "Remember when I told you Bill and I went back into that building because we were told the arsonist had a kid with him?"

A cold chill settled on Libby. "The same boy you found after the arsonist died in the house fire a year later?"

"Yes. Mike Feeney tried to locate the boy after our fire the other night. He couldn't. The kid has basically disappeared." Deke stared deep into her eyes and she could read the concern in his deep-brown eyes.

"And you think Kyle is that boy?" Not the strong, responsible young man she'd gotten to know the past few days. Surely not.

"The boy's name was Kyle Harkin," Deke said, squeezing her hand a little tighter. "We have to consider the possibility that his records were sealed because some judge was trying to protect him from his father's past."

"And you think he could be the arsonist?"

"I don't know. He came to town and suddenly we have an arson fire. What if he learned from his father how to set the fires? What if the firebug is in his genes?"

"You can't believe that, can you?"

He shook his head. "I don't want to. That kid has

been through a lot and seems to have come out for the better. But I have the whole community's safety in my hands. I have to know if he's possibly the one responsible for that fire."

"Just because he was that arsonist's son, doesn't mean he set the fire," she said.

"Elizabeth, I *need* to know." he said. The soft, gravelly sound of the name he alone used for her cracked her resolve. The bleakness in his eyes shattered what remained.

"I can call Judge Rawlins, explain the situation and see if he can overturn the seal on the records." She reached for her cell phone.

At the same moment, Deke's phone went off.

The fire alarm she'd heard two nights ago.

Jarred to his feet, he whipped out his phone and answered, hitting the speaker function. "This is Reynolds."

"Chief, we have a fire called in for eight-three-seven Orchard Lane."

Deke's eyes went wide and Libby gasped. *That was Deke's boyhood home.*

"Excuse me, Brandt? What address?"

"Eight-three-seven Orchard Lane. I've got both squads deployed. You want the GPS?" Brandt Outman, the radioman repeated.

"No. I know where it is. I'm on my way. Call Sheriff Justice for me and Mike Feeney of the arson department, too."

He closed the phone and strode out the door.

Libby grabbed her sandals and handbag then ran out the door after him. "Deke, wait."

He kept going until he got to the elevator. "Libby, whatever it is, it will have to wait until I get back."

"No, it can't." She said, hopping into the elevator with him. "Cleetus and Sylvie are there."

As the elevator descended, he turned to hold her steady while she got the second shoe on. "What do you mean, Cleetus and Sylvie are at my old house?"

"Sylvie was looking for a place to rent. I knew your mom's old place was available." She gripped his forearm tight. "I sent them there this afternoon."

"Fuck!" He said as the door opened, practically pulling her out with him. "Call Clint, tell him to meet me there."

He was running out of the building, but she was right behind him, cursing her choice of shoes for the day. No matter what he thought, he wasn't leaving her behind. He wasn't doing this alone. Not this time. She reached his truck just as he started the engine.

"Dammit, Libby, you're not coming," he said as she wrenched open the door.

"Hell yes I am, Deacon," she said, climbing into the passenger side and pulling out her phone. "So stop arguing and drive while I call Clint."

* * * * *

He slipped into the gathering crowd. He'd worried about hiding his thrill at watching the fiery dance he'd created from those around him, but seeing the firefighters work as a team to move the deputy off the lawn to the neighbor's driveway hit him hard.

How had this happened?

No one was supposed to get hurt. The house was empty.

Why was the deputy there?

Had he messed up? Had someone seen him and reported it to the sheriff's office? Was that why he was in the house?

Maybe he should leave?

Suddenly, more sirens sounded as the second fire truck arrived. He couldn't leave now. His adversary would be here soon. Glee replaced the momentary internal worry the deputy's injuries had caused him. When his enemy saw what he'd done, the other man would know he meant business and stay away from the goddess. *His* goddess.

CHAPTER NINETEEN

Smoke billowed out from blocks away. Deke gripped the wheel tighter as he sped in the direction of his boyhood home. He'd turned on the truck's siren outside the courthouse and hit the gas the minute Libby had her seatbelt fastened.

Whoever this firebug was, and Deke had no doubt this fire was set by the same guy who torched Zimmer's farm, the guy had just made his first mistake. He'd made it personal.

Deke prayed that Cleetus had gotten Sylvie out in time. He couldn't take having another death laid at his doorstep.

"Clint's already on his way to your house," Libby said beside him, slipping her phone back in her bag. "Dear God, I pray they got out. I don't know what I'll do if they're in there." Her voice caught. "I sent them there, Deacon."

Her words mirrored his and suddenly he knew that whatever they found, they'd get through this together.

He laid his hand on hers. "It's not your fault, Libby. You didn't set this fire."

"You think it's the arsonist?"

He let go of her hand and turned the last corner onto Orchard. The house was in shambles. Flames roared from the rubble. Both fire squads were there, working to contain the raging inferno. Deke pulled in behind the quint engine and stared at the rubble that used to be his home.

What the hell was he going to tell Mom?

"Dear, God," Libby whispered. "It's gone."

Suddenly a fist pounded on the driver's window, startling them both.

Colin Turnbill, the eldest of volunteer firefighter Aaron Turnbill's kids and a member of the fire department, yanked open the door. "C'mon, Chief. All hands on deck. Cleetus is unconscious."

The news seemed to snap Deke out of his shock. The next second he was out of the truck and reaching into the back for his turnout gear. "Where is he?"

"Over in the neighbor's drive. Took three of us to move him there." Colin pointed to the far side of the yard.

Libby had come around the truck. "Was Sylvie injured?"

Colin shook his head. "No, the little lady looks okay, but she was trying to move Cleetus by herself when we moved in, so I think she might've gotten some smoke in her lungs. Still won't leave the big guy's side, though."

"What happened to him?" Deke had kicked off his shoes and stepped into the legs of his gear, straight into the boots at the bottom.

"Best we can tell a door hit him when the explosion occurred." Colin said.

"Explosion?" Libby asked, exchanging a look with Deke. That must've been what had sounded like thunder when she'd been holding him earlier.

"Yes, ma'am. Most likely a natural gas line blew," Colin continued. "According to Sylvie, Cleetus was carrying her out of the house when it blew and a door hit him once they were outside the house."

At that moment, a truck drove up. Doc Clint rolled down his window. "Where do you want me?"

"Over with Cleetus, he's been hurt," Deke said, snapping the last buttons of his coat.

"I'll show you," Colin said, jumping onto the truck's running board and holding onto the door.

Libby started after the truck. Deke grabbed her arm to stop her.

"Libby…" He wanted to say so much, to beg her to leave, to be safe.

"You go," she said, turning her hand to hold his a moment. "I'll go check on Cleetus and see what I can do to help Clint and Emma. I'll be safe, I promise."

Deke watched her go for a moment before slamming his helmet on and connecting his radio. "Reynolds, here. Who's on lead?" he asked, checking the radio was working and letting the others know he was here.

"Deke, it's John Wilson. Glad you're here," came the older man's voice over the radio.

Deke jogged past the quint to where the older man stood, directing the hose team where to work the fire with their water. "Where's the other team?" he asked when he got close enough not to use the radio.

"I've got Gage and the second team working the back of the house. Worse part of the fire seemed to be there," John said, pausing. "He said this was your mom's house?"

"Yeah. I'd just finished repairing and painting it to rent."

"Sorry to hear that. Any chance there was a gas leak you weren't aware of?"

"Nope."

John's steady gaze met his and Deke knew he was thinking arson. "Damn."

"Yeah. So, let's try to preserve some of this rubble for Mike to look at later."

"Do our best."

"Thanks. Our first priority, though, is to try to keep this thing from spreading. I'll check on the neighbors. See if they can give us a hand by wetting down their homes and the grounds."

Deke turned and saw that a crowd had formed outside the barrier that Bobby had once again set up. An idea hit him. He went back to his car, grabbed his phone and headed to where Bobby stood on crowd control.

"Bobby, I need you to do something for me," he

asked, turning his back to the crowd.

"Whatever you need, Chief," she said, her brows drawn down in question.

He opened his hand. "Any chance you could get some video of the crowd for me?"

A smile spread slowly as she took the phone. "No problem."

He left her to go talk with the neighbors. By then, Clint should have information on how badly Cleetus was injured.

And hopefully, Bobby would capture the firebug's image on his phone.

He was tired of being played for a fool.

* * * * *

The sight of the big deputy lying limp and unmoving on the driveway was alarming. Clint and Emma were working on him, talking quietly between themselves. Off to the side stood Sylvie, her arms wrapped around herself like she was afraid she'd break if she let go. Libby's heart broke for the little stylist and she hurried over to stand with her.

No one should be alone when someone they cared about was injured.

"How is he?" she asked quietly, putting her arm around Sylvie's shoulders.

Sylvie shook her head. "I don't know. He wouldn't wake up...and there was so much blood...I couldn't stop…" Her voice broke and she turned to clutch Libby to her.

"Doc Clint and Emma are with him, Sylvie. They'll take good care of him." She wouldn't promise Cleetus would be okay. She couldn't. Sylvie was right, there was an awful lot of blood on him and around his head. Even on the cloth Sylvie still clutched in one hand.

"What happened?"

"I'm not sure. When we pulled up outside, there wasn't any smoke or fire. I swear there wasn't." Sylvie trembled and Libby squeezed her shoulders. "Then Cleetus opened the door and the house was just so lovely and homey. I got distracted by something and then he was headed into the kitchen. That's when I could smell something odd…and then saw the flames… and then he grabbed me and ran out…and there was this horrible rumble…and explosion…and we landed outside…somehow I was on top of him…then he turned…" She finally stopped to take a breath and swallowed hard, tears streaming down her face.

Libby's heart broke.

"The next thing I knew, the front door hit him. Then all the blood. And he wouldn't wake up." She clutched the bloody cloth to her and sobbed.

Libby hugged her tighter, her attention torn between where the doctor and nurse worked on Cleetus and watching Deke direct the firefighters, who seemed to be quickly getting the blaze under control. The fact that his childhood home had been reduced to a pile of rubble actually seemed to be helping the men get it put out much quicker than the spread fire in the field. He'd even gotten the neighbors on both sides to water down their houses and yards in an effort to stymie the fire's spread.

That was one of the things she loved about Deacon, always had, his ability to lead others. He could inspire them to set passing records in football, as well as learn to fight fires to protect their community. She knew his heart was breaking over the loss of his home, but his first concern was the neighbors who might lose their houses.

"Oh, look. He's moving!" Sylvie whispered beside her and pointed towards Cleetus.

She was right. Cleetus wasn't just moving, he was trying to sit up at the same time Clint and Emma were trying to hold him down. Clint waved for them to come over.

"Sylvie," Cleetus choked out, still struggling.

"I'm here, right here," she said, dropping down beside him. "You have to lay still and let the doctor work on you."

"You're alright? I didn't hurt you?" he asked, then went into a coughing fit.

She laid her hand on his chest. "I'm fine. Of course you didn't hurt me. You saved me."

"Never want to hurt you," he said, laying his hand over hers. As if her words were medication, Cleetus closed his eyes, no longer fighting the people helping him.

Wiping at the tears in her eyes, Libby turned away from the tender scene to come face-to-face with Deke. He caught her by the shoulders.

"What's wrong?" he asked, his eyes dark with concern. "Is it Cleetus?"

"Yes. No, I mean not in the way you think. He woke up."

"Then why are you crying?"

She gave a shaky laugh. "It's just how he and Sylvie are taking care of each other…I just got a little choked up."

"You always did cry at sappy movies." He lifted the corner of his mouth.

Heat filled her face at his teasing. She glanced over his shoulders at the smoldering rubble. "Is it out?"

Sobering, he turned to follow her gaze. "For the most part. I'll leave one crew here to make sure nothing flares up again."

"I'm so sorry. Did you lose everything inside?"

He shook his head. "It was empty and I'd had the inside repaired and painted for a renter. I've never been so glad that Mom moved to South Carolina last year as I am right now. Anything important went with her, but damn, I hate seeing the house like this."

"Thank goodness she wasn't here." She leaned in closer to whisper so no one else could hear. "Do you think it was the arsonist?"

The look in his eyes told her he believed just that.

Movement from the side yard caught their attention as Gage stalked around from the back of the house, carrying a plastic bag in his hand. The hard planes of his face spoke volumes to his barely controlled anger.

"What did you find?" Deke asked, stepping away from Libby.

Gage held the bag out to him. "Son of a bitch triggered it with a cell phone this time."

"Dammit," Deke said studying the melted contents the bag. "He's changing his MO. Last time it was a timer. This time a cell phone."

"What does that mean?" Libby asked, not liking the men's reaction to the change.

"It means he's escalating." Deke glanced back at his former home. "And it's become personal."

Before she could ask why the arsonist would be targeting him, Doc Clint joined them.

"How's Cleetus?" Gage asked.

"Good news is he regained consciousness for a bit," Clint said. "Bad news is he's confused, refuses to release his hold on Sylvie Gillis and is too damn big for me and Emma to move by ourselves."

"If he's awake, can't he just get on the stretcher on his own?" Deke asked as the group headed over to where Emma sat, monitoring the deputy.

"Nope. He was combative when he came to." Clint shook his head. "Damndest thing. Once Sylvie was by his side, the big guy calmed down long enough for me to get some Propofol into him. I need to keep him calm until I can get him through a CT scan over at the hospital."

"Need some help, Coach?" A voice called out from behind them.

The quartet turned to see who'd spoken. Several of the football players had moved forward.

Gage motioned them over. "Sure could. We're going to have to lift Deputy Junkins onto a stretcher for the doctor. If you guys could help us, the firefighters can continue their work."

"I'll help too," another voice from the crowd spoke out.

Libby looked over and nearly groaned as Todd Banyon walked up to them. The football players made sense, but would Todd be any real help with lifting?

"Glad to have the help, Banyon," Deke said, surprised the man had offered.

Kneeling next to Clint, he helped the doctor roll the sedated Cleetus to one side as Emma slipped a long plastic board under his body. Once it was in place to Clint's liking, they carefully rolled the deputy back until he was on the board. Once Clint and Emma had straps on the board to secure Cleetus' head, arms and legs, the other volunteers, along with Gage, moved into position at the handle holes cut into the board that Cleetus barely fit on.

Deke's eyes met Gage's and he knew they were thinking the same thing.

This was going to be like moving a ton of concrete.

"Everyone ready?" Clint asked at Cleetus' head. Each of them nodded, including Banyon, who had one of the feet handles. "We'll all lift on three and let's try not to jerk him more than necessary."

That got a few half chuckles from the team.

Clint waited for their attention to focus on him again. "Once we have him up, Emma will slide the gurney beneath him and we'll lower him on it. But stay close, I'll need help lifting him into the truck."

"Everyone else move back, we want a clear path to the truck," Deke said, looking around as people moved out of the way. His gaze landed on Libby, who stood by Sylvie, her arm once again around the tiny woman's shoulders. That was one of the things he loved about her, that she knew just what needed to be done and never hesitated to do it.

"...two. Three," Clint counted and as one the team of men and teens lifted the board, with a chorus of grunts.

"Jeez," one of the teens muttered what the others working hard to hold the board and patient steady were thinking.

His muscles straining, Deke just prayed they didn't drop him.

Emma moved quickly and the team finally walked the stretcher to the truck, once more lifting in tandem to hoist him inside.

"Can I go with him?" a soft, southern voice asked

from behind them.

The group parted to see a very worried Sylvie standing near the truck, her eyes glued on the deputy's inert body.

"There's not a lot of room in the back of the truck," Clint started, but stopped when Emma laid her hand on his arm.

"Sylvie was a great help calming him down earlier. We might need her when he comes out of the sedation," she said, then smiled at Sylvie. "You can ride up front with me while the doctor stays in back with Cleetus."

"Unless you two need to talk with her first?" Clint said to Deke and Gage.

They exchanged looks, Deke walking over to the little hair stylist. "Sylvie, I know you want to go with Cleetus and he obviously would do well with you there, but the sheriff and I need to talk with you while the events are fresh in your mind."

"I don't know anything. Really," she said, her gaze still focused on the deputy.

"You probably know more than you think," Libby said encouragingly.

"It might help us catch who did this to Cleetus," Deke added.

That seemed to convince Sylvie. She nodded and took a big breath, straightening her spine as she exhaled. "I'll tell you everything I can remember, Chief."

"Please, call me, Deke," he said, giving her an

encouraging smile and pat on her shoulder. "We'll get you over to the hospital as soon as we can." He glanced at Gage.

"No problem. I'll have Bobby run you right over there, Miss Gillis."

The decision made, Clint and Emma climbed into the truck. Emma leaned out the window and called to Deke. "Anyone with minor injuries can go on over to the clinic. Harriett's there and can handle it."

Deke watched the truck pull out and hoped Cleetus would be okay. Then he looked at the charred remains of the home he'd grown up in.

The guy wanted to make this personal? Well, he had his attention now.

* * * * *

"Elizabeth?"

Libby cringed inwardly at Todd's use of her formal name. But he had stepped up to help Cleetus, so she plastered a friendly look on her face and turned around.

Sheesh! He was nearly on top of her.

Talk about personal-space invasion.

Instinctively, she took one slight step backward to give her some space. Hopefully, he'd get the message. "Thanks for helping us move Cleetus, Todd. That was very kind of you."

"I always liked the deputy. He shouldn't have gotten hurt."

"No, he shouldn't," she said, thinking that was an odd comment. But then a lot of Todd's comments were odd. "Is there something you needed?" she asked, watching Deke and Gage escort Sylvie over to the police car so she could sit and answer questions.

"Could you come over to the Colbert House?" Todd asked, drawing her attention back to him.

"Why?"

"I found some contraband material in one of the rooms. I don't know who it belongs to. Since you're the home's social worker, I thought you might want to talk to the boys."

Seriously? Now? Couldn't the guy see there were more important things going on now? Libby reined in her impatience. "I'd be happy to come by tomorrow and look at it."

He gave a little shrug. "I'd hate to have to kick out the wrong person."

And he would. Probably Kyle, since he was convinced the newest house member was a serial killer or something.

Colbert House was only a few blocks away, but she really felt she should stay to be sure Sylvie and Deke were okay. Whatever Todd had found could certainly wait a little while. But he was right. The young men there would be more willing to talk to her than him. Besides, she might even be able to talk Todd into not dismissing the offender. "I'll tell you what. Let me finish here with Sylvie, then I'll come to the house.

Maybe in an hour?"

"Sure, okay. That will work," he said, looking like a hopeful puppy, then he turned and left, skirting the crowd.

Watching him walk away, she reminded herself he was a good man who wanted to help people. She shouldn't condemn him because of his lack of social skills.

* * * * *

She'd come with *him*.

Clenching his hands into fists, rage filled him to the point he thought he'd explode like the house had.

She belonged to him. After all the time he'd taken planning to show her she was meant to be his, she threw the effort in his face by showing up at the fire with the fireman. Look at her standing there with *him*. She even let *him* touch her.

No one should touch her but him.

Ever.

But today he'd make her his. He had just enough time to get things ready.

They'd both dance to the rhythm of the fire.

Just the two of them.

Then they'd be united forever and no one, not even the fireman, could separate them.

* * * * *

A shadow fell across Deke as he hunkered down in front of Sylvie, who they'd seated in the front seat of the cruiser she and Cleetus had driven over to the house. Even before a soft hand landed on his shoulder he knew it was Libby at his side. It had always been like that between them. Anytime she was within proximity his body became more alert, tuned into hers. He reached up and squeezed her hand briefly as he listened to Sylvie recount what she could remember about the fire and explosion.

"Cleetus was so sweet to drive me over to look at your mama's house. Oh, God, if I hadn't asked him to bring me, he wouldn't be hurt." Sylvie's voice caught on a sob, tears in her eyes once more.

"Sylvie, it wasn't your fault Cleetus is injured," Libby said, reaching over to squeeze the tiny lady's shoulder. "Besides, I'm as much to blame that he was here as you. I suggested you ask him to bring you to see the house."

"Oh, no, Miss Libby, you can't think that," Sylvie rushed to reassure her.

Gage, squatting on the other side of Sylvie, his gaze meeting Deek's. His friend was right. They needed to refocus Sylvie on the crime scene details and away from Cleetus.

"Sylvie, when you pulled up to the curb here, what did you see?"

She blinked. "Your house. It was so cute with the big

front porch and the white flowers all around the front. Oh, and the lovely hostas."

Deke bit back the urge to growl. Libby squeezed his shoulder, reminding him to be patient. Sylvie had been through a very traumatic experience and needed to be guided through the emotions to get the facts.

"Did you notice anyone outside?" Gage asked.

Sylvie scrunched down her brows and stretched her lips into a thin line, then relaxed them, shaking her head. "No, sir, Sheriff. No one was out, not even someone cutting their grass."

"Good," Deke said. "So you got out of the car and went onto the porch. What do you remember there?"

"Oh, Cleetus—um, Deputy Junkins," she corrected herself, her cheeks growing a bit pink, "pulled out this huge ring of keys. I had to wait for him to flip through them until he got the one for the door."

"Did anything strike you as odd? A movement? An odor?"

Again she drew down her brows and pressed her lips in that same thin line. Apparently, this was what she did when she concentrated. "No, nothing."

"So, you went inside. What do you remember about that?" Gage asked this time.

Sylvie's eyes lit up. "Oh yes."

"What?" Deke asked. Finally, they'd get some useful information.

"All the beautiful woodwork. I just had to touch it," Sylvie said with a smile.

Deke wanted to bang his head into the side of the car door.

"While you were inspecting the woodwork, what was Cleetus doing?" Gage said, drawing her attention to him.

"For a few minutes he just leaned against the stair rail going to the upstairs, sort of watching me." She concentrated once more. "One minute he was there, I reached down to pick something up, and when I turned around he was gone."

"Where had he gone?" Libby asked.

"Just into the kitchen. I went to talk to him, show him what I'd found. When I asked him what was wrong, all he said was kerosene. Then his foot slipped, like the floor was all wet. Next thing I knew, the outside of the house was on fire, Cleetus had picked me up and was running out the front the door." She gave a soft little sob and clutched the bloody cloth in her lap tight.

Deke laid his hand gently over hers. "I know this is hard to do, but you're doing great, Sylvie. I have a question I want you to think hard about, okay?"

She nodded. "I'll try."

"Good. Do you remember if the fire started and then the explosion came? Or was there an explosion outside the house then the fire?"

Once more, Sylvie concentrated hard. "The fire definitely came first. Deputy Junkins had us almost out the front door when this horrible rumble started, the ground shook, and we were tossed off the porch.

Cleetus turned so he wouldn't land on me, but then shoved me sideways as the front door flew at us." She gasped back a sob again, her eyes brimming once more with tears. "That's what injured him. The door hit him hard. Then there was blood everywhere. He protected me and he got hurt."

"And he wouldn't have wanted you to get hurt," Gage said, patting her on the shoulder. "Cleetus takes his job protecting people very seriously." He gave her a reassuring smile. "Especially someone he cares about."

His words seemed to ease some of her anguish.

"Sylvie, I have a question," Libby said, and Deke turned to see her head tilted to the side. "You said you went to show Cleetus what you'd found."

"Yes, I thought it odd that something was on the floor of the empty house. Especially something I made."

The hairs on Deke's arms rose. "What did you find?"

"This." Sylvie lifted the blood-soaked rag in her hands, opening it to show it wasn't a rag but a T-shirt. "I delivered these to Miss Lorna over at the café just last week."

Stitched on the front was the Peaches 'N Cream's new logo.

CHAPTER TWENTY

"You found this in the house? Not outside?" Deke asked, gently taking the shirt from Sylvie.

He had to be fighting his anger that someone had destroyed his home and nearly killed Cleetus and Sylvie, but Libby also knew he'd be as careful with the little hairdresser as he could. He'd always had patience with people who had been traumatized.

"Inside," Sylvie said without hesitation. "It was wadded up in the corner of the living room."

"In the living room? Not near the kitchen where the fire started?" Despite the dried blood on it and what looked like circular burn marks the size of cigarette butts, he held the shirt up and sniffed. He handed it over to Gage, who did the exact same thing, then shook his head. Libby knew they were looking for any evidence of kerosene on the shirt.

"No, sir, Chief...I mean, Deke, it was definitely in the living room. It was the only thing in the living room, which is what caught my eye," Sylvie said.

"When I picked it up and realized it was one of mine. I turned to show Cleetus, but he'd already walked away. Do you think it had something to do with the fire?"

Deke exchanged looks with Gage and Libby. So far the knowledge that the two fires were connected and the work of an arsonist had been limited to as few people as possible. Libby knew he'd like to keep it from spreading and sending widespread panic through the town. He focused his deep-brown eyes on Sylvie. "I don't really know, Sylvie, but if you don't mind, I'd like to keep this."

"Of course. I only used it to stop all that blood." She shifted her gaze over to Bobby, who'd come to join them. "Miss Bobby, I didn't know what else to do."

Deke rose and stepped back so Bobby could get in close. "It's all right, Sylvie. You called the fire department and took care of Cleetus. We couldn't have asked any more from you."

Confusion clouded Sylvie's face. "But I didn't call the fire department, Miss Bobby. I was too busy trying to get Cleetus to wake up and stop all that blood."

Deke's gaze shot to Gage's once more. Libby's legs wobbled as she realized what they were thinking.

Whoever started the fire wanted someone to get here fast. Maybe go inside before it exploded. Deke.

Suddenly, his arm was around her back, supporting her.

"Easy, sweetheart. It could've been a neighbor," he whispered in her ear.

Choking on her own fear, she nodded. Whether he wanted her to believe that or just to keep her from drawing attention to the information, she wasn't sure. That he wanted her to remain calm, she understood.

"Can I go see Cleetus…um, Deputy Junkins now?" Sylvie asked.

"I think we're done," Gage said, rising to stand near the car and handing the keys over to his fiancée, who handed him the phone she'd been using to film the crowd. "Bobby will take you over to the hospital."

As Bobby climbed into the driver's side, Sylvie buckled her belt, then held the door a minute before closing it. "I hope what I told you helps y'all find out what happened, Sheriff, Chief."

"You've been a great help, Sylvie." Gage smiled at her. "And I think my deputy is going to be very happy to see you when he wakes up."

The little stylist blushed and closed the door.

"What do you want to do?" Gage asked as the trio stepped back to the sidewalk and Bobby pulled away from the curb.

"I need to talk to Lorna," Deke said, letting go of Libby's side and taking the shirt from Gage. "I need to know how many people she's given one of these shirts to and who they are. Any chance you can finish with the first unit guys here?"

"Yeah. Bobby will keep me posted on Cleetus."

Deke clamped one hand on his friend's shoulder. "The big guy's a fighter, Gunslinger."

"I know. Just hate to see him laid out like that, dammit."

The tenderness and pain on both faces of these strong men for their friend tore at Libby's heart. It wasn't fair that someone so evil could put then through all this. That someone could be so cruel to hurt a kind soul like Cleetus. That someone could target an honorable man like Deke.

Gage turned and scanned the smoldering rubble. "You go get your answers from Lorna. I got this." He clasped hands with Deke. "Let's nail this son of a bitch before he hurts anyone else."

* * * * *

As Deke drove the short distance to the Peaches 'N Cream, his mind tried to put the pieces of the puzzle together.

Whoever was setting these fires had made him a personal target. That fact became evident with today's fire. He reached over and hit the dial number on his phone sitting in the truck's dock.

"Hey, Chief. Everything under control over at the fire scene?" Brandt Outman's voice came over the speaker. A paraplegic war veteran, Brandt had started manning the switchboard a few years back as a volunteer. Deke had lobbied the town council that this should be a paid position, now filled by Brandt full time and three college kids part time.

"Gage and his team are finishing up. Brandt, I need to know something. Did you take the call for the fire?"

"Yeah. Why?"

"Sound like a male or female?"

"That depends on which number you're talking about."

Deke glanced over at Libby, who raised her shoulders in a questioning shrug. Focusing back on the road, he asked, "Exactly how many calls did you get today?"

"Four total. Got the first one and sent the station one team. Then three more…" They heard papers being rifled on the other end of the call. "Four minutes later. Sort of bang, bang, bang. All three of those said there was an explosion. That's when I sent out the second engine. Was there a problem? Should I have called in more volunteers?"

"No. You handled it great, Brandt. Enough personnel to handle the blaze, but not too many to get in the way. Let's focus on that first call. Was it a male or female?"

There was a pause.

"Male, I think. Not real deep though. Not high-pitched like a scared woman, either. That's the odd thing."

Deke exchanged another look with Libby. "Odd how?"

"The person wasn't panicky. They were calm. Like they were reciting something from memory."

"Dammit. That was him."

Libby laid her hand on his thigh. He felt the trembling in it through his jeans. She knew as well as he did that whoever was doing this had planned the fire, coldly calculating to get him to the fire, possibly hoping he'd die in the explosion.

"Him, who, Chief? You think someone started that fire on purpose?"

Fuck. He'd forgotten in an effort to keep panic at a minimum, they hadn't shared the arsonist information with the other members of the fire department.

"Brandt, I need you to keep this just to yourself. Someone may or may not have started that fire."

"Jesus!" the operator's voice barely whispered over the line.

"See if you can get the number of that first call. Then I want you to send it to Mike Feeney at the state arson unit. He can probably get a trace on it faster than we can. Got it?"

"Got it, Chief."

"And Brandt, no one knows about that call or this one. Not the mayor, not the county DA, not anyone from the town council and especially not that new newspaper guy."

"What phone call?"

"Thanks, Brandt." Deke shook his head at the guy's slight humor and hit the disconnect button on his phone as he pulled into the parking lot to the side of the Peaches 'N-Cream. He parked the truck and sat staring out the windshield.

"Deacon," Libby said, her hand still on his thigh. "You could let Gage handle this."

He shook his head. "I could. But from the very beginning this has been about me. This guy is using fire to dredge up my past. Gage might get some answers, but I'm the one with the memories. One person died because of me I'm not going to let someone else I care about get hurt."

"Cleetus will be okay," she said.

Deke clamped his hand on her hand and drew it up to his mouth, pressing a long kiss into her palm. Then he turned until he captured her blue-eyed gaze with his. "I know Cleetus will be okay, sweetheart. It's you I'm afraid will get hurt." His breath caught in his chest and he had to blink at the burning in his eyes. "I don't want to lose anyone else."

Laying her other hand on his face, her lower finger caressing the edges of his scars, she leaned in and kissed him. Softly, tenderly, reassuringly, then finally moving back to gaze at him once more. "You won't lose me, Deacon. I promise."

He nodded, breathing in slowly, the tightness in his chest easing a bit at her words. Releasing her hand, he grabbed the bloody shirt from the seat and handed it to Libby. "Why don't you put this in your bag and let's go see what Lorna has to tell us about how it ended up at my house."

* * * * *

"Deacon, I heard the fire was at your mama's home. Is everything okay?" Lorna asked as Libby and Deke entered the café.

Immediately, they were surrounded by the wait staff and several customers

"No, Lorna," Deke answered, shaking his head. "The house is gone."

"Do you know what happened?" Joe from the hardware store asked.

"I heard it was a gas leak," said Charlie, one of the men who played checkers at the corner stool with his friend Vince.

Vince, who had bad knees, had hobbled over to join the crowd. "We better have the mayor call the gas company to come check for more leaks. You know, once you get one, there's bound to be more."

"Yes," said Annette, one of the afternoon waitresses. "When my cousin May's hot water tank started having a leak a couple of years ago, everyone on that block did, too. Gas company came out and found a leak in the main line. They paid for all the repairs, too."

Deke answered questions as patiently as he could, but the firm set of his mouth and jaw spoke of the frustration he was feeling. Hell, Libby was feeling it, too. They needed to get information from Lorna. The sooner, the better. Maneuvering her way out of the center of the crowd, Libby managed to get in behind Lorna.

Leaning forward, she whispered in the café owner's ear. "Lorna, we need to talk to you privately. It's important."

Lorna studied Libby a minute then raised her arms in the air. "Okay, that's enough. Y'all can have the details later. I've got pies burning in the back." She moved through the group like a bulldozer through dirt. "Annette, you have two orders in the window, girl."

Like birds scattering with the crack of a gun, everyone quickly returned to their seats while Libby and Deke followed Lorna to her office in the back.

"Pete, don't let anyone disturb us," she called to the cook.

"You got it, boss-lady," Pete said, not looking up from the sizzling grill in front of him.

Once inside the office, Lorna closed the door and dropped down into the well-used chair at the main desk. "What do you need from me?"

"Have you any idea how this got into my house?" Deke nodded at Libby. She drew out the blood-encrusted shirt and handed it to Lorna.

She opened it and stared open-mouthed at it. "I have no idea."

"How many of those have you given out?" Deke asked.

Lorna shook her head, confusion in her eyes. "Other than Rachel, who has hers on today, no one."

"You're sure?" Libby asked.

Lorna narrowed her eyes. "I may be getting old, little

Libby, but I can remember what I do with my inventory. We were going to start wearing them at next week's football game in the concession stand."

"Then how did that get into my house just before it blew up?"

"Perhaps Sylvie Gillis kept one or two?" Lorna asked.

Deke shook his head. "No. She was pretty shook up, but swears she gave all of the shirts to you. Any chance Rachel might've given out a few without telling you?"

"Not if she knows what's good for her."

Deke had that frustrated look again. "Any chance we can talk with her?"

"She should be back soon. I sent her and Kyle over to the farmer's market. We needed some fresh produce for the week." Lorna held up the T-shirt again. "What's all this dark red on it? Looks like someone had an accident with some brick-colored paint."

"It's blood," Libby answered. "Sylvie used it to stop some of the bleeding from Cleetus' head."

Lorna dropped the shirt. "Oh dear Lord. Is he...is he going to be okay?" For once the gossip grapevine hadn't gotten the information out ahead of them.

"Doc Clint took him directly to the hospital to do a CT scan," Libby said, putting her arms around her former boss. "He did regain consciousness for a few minutes before Clint had to sedate him. They think he'll be okay."

Deke opened the door. "Pete, have Rachel and Kyle

gotten back yet?"

"No, man. Better get here soon. I need to make more fries and am 'bout out of taters."

"I'll give her a quick call and have her get her keester back here quick." Lorna said, pulling out her phone. "You're both welcome to wait in here. Of course I'll tell her if she's in a spot where she'll get reception. Her phone doesn't always work out in the country."

Libby glanced at the clock on the wall. "Shoot."

"What?" Lorna and Deke asked simultaneously.

She shook her head. "Nothing really. It's just I promised Todd Banyon I'd come over to Colbert House in an hour and it's been almost that."

"Something to do with the fire?" Intensity suddenly rolled off Deke.

"No. He said he found some contraband and wanted me to come check it out or he'd be forced to report it to Gage. That could get all four of the residents removed." She huffed and rolled her eyes. "If I don't get there on time, he'll probably do it anyway just out of spite."

Deke huffed in almost the same way, but moved to let her out the door. "I'll take you over there."

Pausing, she laid one hand on his shoulder. "No. My car's just two blocks over at the courthouse. I'll go see what Todd wants and I'll also give Judge Rawlins a call about that other thing we were talking about before the fire. Hopefully you'll have more answers by the time I get back." She handed him Bobby's phone from her bag. "Here, you might need to keep this."

He took the phone, then grabbed her and pulled her close, claiming her lips in a hard, quick kiss. "You be careful."

Smiling, she stroked her hand down his cheek and scarred jaw. "I promise."

As she walked away, she heard Lorna chuckle and Deke say, "Not one word, Lorna."

CHAPTER TWENTY-ONE

As Rachel drove through the countryside back into town, Kyle couldn't remember a day as good as this one was turning out to be. Yeah, he'd gotten the shit beat out of him last night, but it wasn't anything worse than he'd had happen to him at some of the places he'd lived. Certainly wasn't as bad as his old man would do to him on a nightly basis.

Getting up early this morning and watching the faces of the four teammates when he'd walked onto the practice field had been a definite plus. Getting them to see him as part of the team had been pretty cool. Now, helping Rachel do the shopping for the café, spending an hour or two alone with her just sort of topped the whole day.

As Lorna had instructed them, they'd gotten all fresh vegetables out at the farmer's market on the highway several miles from town. They'd loaded up the back of the van almost to the top. *Who knew the café used so many vegetables in a week?* And Rachel had stopped to talk with every farmer, even the long-bearded Amish ones, taking samples for both of them to try. His favorites were the different homemade cheeses. *Who knew there were more kinds of cheese than the ones wrapped in plastic?*

"We made good time today. Usually takes me all day when I go by myself," Rachel said as she parked the van in the rear of the café, near the service entrance. She smiled at him. "Having help for once was fun."

A funny hitch settled in his stomach and he felt warm all over at her praise. "Yeah, like I was so much help. You knew everything to get and I'm pretty sure most of the sellers lowered their prices for you."

"Oh, that's something Mom taught me to do, sort of haggle with them, but in a friendly kind of way. And it *was* fun having you help me." She opened the door and grinned at him. "Especially to do all the heavy lifting."

Laughing, he climbed out his side of the van, then froze as the sickening familiar acrid odor of burning wood hit him. "Something's burning," he said, scanning the area around them.

Nothing. No smoke. No flames.

"I smell it, too," Rachel said as she did her own look around. "Smells like the bonfire they hold the night before the homecoming game every November."

"Coach Reynolds gave us a talk on fire safety the other day at practice. He said there was a county-wide ban on burning anything outdoors until there was some rain."

"Some people don't think rules are meant for them, I guess." Rachel shrugged. Her phone beeped and she pulled it out of her back pocket. "Crap. I hate the bad reception we get out of town. Mom's called me three times. I'd better go see what has her panties in a twist."

Kyle cringed inwardly. He didn't want to think of Lorna and the word panties in the same image...ever. "You go ahead. I'll get started unloading produce," he said, opening the van door. Suddenly, she was beside him, so close he could see the few freckles scattered across her nose. "What?"

"Thanks for going with me today," she said, then leaned in and kissed his cheek.

As if his feet had grown roots to that spot, he didn't move. Even after she walked away. Even after she disappeared into the back door of the café. He stood there savoring the feel of where her lips had touched his skin.

Yes, this was turning into the best day of his life.

* * * * *

Feeling like a caged tiger, Deke paced the back of the café from Lorna's office through the kitchen area and back.

The feeling that he was missing something important gnawed at him. They'd been lucky so far that no one had been killed in one of these sick bastard's fires. If Cleetus hadn't been as deceptively fast for such a big man, he and Sylvie might've still been inside the house when it exploded. What if he'd taken Libby in there for some reason to check on something?

A sudden wave of nausea rolled over him. He grabbed onto the counter and bent over double. Pain clenched around his heart and he fought to breathe.

"Hey, man," Pete said in his ear, the sinewy man's arms around his shoulders, holding him up. "You okay, there, Chief?"

Deke sucked in a deep breath and forced his body to straighten. Libby was safe. His friend was being cared for by the best doctor he knew. They would catch this SOB before he hurt anyone else. He patted Pete on the shoulder. "Yeah, just got a little overheated, I guess. How do you stand working back here in this heat all day?"

Pete gave him a half-grin. "I like helping people. Making good food that feeds the soul, you know?" He went over, flipped a series of burgers, dropped some potatoes into the fryer and reached into the fridge for a bowl of crisp salad. "Besides, it's like my own little castle. Not even the boss lady messes with me back here."

"I heard that," Lorna said, stepping into the kitchen, pointing at Pete. "I can take back your little castle anytime, don't you forget that."

"Yes, ma'am," Pete said with a grin that said her threat didn't worry him in the least.

Lorna shook her head then grabbed Deke by the

Suzanne Ferrell

elbow and led him into the café. "You find a place at the counter to wait. You're distracting Pete and I have a house full of hungry people."

Sit and wait? The town was in danger. Anyone around him was in danger, especially Libby. He wanted to shout it for everyone to get how serious this was. But he also knew calm, clear thinking was what would catch this firebug, so he took a seat at the opposite end of the counter from the two septuagenarian checker players and bided his time.

"How long ago did you try Rachel's number?" he asked, when Lorna plopped a glass of sweet iced tea down in front of him.

"Fifteen minutes. If she's not back in five more, I'll try her again. But I told you reception out that way is a little sketchy." Lorna patted his hand to still the rhythm of his fingers on the Formica top. "She'll be here soon enough. Drink some tea and calm down."

He strangled a growl that threatened to erupt from him and took her advice, swallowing a long drink of the tea. Closing his eyes, he considered what enemies he had. Quite frankly, the only person he ever thought had a reason to want to kill him was Libby. Could she have decided to get revenge on him with deadly fires?

As soon as the idea popped in his head he dismissed it. Some things never changed in a person. Libby was incapable of intentionally hurting anyone. She'd told him she forgave him for Bill's death and his part in it. He believed that deep down inside.

So who hated him? Hated him enough to try to kill him? With fire?

The son of Leo Harkin. The only person he'd actively hunted and made sure he didn't live to ruin any more lives with his fires. Was fate coming back to bite him in the ass? Had Leo's son come to exact revenge for his father?

The image of Kyle Gordon filled his mind. Familiar grey eyes and a natural wariness he'd only seen in wounded animals.

Was Kyle actually Leo's son? Dammit, he wished he could look inside the kid's sealed records.

"Where have you been, girl?" Lorna's voice carried out of the back of the café. Deke's eyes popped open and he strode back to the office once more.

"Out getting supplies like you told me, too. I just saw your calls. You know how cell reception sucks out of town." Rachel said, standing in the office doorway, wearing one of the new Peaches 'N Cream T-shirts. "So what's up?"

"I need to know if you've given any of those shirts out to anyone," Deke said, coming to stand beside her.

She looked at him, then back at her mother. "I know I wasn't supposed to, but he needed a shirt the other night when greasy water splashed all over him, so I went ahead and gave him one. I know you wanted to wait until the football game, but I figured you wouldn't want him going around shirtless."

"Who?" Deke asked. He reached into the office and

pulled out the shirt and held it up for her to see. "Who did you give the shirt to?"

A loud crash sounded behind them. Kyle stood there, where he'd slammed the box of apples onto the floor of the kitchen just inside the door.

"Don't yell at her." He took three strides forward until he was nearly nose-to-nose with Deke, passion and anger lighting his eyes. "Don't you ever yell at her. She gave one of the shirts to me."

* * * * *

"I understand records are sealed for a reason, Judge. We don't want to know all the details of Kyle's life, just the names of his parents." Libby rolled her eyes and stuck her tongue out at the phone, grateful that video phones weren't the norm yet.

For the past fifteen minutes she'd been sitting in her car under a shady tree two blocks from Colbert House, trying to convince Judge Rawlins that it was in everyone's best interests, including Kyle's, that his records be opened. Whatever it was that Todd wanted to tell her could wait until she'd kept her promise to Deke.

"This is highly unusual, Elizabeth, but you say Chief Reynolds asked to have the records?" The judge asked for the second time.

Libby fought the urge to growl. Her mother's voice filled her head. *You can gather more flies with honey than vinegar.*

Sweet it was.

"Yes, sir, Judge."

"Anything pertaining to the two fires in town?"

How much could she tell him without throwing Kyle under a train? She didn't want to cause him any more troubles than necessary. Especially if he had nothing to do with these fires.

"Chief Reynolds isn't sure, but he wants to check a few things about new people in town."

"Might want to start with that new newspaper man, since the last one turned out to be such a rotten egg, huh?" Normally, his humor would make her laugh, but she was too frazzled about the new threat to not only her town but the man she loved to give in this time. Thankfully, the judge didn't wait for a reply. "Tell Deke I'll see what I can do. Might take me a while. Gotta go through some channels and call in some old favors."

Libby raised her eyes to the sky and mouthed *Thank you, God.* "We understand that, sir. Anything you can do will be appreciated."

"Well, just remember that come election time, Elizabeth."

She promised to do just that, then disconnected the call. Dropping the phone into her bag, she put the car in gear and headed the last two blocks to the halfway house.

One problem solved, or at least one promise kept. Now to see what crazy, petty problem Todd had. The sooner she soothed his ruffled feathers, the sooner she could get back to Deacon.

* * * * *

Deke held the shirt up to the side at Kyle's eye level. "So you're saying this shirt is yours?"

For a moment the teen continued to just glare at him, then he slowly turned his head to the side. He took a step back, taking the shirt and looking at it in confusion. "I don't know. Rachel gave me a shirt like this, but what the hell…er, heck happened to it?"

Rachel stepped closer. "It looks like someone put out a lit cigarette all over it."

"Do you smoke?" Deke hadn't smelled the lingering odor of tobacco smoke on the kid when he'd been around him. Not even just now when he was in his space.

"No, sir. It's a stupid habit."

"When was the last time you saw the shirt Rachel gave you?"

Kyle shrugged. "Yesterday, before I came to work last night. It was folded up and in my go bag."

"A go bag?" Deke knew the term. Military men kept one ready in case they were called out at a moment's notice.

"I've been moved so many times that I've learned to keep things I never want to lose in my bag."

Rachel grinned. "You wanted to be sure and keep the shirt?"

Kyle shrugged again, this time with a half-smile at Rachel. "Yeah. No one ever gave me a shirt before."

Deke wanted to groan. He didn't have time for puppy love 101. He needed them to focus on the problem at hand. "So, you're telling me the last time you saw your shirt that looks like this it was in your go bag at Colbert House?"

"Yes, sir, Coach. That's where it was," Kyle said, all the belligerence out of his voice.

"Then you want to explain to me how it got inside my mother's house just before someone set it on fire and blew it up?"

* * * * *

"May I help you?" the lady in scrub clothes at the ER sign-in desk asked.

"They—I mean, Doctor Clint and his nurse brought Deputy Junkins here?" Sylvie asked. She wished Bobby had come in with her. She'd never been to a big hospital and wasn't sure what to say or do.

"He's being looked at right now. Are you a family member?" the nurse asked.

"I'm, um…" Sylvie hesitated. What should she do? Lie and say she was part of his family? Tell the truth and say she was a friend but was worried about him? Or tell her how much she liked Cleetus and wanted to be sure he wasn't going to die after saving her?

"Hey, Nadine," Bobby greeted the other woman as

she came to stand beside Sylvie.

"Hey, Deputy Roberts. Are you here to check on your friend?"

"Yes, but I also brought Sylvie Gillis, Cleetus' girlfriend, to see him. Doc Clint wanted her to be here when he woke up. She seems to keep him calm."

"Oh, yes!" The woman's smile brightened. "Dr. Preston did say to expect you and that you could come right back." She pushed a button and the door beside her automatically opened. She met them on the other side and led them down the hall past several small rooms containing patients on stretchers. Other cubicles were empty, but the bed was ready for the next patient. Finally, she stopped next to a bigger room. "Emma went to clean up their van, but Dr. Preston went with Mr. Junkins to have the CT scan. You can wait in here. It shouldn't be too much longer."

"Thanks, Nadine," Bobby said and Sylvie gave the nurse a shaky smile. She must've looked ready to cry, because Bobby suddenly put her arms around her and helped her into a chair. "He's going to be okay, Sylvie. Cleetus is a lot tougher than most people think. Last spring he was shot and came through it with no problem."

"How awful," she whispered, wondering at how anyone could want to do a job that was so dangerous.

Bobby sat in the other chair beside her and patted her arm. "It was, but Cleetus is a fighter and he helped us stop a very bad man, then healed up good as new."

Before Sylvie could ask anything more, the curtain was pulled all the way back and a young man dressed in scrubs pulled in the stretcher with Doc Clint pushing the other end. Cleetus' eyes were still closed, but he appeared to be breathing easy. An IV attached to one of his hands dripped clear fluid from the bag hanging on the back of the stretcher. Someone had wrapped a bandage around the top of his forehead down over his left eyebrow. He looked pale and was still not moving.

"Why isn't he awake?" Sylvie whispered, coming over to stand beside the stretcher.

"I'm afraid that's my fault, Sylvie," Doc Clint said, standing beside her. He and the other young man lifting the top of the stretcher so Cleetus was no longer flat. "I wanted to keep him sedated until we were done stitching him up and running the CT scan. I didn't need him hurting himself worse or injuring someone if he thrashed around like before." He smiled down at her. "You weren't here to calm him down like earlier."

Heat flushed her cheeks at the doctor's gentle teasing. She didn't know why Cleetus had calmed down when he held her hand, but she liked that he had.

A nurse stepped in the room. She wrapped a blood pressure cuff around Cleetus' arm, put a piece of plastic on his finger and attached wires to the tabs stuck on his chest.

"Will he be okay?" Sylvie asked as she watched her work.

Doc Clint nodded. "He should be. The CT scan

didn't show any intracranial bleeding."

Sylvie nodded, not quite sure what that was, but very glad Cleetus didn't have any. "Will he wake up soon?"

"Fairly quickly now. I gave him one last dose while they were running the CT scan and it will be wearing off soon. I have to warn you though, he may say some funny things as he regains consciousness. Some of which he may or may not remember saying."

"Sylvie?" Cleetus whispered, almost on cue.

She slid her hand over his free one. "I'm here, Cleetus."

He clenched her hand in his and a smile slowly spread across his face. "So cute. You're like a little pixie. *My* little pixie."

Sylvie felt her cheeks redden again, and peeked over at Bobby, who was grinning, then up at the doctor, who gave her a wink. "He can't help what he's saying, but you can bet it's what he truthfully thinks."

He thought of her as *his little pixie*. Wasn't that the sweetest thing ever?

"Can you open your eyes, Cleetus?" she asked.

Slowly, he turned his head and looked at her, his eyes not quite focusing. "So glad you're here. I was afraid I'd squish you. You're so tiny."

She grinned at his sweet words, said with a slur. "No, you didn't squish me. You saved me."

"Had to get you out of there. Fire outside and kerosene all over the floor."

"You did. You saved me. Carried me out like knight

in shining armor."

He grinned at her a moment. "Your hair is like fire. I like the spikes." Suddenly he scrunched his eyes tight.

"What is it Cleetus? You in pain?" Doc Clint asked beside him.

Cleetus' eyes popped open. "No. Trying to remember something."

"It's okay if you can't. Often people forget things that happened right before a head injury." Doc Clint pushed a button and the machine started squeezing his arm for a blood pressure measurement. "Once the Propofol is out of your system, you may remember whatever it is better."

"It's important, I have to tell Deke and Gage." He squeezed Sylvie's hand tighter, his eyes clearer and more focused. "He could've killed you."

"Who? Did you see someone at the fire?" she asked, understanding the fire hadn't been an accident.

"Where's my phone?" he asked, looking around, struggling to sit up. "I need a phone."

"Hold on big guy," Clint said, pulling out his phone. "You can use mine."

Clutching it in his other hand, Cleetus relaxed back on the stretcher, still holding Sylvie's hand as he breathed deep for a moment. "Gotta warn Gage and Deke."

CHAPTER TWENTY-TWO

"Coach, I don't know where your mom's house is. And I don't know how that shirt got there," Kyle said, standing straighter, his hands clenched in fists at his sides. "*If* it's the one that Rachel gave me. The one I have in my go bag is all white and doesn't have any cigarette holes in it."

Deke studied him—eyes narrowed, the muscles in his jaw and raggedly scarred throat working hard. Kyle knew that look—seen it a hundred times before. It meant the man was going to hit something. The urge to bolt itched up his spine. It took all his guts to stand there and defend himself. Especially with the entire café, Rachel, Lorna, Pete and several of his teammates watching.

Just when he thought the big man was going to grab him and starting swinging, Deke nodded and turned to look at Lorna. "How many of these did you order?"

"I ordered four dozen," she said.

"Let's count them, to be sure this is the one Rachel

gave Kyle," he said, then refocused his attention on Kyle. "The red on it is bloodstains. Blood from the injury to Coach Junkins."

Bile rose in Kyle's throat and his legs started to wobble.

"Grab him, quick," someone said.

"Here ya go, son," Pete said beside him and he felt the cook's hand grab his shoulders. "You sit right down here."

"Is the coach…is he okay?" Kyle asked once he was seated and didn't feel so woozy.

"He's alive, but he's at the hospital and that's all we know," Deke said, pulling up a chair and sitting in front of him. "How do you know these are cigarette burns, if this isn't your shirt?"

"Yeah, you told us you don't smoke," Tanner said from the other side of the counter where the crowd had gathered.

"I don't," Kyle said, narrowing his eyes at the wide receiver and wondering if anyone was going to take his side.

"Show him," Rachel said quietly beside him.

He looked up and saw understanding in her beautiful blue eyes. Dang it, she'd seen his scars the night he'd switched shirts.

Keeping his gaze locked on hers, he reached down and jerked his shirt off, letting everyone see his shame. He knew what they'd see. Old, dark, round pucker marks all over his upper arms. From far away they probably looked like a weird skin pigment. As close as Deke and some of the others were they wouldn't mistake them.

"My old man smoked. He thought a human ashtray was a fun way to put them out. Last thing I ever want to do is light one of those things up." He clenched his jaw hard, then pulled his shirt back on. "Satisfied?"

Deke nodded.

Lorna walked back into the café area from her office. "I have forty-six, Deke. With the one Rachel is wearing and that one, that's all of them accounted for."

"So this is your shirt," the coach said holding it up. "Any idea why someone would steal it and leave it at a crime scene?"

"To blame it on me?" He shrugged. Why not? People had been blaming him for any trouble that came along since the day he was born. Why not here?

"Look, Kyle," Deke said, running his hand over his short cut hair. "I'm willing to believe you didn't do this, but you have to help me out here. I need to know who would target you before someone else gets hurt. Who hates you enough to frame you for this?"

Kyle looked past him to the football team members.

"No way!" Tanner said, holding up his hands palms out.

"We didn't do it." The quarterback Ethan made the same gesture.

Cohn shook his head. "You're one of us now."

"Besides, we're not that sneaky," Riley said, looking

at each of his buddies. "How would we get that shirt?"

Before anyone could say anymore the sheriff walked into the café, holding his cell phone. "Deke, Clint just called. Cleetus is awake. He said Todd Banyon bought kerosene for the Colbert House back in the spring."

"So, that doesn't mean much, Gunslinger. Everyone buys a new supply in case of power outages in the summer," Deke said, and several of the patrons murmured they'd done just that.

Sheriff Justice stared straight at the Fire Chief and Kyle knew what he was going to say. "There's no record of anyone purchasing a generator for the halfway house."

Deke's gaze swung back to Kyle.

Kyle shook his head. "Nothing like that anywhere inside or out."

"Bobby said to look at the video she took at the fire scene." Gage said.

Deke pulled the phone out of the pocket he'd stuffed it into. A moment later, all the color went out of his face and Kyle thought the man had just seen a ghost.

"Oh, God. Libby."

* * * * *

"I was beginning to think you weren't coming, Elizabeth," Todd greeted her as he opened the door. "It's not nice to keep me waiting."

Despite the smile Todd gave her, an odd sense of

unease settled on Libby as she entered the house. She shook it off. He'd always rubbed her the wrong way, even when his intentions were to keep the residents at Colbert House safe and on the path to a better future.

"I am sorry to be so late. I had to wait for Chief Reynolds to give me a lift back to my office to get my car." She didn't think it was any of Todd's business to know the details of Deke's investigation into the fire.

"You could've walked over. The Chief's old home is just a few blocks from here."

Todd's tone once again held a degree of censure, which surprised her. Since the beginning, when they'd started working on managing the halfway house together, she'd always felt he hand an overinflated sense of expectation of her time. It really was time to put a stop to it.

She gave him a look that said she wasn't going to explain her reason for going with Deke instead of hurrying over here at Todd's request. "Well, I'm here now. What exactly was it you wanted to show me?"

"It's upstairs." He started up the steps, turning to wait for her at the landing.

Resisting the urge to roll her eyes at him, she set her bag on the floor and followed him up the stairs. "Whatever contraband you think you've found, you could've just brought it down to show me."

"Yes, but I think you should see it where I found it, then you will understand its importance." He stopped and opened a bedroom door, waving her in. "It's over there."

Shaking her head, Libby walked over to the bed. Lying on it was a box of cigarettes, lighter and an official paper. Ignoring the tobacco and lighter, which she knew was the contraband Todd was upset about, she lifted the document and began reading.

It was a letter from the judge sending Kyle into the state's foster care system after the suicide/murder of his mother and father. It stated that the name of his mother, Katrina Gordon and her common-law spouse, Leo Harkin be kept sealed in order that the child, Kyle Gordon, not be treated with prejudice due to the sensational nature of Leo Harkin's crimes as a serial arsonist that caused not only millions of dollars of damage and insurance fraud throughout the state, but had resulted in the death of a decorated fireman.

Bill.

Stunned, she read the paper again.

How had Todd gotten this? Had it been with Kyle the entire time?

Suddenly, Todd grabbed her from behind and a sickeningly sweet smell filled her nostrils as he slapped a cloth over her face.

The world went dark.

* * * * *

Deke couldn't breathe as he watched the video.

On the edge of the crowd stood Todd Banyon.

Instead of watching the firefighters like the other spectators, his gaze was focused to the right, away from the blaze where Cleetus lay sprawled on the concrete and the medical team was caring for him. But it wasn't Cleetus Banyon was watching. It was—

"Libby."

"Deke?" Gage said behind him.

"She's with him."

"Who?"

"Libby. She went to meet Banyon at the halfway house."

He had to get to her. Fast.

He jumped up from the chair and bolted out the café. Footsteps pounded behind him, but he didn't stop to see who it was as he raced to his truck. His phone in one hand, he tried to hit the button for Libby's number as he opened the driver's door.

A hand slammed it closed.

"What the hell?" He turned to shove Gage out of the way. "Did you hear me? The crazy bastard has Libby."

Gage grabbed him by the shirt and forced him back against the truck. "Yeah, and you charging in there will force his hand."

"Let me go, Gunslinger. I'm not going to let him hurt her." He fought the urge to plant his fist in his friend's face.

"Think a minute, Deke. Right now, he's focused on having Libby to himself. You showing up before we're sure what he's got planned, could make him take the if-

I-can't-have-her-no-one-will route and kill her." Gage gave him a hard shake. "I know you love her, but take control of that panic to get to your woman. Right now time and surprise are on our side."

The words slammed through the panic and anger racing through his veins like an out of control burn. Gage was right. Going in before he knew what Banyon had planned was more likely to get Libby killed. They needed a plan.

He held up his hands. "Okay. Okay. You're right."

"Don't try to call her, either," Gage said, looking at the phone in Deke's hand. "We don't want anything to tip this guy into acting too quickly."

Damn, why hadn't he thought that? As much as he wanted to hear her voice and know she was okay, he pocketed his phone. "We need a plan. Fast."

"How many residents are currently living in the Colbert House?" Gage asked, releasing him and stepping back.

"Libby said four, Kyle and three others. We need to find out if they're in the house." Deke looked over Gage's shoulder to Kyle who'd come with most of the others to find out what had happened.

"Most of them should be at work this time of night," he said. "One works at the bakery, one at the hardware store and the other guy's at that garage/gas station out on the highway."

Gage pulled out his phone. "I'd like to have as many deputies as possible meet us near Colbert, but we have to verify those three aren't in danger, too."

"We can go, Coach," Mike Cohn, the defensive linebacker said, the other three football players with him nodding their willingness to help. "We can split up and check out all three places real quick."

Gage looked at Deke. He nodded. The more help there left more officers to help save Libby.

"Go. Call my cell as soon as you've verified that the guys are at work."

"And don't cause them any trouble at work or accuse them of any participation in this," Deke said, before the quartet could leave. "They've had a hard enough time."

"Yes, sir," they said and took off at a run for their cars.

"How do we get Libby free without triggering Banyon to start another fire?" Deke asked, rubbing his hand over his face and down the scars of his neck.

"I know a way in," Kyle said.

"How?" Deke asked.

"There's an old tunnel that leads out of the house into this dugout that's in the woods behind the house. Maybe fifty yards? Kind of hard to find, especially now that the sun's gone down."

"Come on, you can show me." Deke opened his door. He stopped and turned to Gage. "Give us time to get to the spot and into the cellar, before you approach out front. Kerosene takes a little time to get a big blaze going, so if we're inside before he lights it up, we might have a chance of saving her."

"Will do." Gage said, already on his phone to his deputies.

"Lorna," Deke called to the café owner as he started the engine. "Keep everyone away that you can. Libby's life might depend on it."

She nodded then turned to shoo the crowd back inside. "You heard the man. We'll wait together for our boys to bring Libby home safe and sound."

Deke just prayed he'd be in time to save Libby and bring her home.

CHAPTER TWENTY-THREE

The need to get to Libby drove Deke to press harder on the gas pedal as he weaved his way through the streets of Westen.

"You're sure you can get me into the house without Banyon knowing we're there?" he asked the teen sitting beside him.

"Yes. I tested it more than once," Kyle said.

Deke glanced at the kid, who was gripping the hand-hold to keep from flying around when he took a corner. Refocusing on the road, Deke slowed a little. It wouldn't do Libby any good if they crashed and died on the way to her rescue.

"How did you find this entrance?"

The kid hesitated so long that Deke thought he wasn't going to answer.

"First thing I do whenever I get moved to a new place is reconnoiter the area and look for an alternate escape route."

Kid sounded like a damn soldier or former prisoner.

"Libby said she thought you might be what's called a runner. Is that why they've moved you so many times?"

Again a prolonged silence.

"Yeah. Ever since my mom died, I knew that no one was going to look out for me. I had to do it myself. Most places turn out to be bad on the inside. And if you're lucky to find a good one, something from your past will pop up and you're kicked out."

Deke took the last corner onto Colbert Street, stopping a few houses from the halfway house and killing the engine. "Which way to the tunnel entrance?" he asked as they climbed out of the cab.

Kyle pointed to the right. "We cut through this back yard and into the woods. I'll show you from there."

Deke went to the truck bed and opened the gear box he kept locked there. He pulled out the handgun and two flashlights.

"Whoa." Kyle's eyes had gone wide at the sight of the gun. "You mean business."

"The son of a bitch has Libby. No way does he have a chance to hurt her." He handed one of the flashlights to the teen. "You lead the way, but keep the light off until we're in the woods. No need to get the neighbors curious."

Kyle nodded and took off at a slow trot through the yard.

A low-pitched rumble sounded overhead as Deke followed. A quick glance and he saw the sky finally full of dark clouds. No rain for nearly two months and tonight it decides to end the drought. He hoped the coming storm wasn't a bad omen.

* * * * *

Slowly, Libby felt the hard fog lift. Groggy, as if she'd had way too much vodka the night before, she tried to rub her hand over her eyes, but she couldn't move her arm.

What the hell? Had it gone to sleep while she was sleeping?

And why was she sleeping sitting straight up in a chair?

She shook her head to clear the fogginess and tried to move the other arm. It wouldn't move, either. And she could feel both her hands and arms. No pins-and-needles sensation like when they were numb.

Squinting against the overhead light, she tried to figure out where she was.

Someone's kitchen? Not hers. This was newer. It had the kind of stone backsplash she'd wanted in her kitchen if she ever had the money to remodel it. She'd seen it before. No, she'd helped install it. When the town had chipped in as a group to upgrade the turn-of-the-century house on Colbert Street to make the new halfway house.

Colbert House. Kyle's room. The paper. Todd.

Footsteps sounded just outside the kitchen then the door opened.

Speak of the devil.

"Good. Glad to see you're waking up from your little nap. I was thinking I'd have to slap you to get your attention."

"What—?" She swallowed against the dryness in her throat. Dear God, how long had she been out? Had he raped her? Her pulse raced and she fought against the sick feeling in her stomach.

"What did I do to you? Not what you think, though trust me, I wanted to have my conjugal rights with you, even if you weren't awake to enjoy it. But there just isn't time. In the end this will be so much purer." He gave an eerie chuckle that sent ice skittering down her spine. "In the end. All our sins burned away. Yes. That's what this will be—a perfect ending to our relationship."

Relationship? He thought they were dating or something? Crazy. Yep, totally off his rocker.

Time. She needed time for Deke to find her. Surely, he'd noticed she'd been gone longer than she'd said she would. Her heart settled into a more steady rhythm. Deke would find her.

"You started those fires," she said more than asked. She needed to get him talking.

A slow smile spread over Banyon's face, eyes lighting up with a sickening pleasure. "You did notice. I knew you would."

Dear God, had he set them for her?

"They were amazing. Powerful." She tried to make her voice sound impressed instead of repulsed. The last thing she needed to do was push him farther over the line.

"I wanted you to see the depth of my love for you. That no one could love you more. Not even that fireman."

He walked behind her. She tried to turn and see what he was doing, but the duct tape he'd used had her arms, legs and torso too securely bound to the chair.

"If you set the fires for me, why did you try to blame the boy...Kyle for it?"

"Ah, that was pure serendipity," he said, his voice sounding far off, as if he'd stepped out of the room.

What was he doing? "Serendipity?"

"You know, something not planned for falling into your lap. That's what Kyle was. His background being sealed was a red flag that was just too tempting. I never could resist secrets. The file begged to be hacked."

Great. Todd was a hacker, as well as a crazy arsonist.

Something sounded like it was being poured behind her. Then the smell hit her.

Kerosene.

* * * * *

They found the entrance to the storm cellar with relative ease, but only because Kyle knew exactly where to look.

"You were right," Deke said to Kyle as they pried it open. "I'd still be wandering around out here looking for the entrance."

"It's still a little tricky inside," Kyle said, pointing his flashlight inside and stepping into the storm cellar. "Coach, I have something to tell you. You aren't going to like it. You might want to kick me off the team or out of town because of it."

Deke kept his eyes on the kid's back as he led the way down the earthen tunnel full of tree roots overhead. "This have something to do with your past?"

"Yes, sir." A slight tremor filled the young man's voice. "It's about my parents…my dad, actually."

"You're Leo Harkin's son. The man who started the fire that killed my friend."

Silence reigned between them for a few minutes. The only sound the crunching of dirt, bugs, and who-knew-what-else beneath their feet.

"It's not just that, sir. I was there."

"I know." Deke nearly ran into Kyle, who'd stopped quickly in front of him and was looking over his shoulder at him.

"You knew? And you don't hate me?"

"I never did, son. You didn't start that fire. I saw the fear of it on your face when I looked out the window of the warehouse that night. You're not your father. None of it was your fault. Not the fire. Not my scars. Not my friend's death." He laid a hand on Kyle's shoulder. "You have nothing to apologize for. You be the kind of man you want to be."

Relief flooded the teen's face. "Thanks. I was afraid

you'd think I had something to do with Banyon's fires."

"No, and besides, you're helping me save Libby."
He gave him a nod. "How much farther to the cellar?"

"We're here."

Deke flashed his light beyond Kyle. They'd stopped in front of a wall of wooden planks. No door.

"Hold this, Coach," Kyle said, handing him his flashlight.

With two hands the teen lifted the board and moved it to the side.

On the other side was a brick wall.

* * * * *

Shit. Shit. Shit. He was going to burn her—alive.

Think, Elizabeth. Stay calm. You can do this. You've been trained to get people to talk to you. Keep him talking.

"That's how you found out about Kyle's parents. You hacked into the state's databases."

"Very good. I'd heard the rumors about your brother's death and the fireman's involvement. But finding out the son of the artist who'd created that burn was living in this town, right under the fireman's nose...? It was just too perfect to pass up."

He moved in front of her, slowly pouring a ring of kerosene around her, leaving about two feet of space. "So I decided to emulate Leo's methods. I'd thought to use gasoline for the fast burn, but Leo was a genius. He understood the dance the fire wanted to do on its path to glory."

Todd's eyes took on a glazed look. *He got off on the burn. So not good.*

"Kerosene lets it move, slither, seduce until the heat is too much and the flames shoot higher."

She fought the shiver of dread that arced over her body. "But why not take credit for your creation?"

He finished the circle and finally poured the noxious liquid on his pant legs. Pulling a second kitchen chair into the center of the circle with her, he sat.

"The first fire was supposed to serve as a warning. He wanted what was mine. You are mine. But you didn't listen. *He* didn't listen. So, I needed to make the second fire more personal."

"And leaving the T-shirt?" Subtly she tried to flex and relax her wrists to loosen the tape. Not much more give, but she'd keep trying while he talked.

Leaning back in the chair and crossing one leg over the other as if they were having a casual conversation, he pulled out a cigarette and lighter.

Dear God, he wasn't going to light up now? He truly was crazy.

"When I hacked into the kid's file, I read all of it. Saw how his father was a smoker, used him as a human ashtray, in fact. Why not use the fact to point the fireman after the son of the man who nearly killed him?"

"Why do you hate Deke so much?" she asked

without thinking.

Suddenly Todd was leaning in, inches from her face. All humor gone, his features a caricature of hatred and anger. "Because he wants you and you were a whore willing to let him sniff around you."

Think. How to play him?

"You think I wanted him in my bed?"

"Please, you were like a bitch in heat for him," he snarled, inches from her face.

Make him think we're on the same side. That Deke means nothing to you.

"No. I just wanted to make him suffer more," she said, trying not to choke on the words. "You're right. He couldn't control the fire's dance. And worse, he let it kill my brother."

* * * * *

"I thought you said this was a way into the house?" Deke's heart and temper raced at the idea they'd wasted precious time on a dead end. Then the kid smiled.

"Watch this." He leaned in on one edge and the wall swiveled like on an axis, half into the tunnel, the other half into the cellar.

Deke relaxed and dropped a hand on Kyle's shoulder. "Good job. Now you head back the other way. Out of danger."

"No can do, sir." A stubborn set had come over Kyle as he shook his head. "Ms. Wilson's been nice to me. I want to help you save her."

"I don't have time to argue, son. I can't worry about you and Libby."

"A team works better than an individual. Isn't that what you tell us every day at practice?" Before Deke could argue, Kyle hurried on. "It's like that play you taught us on the field—a delayed safety blitz. Make the quarterback think the pocket is a safe place when the linebackers move to cover the receivers and bring the safety in at the last minute to sack the QB." He held Deke's gaze with his own steady one. "I can do this, Coach."

Deke saw the determination in his voice. Kyle needed to help him rescue Libby, because he hadn't been able to save his mother or stop Bill from dying in that fire.

"Okay, but keep behind me, and if I say get out, you book like a three-hundred-pound lineman is on your ass. Got it?"

"Yes, sir."

"Good. Now where do those stairs lead?" he asked, pointing to the stairs on the far side of the cellar.

"To the hallway between the kitchen—to the right—and the living room—to the left."

Deke slipped his phone out of his pocket and dialed Gage's number. "We're in the cellar, Gunslinger."

"My men are outside," Gage replied. "I've got the fire engines on both sides of the street ready to go. The other members of the house are all accounted for at their jobs. How you want to handle this?"

"Give us three minutes to find Libby. Then you hit the front door."

"You got it. Just be sure to get all three of you out of there."

Deke hit disconnect and pocketed his phone again, heading for the stairs, Kyle on his six. He'd started up the stairs when Kyle grabbed him from behind. He froze and looked back at the kid.

"Fourth step from the top creaks," Kyle leaned in close and whispered.

Deke nodded. When he got to it, he stepped over the creaky board to the one above it. He could hear voices through the door. And the smell.

Kerosene.

Fuck. Banyon meant to burn the house down with Libby in it, like some kind of satipratha—the outlawed Indian custom of burning widows alive on the husband's funeral pyre.

Slowly, Deke turned the doorknob, praying it wouldn't make a sound. It didn't.

Inhale.

Exhale.

He eased the door open. The voices came from his right, toward the kitchen.

"You think I wanted him in my bed?" Libby's voice.

Thank God, she was alive.

"Please, you were like a bitch in heat for him." Todd shouted.

"No. I just wanted to make him suffer more. You're right. He couldn't control the fire's dance. And worse, he let it kill my brother."

Deke's knees nearly buckled at her words.

Had she been playing him? She'd said she'd forgiven him. Had she been lying?

"She doesn't mean it, Coach," Kyle whispered practically in his ear. "It's a diversion. Trying to keep him from hurting her."

Kyle was right. He had to have faith in her. She was buying time, trying to keep Banyon happy and not push him into lighting the place up.

"Is this the only way into the kitchen?" he whispered back.

Kyle shook his head, using hand signals to show there was a circular route through the living room to the other side of the kitchen.

Deke nodded, pointing for Kyle to go that direction. He'd go with the direct route and try to get the madman's attention focused on him.

He showed five fingers for the countdown of how long he'd wait to go.

Kyle nodded and sneaked out of the cellar into the living room.

Deke counted to five in his head, then stepped out of the cellar. Creeping down the hall, his back against the wall so he was in the shadows, he held the gun out in front of him with both hands, just like Gage had taught him years ago.

Relief, fear and anger slammed into him one right after another when he was close enough to see into the kitchen. Libby was alive and looked unharmed. But she was duct taped to a chair in the center of the room, which had been flooded with kerosene. Across from her, as if he were having morning coffee, sat Banyon. In one hand he held a cigarette in the other, a lighter.

Behind Libby was a door. It moved slightly. Kyle was in place.

"Let her go, Banyon," Deke said, aiming the gun at the other man's chest.

* * * * *

Deke.

Libby nearly fainted with relief.

Deke was here. He'd found her. Tears filled her eyes as she tried to focus on the man she loved.

"I said, let her go, Banyon. We know it was you that set the fires. Hurting Ms. Wilson will only make things go worse for you."

Ms. Wilson?

Libby blinked back the tears and finally got a good look at Deke's hard-as-stone face and the cold gaze he leveled at the other man. He took another step closer, standing at the kitchen door opening.

"Don't pretend she doesn't mean anything to you, Chief Reynolds. I saw you two together. At her house. In her living room. You would've taken her there on the couch if her phone hadn't rung."

He'd been watching them.

Suddenly, that tender moment between them felt sordid. Libby wanted to hurl.

"She wanted to give herself to you," Banyon said, holding his hands out in front of him, the old-fashioned lighter out in front of him.

"No, Todd. Please," she begged.

"Put it down, Banyon. I will shoot you." Deke took another step closer.

"Her sins have to be purged. The only way is for her to die with me, the only man worthy of her."

He flicked the lighter on.

A shot rang out.

Libby screamed, struggling against her bonds.

Banyon dropped to the floor like a load of bricks, his entire body engulfed with flames that danced like devilish imps. They jumped to the floor and suddenly a ring of fire shot up between her and Deke.

"Libby!" Deke yelled.

"Get out, Deacon. It's too dangerous!" she yelled. Behind her, she heard a tearing sound. She looked to the side and saw Kyle bending at the chair.

"Coach, I can't get through all this duct tape. I need a knife," he said.

"Got it. Which drawer?" Deke asked as dashed to the side of the kitchen.

"Second drawer to the left of the sink." Kyle kept trying to tear the tape, even bending to gnaw at it with his teeth.

"You have to get out of here. Both of you," she pleaded again.

"Not happening, sweetheart," Deke said as he leaped through the flames, two knives in hand. "Not without you."

He and Kyle quickly sawed through the tape and then she was up and in Deke's arms. Her nose pressed into his neck to hold off the nauseous smell of burning flesh.

There was a crash from the front of the house. Libby looked up to see Gage and two firemen rushing into the house. "Hold on you guys, you're gonna get wet."

And with that the hoses opened full force on the kitchen, the fire and the three of them.

CHAPTER TWENTY-FOUR

It was an hour before the fire was deemed completely out. The clouds had finally opened and a low, steady rain helped the firemen keep the blaze contained to the back of the house.

Once news was out that Libby, Deke and Kyle were safe, the crowd at the café had flooded the area, chipping in to help as needed. Little by little, the extra help and spectators had drifted home.

Now Libby sat huddled in the back of the Peaches 'N Cream truck, wrapped in a quilt one of the neighbors had brought out to her, while the men milled around the house, inside and out. Lorna had sent Kyle and Rachel back to manage the café until closing. Since the house would be uninhabitable for the residents, each of their employers had stepped up to provide temporary housing for them. Kyle would spend the night in one of the two apartments over the café, the other being Pete's home.

"Who knew that Todd was more trouble than the

young men we were trying to help?" Lorna said, handing Libby a cup of hot cider from the thermos she'd brought with her.

"No accounting for crazy," Harriett said in her succinct way.

Libby gave a humorless chuckle and sipped the cider, another shiver running through her.

"The fear will go away," Bobby said, laying her hand on Libby's shoulder. The other three ladies had climbed into the van with her once the rain had started. "It's been six months since I had to climb down into that tunnel for Gage and sometimes, especially late at night when I think about it, the same kind of shudder hits me."

"What do you do?" she asked, feeling like such a wimp that she was reacting now, when all the danger had passed.

Bobby grinned at her. "Well, if Gage's next to me in the bed, I just curl into him. He takes all the fear away."

All four of them were laughing when Deke and Gage stepped up to the van door. Libby looked up to find Deke's intense brown eyes focused on her, his lips pressed in a thin line and his hands thrust deep into his almost dry jeans. She quickly looked down to fight the tears in her eyes and gripped the thermos cup in her hands tighter.

"What's got you all in a good mood?" Gage asked.

The rain had let up and Bobby climbed out of the truck. "Oh, I was just telling them how you help me get over my flashbacks to the tunnel cave-in last spring."

He wrapped her in his arms. "Always glad to help."

Lorna and Harriett exchanged a knowing look, then climbed out of the van.

"Everything settled in there?" Lorna asked, nodding at the house.

Gage nodded. "The ambulance took Banyon's body away and the fire's out. Nothing more we can do until Mike comes to investigate the arson in the morning. But with Libby's, Deke's and Kyle's accounts of what happened, I'm pretty sure we've solved the firebug problem."

Their voices drifted off as the quartet moved to the front of the truck, leaving Libby alone with Deke.

"You ready to go?" Deke finally asked, his usually raspy voice even deeper tonight.

She nodded, setting the cup aside, her hands suddenly shaking. "I don't...I don't think I can drive."

"I'll take you home. We'll get your car tomorrow."

He held out a hand and she slipped hers into it, letting him help her out of the van. He didn't let go once she was out, but walked her down the street to his truck, the quilt still wrapped around her.

They didn't talk, not on the way to the truck and not on the way to her house. There was so much to say, but Libby's emotions were too raw for idle chatter. At the house, Deke parked, then grabbed something out of the back of the cab, coming around to open her door. He dropped her bag in her lap. Tears filled her eyes.

"You saved my bag."

Without saying anything, he reached in and scooped her into his arms. With a swift kick to the truck door, he carried her up to the front entrance. She fumbled in the bag, finally finding her key and unlocking the door. He carried her inside then straight up the stairs to her room. Stopping at the edge of her bed, he let go of her legs so she could stand in front of him.

"Deacon, what I said—" she started to say, but he stilled her with his fingers to her lips.

"It's okay, Libby," he whispered, his voice husky with emotion.

"I didn't mean it." Tears filled her eyes and rolled down her face.

"Shh, sweetheart," he said, cupping her face between his hands and tilting her head until her watery gaze met his. Tears were in his eyes, too. "I know you didn't. You were saying what you thought he wanted to hear."

Unable to say more, she nodded.

"You were staying alive." He leaned in and kissed her softly, briefly. "Waiting for me."

Claiming her mouth again, this time with more force, devouring her lips with his as if he'd die if he ever let go. Wrapping her arms around his body, she clutched his shirt in her hands, straining to pull him into her, needing to feel every inch of him pressed tightly to her. He slid his tongue into her mouth and she met it with her own.

Then the damn shaking started.

He broke off the kiss with a curse, sweeping the damp quilt from her body. "Got to get you out of these wet clothes," he said, working the buttons of her cotton blouse. She tried to help, but her fingers shook too much. He caught her hands in his and stilled them. "Let me, love."

She swallowed the emotions that threatened to choke her and let her hands drop to her sides as he worked the small buttons with his big fingers. It took him a minute or two, but then he was pushing it off her shoulders, his hands continuing down to the button and zipper of her skirt. He pushed it down her legs along with her panties and she stepped out of them, along with her shoes. Finally he went to her bra, opening the front-closing clasp nestled between her breasts.

Standing naked before him, she shivered. He pulled her close with one arm, reaching with the other to pull back the covers. Scooping her up, he slid her into the cool sheets and drew the bed quilt over her. Another shiver wracked her body, and she whimpered at the loss of his body heat.

"Just a second, sweetheart," he said, quickly shucking off his shirt, shoes and socks. Then he pulled a small square packet out of the pocket of his jeans and laid it on the bedside table. His jeans and boxers were next. Finally, he crawled under the covers with her, drawing her up against his body.

The shaking became so hard, she thought she might be having a seizure.

"Can't...stop...shaking."

"Shh, sweetheart," he said against her head, his heart beating next to her ear, his hand sliding up and down her back. "It's the adrenaline. It'll wear off soon. Try not to fight it."

The heat he gave off slowly seeped through the soul-deep cold she'd been frozen in since realizing Todd meant to kill her.

"He was...going to...burn me...alive." She sobbed, eyes clenched tight, but the shaking had slowed.

"I wasn't going to let that happen." He pressed her in tighter. "I've got you. I'm never going to let you go." He pulled back. "I love you, Libby. I always have. I always will."

She stared up into those deep-brown eyes, reading there the love he had and knew now was the time to tell him.

Deke fought the urge to press the issue, to claim her in the age-old way a man claimed his woman, but something flickered in her blue eyes and he found himself holding his breath. "What is it, sweetheart? Don't you believe me? I know I was stupid ten years ago when I threw away what we had—"

She laid a finger on his lips. "No, I know you've always loved me, just as I love you."

Her words should thrill him, but he could feel the tenseness in her body. Something was holding her back. "Then what's wrong?"

"I have something to tell you. Something I should've told you a very, very long time ago." A tear slipped down her cheek.

His chest grew tight at her distress and he wiped the tear away with a finger. "Whatever it is, sweetheart, it will be okay."

She stared up at him for what seemed like forever.

"The day of the fire I had just found out I was pregnant."

The words hit him like a sucker-punch.

"I was going to tell you after you finished your shift. I had a big dinner planned. I was so happy."

"What happened?" he asked, already knowing what she was going to say.

"About a week after the fire, I miscarried. The doctor said it was probably the stress."

"Oh, God, Libby," he whispered, pulling her in against him once more.

"I'm sorry I didn't tell you. I just…didn't know how…then you wouldn't see me."

"I'm so sorry," he said again, leaning down to kiss her face, her salty cheeks, her lips. "So sorry. I was such an ass. You were suffering alone and I was so selfish."

"No, you weren't," she said, returning his kisses, her hand sliding up to stroke the scars on his left side, the other brushing off the tears sliding down his face. "You were fighting to stay alive. I couldn't add to that burden. I'd already lost so much. Bill, the baby. I couldn't lose you, too."

The need to comfort each other over the loss slowly took on a deeper meaning. A need to reaffirm their love for each other. A need to be joined as one. A need so primal they couldn't ignore it any longer.

When she was moist, slick and begging him to come into her, Deke took the time to protect her as he slid the condom in place. As much as they would've loved the child they'd created, the next time they were expecting, he wanted it to be a conscious choice they made— together.

Then he slid into her, joining their bodies as one. Braced up on his elbows he stared down into her beautiful face, not moving, enjoying the hot sheath that held him tight. Home.

"What?" she asked.

He smoothed damp hair off her face.

"This is home. The place I've always meant to be."

"It is," she said, then her lips turned up in a wicked smile. "But if you don't get moving, I may have to rethink—"

He pulled back, then thrust forward again.

"Oh, God," she whispered in a husky rush. Sliding her feet up the back of his legs, opening up wider for him. "Do that again."

"What? This?" he asked through gritted teeth as he repeated the motion.

"Yes. More. Please."

With that plea his control broke. Thrust after deep

thrust he moved faster and harder, covering her mouth with his to swallow each of her small moans of pleasure. Her nails ran over his back, digging in near his spine, her heels locking around his ass cheeks to hold on as he rode her hard.

The tempo spun out of control.

She broke her mouth free.

"Deacon!" she screamed and seemed to spasm all around him.

The next thrust he stayed buried to the hilt as his orgasm ripped through him.

Every inch of her body relaxed and limp from their lovemaking, Libby lay sprawled on her stomach on one side of the bed. Unable to move, she watched Deke climb out of the bed and head to the bathroom.

Outside the low rumble of thunder and the sound of rain hitting the window and roof in a steady rhythm made her smile. Finally the heavens were sending a cooling rain to quench the earth's thirst, same as having Deke with her quenched hers.

A few minutes later he strutted back in, gloriously naked in the bathroom light. She couldn't help but enjoy watching all that hard muscle she'd had her hands and body on earlier. *Mine*. The idea filled that spot in her heart which had been vacant since the day of the fire.

He'd been right.

He was home. Right where he belonged.

Stopping at the bed, he bent to pick up his jeans.

"Where are you going?" she asked. Certainly he wasn't leaving.

He palmed something out of the pocket and then grinned at her. "Nowhere, I just wanted to get something."

Dropping the pants once more, he slid into the bed beside her.

"If that's another condom, I don't think I can take another session just now," she said, only half complaining.

He chuckled. "No. Besides, I put three on the table earlier."

"Three?" she said, leaning up on one elbow. "Rather cocky of yourself, don't you think?"

"Well, it's been ten years." Something in the way he said that caught her attention.

"You mean you haven't? Either? In ten years?"

"Celibate as a monk since the last time you and I were together." Turning on his side, he drew her close and kissed her again. "I told you. I loved you then, I love you now. You're the only woman I've ever loved or ever wanted to make love to."

"Deacon," she whispered before claiming his mouth in another kiss, one that spoke how much she loved him.

Breathless, he eased back, letting their lips part slowly. "Don't you want to know what was in my pants?"

She smiled and reached between them for his thickening cock. "Oh, I know what was in your pants."

Grabbing her left hand to still her movements, he brought it up and kissed her fingertips. Then he slipped a diamond ring on the third finger. "We've waited ten years, Libby. Will you marry me? Soon?"

She didn't look at the ring. She was too busy looking at the most magnificent thing in the world, Deacon, his eyes shining with love—for her.

"Yes. I'll marry you, as soon as you want."

EPILOGUE

The scent of burning wood filled the night air.

Deke stood behind Libby, his arms wrapped around her in the cold November air as they watched the school's cheerleaders lead the homecoming crowd in cheers for the football team.

"Three more games including the homecoming game tomorrow," Sean Callahan said, standing beside them. "What does the Sheriff think our chances are of making the State Championship again?"

"With my son as quarterback and the Tanner boy catching his passes they're a shoe-in," Kent Howard, the county DA, said from the other side of the newspaperman.

"While they make a great offensive threat, it's the defense led by Mike Cohn and Kyle Gordon that's kept this team at the top of the division this year," Libby said.

Deke leaned in and kissed her ear. "You tell them, lady."

A minute later the crowd erupted in a huge cheer as the football team, dressed in their uniforms, ran onto the practice field, led by the five co-captains, including Kyle, who the town now considered one of their own. He had a good job at the Peaches 'N Cream, good grades, friends, and with the college scouts popping in weekly to watch him, the possibility of a college scholarship.

A lump formed in Deke's throat as he watched Kyle jump up and down with the other members of the team, Rachel was at his side.

They *should* treat him like a hero. He was. Without Kyle's help he wouldn't have saved Libby in time. He owed the kid so much. More importantly, he liked him and wanted him to succeed. It's one of the reasons he and Libby offered him a home with them. Not until Colbert house had been prepared, but permanently.

The other residents of the halfway house had finally been moved into the repaired Colbert House and the town had decided to take a different approach to the home. Instead of a hard-fisted, warden-type administrator, the town council chose to use a live-in housemother. On Libby's recommendation, Melissa Compton had gotten the position. Not only had she survived the beatings from her husband and the very public trial, but she'd found her place helping the young men of the home. She understood where they were in their lives. Having someone to mother had helped her thrive.

"So, Gage is whining on a daily basis to me," Bobby said, coming to stand on the other side of Deke and Libby. "He says you guys have your trip all planned."

"Yep," Deke said, pulling Libby in tighter. "Vegas at Thanksgiving, and then she's all mine."

"The football team is the only thing that made this guy wait or we would've eloped the day after the fire." Libby laughed and the sound thrilled his soul. He planned to spend the rest of his life listening to that sound.

"Tell the Gunslinger not to complain," Deke said, then looked down into Libby's eyes. "He only has to wait until close to Christmas for you. I had to wait ten years for the love of my life."

Thank you for reading CLOSE TO THE FIRE!
Want to know more about my books and
when new releases will be coming? Please
consider joining my newsletter mailing list on
my website at:
www.SuzanneFerrell.com
I only send out newsletters when new books
are being published, so only a few times a year.
I promise not to SPAM you.
Your email will NOT be sold to other sites
and is only to be used for the purpose of sending
out my newsletter.

****

Other Suzanne Ferrell Books...

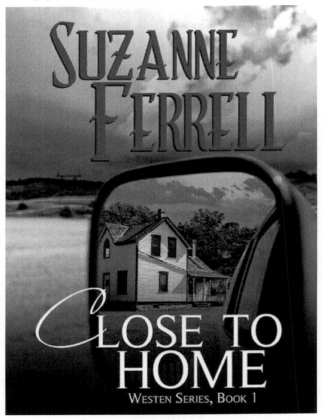

Emma Lewis has a lot on her plate. The single mother of two precocious twin boys and an aging mother who is having trouble getting through each day, the last thing Emma needs is a man in her life, especially a doctor. So when the town's doctor goes on vacation and his handsome nephew takes over, Emma is shocked to not only find him standing in her bedroom, but accusing her of being a neglectful parent.

Clint Preston came to Westen for the year to fill in as the town doc while his uncle took a long needed vacation. Clint also needed a sense of peace and calm to try to find his passion for medicine burned out by long shifts in an urban hospital's ER. Angered to find two boys in his clinic with broken wrists and no accompanying parent, he is determined to confront their mother. The feisty redhead he meets quickly dispels his belief that she's a neglectful mother, but he can see her situation is more critical than she wishes to face and finds himself volunteering to help care for her sons and the remodeling of her home.

As Emma and Clint forge a relationship among the slightly off-beat characters that inhabit Westen a menace from Emma's past threatens her and her sons. Clint and Emma join forces to prevent the loss of either boy and the love they've discovered in each other's' arms.

****

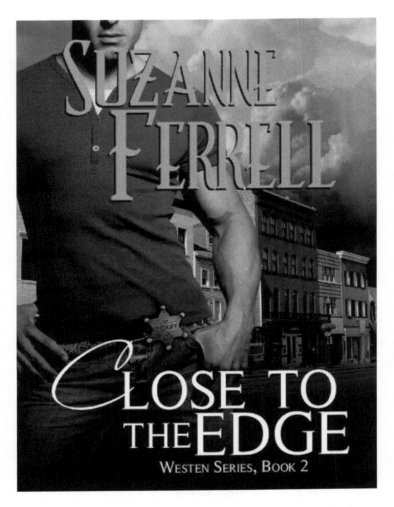

After facing death as an undercover narcotics cop, Gage Justice has come home to heal. His recuperation is cut short by his father's unexpected diagnosis of cancer and subsequent death. Now he's honoring one of his father's last wishes by taking over as the sheriff of his boyhood home, Westen, Ohio. Biding time until his father's term is finished, he fights boredom more than crime in the sleepy little town – that is until one sexy little teacher-turned-Private-Investigator literally falls into his arms.

Bobby Roberts is looking for adventure. After giving up her own dreams to raise her two sisters after the death of their parents, she's been trapped in a schoolroom for nearly two decades. The suffocating claustrophobia of the classroom has set her on a new career path. She arrives in Westen, complete with brand-spanking-new PI license, a handgun and a simple case – investigate a lien on property of a dead man.

Little does she realize her "simple little case" will lead her into the world of one sexy sheriff and the path of a murderer intent on keeping them both from discovering his secrets or stopping his plans that could destroy Westen.

****

The Edgars Family Novels

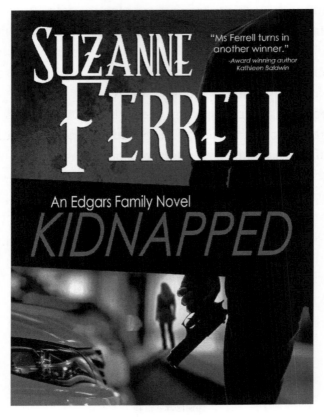

FBI Agent Jake Carlisle is in deep trouble. He's been shot and if he can't get help fast, two lives will be lost-his and that of the young witness whom he's sworn to protect. Desperate, on the run from both the police and the Russian Mafia, he kidnaps a nurse from a hospital parking lot.

ER nurse Samantha Edgars has been living in an emotional vacuum since the death of her daughter. Mentally and physically exhausted following a difficult shift, she's suddenly jolted from her stupor when she's bound and gagged, then tossed into the back of her car. Forced to tend a bleeding FBI agent and his injured witness, she's terrified. But Samantha quickly learns the rogue agent and orphaned boy need more than just her professional skills. Danger is bearing down on them, and she must learn to trust Jake – and her heart – if they're all going to survive.

****

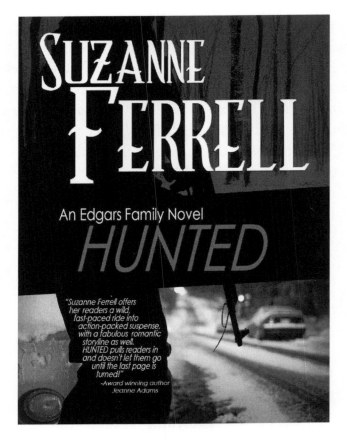

An Edgars Family Novel

HUNTED

"Suzanne Ferrell offers her readers a wild, fast-paced ride into action-packed suspense, with a fabulous romantic storyline as well. HUNTED pulls readers in and doesn't let them go until the last page is turned!"
-Award winning author Jeanne Adams

In one fiery explosion Katie Myers' witness protection cover is blown. Unable to trust the Marshals who've been responsible for her safety, she's on the run from the cult leader she put on death row. In desperation she forces a near stranger at gunpoint to help her hide.

By-the-book patrolman Matt Edgars is shocked when the woman he's come to rescue points a gun at him and demands he help her leave a crime scene. The stark terror in Katie's beautiful eyes has him breaking rules for the first time in his career.

With a hit man on their trail, Matt must break down the walls Katie has built to guard the secrets of her past. If not the cult leader will fulfill his prophecy and take the one woman Matt has ever loved to the grave.

****

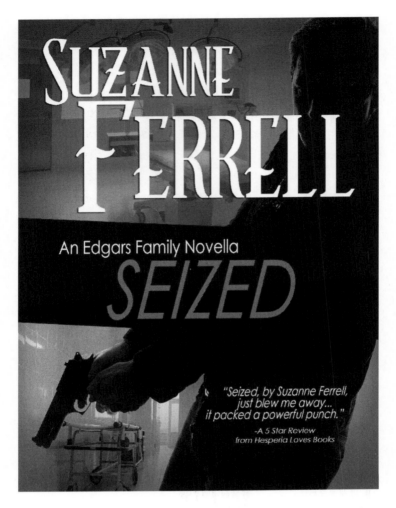

Suzanne Ferrell

An Edgars Family Novella

SEIZED

"Seized, by Suzanne Ferrell,
just blew me away...
it packed a powerful punch."

-A 5 Star Review
from Hesperia Loves Books

Dave and Judy Edgars have always loved each other – they've been married ten years and have three kids. But ever since Dave, a SWAT team member, was shot on duty Judy can't control the intense fear that grips her every time he heads out to work. It puts a strain on their relationship. Dave knows she's scared, but damn it she knew he was a cop the day they met. His patience is wearing thin.

Until the tables are turned...

One icy winter night, Judy, an operating room nurse, is called into work. She's taken hostage by a crazed gunman with an agenda. Now with Judy's life in danger and the SWAT team deployed elsewhere, Dave must face the same fear his wife does on a daily basis. Terrified he will lose her, he and his law enforcement family race to save Judy and stop her captor's plans.

****

This boxed set includes the first two Best-selling Edgars Family Romantic Suspense Novels, KIDNAPPED and HUNTED, along with the fast-paced novella SEIZED KIDNAPPED.